Praise for *The Killer W* D0723715

"Lately it's easier to find someone to hurt me consensually than to make me laugh, so I'm just tickled pink that Laura Antoniou, primarily known for her top-shelf erotica, has decided to render us helpless with laughter in a new comic murder mystery, *The Killer Wore Leather*. No one gets a pass, and no ego goes unpricked. The author has a keen eye for the posturing and paradoxes of the leather world, yet there's nothing malicious here. Because it is obvious that the book is a love letter of sorts. Antoniou doesn't overlook anybody's contribution to making the kinky world go 'round. Not just the contestants and judges, but the harried producers, the dedicated volunteers, and the oft-neglected vendors—all of them get a moment in the spotlight to share their unique perspectives. *The Killer Wore Leather* comes just in the nick of time for me. *Fifty Shades of Grey* stopped being funny around page 34, so thank you, Laura, for giving me something that's supposed to make me laugh!"

—Kate Kinsey, author of *Red*

"If knitters, bibliophiles, and teetotalers can have their mystery mavens, why not the BDSM leather world? And who better to deliver it than Laura Antoniou? Her finely honed rapier wit and keen eye for all things madcap makes *The Killer Wore Leather* one meaty tale of murder, mystery, and mayhem. Frankly, you're suspect if you overlook it."

—Debra Hyde,
author of the Lambda Award–winning *Story of L*

"This may well be the best book of the year—*The Killer Wore Leather* is fifty shades of hilarious!"

—Glenda Rider, producer, International Ms Leather

"Laura Antoniou...elevates the genre of SM erotica... The tales ring true, the dialogue is achingly real, and the sex is as hot as you'd ever hope for. For the novice SM player, the well-seasoned old-timer, and the simply curious alike, these books are the next best thing to being there."
—Kate Bornstein, author of *A Queer and Pleasant Danger*

"One of the funniest books I've read in years; folks will find bits and pieces of themselves and some of their friends in these pages. Antoniou manages to skewer anyone and anything in the leather community equally, all the while weaving good detective work with fabulous writing."
—Viola Johnson, author of *To Love, To Obey, To Serve*

"With *The Killer Wore Leather* Laura Antoniou takes on the mystery genre with aplomb. It's a riveting story set in the leather and kink worlds that doesn't succumb to the sensationalist approaches other, less well-crafted novels might have embraced. I love mysteries, and I love this book."
—Race Bannon, author of *Learning the Ropes*

"Queens-born Laura Antoniou is heiress presumptive to some of the erotic territory staked out by Patrick Califia and John Preston... [Her] writing moves with assurance between genders and sexual orientations, relentlessly exploring the dark side of sexuality."
—Michael Rowe, author of *Writing Below the Belt*

"After decades of delightfully decadent kinky prose, Ms. Antoniou now tantalizes by tickling the funny bone and leading us through a twisty, tangled web of intrigue, leather, murder, mayhem and kink. With a sharp eye and a sharper wit, she manages to draw the reader into the underground world of BDSM, build a mystery, lovingly skewer the denizens of the dungeon, and tell a tale that will keep you guessing until the very end. Whether you're a jaded veteran of perversion or simply a fan of a good whodunit, *The Killer Wore Leather* is sure to enslave you with its charm and humor as you submit to this masterful storyteller!"

—Mollena Williams,
Ms. San Francisco Leather 2009, International Ms Leather 2010

"Antoniou is an elegant stylist of erotica."

—Patrick Califia, author of *Sensuous Magic*

"If you've ever experienced a leather contest—from the inside, outside, or somewhere in between—you must read this book. A perfect parody (or should I say, telling lens?) of the community, with a gripping murder mystery wrapped around it. I was hooked immediately, in between my knowing head-nods and embarrassed guffaws."

—kd, International Ms Bootblack 2011

"Laura Antoniou has a winner in *The Killer Wore Leather*. Her grasp of the leather contest scene is eerie. She captures all the fun and all the drama of these events. You'll swear you've already met many of her characters. I thoroughly enjoyed reading this book—it really made me laugh."

—Chuck Renslow,
executive producer, International Mr. Leather

"Bravo, Laura, for holding up a funhouse mirror to the leather community! Like all good humor, these pages contain a bone of truth that makes us laugh at ourselves while delivering a satirical bite. Titleholders, this is a great read when traveling to your next contest or run, with caricatures of almost every type in our community, from the controlling slave Bitsy to the self-important gay titleholder Mack Steel. Download it to your Kindle and enjoy it en route."

—Hugh B. Russell, International LeatherSIR 2010

the
KILLER
WORE
LEATHER

the
KILLER
WORE
LEATHER

A MYSTERY

BY LAURA ANTONIOU

CLEiS
PRESS

Published in the United States by Cleis Press, Inc., 2246 Sixth Street, Berkeley, California 94710.

Printed in the United States.
Cover design: Scott Idleman
Cover photograph: Tore Johannesen/Getty Images
Text design: Frank Wiedemann
First Edition.
10 9 8 7 6 5 4 3 2 1

Trade paper ISBN: 978-1-57344-930-4
E-book ISBN: 978-1-57344-947-2

DEDICATION

Karen Taylor and Kim Attica—my loyal beta readers who tie for #1 fan, sounding board and inspiration.

Ketzer (who drives too fast) for phrasing and Frey Ray for her academic expertise.

To Sharon McCrumb for *Bimbos of the Death Sun*, which taught me that mysteries could be funny.

To Lori Perkins, who believed in this the moment I mentioned it.

To Sky Renfro and Chuck Renslow, who must take credit for the modern title culture. International Mr. Leather and International Ms Leather might have been the first, but oh, did they have a large and colorful array of offspring...

To Glenda Rider, who competed in my contest and then went and made some of her own. Masochism is not limited to those who play hard on the bottom.

To Tyler McCormick, because you won, dude.

And to all the winners and the runners up and to every person who bared it all on stage or strutted down the boulevard; to the producers and performers and stagehands and nannies, to the security staff and the schleppers, the ASL interpreters and the tailors, the builders of sets and the designers of web pages, the ones who donate goods and the ones who deeply discount, the artists and writers and singers and dancers, the sound and lighting engineers, the bag stuffers and raffle ticket sellers and the drivers of vans and trucks and everyone who works so hard to produce events that entertain, inform, enlighten and enrage this amazing community. May you all get what you need and desire. And to the burnouts...

CHAPTER 1

THE MULTISTORY ATRIUM OF THE GRAND STERLING HOTEL was buzzing with arrivals lining up at the registration desks and at the purple and black draped tables still being set up before the main elevator banks. Five people wearing black T-shirts emblazoned with VOLUNTEER were frantically stuffing stacks of postcards, bookmarks, safe sex kits packaged in little matchbook-like folders and samples of flavored body oils into plastic bags while others were struggling to make label printers and laptops share outlets and table space. Above them, suspended on wires, was a large flag with alternating black and blue stripes and one white one in the middle; in the upper left-hand corner was a bright red heart.

It clashed slightly with the purple draping on the tables.

"I registered online under the name Glasser, but I want Lady Stringent on my badge."

"Did you get my email about needing adjoining rooms? I need it for my Daddy's two slaves, they're arriving tomorrow and they might bring a service dog."

"Where do instructors register?"

"Your website never worked for me, can I still get the early bird discount?"

"When are the NA meetings?"

"Where are the quiet rooms?"

"Where are the dungeons?"

"Is the sit-down dinner formal leather, or can you wear casual clothes?"

A frighteningly large woman rose up from where she'd been unpacking a box of lanyards and shouted over the din. Her high, quarterdeck voice easily overwhelmed the crowd of questioners, and her sheer bulk intimidated most of them as well. Maureen Olmstead was a hell of a lot of woman—almost five foot ten and easily two-hundred and seventy pounds, much of it molded into a plus-size corset that hefted her generous, pale breasts into a stunning display of cleavage. A net of colorful beaded wire was draped over her long auburn hair; her dark brown eyes narrowed as she took control of the situation.

"Registration will begin in ten minutes! A through M over *there*, N through Z over *there*! Instructors, judges, contestants, press and guests, in the office behind me! Printed schedules are late; either check the master schedule on the website or keep your panties on until we get them here! Street legal clothing everywhere but the dungeons and no discounts, *we are sold out*!"

For a moment, the small crowd just stared at her, perhaps buffeted by the sheer force of her personality. Then, meekly, most of them sorted themselves out into appropriate lines, checked their smart phones and tablets or wandered off.

Maureen adjusted her designer gold-framed glasses and handed the box of lanyards to one of her volunteer force.

"I don't know what we'd do without you, Bitsy," said a harried looking man behind her.

"That's *Slave* Bitsy," she corrected. "And don't you forget it."

At thirty-nine years, Ms. Maureen "Bitsy" Olmstead was getting sick and tired of looking for the right partner, and she wanted to make sure everyone knew she was a slave, just in case Master Wonderful showed up. She plumped up her ample breasts, fluffed out her hair a little under the beads and checked her nails. Impeccable. "Hey!" she cried, pointing. "Don't touch the bags! You'll get one when you register!"

The man in leather pants, shirt, tie and cap drew his hand back quickly and muttered, "Sorry." He obediently shrank back into the line, a bundle of keys jangling on his left hip, and Bitsy turned her attention to her staff. It takes a real slave to run things, she thought for the tenth time that day.

In the conference room behind Bitsy and her army of volunteers, Earl Stemple, producer of the Mr. and Ms. Global Leather (and Bootblack) Contest, stared at the logistics board and checked off boxes as voices reported to him over the headset he wore crookedly. A Bluetooth earpiece was stuck over his left ear; the radio headset was adjusted so one earpiece was on his right. His tight blue Levi's were marked with different colored inks, as he would absently wipe the markers across his waist or thighs as he toggled the talk button for the headset or searched for his holstered cell phone. A stocky yet surprisingly agile man, he went back and forth from charts to laptop and conversation to commands, his thick fingers twirling the dry erase markers or stabbing at keyboards as necessary. Twelve half-drunk cups of coffee were scattered over the large conference table, all of them his.

"Tell the dungeon crew we need a spanking bench in the Seneca Room by ten A.M. tomorrow. They can have it back later." Click. "Where's our shuttle from the airport? Have him call in please." Click. "What do you mean, there's no hospitality suite? It's room 2001! Call Roger at the front desk; they should be setting up coffee service in there now." Click. "Send all contestants to the

Oneida Room; tell them to see Boy Jack. No, the other Boy Jack. Send any judges to me in the main office. Where *is* the other Boy Jack, anyway? I got arrivals stacking up!"

Earl sighed and shook his head, circling a few names on his board. As usual, important people were missing. That was the problem with any event managed by a volunteer staff; people giving their time mostly felt it was theirs to take back as well. Not that he was a volunteer; he had the honor and curse of being the sole paid staff member of the Global Leather empire, consisting of the contest(s) and fetish ball, the souvenir sales, and the Global Leather Foundation, which gave modest amounts of money to several well-chosen modest charities. Estimates of how much he made were often wildly off base, as his regular hate mail would attest. Just this morning, he'd gotten a message on KinkyNet, the largest pansexual online space for the BDSM crowd. It read, in typical online style, "u suk! Bloodsucker making millions off the community, u shuld give tkts to people who cant afford them not everyone is rich like u. titles r shit."

Yeah. Titles are shit, but you want a free ticket, you ass. Millions! Wouldn't that be nice? They complained at the registration and contest fees and the prices of the T-shirts, but they never wondered how much money it cost to get a hotel in midtown Manhattan, purchase event insurance, cater dinners, rent stage and dungeon equipment, fly in dozens of famous names, and feed hungry judges and contestants. Plus, he had to staff and supply the hospitality room full of free snacks and drinks for volunteers, instructors, entertainers, and print thousands of flyers and brochures and schedules...speaking of which...

"Bitsy, did the schedules come in yet?" Click.

"Yeah, we just got 'em now!"

Last minute changes, of course, due to the flakiness of some of the instructors. Earl scratched his scalp under thinning sandy hair. It was probably best that the person originally scheduled to

4

teach "Dark Fantasy Role-playing" decided to stay home because he was having a panic attack. Earl made a note to take that name off the potential invite list.

"Earl! We got a problem," crackled a voice over the radio headset. "Dr. Westfield never made his flight."

The keynote speaker? "Repeat that?"

"I just heard from Greg in the van. He's at the airport. Westfield was not on the flight we booked for him! What should he do now?"

"Tell Greg to continue the pickups." Earl clicked a few times and called his judge and special guest wrangler, Boi Jack. "Jack! Where are you?" He muttered more curses and called Bitsy again. "Bitsy, I can't find Boi Jack. The other one! Would you call Westfield and find out where he is, he missed his damn flight. If he needs help rebooking, can you handle that?"

"Sure, Earl, in my spare freaking time!"

"Well, can you at least send someone to find her?"

"Hey, you! One badge per person—no, your damn service dog doesn't need one! What part of *person* didn't you understand? And I need a runner to find Jack!" She abruptly clicked off, which was fine, since it gave his ear a rest. But he needed Boi Jack. Because any minute now, assuming the previous airport run to JFK was on time and the volunteer tasked to drive out to Newark was also on time, his biggest headache was about to walk in the door. He stared at the furious red arrows added to his master chart and wondered how on earth no one noticed that Ravenfyre and Steel would be arriving at the same time.

"Lick it. Kiss it." The words came in whispered breaths and the smell of anise and leather and, sadly, the strange, medicinal scent of industrial cleaners. But Boi Jack never minded the intrusion; the leather was the thing, and the leather was molded around two strong legs and an inviting bulge between them, and a belt

5

wrapped around her wrists, and the slick, soft texture against her lips and tongue as she worked her way from calf to knee and then to thigh.

The exploration had started with the traditional boot kiss, but Boi Jack was never one to leave a kiss by itself, and privacy was going to be at a premium soon, so why not go for it? When sexy Skylar gave her the cruise of death, why not take advantage of a master key that could unlock the classrooms? They could hear the thuds and bangs and shouts of the vendors loading in, but behind this one door, they were alone for as long as they could manage it.

"Yeah, you want it, you bad boy. You hungry, naughty boy. Come on up nice and slow and see what I got for that sweet mouth."

Jack eagerly zoomed in to the package pressing against the button fly of the soft leather jeans and tongued against the waiting treasure, forgetting the bondage on her wrists as she tried to hug one leg, tried to work her own legs around a calf, rub herself so nicely against Skylar while Skylar whipped that tasty bit of…

"Hey, Jack? Jack? I think your phone is ringing. And your radio has been blinking for a while. Do you need to check that?"

Dammit, dammit, dammit! Jack sighed, shook the belt off her wrists and looked at the time. Then, she paled and almost fell forward into Skylar's legs. "Oh Em Gee! I am so late! I am so dead! They're gonna kill each other! Oh Em Gee!"

Nancy Nichols wanted to be somewhere else. A crane collapse maybe, or a nice, juicy story-of-the-moment that would guarantee a front page burst, a page-three story and a nice pick-up by AP. Maybe this hotel has bedbugs, she mused hopefully, peering up through the layers of suspended light fixtures in the atrium. For some reason, readers were just fascinated by bedbug infestations. That would be a funny headline: Bedbugs Frighten the Freaks!

A…person…walked past her dressed in a fox costume. Head-to-foot, big bushy tail, velvety paws on their hands, pointy nose and ears. What on earth did that have to do with leather? Or the big girl behind the desk in her enormous corset and medieval headwear—Victoria's Secret was safe from her. Where did one find lingerie in huge sizes? Almost everyone else seemed dressed in fairly standard street clothes, many of them dragging fairly standard cheap luggage as they waited patiently in lines. Not exactly the corner of Sodom Street and Gomorrah Avenue.

Not that she expected it to be. "For crying out loud, Vic, this is so tired! No one cares about a bunch of freaky people getting dressed up and playing spanking games anymore. Don't you watch TV? There had to be ten *CSI* episodes alone about how normal these people are! All in prime time!"

Vic, her editor, boss and nemesis, didn't even argue. "Then do a story about how normal it all is. The fashion show is Friday, and there's a fetish ball, whatever that is, on Saturday; you'll get Donny for two hours. Get some nice PG-13 pictures for a slide show."

The *New York Record* loved slide shows and videos on their website. Every story seemed to need one, especially if it involved celebrities, fashion, cooking, accidental nudity or gory tragedies. Stories in the physical paper even had little code boxes people could scan to take their mobile devices right to the in-depth online version. So far, tracking showed that most readers would stay for up to fifteen seconds of advertisements to see ten pictures of, oh, a crane collapse or the latest antics of a celebrity chef having a kitchen accident. Longer, one assumed, if it involved their fashionable clothing being set on fire and falling off.

I shouldn't have come today, she thought. Tomorrow is when the actual event starts. She had thought to get some behind-the-scenes color, but so far there were few opportunities to talk to anyone connected to the event. Miss Massive seemed to be running the show at registration, and all she'd managed to snarl out was that press passes would be available shortly. Nancy had pulled some names off the website for the contest, amused by some of the *noms de kinky*—she couldn't *wait* to meet Lord Laertes or Chava Negilla.

"Excuse me, but I think we are colleagues," said a thin, reedy voice from next to her. She turned, hoping it wasn't someone from the *News* or *Post*; this might be a stupid story, but it would be hers, dammit. She immediately knew she was safe. The man standing next to her was dressed in badly fitted black leather pants, cinched around his tiny waist and adding to the wrinkles on his black cotton uniform shirt, which was buttoned all the way up to his scrawny neck. A black leather vest was layered on top of the shirt, covered with small cloisonné pins, like the ones you picked up at Disney. These seemed to lack cartoon characters.

Intense dark eyes circled by deep shadows gazed at her with a fascination she read as a kind of hunger. Oily black hair was plastered on his skull; if he'd owned the slightest bit of menace at all, he might have carried off a role as a sinister Nazi interrogator. Instead, he gave off waves of neediness. He was extending something to her; she took a business card and glanced at it.

"I'm Cary Gordon, *Leather Today*. The *official* newspaper of the leather/BDSM community."

Oy, Nancy thought. *Took Journalism 101 in college twenty years ago, did you?* But she plastered her reporter smile on. "Nichols, *New York Record*. Good to meet ya, Cary. Since you're in the know, maybe you can introduce me around." Because masochism doesn't just belong to you whips and chains people, she added silently. And sometimes, a local guide would manage to cut down the legwork real fast. Find two, three colorful people who look good in their sexy clothing, get a few quotes, and knock this puppy off before dinner.

"I'd be delighted!" he gushed. "It's so rare to see mainstream press attending our little affairs. I hope you aren't here for some sensational look-at-the-freaks story?"

You and me both, brother. "Nah, I think we're beyond that these days, don't you? At least in New York. I'm more into human interest—who are the people who go to these things, what do Mr. and Ms. Global Leather actually do the rest of the year? That sort of thing."

"Well, you're in luck! I know everyone!"

Nancy caught movement out of the corner of her eye and pointed. "How about them?"

It looked like a meeting of the Jets and Sharks. On one side, two men; on the other side, two women and a man. It was instantly clear who the gang leaders were.

"Those are last year's winners!" Cary supplied earnestly, taking pictures with his cell phone. "That's Mack Steel, with the sash on, and the woman with the red hair is Mistress Ravenfyre. They're judges for this year's contest, you know, the old winners are always judges for the next year."

Nancy watched the man in the black leather, silver studded sash and the woman in the very tight emerald green sundress and strappy sandals and knew something else about these two.

"They *hate* each other," she said, with some measure of delight.

Cary sighed with a hangdog nod. "I'm afraid they do," he said.

Nancy chuckled and snapped a few photos herself.

"Nice dress, *Wendi*. Buy it new?" Cormac "Mack" Steel asked with a smirk. Behind him, his loyal boy smirked exactly the same way, balancing two shoulder bags and dragging a large rolling suitcase.

"How original. Did you look that one up on the Internet first? Oh, wait; you'd have to be literate to do that." She eyed his ensemble of leather jeans, bar T-shirt and title sash and raised an elegant russet shaded eyebrow. "Did you impress all your little fans at McDonald's when you went in for your McMuffin this morning? Some of it is still on your...studs." She turned away as Mack glanced down, and her entourage of two laughed as they followed her.

"Mistress Ravenfyre!" called out a short, androgynous figure in jeans, chaps, a leather shirt and ubiquitous vest covered with pins. A leather baseball cap was emblazoned with the stitched word "Boi."

"Ah, *Jacques*," Ravenfyre said, extending a hand. Boi Jack pounded to a stop and made an awkward bow over that hand and kissed it.

"How good to see you," Boi Jack gasped, out of breath. "Both of you! What a surprise to see you, um, together!"

"You mean what a surprise to see *him* on time and *sober*."

Mack finished wiping the crumbs from his sash and snarled, "What a surprise she isn't trolling for hourly clients over in Penn Station."

"Wow, it's such an honor to have you here," Jack said more firmly. "Wouldn't it be great to get you all registered?"

"And apart," muttered Ravenfyre.

"You mean medicated," said Mack. "Got a good supply of Mistress's Little Helper?"

"Let's get you all out of the lobby," suggested Boi Jack, gesturing in desperation at Ravenfyre's attendants. They got the hint and started moving five pieces of matching lavender luggage toward the hotel's front desk. Mack and his boy started to follow, but by then, Earl Stemple had reached them, and he inserted himself neatly in front of them.

"Mack! Paul! How good to see you!" He gave Boi Jack a chance to hurry the Ravenfyre crew away and shifted Mack toward the conference registration area.

"You should have taken her sash away five minutes after the judges accidentally gave it to her," Mack said. "And sent those judges to a psychiatrist!"

The same judges picked you, thought Earl, as he made a noncommittal sound. "Is it too much to ask for some civility for one last weekend, Mack? As a personal favor?"

"I don't owe you anything," snapped the titleholder, adjusting his sash. "I gave you guys good value this year and you know it. If anything, you owe me, big time, for all the hours I wasted with that harpy in high heels."

Earl handled the paperwork for Mack personally, since Boi Jack was taking care of Ravenfyre. He pulled out two envelopes containing badges, meal, shuttle and drink tickets, and the three-page, small-print waiver stating that the person attending understood they were at an adult convention for kinky people. He handed the envelopes to Paul, Mack's loyally submissive boyfriend, and handed the shiny black and purple gift bag to Mack, hoping presents would distract him. As expected, they did.

Mack Steel was easily distracted with shiny things.

He was right about one thing—he'd given the Global Leather empire a pretty good year from a financial point of view. The calendar and video shoots had sold very nicely, along with signed copies for higher prices. His personal run pin, a stylized truck grill with his nickname stamped over it and a gold ring with the contest title circling it, sold rather nicely for five bucks. Made in China for about sixty-five cents each, they went through buckets of them at some events.

But what he cost the event in goodwill was...incalculable. A string of insulted bar owners, underpaid bootblacks, event producers stuck with five-hundred dollar hotel room service bills and a whole tribe of disappointed, annoyed, disoriented and snarky sash-lovers who found out their idol was somewhat less princely than his fashion shoots suggested.

Because Mack Steel certainly looked the part of a studly leatherman, people mistook the image for substance. A little over six feet tall, with broad shoulders and a firm chest and stomach, he made chaps and a vest look sharp. His wavy black hair was kept just long enough to show it was wavy, and he maintained a retro mustache that was making other men start to grow theirs as well. In one of his best calendar shots, he was in a leather jockstrap, a motorcycle jacket thrown over one shoulder, a cap pushed back on his head. He had one hip up against a beautiful loaned Harley. It was called his Brando shot, and he must have signed and sold a thousand of them, easily.

Although Brando rode a Triumph in that movie, Earl thought. Not that Mack would know that. Or care. Mr. Global Leather was rooting through his gift bag, shoving aside the T-shirt, engraved pewter mug and baseball cap. He pulled out a hand-cut leather belt with his title stamped on it, unfurled it, grunted, and shoved it back into the bag.

"That's handmade, from Medusa Leathers," Earl said. "They're vending here. It would be nice if you stopped by the booth."

"Last year's winners got *jackets*," Mack said. "God, I have so much crap. I throw out tons of this garbage. They should thank me for letting you list it in the program as a freaking prize. It probably doesn't even fit." He shoved the bag at Paul, who took it and put it with their other luggage while he slid papers over for Mack to sign.

Earl didn't know how Mack could get from point A to B without his boy Paul. Paul was like a lot of nominally submissive partners out there—kind of quiet and shy in appearance, but as organized and regimented as an English nanny. He spent as much time in the gym as Mack did, but he had a slender swimmer's build and a classic blond/blue midwestern coloring. He wasn't in the calendar, of course, not being part of the contest, but he had been photographed with Mack for many websites and a few magazines, mostly on his knees beside his master/lover/daddy/whatever they were. Earl never asked for particulars. He was just grateful Mack had someone to make sure he turned up on time.

And relatively sober. He hoped whoever stuffed the envelopes remembered to shortchange Mack's drink tickets. With a smile, he assured his troublesome titleholder of a fabulous dinner that evening, exciting meetings with fresh new contestants, a good night's sleep and lots of adulation to come. He would get Mack off to the front desk as Boi Jack brought Ravenfyre and her family back here and hopefully, they wouldn't see each other again until the meet and greet later in the evening. They were even on different floors. On different sides of the hotel.

His messages were lining up on the computer screen; there were at least six waiting on the phone, and his muted headset was blinking madly. But he smiled.

Earl Stemple was a professional. And on Sunday night, Mack Steel would be nothing but a memory, and he'd have a new and hopefully much nicer Mr. Global Leather to promote and sell for a year.

It beat selling vacuum cleaners. By a very *slender* margin.

CHAPTER 2

Boy Jack counted heads one more time and came up with ten. Still missing one of the men. He sighed and toggled his headset. "Guys? Anyone seen a little lost contestant?"

"He's an hour late already. Disqualify him," insisted Lennon Munro. Len was always insisting on something that would disqualify a competitor. Today he was wearing a rubber belt, studded with the words Mr. Fetish, 2007, a leather sash emblazoned Mr. Leather Blaze (accented with red leather flames), and a medallion pronouncing him Mr. Ganymede Cruises Leather. Boy Jack thought they were all lucky Len hadn't also decided to wear whatever the Mr. Tighty Whitey contest had given him. This was Len's fourth try at Global Leather. His list of bar, club, one-time, and oddball contest titles took up an entire page of his profile. The closest he'd ever come to an international title was fifth runner-up.

Boy Jack thought it was nice Len had a hobby.

While he ignored the demand to disqualify another contestant, he ran through his notes, making sure he had everything organized. He usually did; and unlike his counterpart, Boi Jack, his charges were more likely to be obedient and eager to do what he told them. He'd rather handle contestants than judges and special guests any day!

Like Boi Jack, Boy Jack was short, slender, dark haired and dressed in well-fitted leather. They liked to play off their similarities and did in fact check in with each other about what they were wearing day-to-day. Lots of people asked if they were twins, or at least brothers, which was kind of funny since Boi Jack wasn't a guy and Boy Jack was. Still, they were brothers in leather, sort of, and best friends, and knew that Earl depended on them to keep his judges and contestants shepherded around and out of his way.

"Jack, he's on his way now! Had some issues with the front desk, we're handling it," came a voice over his headset. Boy Jack nodded and clapped his hands.

"Okay, folks, we got our last contestant on his way. Does everyone have a bag with your binder and badge? Let's get settled in, and I'll tell you the tortures in store for you this weekend!"

The contestants seated themselves at the conference tables in the small, windowless room. Some of them, like Lennon Munro, were in their contest regalia. Most were in neat street clothing. The door behind Boy Jack opened and a white-haired man in his sixties came in, a little out of breath. He was wearing a black rubber sash that read MR. PALM SPRINGS RUBBER. He looked around and settled on Boy Jack. "You can all relax! Maurice is here!"

Boy Jack grinned. "Welcome, and grab a chair, we're just starting."

Maurice nodded and waved at the man in the chair closest to the door. "Budge over, boychick, I'm old and you're spry." The much younger man looked surprised but hopped over one chair, and Maurice levered himself down.

"Okay, welcome to the Mr. and Ms. Global Leather and Bootblack contest. The bootblacks are getting a different orientation, but you will meet them all later at the meet and greet. There's a purple binder in your bag that should contain your master schedule, the conference timetable, your drink and meal tickets, the shuttle bus wristband and your badge. You must wear your badge at all times, and it must be above the waist and visible at eye level. Any judge who sees you without a badge can disqualify you right there."

Nervously, they all checked for their badges.

"My name is spelled wrong," two people said simultaneously.

Boy Jack sighed. "Okay, I'll take you two down to registration and we'll print out new ones. Next—anything you *must* be at has been highlighted in red on your schedule. If you don't show up, you get disqualified."

"Wait, wait," said one woman, contemplating her badge with an air of confusion. "We have to, like…wear this all the time?"

"Any time you are out of your room," Boy Jack amended.

"But…like…what if I am…you know. Out getting coffee or something." She blinked under the harsh lighting of the room, showing off the slight wariness of someone not used to being up at ten A.M. Boy Jack checked his roster. This was Ms. Idaho Leather, Bobby "Blade" Guthrie. She was dressed in skinny jeans, worn but well-shined engineer boots and a long-sleeved concert T-shirt for the Violent Femmes. The unrelieved black of her clothing matched her unnaturally black straight hair and the dark shadows around her eyes. It was hard to tell if she was Goth, punk, or merely hungover.

"If you are anywhere outside your room, you must wear the badge. Judges might be out getting coffee, too, although seriously, if you need coffee? Tell me and I will send one of our contest slaves to get you whatever you want. You all have tickets for three lunches and two dinners, and breakfast will be here every morning."

Boy Jack waved the binder at his charges. "This is your bible. The contest rules are in here. Review them when you get the chance. Tonight is your first required event, the pre-conference meet and greet. It will be held at the Shaft."

"Woo hoo!" hooted Mr. Shaft, pumping his fist in the air.

"There is a special shuttle just for you guys at seven o'clock sharp. Dress for a leather bar. This will be your first formal meeting with the judges—you are encouraged to schmooze like crazy. I am not supposed to give you guys too many hints, but listen to this one very carefully—make sure you meet every judge. Do *not* skip one because you think they know you. Judging starts the minute you go through that door."

They all nodded, some with more confidence than others.

"Now, I am sure none of you contacted the judges before the contest, right?" Boy Jack grinned and a few contestants grinned back.

"Only to say hi on KinkyNet," said Mr. Alberta Leather, the single Canadian titleholder competing this year. "It's the polite thing to do."

"This one sent her slave bio to each judge," said one of the four women. From her self-reference style, Boy Jack deduced that this was slavegirl phyl'ta. This style of speaking, along with the "ta" at the end of her name, identified her as a Zodian. In fact, she was the first Zodian contestant, ever.

She was a shade under five foot three and could have used some help from firmer support garments; the colorful layers of chiffon and silk that made up her costume were draped somewhat haphazardly over a rather plump body. The Zod books featured a special slave dance, Boy Jack knew, having researched this for all of ten minutes when he got the bio for this contestant. It was like a striptease, with each color and fabric choice having some sort of coded meaning to it. It all seemed very...girly. So did phyl'ta, with her strawberry blonde hair, multiple dangling earrings and bracelets, all decorated with colorful crystals, and her wide, rapidly blinking eyes.

17

Of the four female contestants, she was one of the two who did not have a title. Instead, she was sponsored by the Nevada Zodian Confederation, one of the larger Zod groups in the country.

"Well, all the judges have your bios in their binders, so no problem there. Judges can ask you questions anytime they want, anywhere. So be on your best behavior and be ready for some of the trickier ones. Some judges really like to try and catch you off guard; just relax and be yourself—or failing that, be polite." He grinned to the polite laughter.

Mr. Newark Leather raised his hand. Boy Jack checked his list; the man's name was Giuliano Ferri. "Yo, we can hang out with the judges?"

"You can't be *alone* with any of them," Boy Jack said firmly. "In any public space you can chat, or they can pull you aside for a few minutes. But no taking meals with them, no running errands for them, and under no circumstances should you be in their room, or one of them in yours. No tricking! Until after the contest, when you can knock yourself out."

"Yes, because no judge ever slept with a contestant," sniffed Ms. Bayou Leather, whose badge read Jazz Dean. She was dressed in classic leather: chaps over Levi's 501 jeans, Harley boots, and the colors on her vest were for the Baton Rouge Harpies. She had a severe buzz cut, showing off the silver steadily growing through her dark brown hair, a knife in her belt and a reputation of being quite the studly lady-killing butch.

Boy Jack shrugged. "Well, it'll get you disqualified here, if we even think it happened. If any judge suggests something like that to you, or hints there are ways to sway them, you call me." He waved his cell phone. "Any time, day or night. My number is in the binder. Program it in your phones now, and then erase it Sunday night, okay?"

Each of the contestants immediately whipped out a phone and started punching numbers. Except for Ms. Idaho Leather, who patted her pockets and shrugged. "I think I left it somewhere," she said with a yawn.

Boy Jack made a mental note to keep a runner on hand to collect Ms. Idaho Leather. There was always one who didn't have a phone or forgot to bring it, or left it on mute.

"And finally, folks, remember this is supposed to be fun! This will be an amazing weekend for you, maybe life changing. Everyone who has been through this contest can tell you so, right, Len? Right, Kelly?"

Lennon Munro nodded smugly and avoided looking at Kelly, who was grinning.

"Well, I have a sort of unique perspective on the whole thing," Kelly said.

"And I am sure we'll hear a lot about it over the weekend. Does everyone understand their responsibilities and what the contest rules are?"

There was a rustling as the contestants flipped through their binders. Then the room exploded in questions.

"Are there vegan options on the menus?"

"What if my best friend is a member of one of the judges' ex's clubs?"

"Can my handler be alone with the judges?"

"Where are the AA meetings? What if I need a meeting but it's during the interviews?"

"Can I get an extra T-shirt for my girlfriend? And my other girlfriend?"

"What does the first runner-up get?"

"I'm raising money for a cat shelter, and I'm selling little kitten pins. Can I give them to the judges for publicity, or would that be, like, bribing them?"

"How often are bathroom breaks?"

"May this one's Master be formally introduced to the judges? This one is not allowed to speak to others without permission."

"Is there media here? Can I blog about the process if I don't name names?"

Boy Jack sighed and pulled up a chair to start answering.

CHAPTER 3

The Shaft was a sprawling bar housed in one of the few remaining half-empty warehouses in the infamous meat-packing district of lower Manhattan. Back in the day, that neighborhood had been a seedy, dangerous place, smelling of old blood and sour river water flowing through the myriad sewer pipes and old bootlegger tunnels under the cobblestone streets. Transvestite hookers, junkies and thrill-seekers congregated there among the truckers and butchers who moved thousands of animal carcasses into vast refrigerated trucks and then onto dinner plates across the tri-state area.

In those days, sex and BDSM clubs operated alongside (and sometimes below) the SRO and hourly motels with broken neon signs advertising continuous vacancies. Suburban tourists would daringly risk parking their expensive cars on the streets while making their way down steep, dark stairs into dank basement palaces of perversion. Less culturally and financially secure people would come down to those streets and just never leave, finding crowded shares in illegal loft spaces or a sugar daddy or mama to take them in. When filmmakers wanted a picture of a dangerous, sexy and violent Manhattan, they would send their crews down to the meatpacking district.

Then, gentrification happened. And HBO's *Sex in the City*, whose main character moved just three blocks away from where the notorious sex clubs used to be.

Real estate prices skyrocketed. Refugees from the blocks around the World Trade Center moved uptown and bought new lofts in old buildings and spent millions in renovations. Empty lots suddenly had construction walls and permits and gorgeous watercolor renderings of future luxury apartment buildings. Diners, bodegas and after-hours clubs became bistros, cupcake bakeries and gyms. Whole Foods moved in, and that spelled the end.

The Shaft resisted with all its might. Having survived previous incarnations as a warehouse, a series of smuggling tunnels for speakeasies, a slaughterhouse, a squatter/sex worker shelter and very briefly an art space/dance club, a consortium of investors fronted the money for a leather bar after the previous Levi/leather drinking hole closed, leaving New York bereft. The managers were canny and persistent. When the no-smoking laws closed other bars, they installed an elevator and got a permit for a rooftop space where their men could smoke their cigars. When the rents went up, they leased their bar during the day for everything from porn shoots to tai chi classes. They instituted theme parties and nights for every taste and identity, even filling up on Monday nights with their women's party, hosted by the Women Into Sadomasochistic Expression lesbian BDSM group. And they promoted the hell out of their bar title, Mr. Shaft.

"So, there're bar titles, fetish titles, club titles, city titles, state titles, regional, national and international," explained a pretty woman with curly, light brown hair. She wore a large pendant over the low neckline of her red leather minidress. It proclaimed her to be *Ms. Global Leather, 2008*. She had introduced herself as Phedre Lysande. "Before I was Ms. Global Leather, I was Ms. Keystone Leather."

Nancy Nichols nodded, absorbing both the facts her latest informant delivered and the steady stream of leather-clad bodies filling the bar. This was already a much more photo-friendly event than registration; she'd gotten her press pass, pried Cary Gordon off of her, and escaped to write up a quick intro to her piece and take a nap. She filed a quick little bit of filler she dashed off on one of the vendors; someone would find a use for a story about a modern corset maker, especially since they did plus sizes. It wasn't news, but it was writing and she'd get paid for it and in the end, that was what mattered.

"So what do you know about last year's winners?" Nancy asked, pausing a lecture on the history of leather contests. Phedre was a font of information; maybe way too much of it. So far, it seemed that these people were either publicity shy, hiding their faces with one hand as they passed anyone with a camera, or they were desperate for someone to listen to everything they had to say.

"Ravenfyre is a wonderful lady. Really very nice! She's a life-styler; she really lives what she says, she has a husband and a 24/7 slave. She raised over ten thousand dollars for an anti-violence project last year." Phedre waved to several people who called over greetings.

"So, she's into S and M and raises money for anti-violence?" Nancy asked. "Isn't that a little...odd?"

"No! S/M isn't violence; we're all safe, sane and...hi, sweetie, over here!" Phedre waved to a tall black woman, who weaved her way through the sidewalk crowds. "I think I have a pamphlet, give me a second...here! It's from the American Sexuality Society." She shoved a piece of paper at Nancy and said, "Give me just one more second; I have to get my vlog in."

The approaching woman was already holding up a small video

23

camera, and as soon as she was close enough, she gave Phedre a thumbs-up sign. "Hi, perverts!" Phedre said brightly. "We're here live at the Global Leather meet and greet at the Shaft. So far, looks like everyone is here except no one's seen Dr. Julian Westfield, the keynote speaker! Lennon Munro is wearing his Mr. Buckskin outfit, designed by Weird Out West, and just wait until you see Angelina's latex vampire outfit; it is totally amazing, from Silky Smooth Latex Productions. They'll be starting the contestant number draws so I'm on my way in soon, but get this—we are being covered by traditional media this year! There's actually a reporter from the *New York Record* here, and she is totally cool with us and not writing the usual 'hey look at the freaks' piece of trash. See you inside!"

"Got it!" said the videographer. She slipped the camera into one of the many pockets of her vest and stretched.

Phedre said, "This is my primary, Dorcas. Dorcas, this is Nancy, from the *Record*."

Dorcas gave Nancy a cool, measuring look and then broke into a grin. Broad shouldered as well as tall, she was bulky and assured in her movements. "You really gonna cover this straight?" she asked.

Nancy shrugged. "Unless you do something really weird."

Dorcas and Phedre laughed. "We're dead then," Phedre said, linking arms with her lover. "Because guaranteed, there will be something weird. Okay, we gotta get inside and near the stage. Nice meeting you!"

"Wait, one more question," Nancy said, holding up a finger. "What do you think of Mack Steel, the current title...man?"

Dorcas sneered and Phedre put on what Nancy immediately recognized as a neutral smile.

"He's a *dick*," Dorcas said. "A jerk, an ass, a real mother-"

"He's got a *strong personality*," Phedre said firmly. "Never afraid to say what's on his mind. We have to go now!"

24

Everything ran late, as usual. One of the judges missed the bus, one of the contestants had stage fright and threw up, the owner of the bar wanted more stage time to make announcements for upcoming events and promote the new cocktail they'd made to honor their contestant, Jason Asada. Earl nixed the *Asada Colada*—offering discounted drinks with the name of a contestant on them seemed against the spirit if not the letter of the rules. The MC mispronounced half the names of everyone introduced and told rambling, misfired jokes of dubious taste, even for a crowd of kinky people. Asking whether George Santos, a judge and the current Señor Cuero (representing Spanish-speaking leathermen) was in the country legally almost made Earl knock the idiot off stage personally. Luckily, the hisses and boos seemed to get through, and the MC quickly moved on and continued to stumble his way through the necessary formalities.

"I thought he was funny," said Mack, holding a hand out for a fresh drink. Paul put a cold bottle of beer into that hand and then replaced his hands behind his back. He was dressed in tight leather shorts, lace-up boots, a narrow black leather collar and a chest harness. In contrast, Mack was in leather from cap to boots. The judges were clumped together waiting for the sponsorship announcements to finish so they could go out and do their mandatory socializing.

"He didn't know how to work the crowd," sniffed Chava Negilla. Taller than Mack in her four-inch heels, Chava was in full drag regalia. Her beaded amber-colored gown had a tall lace collar and shot off lines of reflected light every time she turned. She was drinking a cocktail to match her radiant ensemble, with the flecks of gold floating in the martini glass. "I could have done better. There's a reason why you leather people need drag queens to run your shows. You have all the style and charisma of a discount sofa bed."

"Better not let anyone hear that," rumbled Lord Laertes. A burly man, his bulk was emphasized by his own costume. Brown leather trousers were tucked into cross-gartered fur boots with some kind of horn attached to each tip, pointing up. A broad belt was hung with a coiled whip on one side and a long-handled flogger on the other, its tails made of thick, umber moosehide. A red pirate shirt was open over his hairy chest, and over that was a vest decorated with strips of black and brown fur. A medallion in the shape of a crescent moon crossed with a double-bladed axe around his neck proclaimed him to be the Khan of the Eastern Kingdoms. "People will think you are prejudiced against the scene." He wiped beer foam off his goatee with the back of his hand after draining a mug and slapped his free hand against his thigh. A small, delicate looking woman came over to him to make a stylized curtsy, and he thrust the empty mug at her. She placed it on the palm of her hand and asked, "May this one fetch another for the Khan?"

Mack guffawed. "Jesus, you are the last one to talk about being prejudiced, Lord—Khan—whatever your real name is. I always knew you Zodians were weird, but puh-leeze. Only a moron would believe you aren't going to go all out for your fellow weirdos."

Behind him, Paul cried out, "Khaaaaaan!" in a bad William Shatner imitation. Mack laughed even harder as Lord Laertes turned away from him.

"The Zodians have been in the scene for over twenty years, which is more than anyone can say for you," said Mistress Ravenfyre.

"I need a drink," muttered the other woman on the judging panel, a short bespectacled woman in a Hawaiian shirt with a leather vest over it. She stalked over to the bar by herself.

"Try to get a sense of humor while you're there," Chava called after her.

"Worst. Judges. Ever," Boi Jack muttered into her headset.

"Roger that," Boy Jack responded.

"So, you are not all into that master/slave stuff?" Nancy Nichols asked, curious despite her continued reservations. This was turning out to be one of the strangest things she'd ever seen, and that included the evening she spent with a group of chicken fanciers—breeding them, not doing kinky things with them. Those people were as passionate about something as tiny as an array of little feathers on the back of a chicken's leg as these folks were about their array of strange costumes. These kinky people had actual philosophies. Or delusions masquerading as philosophies. The little pamphlet Phedre had given her was quite illuminating.

"Oh, lordy, no," said the small but well-shaped man in front of her. His dark brown hair was buzz cut almost to the scalp, and he wore a delicate chin beard and mustache groomed to exacting precision. It outlined his jaw nicely, and he had terrific, smooth skin and dark green eyes to die for. Nancy thought they might be boosted with colored contacts. He wore what looked like a motorcycle cop's ensemble in black and blue leather, complete with tall boots, cap and badge. All in all, he was a damn pretty man, lacking only a few more inches to make him gorgeous. He had introduced himself as Kelly Manning.

"You'll find most of the people in the leather/BDSM scene are into fetishes, like clothing, role-playing, sex games, fun things they do to spice up their relationships. The folks into that 'me master, you slave' stuff are a minority. And a lot of them actually don't do it much when they're not out showing off." He grinned with disarming ease, showing off a slight chip in one front tooth. Nancy was half relieved that there was something to mar his clean-cut prettiness.

"How do you know this? And how do you know who's into what?" Nancy cast a glance around the cavernous bar, taking in people dressed in everything from jeans and sneakers to the ubiquitous chaps and boots look, more cops and soldiers than she could count, the person in the fox costume she'd seen earlier, a few people in kilts, and bunches of men dressed in barbarian splendor, seemingly accompanied by girlfriends wearing draped layers of pastel cloth from the discount bin at Fabric Barn. The vast majority were just in some variation of all black, with lots of jeans and T-shirts, boots and vests and caps. There was a fair amount of skin on parade—lots of bare chests on men and corsets on women. And while some of them appeared weirder than others, most of them looked fairly, well, normal; just people out for a night at the bar, drinking, hanging out, shouting and exchanging phone numbers. Lots of people hugged when they saw each other; clearly many of them were friends already but probably only saw each other at events like this. Nancy found it disturbingly comfortable and friendly.

"You don't, really, until you ask. But you can always get a few hints, I guess. Like, if you see someone wearing a collar with a lock around their neck, it's a pretty good bet they're someone's slave. And the guys in the fur vests? They're Zodians; they are sort of heavily into role-playing, although, don't let one hear you say that. They live the Zodian lifestyle, heh. It's based on some old science fiction books, I think." Kelly's voice was rough and pleasant on the ear as he pointed out more examples. "And then you have the rubber guys—one of the other contestants is Mr. Palm Springs Rubber. He's, like, in his sixties or something. That's all about the clothing and texture, no role-playing. We also have a few guys who are into the whole furry thing. I don't know how they wound up in this scene, except we're pretty welcoming to almost anyone. They'll be wearing full-body costumes—the only one I know outside his fur suit is the one dressed like a fox. They'll do some role-playing too; it looks kinda fun."

"And you? What is your special interest?"

"Oh, I'm strictly reality based! I'm kinky, sure, but it doesn't rule my life. I just like the leather, the contests, and I love working in the community, going to events, playing around, having fun."

"And you were…?" Nancy glanced at the medallion around his neck to identify what previous title he once had. She did a double take.

Kelly grinned. "Yep! I was *Ms.* Global Leather, 2003. Since then, I transitioned. I thought it would be fun to see if I could win it again."

Nancy blinked and tried to form another question, but then Kelly looked up at someone approaching and winked at her. "Gotta dash, it's time to impress the judges!"

He used to be a woman? Nancy thought, her mind quickly making a brand new story. Maybe she could get a few different pieces out of this silly event. She began to forgive Vic for the assignment. This was more than just spanking and fashion—this was sex changes! Rivalries! Bizarre in-group politics! Visions of a series tempted her. "Notes from the Leather Underground." "Sex and Longing in the West Village." "The Kinky Among Us."

Nancy moved through the crowd on a renewed mission.

Bitsy was officially off duty as a volunteer and on the hunt for The Master of Her Dreams, but that didn't stop her from passing bad news onto Earl and his nighttime staff. She was helpful that way.

"Aphrodite organized the clean-and-sober people, and they're picketing outside the bar," she said, ticking the first complaint off her fingers. She had changed into a dark green leather corset with gold laces over a black velvet full-length skirt. "Brittney says she's joining in solidarity."

Earl sighed. The two women in question were continual blessings and banes upon the leather conference world. Aphrodite Turner was the queen of addicts—she managed to convince every event to make space available for attendees struggling with issues around alcohol, narcotics, meth, overeating, sex addiction, and dysfunctional relationships.

That would cover a *lot* of people in the kinky scene. So, organizers were usually happy to provide a conference room or two for her people to use. But Aphrodite was also a bit of an activist. Whenever an event was held in a bar, or allowed alcohol to be served, she was there with her protest signs, saying it was unfair to people in recovery.

Brittney was Aphrodite's counterpart in another segment of the community—the under-thirty demographic. They called themselves NuKnk, or "new kink" in cell phone speak. Under-thirty was no problem, until they reached under-twenty-one.

You had to be twenty-one to attend the Mr. and Ms. Global Leather (and Bootblack) Contest and all of its events. Hell, you had to be twenty-one to go to the Shaft! One of the female contestants was very active in NuKnk, leading a chapter somewhere. He couldn't remember which one, and didn't much care.

"Not my problem," Earl said firmly. "Let 'em protest. In fact, see if you can get someone to bring them some soda or iced tea; it's hot out there."

"Aw, you are such a sweetheart, Earl. I'll take care of it. But you ought to know the bootblacks have already complained about Mack."

Earl nodded grimly. "They'll be taken care of," he said. "Go have a good time, hon. Good luck finding a new master."

Bitsy looked around the bar with skepticism. "Good luck finding a straight guy here tonight who isn't already married, a loony, or a Zodian."

Earl silently agreed but wisely said nothing.

Boy Jack slipped contestant Timmy the Bootblack a ten-dollar bill. "I'm sorry about that," he said, hoping the budget for these things would be sufficient.

Timmy, a whipcord slender man with powerful arms and black polish embedded in his nails, tucked the money away with a bitter smile. "You know, I'm only taking this because I know it's not from him. I'm warning you, if he or his smarmy little boy come to the chairs again, none of us are going to do them. We're boycotting his leather."

Boy Jack nodded, understanding. "Well, I'm sure Earl will have a chat with him."

"I'd rather lose than even *touch* his boots, okay?"

"Got it. You don't have to. Just...try to keep it quiet?"

Timmy folded his arms stubbornly. "Word is gonna get out, Jack. No bootblack here will ever work on that man's leather, period."

Boy Jack continued to make soothing noises until Timmy agreed to not discuss the fact that Mack Steel not only refused to tip any bootblack who worked on his—or his boys!—leather, but instead sat there insulting their work and telling them how honored they should be by the experience. Not to mention what he said about bootblacks who had the temerity to be *female*.

"Where did all these hets come from anyway?" Mack was asking from his spot at the end of the bar. He did not circulate. Contestants came to *him*, dammit. "Jesus, this used to be an event for gay *men*. Then we let some lesbians in. Next thing you know, we're overrun by breeders from the suburbs." He said this as he spotted the one straight man running for the title and didn't bother to lower his voice. His phone buzzed and he took it out of his pocket, read the screen and thumbed a response before shoving it away with a yawn.

"Actually, I think he's from Chicago," offered Jazz Dean, who had been trying to do her contestant duty and allow Mack to ask her questions. She was still in her afternoon ensemble of chaps over jeans, but had replaced her club colors vest with her title vest.

Tall and stocky, her firm biceps showed under the sleeves of her tight black T-shirt, her left arm decorated with a tattoo of intertwined winged snakes.

"Whatever," Mack said, taking a long drink. He groaned melodramatically as the man turned to head their way.

"Kevin McDonald," he said, extending a hand. His sash read PRAIRIE MASTER, 2010. It's an honor to meet you, Mr. Steel."

"I'm sure," Mack sneered. "Prairie Master, huh? How many cows did you have to screw to get that one?"

Kevin McDonald blinked and then gave a forced laugh. "Yeah, it is a silly sounding title, I guess. But it was a tough contest, and my slave and I are honored to have won." He glanced around and pointed out a woman who was in a group of other women, watching the footage from previous Global Leather Contests on one of the large flat screens around the bar. "That's my slave in the middle."

Mack eyed the group of women and laughed. "Well, you got your cows right there!" Next to him, Paul started to moo.

Kevin stiffened and drew himself up. "Excuse me?"

Jazz grabbed her seltzer with lime from off the bar and beat a hasty retreat.

"So, the guys at the bar said they only had one contestant, what are they going to do, *oy vey*, like it's the end of the world! So, I said, look, I'll put on my rubber suit, I'll come down, he'll have someone to run against. And then I won! Who knew?" Maurice gestured to his own outfit, black rubber pants tucked into tall rubber boots, and a long-sleeved rubber uniform shirt, trimmed in red.

"So what made you want to run for this title, since it says leather?" Nancy asked.

"Leather, rubber, what's the difference? When I came out, sweetheart, it was all just kinky. We had cowboys and uniform guys, the motorcycle look, you name it. And the guys at the bar said I had to run for this because it was part of my winner responsibilities. So, I thought, hey, free trip to New York, why not? I grew up over the river you know, in Jersey."

Nancy was already composing "Gay and Grey," her story on aging in the homosexual community, when loud voices rose above the deep thumping of the bar music and the steady buzz of conversation.

Over by the bar, Mack Steel was shouting, "You'll be Mr. Global Leather over my dead body!"

It just keeps getting better, Nancy thought with glee.

"I *insist* he recuse himself!" said Kevin McDonald, safely hustled away from the bar by helpful volunteers. His face was still red with outrage. "He's clearly prejudiced against straight people!"

"We're talking to him right now," assured Boy Jack, wiping beer off his chaps. There had been some spills while getting the two men separated. "You're right, you are completely right."

Faced with hearing he was right, Kevin had no choice but to calm down. Top, mistress, master, daddy, khan, whatever, thought Boy Jack, gesturing for another volunteer to come over with glasses of water. Doesn't matter, you are all programmed to calm down when someone says you're right.

He wondered what the hell Earl was saying to Mack, though. He couldn't wait to get the dish from Boi Jack.

Mistress Ravenfyre sipped delicately from her diet soda and smiled as her husband and slave sang the chorus from "Na Na Hey Hey Kiss Him Good-bye," complete with choreographed waves. "Thank God, he'll be off the panel and we won't have to spend the entire weekend with him," she said to Cary Gordon, who looked about to faint from all the excitement.

"I don't remember any time a judge was disqualified," he said typing madly on a tiny netbook he propped up on the bar. "This is amazing. I'm going to put a big splash page on the website! I think I got a shot of him hitting those beers, which should look incredible."

"Oh, Cary, dear, don't give the man more publicity!" Ravenfyre said in horror.

"But...it's *news*!"

"Of course it is. But don't put his picture up there—put a group shot of the *other* judges. The well-behaved ones." She adjusted her sash and smoothed down the sides of her red leather bolero jacket and matching skirt. She smiled at the gathering of bootblacks who were all raising a toast and starting to sing along with her family. "Hey, hey! Good-bye..."

"And make sure that's Master Zenu, not Lord Zenu, okay?" said the big man in front of Nancy. His sash read LONE STAR LEATHER MASTER, and his badge showed him to be a judge. "I know, it sounds ridiculous, but we get mixed up a lot."

"So what happens now?" Nancy asked, not really caring enough to ask why he didn't just make up a new name if he kept getting mixed up with someone else using a silly name that sounded like it was cribbed from a *Star Wars* movie.

"I suppose he'll have to recuse himself from judging that contestant," Master Zenu said, stroking his rusty beard. He looked to be almost six foot five, and probably weighed in at nearly three hundred pounds, but he carried it like a football player, boots planted as wide as his broad shoulders, chest and belly stretching the snaps of a leather shirt. "Worst case scenario for him is they just take him off the judges panel, and although we're probably not supposed to say these things, good riddance."

"Why didn't he like that contestant?"

"Oh, he never met the guy before in his life! It's just that he's straight."

"Straight men aren't allowed to run?" Nancy was amused by the thought. Reverse discrimination!

"Well, see, there was nothing in the rules that said they couldn't. I mean, my title is gender neutral, even women compete for it. But Mack thinks all the leather titles should be gay only."

Nancy filed away the concept of female "masters" for a future question. She had so much to work with now it was getting difficult to choose her lede. "Fear and Loathing at Mr. Global Leather" was making her giggle.

Boy Jack found Boi Jack near the coat check and made a WTF? gesture. Boi Jack beckoned him into a corner and whispered, "Earl talked to Mack alone! And then said there wasn't going to be any announcement about recusing or anything tonight. Mack is just gone, and the weird thing? Paul is still here!"

"Well, damn!" Boy Jack said. He wondered if he should gather the contestants again to try and keep them from making any unwise statements. He scanned the room, taking a headcount. After a few minutes, he asked for help. About fifteen minutes after that, he knew he had a problem. One of the contestants was missing.

What else is going to go wrong? he thought. He passed Boi Jack trying to pry one of the judges away from the bar, and there was his answer. Dr. Mickey Abraham, the famous sociologist/author, well known for her Hawaiian shirts at leather events and mind-numbingly dull books looked completely plastered.

Pissed off bootblacks, a pissed judge, a missing judge *and* a missing contestant, an offensive MC, angry groups ranging from the alcoholics to the Zodians—this weekend was shaping up to be the most disastrous Global Leather of all time.

And it was only Thursday.

CHAPTER 4

MACK STEEL LAY BACK ON THE KING-SIZE BED IN HIS SUITE, arms folded behind his head and laughed out loud. What a night! He was certainly going to surrender his title with a bang.

He didn't regret his outbursts at the Shaft; that whiny, pathetic bunch of losers deserved his scorn and much worse. Those heterosexual fantasy role players in their furry vests and the clueless straight-from-the-Internet couples trying to dress and act like gay men just infuriated him.

Sharing his title year with one had just been humiliating. And she could have at least *pretended* she was queer—she had a female slave. But she dragged her boring husband around everywhere, talking about "living the lifestyle," giving out tacky weaponry and selling videos of her flogging her slavegirl and delivering safety lectures.

Living the lifestyle! How people could take something that was about hot sex and turn it into workshops and demonstrations and meetings and endless chat and posts on KinkyNet was just a mystery. Just shut up and get nasty! And take your fat, pale asses out of my bars and clubs so I don't have to watch. And take the pony people, the role-players, the spirituality seekers and their drums, and for crying out loud, take the freakin' furries with you!

Glad he was alone for once, he giggled. After this weekend, he could say whatever he wanted and do whatever he pleased. Especially after the miracle that happened tonight! JB back after all these years! And what a brand new JB, too. Soon, Mack Steel would have everything he could ever desire, with no one to limit his fantasies or his actions.

He scratched himself idly, pleased with how the evening had turned out. Yeah, Earl would have to make things okay with the rest of the judges and the contestants, but that was his job, wasn't it? Maybe the straight contestants would quit in protest. Maybe the straight judges would quit! Oh, that would be perfect.

Over this interminable year, he had judged over a dozen contests, and each one had been a nightmare. Gay male contestants would suck up to him before he even got into town, and some of them were damn tasty morsels, too. But he wasn't supposed to touch them, oh, no! Stupid rules. Only an idiot wouldn't take advantage of the endless array of hot bods delivered in kinky packages!

Mack Steel was not an idiot by any means.

And half of the events he went to had Ravenfyre, too. Raven-freaking-fyre! Her real name was Wendi Schneider. No doubt she regretted telling him that back in the first few hours they shared as co-titlists. Oh, she'd sucked up to him too, knowing that the Mr. Global Leather got more invitations to events than the Ms. She gave him stupid trinkets, made up postcards with both their pictures on them, spoke glowingly of her "leather brother," and "sash husband."

Disgusting. It had taken her almost a month to realize he was dishing her behind her back and that he had no intention of talking event producers into booking her as a star. Not even the weird-ass Zodians.

He got up to grab another little bottle of vodka out of the minibar; he intended to stick it to Earl and the Global Leather company this weekend. It was going to be steak and lobster every night and a lot of little bottles, yessirree. He admired himself in the mirror. Oh, yeah, he still had it. Taut muscular body, a light trace of silky chest hair, a respectable package and great legs. He turned, flexed and grinned at his reflection. There would be more modeling in his future and maybe a couple of movies, too. He'd outsell that bitch, that's for sure. And have the last laugh at every one of the sash-suckers who begged him for attention and then blogged like twelve-year-old gossip girls the next day. They never even knew *half* the man he could be.

He checked the clock on the DVD player in the corner of the room and frowned as he tossed back the rest of his mini-vodka. A little bit of alone time was fine, but this was ridiculous. Despite having romped quite recently, he was ready for another bit of release. Maybe he should call his new discovery and summon him back. Stay up until dawn enjoying himself—it wasn't like he couldn't nap a little during the judging.

He heard knocking on the outer door and stretched. Did Paul leave his key in the room? Maybe it was JB being polite. Or a crazed fan, desperate to suck off the hottest man at the show before he gave up the title. Or, maybe it was that freak he chased away earlier? He sighed, stood up and spotted the memento JB had brought to him. Stifling another giggle, he put that on. "There'd better be a *damn* hot man at my door," he called out, as the knocking came again. Paul, JB or some new asshole was about to get a good eyeful. And one way or another, he'd get a charge out of it!

Josh Grover, or as his badge read, Slave Joshie, walked slowly through the hotel corridor, exhausted and wrung out. Self-disclosure as an alcoholic was always trying, even though he'd been clean and sober for almost ten years now. Part of it was the hour of the meeting. Two A.M. was great for those who stayed late at the bars or clubs, but now he needed to find the room he was sharing with three other guys, tiptoe in, get some sleep and be up for a class he wanted to go to, "Seeing Through Walls: Anticipating Your Top's Needs." Not that he had a top, a dominant, a Daddy, a master or anything that looked like one. He'd like one. A guy into rubber, maybe, or latex, and rope bondage. A master with experience, who knew how to treat a slave, guide him, use him, nurture him. Even better, someone with a job. Maybe this weekend...

Joshie blinked to clear his vision, seeing someone ahead of him down the corridor. He waved, but the guy turned and went in the other direction. Joshie looked at the room numbers and sighed. No wonder he couldn't find his room, he was in the wrong tower! He turned and started back toward the central elevators. Before he got there, he found his eyes drawn to an odd stain on the carpet outside one of the rooms. Wow, he thought, shaking his head. Someone had *way* too much ketchup on their twenty-dollar hamburger. For a minute, against the gold tones of the patterned carpet, it *almost* looked like a splash of blood.

CHAPTER 5

BOI JACK HIT THE SEND BUTTON ON HER PHONE AGAIN AND heard the steady buzzing that went on and on. She switched to the other number and called that again, and went straight to voicemail. The restlessness in the room was growing, and she felt every judge staring at her. *Almost* every judge. Cups of coffee and herbal tea had been drunk, bagels and pastries and fruit salad devoured, and there they were with their yellow legal pads in front of them, ready and waiting.

Time to escalate this. She clicked her headset. "Earl, Mack still hasn't shown up, and there's still no answer on his or Paul's phones or from knocking on their door."

Earl sighed and went to the twentieth floor with Roger, one of the many assistant managers of the Grand Sterling Hotel. Roger was the always-patient liaison for Global Leather, amused by the nature of the event and happy to accept complimentary tickets to the fashion show and contest. Last year, he brought his wife. She had been quite the heavy tipper during the drag queen performances.

"It's always something, huh?" Roger said with a chuckle. "He's probably hungover, phone turned off."

"I'd almost rather he packed up and left," Earl growled. It was too early in the day to handle this, what with the rest of the judges and most of the contestants already angry with him. Plus, his keynote speaker was still MIA! Maybe he could get Mickey Abraham to step up. It might just keep her distracted and away from the Zodians and the cash bar, which would be an added bonus.

They stopped outside the suite and Roger knocked hard. "Mr. Steel? This is hotel staff. Please respond if you're in there!"

Silence. The two men looked at each other, and Roger reached into his pocket for a master keycard. As he did, he glanced down and froze. Earl looked down too, at a dark brown stain on the carpet, just outside the door.

Earl felt the acid of his morning gallon of coffee suddenly churn in his stomach. "That isn't...I mean, it can't be..."

Roger reached for his two-way radio and hit a number. "Security," he said when he connected. "We have a possible Code Three in room 2040."

Two security guards arrived within five minutes, and Roger handed the keycard to them. In those minutes, Roger tried to soothe Earl with assurances that it was probably just *au jus* from a sandwich. Earl, having given many a soothing talk in his lifetime, had gone quite pale and had muted his cell phone and headset.

One of the guards opened the door, and Earl groaned as he saw more splotches on the interior carpet. The guard called into the room, "Is there anyone in here? I'm coming in!"

Silence. And worse, a faint, sickly-sweet rusty scent reached the doorway and Roger, who had been managing hotels for over twenty years, dialed 911.

As the door swung open wide, Earl could see through the living room area into the bedroom beyond, with its massive king-sized bed piled high with pillows. It made a perfect white backdrop to Mack Steel's magnificent, beautiful body. He was sprawled in abandon in the center of the bed, wearing only a skimpy, lacy, bright yellow bikini brief. Surrounding his body was a pool of blood.

Mr. Global Leather was very, very dead.

Earl backed away from the door and turned away from the horrid scene, thumbing his headset on. "Jack," he croaked out, his mouth dry. "Both Jacks. Um. Go ahead without Mack. He's... indisposed."

Then he slid down to the floor and sat there, dazed.

Worst. Contest. Ever.

CHAPTER 6

Detective Rebecca Feldblum walked carefully around the bed, stepping over the markers on every bloodstain on the floor. She turned to the uniformed patrolman who was the first responder; he was a just-out-of-the-academy gawky thing who was way too excited to have ever been at a murder scene before.

"Okay, so run this by me one more time," she said, beckoning.

He flipped open his notebook and read from his notes. "The stiff is named Mack Steel. He's some kind of kinky celebrity—this is like a gay beauty contest thing called Mr. Global Leather, and he won last year. Here's a picture—the guy had a stack of 'em here." He pointed to an 8x10 print on top of the dresser among many other scattered items.

Rebecca glanced at it. In the photo, he was wearing tight leather pants and tall boots, bare-chested under a broad sash draped across his body with the title on it. It was signed; apparently he was some sort of star.

"His, uh, boyfriend, is in the next room; he *says* he wasn't here last night." The uniform looked up meaningfully and Rebecca nodded for him to continue.

"Hotel security discovered the body; they were called by the manager, um, Roger Clarendon, and he was asked to open the room by the producer of the contest, a guy named Earl. Seems the vic had to be judging the people for this year's contest and didn't show up on time. Earl is downstairs, running things; I told him to stay in the hotel and wait for your call. Anyway, I just slapped some tape up after I saw it was clear he was dead and called it in."

"Good work," Rebecca said, slapping his shoulder. "Outstanding. Thank you! I'll take a copy of everything before we start the room canvassing. And what do *you* have for me, Eduardo? Have you solved it yet? They would have on TV, you know."

Her favorite crime scene detective looked up from his visual inspection of the wound and rolled his eyes. An assistant was taking close-up photos.

"And on TV you'd be a blonde wearing three-inch heels and a miniskirt. I guess we ain't all gonna be rich and famous soon. Where's your partner?"

"Sprained or strained ankle from a basketball game gone terribly wrong," Rebecca sighed. Not that she liked Grant very much; her third partner in her time in homicide, he was equally not happy with a female coworker, let alone a gay one. The fact that she was in better physical shape than he was made his eternal complaints about the lack of upper body strength and stamina in "lady cops" a joke. What he'd been doing on a basketball court was questionable. Rebecca suspected he tripped over an ottoman after a few beers.

"That's a shame," Eduardo said. "But I can at least get you started off with some real good intelligence here." He returned his gaze to the corpse and pointed. "Looks like Mr. Steel was stabbed one time, but I see three entry wounds, awful close together, all lined up. That's weird. It's like someone stabbed him with…a garden trowel, something with three blades on it hitting all at once, *chuck*! Otherwise, it would have to be someone with a scary kind of precision. It looks like they might be of different depths, with the one in the middle the longest blade, but the M.E. will have to give you the data on that. Another thing—your perp might know his anatomy very well or just be really lucky—whatever it was went right between the ribs, neat as can be, from an angle…down here, so he was thrusting up. From the state of the blood and his body, I'm thinking sometime between midnight and five A.M. If there was a struggle, it wasn't much." He shrugged and adjusted his glasses. "He might even have been passed out. I found four of these." He held up an evidence bag with little vodka bottles in it.

"Four isn't enough to make a man his size pass out," Rebecca said. The deceased had been an impressive specimen for a man, well-built and muscular, with beautifully sculpted legs and a respectable endowment, quite visible through the scant yellow briefs he was wearing.

"No, but he might have gotten well-lubricated before coming back to the hotel room." Eduardo realized what he said and coughed, and a faint blush showed under his olive skin. There was in fact a large tub of some sort of "personal lubricant" on the bedside table along with some leather cuffs, a blindfold and a sizeable silicone phallus. "I mean, he might have drank somewhere else."

The patrol officer snickered. "Yeah, well, if this is some kinda kinky thing, maybe he was all lubed up, too. Any gerbils missing?"

Why do I end up with these cases? Detective Feldblum asked herself, glaring and holding her hand out for her copy of the patrolman's notes. He pursed his lips and tore a page out of his book. She took it and nodded for him to wait for her in the hall, and sighed, knowing she could have been nicer to him. Because she knew damn well why she was lucky enough to snag this beauty of a case.

"They're *your* people," Lieutenant Ludivico had said, when he handed her the assignment personally.

Sometimes, it was an extra challenge being one of the only out lesbian detectives in homicide. Not that Ludivico gave her *every* potentially gay corpse their precinct covered. That would show a pattern. No, he just made sure to hand over some of the weirdest ones. Her people? She knew nothing about this leather stuff, except that there was always a large number of men and women dressed like bikers who marched down Fifth Avenue the last Sunday in June. And that they, like the drag queens, made many of the more mainstream gays consider them slightly embarrassing. Personally, she never gave it much thought. If they obeyed the law and didn't make a nuisance of themselves, why should she care? They were no stranger than many other special little populations in the New York City area.

Eduardo rose from his examination and stretched. "Well, there's been *some* conventional sexual activity going on here. I got four used condoms in the trash; we'll get some cells from the boyfriend just in case we need 'em for matching later. Wallet, watch, keys, cell phone are all here. In fact, we got two cell phones and two laptops in the room and about a hundred bucks in cash; this was no robbery. Nothing else too complicated here; no special imprint I can see from the blood on the carpet, but we have a ton of photos to look through anyway. No sign of blood in the bathroom drains, but we have some swabs to test. There *is* something funny about his, um, lingerie there."

Rebecca looked down and cocked her head. "Kinda frilly," she noted.

"Yeah. I'm no expert on this, but isn't that weird for these motorcycle guys? I thought they were all, you know, macho, macho men."

This was one of the many reasons why Rebecca loved Eduardo. Some other guy would have said "leather fags" or "kinky perverts" or waggled his brows at her, implying that indeed, these *were* her people, and she should know all these little details like what underwear they might prefer. Four years in homicide and there were still plenty of men who loved to see if their locker-room talk or dirty jokes or blatant weenie wagging would get to her.

Instead, Eduardo just about admitted that he knew his way around the Village People. "I'll be sure to ask about it," she said with a slight smile. "Thanks, Ed. Check in with me if you guys solve the case before dinner. Try to hold down the high-speed chases and explosions."

"Ha! You'll be lucky if we get to look at him before Monday," he said. He pointed, and another member of his team bagged the sex toys. "But if a slot opens, I'll call you with anything interesting. Okay, folks, let's wrap this up and get him outta here!"

Rebecca scanned the room one more time, noting an unopened box of condoms, a stack of candy and protein bars and crumpled receipts all on the dresser top, and asked for those to be bagged as well. Then, she went to go talk to the boyfriend who was mysteriously not with the victim between midnight and the body discovery.

He was ashen, with swollen red eyes. He clutched a black bandana in one hand, his fingers tightening and then shaking it out. From a quick glance, his hands looked clean and unbruised, no scrapes on the knuckles. In fact, his nails looked so pristine, she suspected he had gotten a manicure recently. Paul Helms, twenty-five years old, home address same as the victim, in California. Another handsome man, in a less striking manner than his late boyfriend; his eyes were a lovely dark blue, his hair a honey blond, trimmed in a short ivy league. He was dressed in very tight jeans with the bottoms turned up in cuffs over scuffed harness boots and a baggy contest logo T-shirt. He had a thin chain collar with a lock dangling from the front around his neck. A piece of luggage was open on the floor, most of the contents still packed inside; Steel's clothing and belongings had already been packed up for the lab. There had been quite a lot of leather, and notably, no other panties.

"I'm very sorry for your loss," Rebecca said, sitting down across from him. "But I need to ask some questions."

He sniffed and nodded, and wiped his eyes with the bandana.

"I understand you were not in the room last night or this morning. Why not?"

The young man looked down and took a deep breath. "My... Mack and I...it's hard to explain."

Oh, goody. "Go slow and I'll try to keep up," she said encouragingly.

"We're not monogamous. I mean, most of the time, we are. But Mack, he, um." He rubbed his forehead, trying to focus, his eyes screwing up. "Okay, so we're into BDSM. Know what that is?"

"Yeah, the whole bondage and leather thing."

"Right, well, there's more. Like, Mack, he's...he was...my master. He was in charge of things, okay? I was his slave. But it was a good thing, completely consensual. I *liked* it that way."

Rebecca nodded.

Paul gathered himself, thought, and then started again. "See, when we go to events like this, sometimes Mack would...pick up someone new. Just for the night. And, well, I'd get out of the way. Or, he'd tell me to go out and have some fun on my own, because we're kind of poly. And that's what happened last night."

"Which one?"

Paul looked at her blankly.

"Did he find someone new, or tell you to go out and, uh, do the same?"

"Both."

"Okay, then, let's start with who he was with last night." Rebecca clicked her pen, thinking maybe this *would* be solved before dinner.

"I don't know."

"Seriously?"

Paul shrugged. "He didn't always tell me. They usually...didn't matter."

"All right. Then tell me who *you* were with."

Paul looked uncomfortable. "This is going to sound weird. I sort of wandered around most of the night going to room parties. I can find some of the guys who would have seen me, I guess. I spent most of the night in this room on the fifth floor, with this guy who calls himself Wolfboy. I know. Obviously it's not his real name, but sometimes, people are only known by their scene names. That's where I was this morning...when...when they called me."

"I see." Rebecca pinched the bridge of her nose and asked, "I'll want to have a chat with...Wolfboy, so you'll have to find him for me. Do you think anyone else might have known who Mack spent the night with? Would he have told anyone else? Would he have gone to one of those room parties?"

"I don't know," Paul said, blinking. "I don't think so. He wouldn't tell anyone something he...he...didn't tell me!" He burst into a harsh sob, and Rebecca pressed her lips together. When the young man got himself together, she would ask about nearest kin, those yellow panties, and then if the deceased had any enemies or rivals at the event. After all, if people killed each other over roles in community theatre and slots on cheerleading squads, why not Mr. Leather Whatever?

She would get the uniforms to do a canvass of the rooms surrounding this one, ask for the security images to be downloaded onto a disk or flash drive for her, and then talk to the hotel manager and the contest producer who discovered the body together. The producer would certainly have a list of the event's attendees, and, hopefully, know everyone's real name. By then, maybe she'd have another detective or two to help the expanded interviews. She glanced at her notes.

Wolfboy. Non-monogamy. BDSM. Frilly panties and leather contests. Room parties. Scene names. Masters and slaves.

Her people?

My ass, she thought.

CHAPTER 7

DOM. SUB. SLAVE. PUPPY. SWITCH. ALPHA. PRIMARY. BOY OR boi, master, mistress, or sir and ma'am, top and bottom, 24/7, twink, tourist, Zodian, polyamorous, lifestyler, leather, latex, gear, rubber, cyberpunk, steampunk, uniform, vampire, furry...

Nancy Nichols hadn't had such an extensive vocabulary list since the fourth grade. Arriving bright and early to discover the fallout from the meet and greet debacle, she was armed with a scene guide she'd discovered online, scrolling through the wonderful cheat sheet on her smart phone. She hadn't bothered to do much research on the leather community before—who had the time for real work on a turkey-ass story like this one? But now that it seemed full of filler pieces she could spread out long past the actual event, it was worth it to get a grip on the lingo. She already had outlines for three lifestyle pieces and the bones of her big story on the event itself.

Nancy also had joined KinkyNet; she'd picked the screen name TELLMEKINKYSTORIES after she found out there were no less than eighty MISTRESSNANCY and LADYNANCY accounts already registered. The chat boards there had been full of outraged and delighted recounts of the Mack Steel outburst, many seeming to be from people who were not actually present. Someone had started a petition demanding he be fired, or recused or censured— often misspelled *censored* in the comments. That seemed to lead directly into cries against censorship, supporting his freedom to say whatever he wanted.

KinkyNet did not seem like a place she was going to get a lot of useable material if so many of the users were morons. On the other hand, merely stating that "the online bizarre sex community, represented by the million-user KinkyNet, erupted in fury over the controversy..." seemed like a fair statement.

But as she got to the hotel, ready to hit up the producer of the event for an interview, she spotted the police, paramedic and fire/rescue units out front and her heart quickened. With luck, maybe the Steel guy got into another fight, and this time, she'd get the pictures out of Cary so fast they'd be on the website before the man finished thanking her for the opportunity.

But when she worked her way through the lobby, now even more filled with leather/latex/lace/barbarian fur-clad conventioneers, she knew at once this was not a follow up to a brawl. Hotel security was buzzing around, managing to look both officious and a little panicked at the same time, and there were more than four uniformed cops with no trouble in sight—which usually meant there were more somewhere else. The registration desk was still doing business, but there was a steady undercurrent of curiosity that had nothing to do with the schedules now being posted and stacked around the room; Nancy grabbed one and sidled over to one of the patrol officers. She showed him her press card immediately.

"Good morning, Officer...Ramirez! What's the fuss? Did the leather people scare some tourists from Des Moines?"

Officer Ramirez, a stocky Puerto Rican with one palm resting against the radio in his belt, looked at her with the wariness of a veteran. Dammit, she should have picked a greener one. But he shrugged and said, "Maybe you wanna talk to Detective Feldblum."

The Dyke Detective herself? Nancy Nichols nodded, smiled, thanked the officer and suppressed a cackle of sheer joy. A detective could mean a burglary, an assault, some party drug dealing. But Feldblum was in homicide—someone was dead as Elvis, and probably all trussed up like a kinky turkey, to boot! Deep inside, she knew that feeling glee over a murder was probably not the best response humanity expected of her, but now her piece-of-poop story had officially become headline quality, and she was the only reporter here!

Trying to figure out where to find the corpse, the killer, and the famous lesbian homicide detective was next. As she moved, she hit speed dial on her phone and called her photographer. She'd call editorial *after* she filed her first piece, before they decided to give it to someone else.

"How can we judge with an even number?" Master Zenu asked, scratching his pen against the yellow pad in his folder. "What if there's a tie?"

"There are procedures for that," Boi Jack said for the fifth time. "Really, it'll be all right."

"Jesus Christ, Zenu, give it a rest," moaned Mickey Abraham. She was dressed in a vintage Hawaiian shirt featuring a multitude of guitar players and hula dancers against a vivid blue background, and her eyes were dark circled behind thick glasses that did not hide the red streaks of overindulgence. "The world won't end if we reach a tie. Screw it, let's give everyone a sash and go home."

"Clearly, there should be a back-up judge," said Mistress Ravenfyre, sipping her tea. She appeared tired as well. "How rude of that man to just drink himself into a stupor and leave us like this."

"We don't know that's his issue," Boi Jack said nervously. "Maybe he's sick."

"No great loss," rumbled Lord Laertes. There was a murmur of agreement, and then the judges seemed to finally settle down. Boi Jack sighed and got ready to call in the first contestant; while in the hall, she felt her phone buzz. She checked the screen and read what was on it three times before it truly registered.

Sorry, dude, I flaked.

"I flaked," Earl read, with an exasperated giggle threatening in his throat. That was the excuse of Dr. Julian Westfield, celebrated author of *You're Kinky and That's Okay!* Familiar on daytime television screens and morning radio shows and college campuses, he was the highest profile pervert in the United States. In fact, he was the telegenic opposite of Dr. Mickey Abraham, who also wrote books on being kinky. But Julian was tall and long-haired and media savvy and smiled a lot, using easy language and humor to disarm straight and vanilla audiences from coast to coast, whereas Mickey was short, gloomy, dark and sarcastic and the author of thick tomes required for her sociology classes. People in the leather scene pretended they read Mickey's books but probably didn't; they pretended to disdain Julian's, but probably owned them on every electronic device they had. Julian got up and said things that boiled down to "We're having kinky sex! Isn't that super?" Mickey discussed the neurolinguistics of safewords and passive-aggression in negotiation for sex play. Julian *was* flaky, loved every fetish with equal passion, and chased skirts while loudly proclaiming the superiority of polyamory. Mickey was bitter, ridiculed community mores and sub-groups and chased skirts while drinking a bit too much.

This was why one was a keynote speaker and the other a judge.

But Julian was re-booked on a flight that would arrive tonight, just in time for the opening ceremonies, although what to do about, well, everything, was now up in the air.

With phone and radio headsets on the table, Earl stared at his master schedule and sipped his cold coffee. The young police officer had told him to expect a detective for a formal statement soon, and Earl had been only too happy to say yes to anything to get away from the awful sight of Mack sprawled and bloody. And when Paul finally showed up! Oh, God, what a scream from that boy, and the sobbing! Where had he been, anyway? He picked a hell of a time to go tricking and turn his phone off. Oh, dear God, what if they'd had a fight or something? Wouldn't that look *splendid* for the community?

Earl shuddered and slumped in his chair. What now? Continue with the contest? He'd told the Boys Jack to keep it going; thank goodness for them and Bitsy and the rest of his army of volunteers. The vendors were all set up, the classes had begun, and as far as he knew, no one else knew Mack was...dead. Yet. But they would soon. And then what?

Canceling the event was out of the question. He'd lose everything he had, he'd have to declare bankruptcy. But to go ahead seemed... disrespectful? Or maybe he could slap some lipstick on this pig and say the contest was...a memorial. To Mack.

Another giggle threatened. He could just imagine getting up to proclaim this weekend a memorial to the single most-hated Mr. Global Leather there had ever been. The blinks of disbelief and the snickers that would ripple through the crowd. Oh, lord, would they cheer? How would that look to the rest of the scene? Hell, to the rest of the world! Like...to the cops?

What would he tell the police? Surely, they'd ask him if the man had any enemies! He groaned, emptied his cup into the trash and poured a fresh round of hot coffee from the urn. Then, with a sigh, he picked up his phone and started texting his staff to let them know. He would tell them to keep it quiet for as long as possible.

"As a doornail!" Boy Jack whispered to Boi Jack as they stood together in the hallway between the two rooms being used to house the contestants and the judges.

"Oh Em Gee!" Boi Jack squealed. She lowered her voice and swept a hand through her hair; both of them were capless today, wearing grey T-shirts that read JACK under their leather vests. "Who did it?"

"How should I know? But the cops are all around his room; Greg texted me that he can't even get back to his own room because of real crime scene tape and everything!"

"Oh, my freakin' God, I am totally being first to post this on KinkyNet."

"I was first on Facebook."

"Let's tweet it at the same time!"

They texted furiously for a moment, their thumbs moving at lightning speeds, and then their phones beeped at the same time and they glanced down to read Earl's message, and then back at each other.

"Oops," they said simultaneously.

All over the hotel, and from there all over the world, phones, tablets and computers lit up, beeped, clicked, rang tones and otherwise heralded the passing of Mr. Global Leather.

CHAPTER 8

"So, was it a kinky sex thing?" Nancy asked, microphone clipped to her jacket lapel while she took notes at the same time. Her target, a hotel security guard named Farid Ghorbani, had remained silent and stoic until a twenty found its way into his pocket and she swore she could call him an unnamed source. "Was he all tied up in a gimp hood?"

"No, not tied up. No hood. But he was on the bed all spread out, blood everywhere. Someone stabbed him right in the heart, looked like. But there was this big..." he gestured at his own crotch and then looked away for a moment. "A fake one, rubber one, right by the bed! And he was *naked*!" The man was whispering, apparently torn between the joy of telling what he saw and the fear of getting caught.

"Do you know if they arrested anyone?"

He shook his head. "No. His fag boyfriend was all crying like a little baby. He didn't look strong enough to do something like that. It's their cursed lifestyle, you know. If they don't kill each other with diseases, they do it with knives!"

"You don't say," Nancy murmured, amused by the casual contradictions of bigotry. The gays were all weak, limp-wristed fairies, *and* they were all vicious killers. "Well, thanks, Farid. Look, here's my card. You call or text me if you remember anything else, or find out anything new, and I promise, there's more in it for you."

He strode off and she pondered her options. Elevators were not being allowed to discharge passengers on the 20th floor unless you had a room key and then you were walked to your room and presumably into an interview. Her credentials didn't even garner a moment of hesitation; every uniform she met said quite firmly that no press was allowed on the scene and the detective was too busy to talk. Donny the photographer was annoyed at being awakened so early; he hadn't been scheduled to come out to this thing until tomorrow night. But when he heard the magical *murder* word, he hit the ground running so fast his text read like he'd accidentally stepped on his phone. Kinky killings trumped fashion shows any day! He had the service elevator covered on the first floor, trusting them to bring the body out the back way.

How to get to Detective Feldblum, though? She was known as a pretty meticulous, by-the-book investigator with a solid solve rate, despite the handicap of being a gay woman in what was still a very male-dominated, paramilitary organization. She was also notoriously publicity shy.

You'd be too, if they called you Detective Dyke, Nancy thought with a nanosecond of sympathy. But business was business.

Where would she go after checking out the crime scene? To the event producer? That sounded reasonable. And if Feldblum wasn't there yet, he'd be good for a quote or two.

But by the time she got down to the lobby, she could see the rest of the world was already finding out the news. Dozens of people in their leather pants and miniskirts, their corsets and spikes, their furry vests and romantic gowns, were all converging at the registration desk area and loudly demanding to know what was going on. A ring of cops blocked the way to the convention office.

Ah, well. Time to get some statements from the dead man's community, then. Or, find a spokesperson from their array of local celebrities. She flipped through the program and spotted a class titled "Edgeplay: Dangerous Practices for Beginners." That sounded just absurd enough to be promising. She quick-texted Donny to come and get some pictures of anyone who might allow it and scanned the lobby for more inspiration.

Earl sat down at the conference table with Detective Feldblum, and they looked at each other for a moment in silent appraisal.

He knows a ton and doesn't want to say anything, she thought, flipping her notepad open. The smell in the closed, windowless room was coffee, heavily salted with sweat. Charts and folders and stacks of paper were everywhere, but displayed some basic order; it was the man himself who looked disarrayed, his fingers twitching as he played with his coffee cup, a pen, his phone. Although he welcomed her and announced his intention to help, he was afraid of saying something.

She knows how nervous I am, he thought with a twinge of despair. At first, he was confused; didn't all New York homicide detectives look like grizzled Brooklyn thugs or gorgeous, square-jawed models? This one was just about five foot five, with curly chestnut brown hair that just hit her shoulders, an arched nose and dark eyes under even darker, feathered brows. Her makeup was light, if she wore any at all, but the light olive tone of her skin looked smooth and even. She was dressed in a dark blue pantsuit that looked nicely tailored, showing her strong looking shoulders and curved hips. She had refused his offer of coffee.

"First, Mr. Stemple, let me say I am very sorry for the loss of your...winner?"

"Titleholder?" he suggested.

"Titleholder, then. Thank you. This is a new world to me, and I sure will appreciate any help you can give me in navigating around this." She paused and let that sink in, then continued. "I'm going to have to ask you some questions, though, that might seem like I am questioning your..."

"Lifestyle?" he offered. Then he laughed. "Although, God, we hate that word, too. Our culture, let's say. Thank you. I know, we look weird. Maybe we are weird. I mean, I'm sure some of us are. But...we're not killers. Not generally. I mean, not more than anyone else!" He braced his forehead against the heel of his left hand and pressed. "God, I sound like an idiot."

"No one is expected to sound logical and clear after something like this," Rebecca assured him. "What can you tell me about Mr. Steel? Were you personal friends?"

"He, ah. No, not exactly. Okay, not at all. He was not one of the most popular titleholders we've ever had," Earl said haltingly. "I hate to say it, but it's not like you won't find out in five minutes talking to anyone else. He was obnoxious, self-centered, rude, and very, um, outspoken about some of his opinions."

"So he might have had some enemies?"

"Enemies. See, I don't know. He had plenty of people who didn't like him. But not liking someone doesn't mean you're going to go kill them!"

"No, but it's generally a good place to start looking," Rebecca said gently. "Could you give me some names?"

"I don't know! How can I do that?" Earl sprang up, wiping his hands against his hips. "These are good people here, safe, *consensual* people! I mean, it could be just a random killing, right? Robbery! Gay bashing! Just because we look threatening doesn't mean we're murderers!"

Personally, Rebecca didn't think anyone she'd seen so far looked threatening, leather clothing aside. Earl himself reminded her of her seventh grade science teacher; most of the costumed people she'd seen in the hallways seemed pretty normal looking, no matter how gussied up in leather and steel studs. At first, she had taken the event to be all gay male, but it was clear that this was no purely masculine enterprise. Neither did it seem all-gay, despite the relative popularity of the leather clone look among both genders. There were quite a few women sporting the leather jeans and motorcycle chaps and jacket style, and Rebecca would turn in her own gay agenda ID if she hadn't spotted plenty of straight people, some of them looking slightly defensive, others merely cheerful in their fetish finery. But scary? Not really. She filed away a desire to be *perceived* as scary, though; people who wanted others to think they were threatening could be a potentially annoying aspect of this investigation.

"Tell me more about...this leather, this BDSM stuff. I looked through your program, but I can use some explanations. For example, what exactly do you have to *do* to compete in this contest? Paul Helms, Mr. Steel's boyfriend, said Steel was his master. What does that mean, exactly? Is it necessary to be a master to run for this title?"

"Oh, no," Earl said quickly. "Anyone can run, as long as they're into leather."

"Leather...clothing?"

"Well, yes, but not just that. It's more a state of mind? God, you can get into such fights over what *leather* means, or who a master is or the difference between a sub and a slave or a dom and a master. Or mistress, or daddy or whatever. But for the purpose of the contest, you are leather if, um...you say you are. And as for masters and slaves, we don't require a contestant to be in a power exchange relationship to run. How could you judge that based on a weekend? There are different contests for that stuff anyway. This one—it's for the image? Not *just* the image of course, anyone can dress up. But...ah...Miz?"

"Detective Feldblum."

"Detective...it's hard to define. Our judges spend two days asking the contestants questions about it and I promise you, everyone has different answers. It's like the dom-sub stuff; you can't just have a list of these ten things that make a BDSM relationship, because it's all very...subjective. You can only judge based on what you see out in public. I mean, I think a lot of people actually *pretend* they're into it, or do it for the weekend, then go home and lead perfectly normal lives, like anyone else!"

"And was Steel one of those people?"

"I don't know. Honestly." Earl ran a hand through his hair and paced. "I suppose so. Paul always seemed to do what Steel told him, he was quiet, respectful...to Mack, at least. And he really took care of Mack, made sure he always had the right clothes and gear for an appearance, kept his calendar, answered his email. I guess they were real enough. And they've been together for three years—a lot of couples actually break up during a title year, from the stress."

"Really? What kind of stress?"

"The travel! Mack did over sixty appearances and photo shoots last year, not counting remote interviews on blogs and Internet radio shows. And the fundraising—we give the winners a travel fund, but it's not really enough for more than three or four trips, especially if you take a partner with you like he always did. Both of our winners this year did, actually—I think Mack had to raise between ten and twelve thousand for his travel expenses and his charity. And people ask you to give speeches, judge contests, perform in fantasies, do a million fund-raisers, write editorials—you're expected to promote the title as well as yourself, and it's not that easy."

"But you said Steel was one of your most unpopular winners," she repeated, leaning back to look up at him while he paced. "So...did you get complaints? Did he ever get any threats, or hate mail?"

It was his nightmare! Earl clenched his teeth, thinking of the folder of Internet hate mail he had accumulated, for himself and for Mack. And as for threats...what had Mack been screaming last night? That one of the contestants would win over his dead body? He groaned, trying to figure out some way not to incriminate anyone.

"Mr. Stemple," Rebecca said, remaining seated. Her voice was soothing, patient. "If it's like you say, I can go out there and just start asking around. I'm asking you to help me out here. Think of it as helping me eliminate suspects. This is a big event, right? Lots of people here might have a grudge against Mr. Steel. Let's get the obvious ones out of the way; I'm sure most of them have solid alibis. But I'll need to work fast. How many guests are here for the event? And how many of these people will have come from out of town?"

"About three thousand, including people just coming to the ball and contest. And, er, about three quarters of the attendees would not be from around here," he admitted.

"And you wind up on Sunday night? That leaves me three days, tops, to figure out if there's one bad guy mixed up in your... culture. Someone who *doesn't* belong, let's say."

That sounded reasonable. Earl stopped in mid-pace and considered. She was right. Hell, all she'd need was one minute with someone like Phedre or Cary to get the entire history of the contest and everyone associated with it.

"And by the way, where were you last night, after midnight?"

Earl turned to her and swallowed. Her face was a polite mask of curiosity, one eyebrow raised, pen poised to write.

"M-me?"

"If Mr. Steel just spent a year being so unpopular, that can't have been much good for you, am I right?"

"Well—certainly—we had our differences. But I didn't kill him!"

She waited. He thought, quickly, putting the evening together frantically. "I was...I was at the bar, the Shaft, until almost two in the morning. After that, I came back here, no, wait, I stopped at a deli on Park Avenue and got a sandwich and some salad and then came back here. I have my cab receipt! I have the deli receipt!" He sat down again and flipped through the folders and envelopes on the table. "I save them...business expenses, you know..."

"Of course, of course. And then maybe you could give me some names of people I might want to talk to?"

As he emptied an envelope full of crushed receipts, Earl was already speaking, hating himself.

"Last night at the bar, Mack almost got himself into a fight with one of the new contestants," he said, shoving over the scraps of paper. "I sent him back to the hotel early because of it. But that contestant stayed at the bar; he didn't leave until they all did, later on!"

Rebecca nodded. "And his name..."

"Kevin McDonald. But you'll see, he's a perfectly nice man, married, middle class, he sells electronics in Evanston, for crying out loud!"

"I'll want to meet him."

"Yes...right. Well, I can send a message to Jack, get Kevin up here, I suppose."

"That would be great, Earl, thank you. And is there a way I can maybe see all or most of the attendees? At one time?"

"Oh! Tonight is the opening ceremonies and fashion show," he offered weakly. "I thought about canceling...but with so many people here...and the contest..."

"You're going to continue the contest?"

"Yes," he said, not realizing he'd decided. "Yes. We're here, and the other contestants came all this way. I have to. We'll find some way to, ah, make it a memorial to him."

Rebecca cocked her head and raised that eyebrow even higher.

"To one of your most unpopular winners?"

Earl shrugged helplessly. "Sometimes it *is* all about image. Do you want me to ask Kevin to come up here? Or, maybe you can just go and meet all the contestants at once; they're together all day today, for the judging. And, er, there are other groups meeting all day—classes, workshops, there's a drumming circle at five, some AA meetings and a couple of affinity and D/S groups are having their meet-ups here, too. There's an erotic fiction and poetry reading after dinner. Tomorrow night is the fetish ball with part two of the judging. Most of the attendees will be there for that; it's more popular than the contest itself. But the puppy and pet show is in the afternoon, along with the high tea and the Zodian scarf dance contest. And, uh, yeah, I have a little bit of hate mail I can copy onto a disk or something for you."

For a second, he thought he saw just a glimpse of frustration or annoyance in her eyes. But she sighed and got up. "I'll be sending some other officers around, then. I'd appreciate a few more copies of your schedule and program. But let's start with your contestants, shall we? And then I'll figure out how to find the rest of the folks I'll want to talk to."

But as they stepped out of the room, finding a large group of attendees was made absurdly simple. The lobby was packed with milling conference goers, some shouting questions at the registration desk or the uniforms behind it; others were loudly and slowly repeating the story thus far into cell phones; and still others were texting away, completely disobeying the signs taped to the walls forbidding the use of cell phones. Bitsy was trying desperately to maintain order, but her own staff was fully involved in the dissemination of questions, theories, facts and guesses.

And finally making Rebecca scowl, she could see and hear professional cameras. The press had discovered the story already, and she was still on her own.

CHAPTER 9

IN THE ONEIDA ROOM, A WELL-ENDOWED WOMAN IN A BRIGHT red corset, deeply slit silk skirt and impossibly heeled boots was crossing her leg and holding her hand out while a tall man in a black and white maid's costume bowed to that hand and extended a laser pointer on the tips of his fingers. She took it and casually waved it at the PowerPoint screen projected next to her and asked, "Now, how did Flossie know I needed this?"

Because you rehearsed it, thought Slave Joshie with a deep sigh. He got up early for this? He should have read the description better. He was sure that Lady Esmerelda was very popular among her tea-serving sissy maid crowd, but this was just not his scene. He drifted off as the lecture/demonstration continued, and woke up when the door opened to let in a hot looking guy in the best copy of a NYPD uniform he'd ever seen. Then he saw the gun and radio on the man's belt and realized that oh, shit, this was real.

Esmerelda turned a slow, icy stare toward the man and said in her lofty, oh-so-dominant voice, "Excuse me, we are having a closed class here!"

"Sorry, ma'am, but I need to have everyone's attention for a minute," said the man, taking in her garb and Maid Flossie's ensemble with typical New York *sangfroid*. He turned to the class and continued speaking. "Excuse me for interrupting, folks, but there's a police investigation going on here today and we need your help. Someone was killed up on the 20th floor last night, and we're trying to find out if anyone might have seen or heard anything that can help the detectives find the killer."

The room erupted into shocked cries and immediate questions, some people raising their hands and others simply shouting them out. The officer raised his hands for a moment and said, "There's not much I can tell you now, except that the deceased is Mr. Mack Steel, and he was in room 2040. We're looking for anyone who might be on that floor, or might have seen Mr. Steel last night after midnight..."

A woman screamed, covering her mouth as though shocked that she could make such a sound. The buzz of questions grew into shouts and cries of "Oh, my God," and "Holy shit!"

Wow, the winner from last year murdered! Joshie sat there shaking his head; what irony! He'd never met the man, but he did buy his calendar and had one of his run pins, and remembered quite well the grace and beauty of the man under the contest lights the previous year. What a shame! But wait...something was nagging at him. He frowned and tried to concentrate over the din. As his thoughts clarified, he stood up gingerly and raised his hand.

The cop was busy shaking off questions asking for more details, while passing out business cards. Joshie cleared his throat and waved a little, and muttered, "Excuse me? Sir? Officer? I think...I might have seen..."

"Hey!" barked a short, stocky lesbian next to him, over the staccato noise of the classroom. "This guy saw something!"

Everyone turned to him, and Joshie felt suddenly very embarrassed. But the policeman came over to him and said, "Is there something you can tell us, sir?"

"Maybe?" Joshie squeaked.

"Come on, sir, let's get you hooked up with the detective," the uniformed man said, and for a moment, Joshie thought having a master into uniforms might be pretty hot. He nodded as helpfully as he could and said, "Okay, sure. But, um, please don't call me *sir*. It's just not right. See, I'm a sub."

The officer blinked and nodded. "Whatever you say, sir."

Joshie sighed. Life was full of disappointments.

CHAPTER 10

"HE WAS A DICK AND A JACKASS, BUT I DIDN'T KILL HIM," SAID Kevin McDonald, the minute they were alone.

"He did threaten you last night, though?" Rebecca asked, watching the man's eyes. They were dark grey, almost black, and his hair was a buzz-cut nest of salt and pepper. In his midthirties, his body was trim and fit in a black *kilt* of all things, a black, silk button-down shirt and a leather vest. Rebecca had never seen a man in a kilt outside of the Emerald Society Drum and Pipe Corps. Dangling from his left hip was some sort of whip unlike anything Rebecca had ever seen. Instead of being a single braid or even a cat-o'-nine-tails, it was a thick bundle of green strips of leather, attached to a handle displaying a complex woven pattern. He was also wearing a medallion on a leather strap around his neck that read PRAIRIE MASTER.

This case was just getting better by the minute. What's that, Lieutenant? Who are my persons of interest? Wolfboy and Prairie Master.

Yeah, that would go over well.

"No, he never threatened me. He said I'd be Mr. Global Leather over his dead body."

Rebecca waited a moment, letting the silence make its own comment. Kevin grimaced and waved his arms. "Oh, seriously? You think I killed a man because I wanted to win Mr. Global Leather?"

"We're trying to track down *anyone* who might have an issue with Mr. Steel," Rebecca answered. "And apparently a lot of people saw your altercation with him last night."

"Yeah, well, if you want to see a lot of people, try asking who else he pissed off. You'll need a database to keep track of them!"

They were in the corridor running between meeting rooms on the first floor. Rebecca had commandeered several uniforms to start rounding up potential witnesses and called the precinct to ask for backup, and fast.

Working her way through the panicked crowd in the lobby, she'd heard several people loudly demanding refunds and announcing their intentions to leave. This was bad, very bad. With no broken door and no theft, the victim was almost certainly killed by someone he knew and trusted enough to allow into the room while he was almost completely naked. And Eduardo was right; yellow, frilly women's panties did seem jarring in the context of this...culture. There was no other underwear like that in the room. In fact, there was little underwear at all, except for a few jockstraps.

Did he wear them for kicks? Did the killer put them on him after killing him? As uncomfortable as it made her, she realized she'd have to ask his lover about that in a little while. She'd cut her interview with Paul fairly short, after determining there was no other next-of-kin to be contacted. He was distraught and couldn't quite manage to get out of the spiral of grief her first questions had produced, so she'd quickly looked through his luggage and let him get back to the business of moving to another room. But she needed to question him not only about the panties, but whether he had the passwords to Steel's phone and email.

And of course, she needed to talk to him again because you *always* looked at the boyfriend or husband first. Even if they said they were slaves into *complete surrender of power,* whatever that was. It seemed to pop up a lot in the program book.

"If you can help us out with the names of other people who might have had a grudge against Mr. Steel, I'd sure appreciate that," Rebecca said to the Prairie Master. "But I'd still like to know where you were between midnight and about six this morning."

He instantly relaxed, his brows unfurling from his panicked frown. "Well, that's easy. We were at the bar until after one, and then my wife and I came right back here. We're on the fifth floor; we went to sleep and I was up at seven—we had coffee from room service, I was online for a while, hit the gym, and then I had to get here for the breakfast meeting with the other contestants."

"And if I speak to your wife, she'll say you never left the room last night?"

"Absolutely. Call her. I'll call her! She can get a room service receipt from the front desk! It was eighteen dollar coffee; believe me, they'll have a receipt. Can you believe that? Eighteen dollars for a pot of coffee? I could have gone out to a fancy coffee shop and bought two giant cups of latte or something like that *and* breakfast for that much!"

An excitable man—he looked about as passionately outraged by the coffee price as he was at being suspected of murder. "Just one more question; your title is Prairie Master, so does that mean your wife is…"

He flushed a bit and smoothed down the front of his shirt. "Okay, well. Yes, she is my slave, but you have to understand, this is all consensual…"

What was that, some sort of mantra among these people? Rebecca thought. The magic word that makes everything okay—*consensual.*

"So, really," he was continuing with earnest deliberation, "what we have is a *negotiated* relationship. We're mindful about power. That's what makes us different from the vanillas out there. We see patterns, we *embrace* roles, instead of just going along with what society expects. We actually teach a class about it, called 'Whatever You Like: the Romance of D/S.' That's dominance and submission. My wife and I—our marriage is probably just like what your parents had, except my wife chose to do this. She wasn't raised to be submissive to men; she's just submissive to *me*."

Rebecca thought briefly of her mother, the rabbi, her father the frustrated artist who left them when she was seven, and her stepfather the credit-extending caterer. At no time had her mother been subservient to either of her husbands; in fact, Rebecca and her sister had grown up to hearing how strong and independent and wise and clever they were as girls and women. Now Rebecca was a lesbian detective and Naomi was a heterosexual doctor, neither one married. Naomi had her boyfriend, Oscar, an oncologist, and right now, Rebecca...was a detective.

"When you say submissive, you mean she does what you tell her to?"

"Yes. Absolutely. Within reason."

Rebecca smiled slightly. "You mean she wouldn't go out and kill for you?"

The man snorted in spite of himself. "Of course not! Not that I'd tell her to do anything like that, anyway. We're not crazy, just kinky. Besides, like I said—we're into old-fashioned gender roles. I'm the alpha male, the head of the household and she's submissive to me. It's my job to defend *her*. Like that stupidness last night. You want to know what that fight was about with Steel? He called my wife a *cow*. My wife! I would have slammed him a good one if people didn't immediately break us up, but that's because I was defending her honor. But I didn't need to kill him, jeez!"

"She's your slave and you defend her honor?"

"Hell, yeah! I love her. When she obeys me, it's...a gift, from her heart, from her soul. She would do anything I asked her to, trusting me, and believe me, that kind of trust is rare. It's a treasure. Every time I give her a command, it's an opportunity for us to show love to each other. She *wants* to serve me, obey me."

"So...why didn't you send her out for coffee?" Rebecca found herself asking without thinking. Kevin opened his mouth then closed it, then managed a shrug that spoke volumes.

Rebecca quickly nodded; what was a successful marriage anyway, but an agreement on a shared reality? "I'd like to speak with your wife, please. And if you can think of anyone who might want Mr. Steel dead, please don't hesitate to call me, or grab any officer you see and ask them to contact me."

And in fact, one of the uniforms was ushering someone to her right now; she turned to see a nervous looking, pale young man with a wisp of a pale brown beard and a heroic attempt at a mustache that would probably come in much better given a few years. He was wearing very tight jeans and polished military boots and a black T-shirt that read STICKS AND STONES MAY BREAK MY BONES, BUT WHIPS AND CHAINS EXCITE ME, complete with a muscular looking half-naked man holding a bullwhip. In addition to the plastic bag given to all attendees at the front desk, he had a knapsack over one shoulder. His eyes were light brown behind rimless glasses and as he approached, he actually wrung his hands. A huge bundle of keys dangled from a belt loop on his right side; come to think of it, Rebecca reflected, she'd seen a lot of people carrying keys on their belt loops. How weird.

"This gentleman says he might have seen your guy, Detective."

She turned to him and extended a hand. "What can you tell me, sir? Mind if I get your name?"

"Josh. Joshua Grover. Um. My friends call me Joshie." Why did he wince when she spoke to him? She glanced at the patrolman, who shrugged and gave her a crooked smile.

"Joshie, then. What have you got for me?"

"I was kind of lost in the hotel last night. I was in the wrong tower, because I got on the wrong elevator. I get turned around in new places. Anyway, I was up on twenty near...that room. Where Mack was? And I saw a guy."

"What time would that be, sir?"

He winced again, like she'd been rude to him. "Around two in the morning? Or, maybe two fifteen, because the meeting let out just before two and then I got lost."

"Meeting?"

"AA. I'm sober for almost ten years, and sometimes I go to just, you know, support the newcomers? But I was so tired...I forgot which elevator to take and that's when I was wandering around. And I saw this guy up there...I was going to ask him if he knew how to get to the other wing, but he moved fast. And then I just rode the elevator down to the first floor and found the other bank. It's tricky, see, because they're both behind registration, but..."

"Let's concentrate on the man you saw," Rebecca said, flipping her book open. Just after two A.M. was right inside Eduardo's window, and she trusted his guesses. "It was a man?"

Joshie blinked and seemed suddenly lost in thought. "Oh. You know, I guess it might have been a woman. A butch woman. Or, you know, maybe a transgender person? Wow. I never even thought of that."

"What made you think it was a man?"

"He was dressed in leatherman stuff?"

"Like?"

"His pants were black, shiny—so, probably leather. Heavy boots, like maybe they had straps or something on 'em. And he wore a cap, too, and that was black, probably leather...and a jacket. Motorcycle jacket." He thought some more, trying to remember. "Black shirt under it, I didn't see any color at all. Shirt might have been leather too, actually."

"Was the person tall or short?"

"I don't remember," Joshie sighed. "It was a only a moment when I saw him. Or, her."

"Well, how far away was this person when you saw them?"

Joshie pointed down the hall. "They would be down by that exit door."

Rebecca pointed and spoke to the patrolman. "Would you mind stepping down there for a moment?" When he got by the door, she turned to Joshie. "Okay, so he's about six feet tall. Was the person you saw taller, or shorter?"

"Oh!" Joshie cocked his head. "Shorter! Hey, that's a good trick."

"Much shorter, or close?"

"About…maybe…four, five inches shorter. Maybe even a little shorter than that."

"You're doing great, Joshie, thank you. Now…black or white? Did you see any skin tone at all? Facial hair, or hair on the head?"

"White. And…um…I didn't see any hair. Not that I can remember."

"You said they were wearing a hat. Like a baseball cap?"

"No, a Daddy cap. I mean, like, a uniform cap?" He looked around the hall and pointed at one of the other contestants, waiting for Rebecca to speak to them. "Like that guy is wearing."

"Someone between five foot six and nine, skinnier than that officer, or heavier?"

Joshie squinted and shrugged. "Maybe a little heavier? Hard to tell under a jacket."

Rebecca looked down at her notes. A white person, probably a man of average height, average weight, and wearing black leather pants, shirt, jacket and cap.

At a contest with three thousand attendees where this ensemble seemed to be the default casual wear.

"Thank you, sir," she said with a grim smile. "If you remember anything else, please call me at once." He looked a little disappointed when he slouched away.

The remainder of the contestants were an education in themselves, although not very useful in actual data concerning the case. Their real names did not always match what they had on their badges, but she had a list Boy Jack thoughtfully copied for her.

"This isn't going to be in the news, is it?" fretted a tall dark-skinned man, dressed for effect in white leather jeans and a white leather arrangement of straps across his chest. Franklin DuMont of New Orleans had the title of Chevalier, something granted to him by a group called the Queer Cuir Krewe.

"Holy shit, of course it is," piped up Angelina Swiderski, whose business card reported her to be a world-famous sex blogger. "Could you make sure they mention my blog?"

"I've got no control over the press," Rebecca said firmly. "And all I'm interested in are facts. Did anyone see or interact with Mr. Steel after midnight last night, or know of anyone who might have wanted to do him harm?"

They all looked at each other in various modes of apprehension, waiting for someone to start. Then, a short, thin young man wearing a T-shirt that read JACK said, "Look. You're going to hear this anyway, so I might as well get it over with. Mack was..."

"Not the most popular guy, I know."

"Oh!" His dark eyebrows went up in surprise and then he shrugged. "Then I might as well start. Mack went out of his way to piss off a ton of people last night, but almost all of them were in the bar long after he left. And everyone here was on time this morning at eight thirty, in fact, most of them were early."

Nods all around the room, the group eager to show they'd been on time. "I just want to say I had no beef with Mack," insisted Lennon Munro, whose handshake and smile reminded Rebecca of the used car salesman she'd gotten her last clunker from. "He's always been polite with me."

"He's dead now, Len, you don't have to kiss his ass any more," sneered the woman who introduced herself as Jazz Dean.

"There's no need to...demean his memory!" the man insisted.

"There's no way anyone in the scene could have done this," said the shortest man there, Kelly Manning. "We don't kill each other. We spend a fortune on toys that don't damage the body; we spend hours learning safe ways to tie knots. We negotiate everything to death sometimes...oh, shit, that came out wrong." He flushed and slapped the side of his head. "Sorry. But really, our motto is safe, sane and—"

"Consensual, I know."

There was a ripple of surprise among them; some of the contestants looked impressed with her. A few seemed to relax. Score one for the flexible, understanding detective.

"But it appears that Mr. Steel might have known his attacker," Rebecca said. To this news, they responded with near universal dismay, looking down, fingering their sashes and medallions. The oldest man there, a deeply tanned gentleman strongly reminiscent of her maternal grandfather, sighed and murmured, "Oy, such a mess."

Then, a well-built man dressed in the all-leather getup standard to the leatherman look asked, "Where was his boy?"

Rebecca glanced at her list. This was Giuliano Ferri, from Bayonne, although his title was Mr. Newark Leather. His dark curly hair was lightened with a little amber for highlights, and he had an extremely narrow, trimmed beard expertly barbered to a thin chinstrap to emphasize his strong jawline. Of them all, he looked the most shaken. His eyes, under thick brows, were slightly reddened and tired, his voice hoarse.

"Mr. Helms was out for the evening."

"Lucky him," said Jason Asada, Mr. Shaft. He was Japanese; his hair was long and tied back in a ponytail, his leather tank top a little ill-fitting. He had a tattoo of some kanji text on one arm and a ring in his nose. "Paul's a little guy. Anyone strong enough to take down Mack had to be big. He was built."

Kevin McDonald snorted. "Lifting weights and building muscles means nothing in a fight. Mack was a coward; he insulted women! I bet he went down sniveling."

"Hey, good move, Kev; why not hang a sign over your head that reads 'I fucking did it,' huh?" Jazz rolled her eyes.

"I have nothing to hide! Whoever killed him did the community a favor!"

That got them all shouting at each other, and Rebecca barely felt the buzz of incoming messages on her phone. Despite having left jobs with half a dozen uniforms and messages back at the precinct, her first thought was more to the tune of *now what* than anticipation of anything helpful.

"People, please! Let's focus here. Did anyone here spend any significant time with him last night? Talk about anything with him? Was he nervous, or concerned about anything? Do you know of any close friends and associates? Even unpopular people have some friends."

"I don't know anyone who says they're friendly with him, except for his boy Paul," offered Jack.

"And we're not allowed to talk to the judges anyway," added Jason. "It's against the rules to be alone with them or have conversations outside of what they're supposed to be judging us on."

"Not that it stopped him from offering his stupid opinions about Zodians, heterosexuals, women, furries, NuKnk, cybers..." Jazz Dean ticked off the groups on her fingers. "I tried to get him to talk contest stuff, but it just looked like all he did was bitch about anyone who wasn't male, young, and interested in *him*.

Everyone knew he played with contestants in other contests, even when it's not allowed."

The woman next to her nodded sadly. She was soft, quite round in body, and more feminine. She smelled of something musky and spicy.

"It pains this slave to say this about an alpha male dom, but Master Mack only said this girl should never speak to him and laughed at this one's attempts to be respectful."

Rebecca blinked, tried to formulate some sort of question about that strange way of talking and failed to come up with anything.

"That's because he hated women!" said Jazz.

"Well, some more than others. It didn't help that phyl'ta is Zodian."

"Seriously, phyl'ta, you picked the wrong year to run, with him *and* Mickey Abraham on the panel. She hates Zodians more than anyone!"

The plump little blonde lady shrugged with a tingle of jewelry and a shimmer of silks. "This one hopes to do her best to represent the honor of her clan and kingdom."

There was a moment of silence as everyone in the room glanced at Rebecca, who was keeping her mouth shut. Their eyes shifted nervously from one to another.

"Well," said Kelly thoughtfully, "It's true he hated straights and Zodians and furries and all, but he *really* hated Mistress Ravenfyre."

"And Phedre! He called her a cyber-snatch in that interview on LeatherHeart radio."

"Wow, I am so glad to know you guys will bad-mouth me the minute I kick off," snapped Len.

"What are we supposed to do, stand around and tell her he was a freaking hero to the scene? That he loved everyone and gave out puppies?"

"Oh, my God, remember what he said about puppy play in

that interview on *Scene About Town*?"

"Mickey called him the stupidest titleholder *ever*."

"Slave Willow said she wished he'd fall off the stage."

"The bootblacks said they were going to piss on his leather if he came back to them again!"

"Guys? Maybe we shouldn't be so, um, forthcoming about *everyone* who ever said anything bad about him? We could be here all day," pleaded Boy Jack.

Rebecca excused herself and left them arguing the merits of talking about the deceased. She clearly needed to speak to the judges, especially the Ravenfyre woman. Checking her text messages, she discovered that the surveillance footage had been made available for her to pick up at the hotel security office, and she was in fact getting some help—two detectives were on their way to conduct more interviews and one was to be her "temporary" partner. Dominick DeCosta, the text message read. Not a familiar name, but she could picture him already, a thick-necked, swaggering Bensonhurst bad boy in a shiny suit.

Two people passed her in the hallway; he was a slender pale-skinned man dressed like some sort of barbarian, complete with horns on a metal helmet, a vest covered with fake black fur and what looked like an axe stuck through a wide leather belt. She was a lovely, Rubenesque woman in very high, pink stiletto heels bound together with about eighteen inches of slender gold chain decorated with paste jewels; her garb, several layers of brightly colored chiffon. A necklace matching the ankle chains was around her neck with a large lock dangling in front. The lock looked like it had been covered with little sparkling beads. From her layers of rainbow sarongs wafted a scent somewhat reminiscent of the sort of earthy, musky perfumes sold at organic food co-ops...almost exactly the same one the contestant was wearing. They could have been sisters, in some odd, extended gypsy family.

Behind them was a man wearing a leather mask that sort of

made him look like a horse; his badge hung from a thick, studded chest harness proclaiming his name to be STARFOOT. His heavy boots seemed to clomp louder than boots normally would; as he passed by, he snorted and threw his head up and down, and then...trotted...down toward the lobby. He was followed by about a dozen people all wearing black clothing with different pieces in leather, latex or various other shiny materials. Behind them were two men wearing running shorts and no other clothing, although each carried a black canvas bag over one shoulder. Perhaps they were going to the gym. Their event ID badges were dangling from rings going through their nipples. But in this hallway, stripped down like that, badges, nipple rings and all, they were the most *normal* looking people.

And Rebecca was getting a new temporary partner.

Oh, good. This was just the sort of case to bond over.

CHAPTER 11

"All press passes are revoked! You can fill out another application for one, but until we figure out what's up, no pictures, no interviews and no access to the event!" Bitsy issued this fiat with stern dominance, making the crowd around her table cheer or mumble assent, with three exceptions.

"But...not *me*, Bitsy!" cried Cary Gordon, clutching a camera to his chest in horror.

"And what about me?" demanded Phedre.

"Fill out a new application, like anyone else," Bitsy insisted. "Look, I'm sure it'll be fine, but we have to be fair and make everyone apply again."

Nancy raised an eyebrow and chuckled. "Make everyone apply, so that you can keep the mainstream out, you mean?"

Cary had the decency to look a little ashamed but Bitsy scowled. "I didn't think it was a good idea to issue *you* a press pass to begin with. We can't trust outsiders to cover us fairly!"

"Oh, yeah? Well, let me tell you what's going to happen in about," Nancy checked her watch, "fifteen minutes. The rest of the 'outsider' media is going to show up, way more than the two or three bozos who're bugging your people out front right now. I'm talking TV here, the big boys, maybe cable. And they're not going to care about your slogans and safety workshops and your contest and charities. They'll never have heard about your whole safe, sane, risk aware, totally awesome whatever thingie. What they're going to talk about is a kinky gay guy murdered at a kinky convention, and they're gonna find *someone* to talk to, preferably the weirdest looking guy they can find, or the woman with the least clothing and highest boobage factor. Or, you can hook me up; I've been here since yesterday, I've already met a lot of your people, I know your lingo. Your choice."

Bitsy sniffed and turned away to spur her table volunteers to greater productivity. A skinny little leather-clad man was asking her where the memorial service would be; she snapped, "Can't you read?" and pointed at a large handwritten sign with schedule updates on it. He dutifully examined the sign while sneaking glances at her stunning black and gold pseudo-medieval dress, with the crossed lacings barely constraining her big breasts.

Cary looked thoughtful, and Phedre started to nod. "You know," she said, "that's not a bad idea."

"No interviews! No interviews!" shouted a man forcing his way through the crowd around the table. He was dressed in a dark brown suit that looked slightly old fashioned, his dark goatee and a natty bowler hat adding to the almost Edwardian feel of his garb. He shoved a card at Nancy, who took it reflexively.

"I'm here from the Pansexual Institute for Sexual Studies," he announced with authority. "Any interviews should only be conducted with one of our media interface team."

"You're from...PISS?" Nancy snickered.

He flushed. "We're a serious, nonprofit educational and advocacy agency standing up for the rights of sexual minorities. And no one here may be interviewed without one of our observers present."

Several people in the crowd cheered and he stood straighter.

"And are you part of the media interface team?" Nancy asked.

"Yes, I am. I'm Reginald Fairway."

"Excellent! Then let's talk, Reggie. Always happy to connect with an interfacer."

"Hey, wait, she was going to interview me!" objected Phedre.

"You have to leave this to the *professionals*," said Reginald. "You don't know how easily the press can twist what you say!"

"Hey, I know just as much about dealing with the vanilla world as you do, Reg! I'm teaching 'Flog Your Blog,' my class on publicity and outreach this weekend! I did the two-day media training with the American Sexuality Society."

"They're a joke! They only got started because we threw half of that board off *our* board."

"I'll tell you what a joke is, coming into an event you aren't registered for to take over press duties. Does Earl even know you're here?"

"I texted him! And I came over as a volunteer the minute I heard, to help! And it looks like you need it because you were probably about to expose us to—"

"Guys, guys, don't fight," said Cary, waving his hands.

"Let's let them sort it out," Nancy said quickly, grabbing Cary by the arm. "I wanted to talk to you, anyway."

"You...you did? But Reggie—"

"Hey, Cary, are you an insider, or not? Do you work for *him*? I just want to establish some facts with you, pro to pro, since you are obviously the guy in the know."

Cary puffed up immediately and came away with her like a starving puppy. "Look," she said, lowering her voice as they ducked behind a column away from the registration tables. "You know how it's going to be. In a way, Reggie was right, the press is gonna swoop in here like vultures and look for the scariest, weirdest pictures they can find and hook it up with a scene from *Pulp Fiction* for the evening news. You don't want that, do you? So, see, it's in your best interest to get the real facts to me. You can trust me."

"Oh, lord, *Pulp Fiction*! The damage that movie did to us! Do you know, it's not even called a 'gimp hood,' which is offensive to the differently-abled community and to us at the same time?"

"Yeah! See, I knew that!" She hadn't known that, and would have to make sure she didn't use that phrase, but fine. "What I want to know is the *real* background to this story. I bet it wasn't even one of your people who did it."

"You're right! It couldn't have been. It was probably some right-wing homophobe out to get us, make us look bad." He sputtered, dug into his shoulder bag for a little computer. "You should see some of the horrible things they write about us! I link to them all the time. There's one guy who even dresses up in leather—cheap crap, mail order stuff, really—and sneaks in to the conferences to take pictures of the vendor room and the fashion show and the...uh, dungeons. Which I know sound scary, but really, it's all safe, sane..."

"I know, I know," Nancy said soothingly. "You know what's been puzzling me, Cary? That little scuffle we saw together yesterday, between Mack and Ravenfyre and then at the bar, with the other guy? Mack seemed to make himself a lot of enemies."

"He was not...a nice guy," Cary said with one of his hangdog sighs. "I interviewed him right after the contest last year, and one of the first things he did was bad-mouth the other contestants. That's just rude! I mean, it is a competition, but generally contestants have a good time and make deep connections in their contest years."

"So how did he win?"

"Ah! Well, that was part luck and part coaching and part the perfection of his leather fantasy image performance."

"His what?"

"The contest has four components," Cary explained, looking much more confident. "The interviews, the three style requirements, the pop question at the ball, and the leather fantasy image. Although the interviews count for a lot, the other three categories together can push a contestant to win even if they tank in the interviews."

"No kidding."

"*Right*? This is one of the weaknesses of the system. Personally, I prefer the North American Owner/owned Contest, where if you fail the interviews, you can't possibly win. Of course, they're having problems getting enough contestants these days, due to their requirement that you be in a full-time relationship for more than a year."

"Yeah, I can see how that could be a problem," Nancy said. "What a shame. So, the leather fantasy thing...was it violent? Bloody?"

"Oh, no! It was a coming-of-age theme, actually, very well-staged. To be fair, it was much better than most of the others. There was one contestant who, I swear, must have come up with his fantasy on the airplane ride here!"

"Okay, so clue me in. This fantasy, they act it out on stage? Whips and chains and knives, that sort of thing?"

"They don't act it out, no. There's a long story about that—some other contests still have fantasy segments and this one used to. But oh, my God, the troubles! Bad dubbing on music or pathetic original compositions, no lighting or staging cues, or even no script! Props that got damaged on the way, or fell apart on stage, bad acting, overblown voiceovers and the same scenes repeated *ad nauseum* year after year!" Cary waved his hands around in horror. "How many times can you sit through another flogging, another Japanese bondage setup, another naughty little girl or puppy scene? Endless Enya, Nine Inch Nails, Enigma, Depeche

Mode and those awful chanting monks for years, just years. Or some weird Death Metal thing that would set your back fillings vibrating. So, Earl had this idea, that instead of having them actually act out a fantasy, they'd set up a fantasy *image*. It's just a pose, long enough to show off a nice costume, a few props. No speaking, no singing, but you're allowed prerecorded music and a voiceover of no more than twenty-five of your thirty seconds. It's designed to show a certain esthetic, a sense of time and place..."

"A tableau," Nancy said, impatiently. "Like in *The Music Man.*"

Cary widened his eyes and nodded eagerly. "Precisely! I'm sorry for blathering on—so many contestants don't even know what a tableau is, let alone can reference *The Music Man*. A shocking lack of education in American musical theatre, really."

Nancy considered mentioning trying out for Marian in college and being cast as one of the Pickalittle ladies instead, leading to her change in majors from theatre to communications and journalism. But maybe she'd better save that for leverage later. Cary was going on, now completely in her corner.

"Well—Mack had a fabulous fantasy image, him in gorgeous bar leathers, oiled up and confident, everything custom-made. But next to him, stage left, there were two other men, representing him as a...a lost, confused sort of teenager, and a young man just out in the scene. The progression was just note perfect. I can show you pictures! Thirty seconds, the voiceover is some sexy little poem about becoming a man. He was a clear favorite of the audience. Also, his pop question was just a lucky softball, something about discovering what turns him on. It just dovetailed so perfectly with his fantasy image, anyone who hadn't actually spoken to him thought he was just all that!"

"And then he spent a whole year pissing people off? Isn't it possible he just ticked off the wrong person?"

Cary shook his head, but she could see his heart wasn't in

it. "Oh, Nancy—may I call you Nancy?—you know, anything's possible. But it's so unlikely! And frankly, I don't envy whoever has to question everyone who ever said a bad thing about him. Some people in the scene can be very, er, theatrical in their passion. Especially when they're online, behind a scene name."

You mean they can sound like complete lunatics, Nancy mused, reflecting on her quick scans of KinkyNet. The posturing and obnoxious braggadocio she'd spotted made gang members seem shy and retiring; the role-playing personas almost matched the intensity of the people who glued rubber prosthetics onto their foreheads and pretended they were aliens at science fiction conventions.

Oh, that was an interesting comparison. Kinky people as alien cosplayers who actually got laid! She could already see a sale of that piece to one of the high profile news and culture websites.

"And just how many enemies did he have? Like, what about his co-winner, Mistress Ravenfyre?"

"Ah. The poor woman. She did not deserve a year of playing second fiddle to Mack. And he was just horrid to her; he did one of the worst things we can do to one another..."

"Die, fags, die! Die, fags, die!" came a screaming chant, cutting through the buzz of conversation in the lobby.

This, Nancy thought, is what they call a target-rich environment. She felt her phone vibrating even as she pushed her way toward the front doors, uniformed cops and hotel and event security pushing along with her as conference attendees stampeded in the opposite direction.

CHAPTER 12

REBECCA WAS HEADING BACK TO THE ELEVATOR BANKS TO SEE if Paul Helms was composed enough for some more questions when she heard someone calling "Detective! Detective!" behind her. It was one of the contestants, Len Munro.

"Yes, Mr. Munro, what can I do for you?"

"This is very awkward," he said quickly, not looking awkward or flustered in the slightest. "But I feel as a citizen, I need to come forward to aid you in the investigation even if this puts one of my own leather brothers in a bad light. Not that he's alone! As you heard, a lot of people had their issues with Mack, even though I'm not one; I get along with everyone. Even some of his fellow *judges* hated him, like Mistress Ravenfyre and Lord Laertes. But Jack said we contestants were all in the bar late last night, and I'm sorry, but that's just not true. I'm sure it means nothing, but maybe, like you said, you can eliminate him from the suspects even though what he did looks *very* suspicious!"

"Thank you, Mr. Munro. And who, exactly, are you talking about?"

He glanced from side to side and adjusted the large badge identifying him as a contestant. "It was Ferri. Mr. Newark Leather. Last night, all the other contestants stayed late, but he went missing at about the same time Mack left."

"I see."

"I don't know why Boy Jack didn't mention this; half the contest staff was out looking for him! Maybe they thought he would tell you himself, that would be the *honorable* thing to do. You know, the leather lifestyle is about honesty and being true to a code, and any *real* leatherman would come clean, I'm just saying."

"That is helpful, sir, thank you."

"I think it's our civic duty to be involved in supporting public employees," he said righteously. "Frankly, I've seen Ferri's contestant bio sheet, and he hasn't even been in the scene for more than a year or two, let alone done meaningful community service. This isn't just costumes, you know."

"Yes, I am seeing that."

"You know what I think?" Len leaned in toward her, and she made a responding move to listen, catching a whiff of mouthwash and one of those young men's body sprays. He lowered his voice, glancing around again. "I think he should be disqualified."

And that was when an awful lot of shouting and screaming started coming from the lobby.

Four white people, all with light brown hair, one going steadily white with age, all wearing red shirts with the word FAGS stenciled on the front with the international "no" red circle with a diagonal slash through it over the word, were standing in the hotel lobby holding signs. Two men and two women, the eldest in his late sixties, the youngest in her teens. The patriarch's sign read THANK GOD 4 DEAD PERVERTS!!! The older woman, eyes wide with passion behind thick glasses, her hair frizzy and barely restrained inside a scrunchie studded with little gold crosses, held two. One proclaimed New York City to be GROUND ZERO FOR SEX PERVERTS!! with a picture of the World Trade Center in flames, while the other merely urged DIE FAGS DIE! The teenager, chewing gum and rocking back and forth on her heels, switched back and forth from a stack of signs; when Rebecca pushed her way through the shouting, angry crowd facing the protestors, the two signs the young woman held read MUSLIMS, JEWS, FAGS, QUEERS, PERVERTS = NAZI!!!! and a simple DOOM! printed in black text on a background of explosions.

Oy. The Western Harrisburg Alliance Church of Our Savior. They were notorious for showing up at public events featuring anyone who might be on the news—gays, Jews, Muslims, politicians, sports figures, pop singers—and promoting their unique brand of insane interpretation of scripture. Even the most die-hard, right-wing extremists declined to associate with them. The Ku Klux Klan issued a cease and desist order against them when the church started showing up to support the Klan's various protests. The tiny church seemed mostly made up of a core group of blood relatives infected with serious delusional issues and blessed with an excess of legal degrees and time to spend both fighting and planning lawsuits.

How do they get to New York so fast? Rebecca wondered. Several of her colleagues thought the group had an insider in law enforcement who sent them messages as soon as something newsworthy hit the police scanner.

Several of the uniforms were keeping the more outraged and shouting convention-goers from getting too close to the church members; hotel security was surrounding them and shouting at them to leave. Rebecca was about to start directing arrests for trespassing when an extremely handsome black man in a well-draped, dark grey, chalk-striped suit stepped in the middle of the whole mess and turned his jacket back to reveal a badge.

"I want you four folks to remove yourselves from this place of business immediately and then down the sidewalk a distance of at least twenty feet from the main doors, do you understand me?" His voice was deep and rumbly, and he had an accent Rebecca couldn't place anywhere except "Southern." His hair was clipped short against his gently rounded skull, revealing a wide forehead, nose and cheekbones, with dark coffee-colored eyes against significantly lighter skin. His tie was the only thing not perfectly in place; the yellow silk looked hastily knotted. Like Rebecca, he favored a shoulder holster, and she noticed at once the telltale signs of a suit jacket tailored to make room for it.

"The wages of sin is death!" cried Obal Croyden, the elderly man leading this pack.

"Romans, chapter 6. And the gift of God is eternal life," finished the newcomer placidly. "Now, sir, I am directing you one more time to take your preaching out of this hotel and down the sidewalk."

"God calls us to speak the truth to these perverts-who-will-burn-in-hell and all their enablers," shouted Croyden, his face red with exuberance. "By protecting them, you'll go right to hell, too! God hates the NYPD!"

"Mmm-hmm. Well, I 'preciate your witnessing and all, but you are *still* moving your ass down the street like I told you, or you are gonna find out what eternity means in a holding cell!" The man gestured to the uniforms, and the church members immediately grabbed their signs and started marching to the door on their own, chanting, "Per-verts-DIE!" on the way.

"Makes a mockery of the Word," the nicely dressed officer said, brushing his lapel. He looked way too pretty and young and fresh to be in homicide. "Say, any of you fellas know where I can find Detective Feldblum?"

"Right behind you."

He turned with a start and then adjusted his gaze down; he was a good five inches taller than Rebecca's five foot five plus her low heels. Up close he smelled like bay rum and cloves and gun oil all at once, spicy and dangerous.

"Dominick DeCosta," he said, sticking his hand out. "Dom, if you like."

"Tell you what, DeCosta; no matter what I like, they're gonna *love* you here." He squinted and cocked his head in puzzlement, and she was about to explain about *doms* and *subs* but then he swiveled his head at some movement in the crowd and spotted a woman dressed in some sort of formfitting bodysuit of white with black spots and a strap around her hips with a long dog's tail hanging from her rear end; public modesty rules saved them from seeing *exactly* how it was...attached. Another harness on her head was decorated with two long, floppy black ears. DeCosta's lips curled in distaste.

"Good lord, I've got no use for those false preachers out there, but that's some sick shit. I understand one of these freaks killed another playing their kinky little sex games? What a surprise."

Rebecca slammed her mouth shut on her friendly chitchat. Great. A Bible-quoting Southern black man. Homophobic as hell. She would have preferred the *paisan* from Bensonhurst. Was this yet another little gift from Lieutenant Ludivico? Maybe he had been offended to find a man with such an obvious Italian name was not exactly from the local families of Italian cops, and figured pairing him with the lesbian would be a laugh.

Ha-ha.

"We have video and a ton of interviews, but we still need to interview the judges," she said with cool professionalism. "If you want to see the scene, we can take a quick look, or I can make copies of the notes and reports. But this convention ends on Sunday, and the deceased was not a popular man. I'm on my way to find a potential suspect, but I need eyes and ears on about a dozen others as well."

He tore his eyes away from a man dressed in crinolines accompanying a woman in a tuxedo, and two tremendously hairy men with only leather codpieces under their ass-baring chaps. "Only a dozen? I bet if we line these freaks up we'd find a dozen killers and pervert victims who don't even know they're targets yet. Whoo-ee. Let me play catch up with your notes and I'll eyeball the scene; then I can see where I can help best, that all right by you?"

It sounded like, "thaht awl-rite bah yoo?" She might have found it charming if he managed to stop referring to these people as freaks.

But they are, she reminded herself.

Which is none of my business unless they break the law! She argued back. Or, his, with his backward, Southern Baptist, right-wing bullshit.

She briefed him as she walked him up to the twentieth floor.

CHAPTER 13

PAUL HELMS LOOKED SLIGHTLY MORE COMPOSED BUT A LITTLE puzzled to Rebecca. He seemed lost among the luggage that was not claimed by the crime scene team, relocated to a new room one floor down from the room he'd shared with Mack. His eyes were still red-rimmed, and he was pale under his light tan. When Rebecca asked if he'd eaten anything yet that day, he blinked, and shook his head.

"I...I don't want to go out; I don't want to talk to anyone," he said with a slight sniff. "I just can't stand the idea of what they'd say..."

"That's one of the things I need to talk to you about," Rebecca said, sitting down on the hard little sofa in the room. Paul was perched on the edge of the bed opposite her, hunched over. "Mr. Helms—the people I've spoken to seem to think Mack had a lot of enemies."

"Paul," he said. "You can call me Paul. And you know what? Mack didn't have *enemies*. He had people who were jealous of him! Snipers...bitchers and moaners, guys who couldn't stand how he kept winning, and how *real* he was!"

Real. How real someone was seemed very important to these people. Rebecca underlined the word and waited for more. Paul did not make her wait long.

"There were fourteen contenders for Mr. Global Leather last year, and do you know how many there are this year? Seven! Half! And you know why? Because no one thinks they can be as good as Mack was. There's like, two thousand guys here who think they're leathermen, but let me tell you—they're mostly poseurs and fakes, losers who play dress up because they think it looks hot. Then, when you get them alone, they're all..." he paused, looked over at her and then down at the bedding, running his hands along the velvet decorative trim at the edge. "Not real," he finished with a shrug.

"Not like he was with you? As a...master?"

The young man sighed and lowered his head even further. "You wouldn't understand."

"I understand it's a very intimate relationship."

"The most intimate you can get! I mean...it's not just trusting someone with, like, your secrets, or even your bank account, you trust them with your body, your feelings. I...I would have done anything for Mack. He was everything a man was supposed to be."

Rebecca studied the younger man and his rising passion as he eulogized his partner. There was certainly some outrage there, some offense, but also, underneath, she could feel the defensiveness. This was clearly an old issue. The right time to ask her sensitive question was now.

"Paul, Mack was wearing what appeared to be yellow ladies' panties. Was that something he enjoyed?"

Bingo. Paul's face immediately reddened, his eyes narrowing. "Never! That was some sick, disgusting way to try and humiliate him! Look, look!" He sprang up and grabbed an accordion-style folder from the desk against the wall and jerked a fistful of photos out of it, tossing them onto the bed. "Look at those! Does this look like a guy who wears *panties*?"

They were studio shots, mostly color, although a few were stylized in black and white and one in sepia tones. Mack Steel was posed on and by motorcycles, ladders, dangling chains, coiled ropes, bondage furniture and gym equipment. He was in many styles of dress, from jockstrap and skin to full leather and lots of staged theme images as well. There he was wearing football pads over his bare chest while he leaned against a locker; in camouflage pants and military boots outside; in heavy jeans and a carpenter's belt hefting a hammer. Bright colors, silk, satin or lace were not present in any of them.

What was it Eduardo said? "Quite the macho man," Rebecca offered. "What are these from?"

"Mack was going to put together his own calendar this year, with just him, and no Ravenfyre or bootblack stuff. You know that's the only reason why people bought the Global Leather calendar last year, for *his* pictures? But yeah, he was macho, but for real macho, not just, you know, posing. He'd never wear anything like...panties. *Ever.* Someone brought them and put them on him!"

"That would certainly suggest someone who had a very serious problem with him, Paul. Someone who came prepared. Did anyone ever threaten him?"

Paul hitched one shoulder and nodded. "Yeah. I guess. He'd get hate mail all the time, mean messages on KinkyNet, that sort of bullshit. But we never took it seriously. I mean, who takes any of these people seriously? Most of them don't even use their real names...oh, God, God!" He ran a hand through his short hair and tugged at it helplessly. "Oh, my God, what if it was one of them, and no one knows who they really are, all posting anonymously under bullshit names!"

"Did you ever see his email, or these messages?"

"Yes, all the time! It was part of my service to him…but I deleted so many! You can trace them, right? Get their IDs off his hard drive or something? Like on TV?"

"If you have his passwords," Rebecca suggested.

"Sure, sure," Paul said, nodding. "Easy. For his email, it's MGLMack…wait, I'll write them down. You'll find them all on KinkyNet, you'll see!"

"That would be a great help, Paul. And can you think of any particular person who might have threatened Mack, or gotten into an argument or fight with him that might have gone a bit too far?"

"Well, there was that straight guy at the bar," Paul said, scrawling a list of codes. "And of course, Wendi."

"Wendi?"

"Mistress Ravenfyre," he sneered. "She hated him from the moment they met. Her slavegirl and her husband, too, and he has *guns*!"

"How do you know that?"

"They brag about it on their website! He shoots deer. Like, what did a deer ever do to him? The three of them are a bunch of weirdos."

The irony escapes them all, Rebecca thought, checking her text messages. DeCosta was rounding up the videos and doing more interviews; he could check in with the lab techs as soon as she sent them the passwords to the victim's phone and computer. Next up, the fellow judges, and the contestant who went missing last night, Ferri, and she still needed a real name for Paul's supposed alibi. She circled "Wolfboy" and added "Earl?" as a note.

The apologies from the Boys Jack were sincere, if somewhat belated, but now that everyone knew, Earl had bigger problems.

"I quit! I can't stay here, Earl! I'm a teacher for crying out loud! What if one of those TV people got my picture? I'd lose my job!"

Terry O'Keefe, known online as The Headmaster, looked the role, with his white hair and close-cropped beard; his glasses often slipped down his nose to add to his demeanor of constant disapproval. His assistant/slave/girlfriend Gayle was stuffing adult-sized Catholic school uniforms into wardrobe boxes.

"Terry, Terry, think! No one's coming in here, we canceled all press passes. But if you leave the hotel now, they'll get your picture for sure! Look, it'll all be over in a few hours; there's nothing to see here, the lobby's been walled off by security, the press will just go find something else to gawk at."

"Then I'll stay in my room until they're gone," Terry snapped. "And I want a refund of my table fee."

Earl stiffened. "No refunds. If you back out, it's your loss—no sales and no presence in the fashion show!"

Terry gawked. "Are you insane? I brought five thousand dollars worth of specialty items for the show! I even have that damn *magic* school stuff you said everyone wanted!"

"And you're deserting the event! Why should I support you when you won't support me?" Earl saw a few of the other vendors crowding in close to eavesdrop and slapped his fingers down on the insistent beeping of his headset. "Look...now is the time we have to stick together! As a community! We need to...uh...go on like, well, Mack would expect us to."

Dr. Mickey Abraham, sitting at the table to Terry's immediate right laughed her low, bitter laugh, tapping her pen against the tabletop. Three of her textbooks were in short stacks to one side; it didn't look like anyone had been buying. Other books were lined up across the table and on racks behind it for browsing, with titles like *A Pretty Package: Cock and Ball Bondage for Beginners*, and *Like a Rented Mule: Beating for Productivity*, and *BDSM Magicks*. Three novels with similar covers were stacked in front of a bored-looking man who had edged far away from Abraham, but seemed to be about as successful in sales. Earl could see that the first book was titled *The Mistress*, followed by *The Mistress Returns* and *Revenge of the Mistress*. The cover model, posed in a latex catsuit against the same grey dungeon wall background, looked as bored as the author as she pouted and gestured with a riding crop. Also prominently on display were copies of *You're Kinky and That's Okay!*, with a large sign indicating that Dr. Westfield would be there to sign them "later."

"Like Mack would expect," Abraham echoed. Over her Hawaiian shirt she wore a leather bar vest with only one pin on it, reading ASPHYXIOPHILIA—THINK OF IT AS EVOLUTION IN ACTION. "Mack would expect you to build a shrine and have us all bow down to it. The idea of doing anything but igniting a pyre of his leftover self-promotional crap is a joke."

"Isn't it time you went back to the judges room?" Earl snapped.

"Ah, yes indeed it is, to meet with the poor detective assigned to this carnival of the grotesque and continue being amazed by this year's best and brightest contestants." She tossed the pen over to the bored author and strolled off.

"Look," Earl begged, turning back to Headmaster Terry. "You know sales will be amazing now, with everyone afraid to leave the hotel. All they're going to do is shop!"

"Oh. Hm." Terry considered this, glancing around the room in speculation. "Well..."

Fine, thought Earl, already moving on to the next problems. Two vendors were in fact selling Mack memorabilia at inflated prices, and there were both serious and farcical tribute events being circulated. One cabal of Mack-haters was planning a Memorial Haiku and Drinking Contest. He had to put a stop to that before things got way out of hand.

Even if it sounded kinda fun.

In the meantime, police were interviewing people all over the hotel, causing disruptions in the judging schedule that would send ripples throughout the event, changing meeting times, classes and rehearsals. Three volunteers had abruptly quit; Bitsy had managed to strong-arm two more from following, but there was a distinct scent of desertion in the air.

Also, the Southwestern Association of Submissives/Slaves wanted to do a fundraising auction for Paul, even though no one knew what his financial stability was like; Loving in Leather, the organization of kink-friendly mental health professionals, wanted to hold free grief counseling in one of the rooms set aside for religious/spiritual/recovery purposes; the instructor for a scheduled class called "Daddy Knows Best" wanted to change it to "When Daddy Goes Away," and most worrying of all, his lawyer had left him three voicemails.

If meeting the contestants was strange, the judges just sent the whole case into a new level of surrealism. Like the contestants, once they realized that Mack's unpopularity was already accepted, they wasted no time in assuring Rebecca that although none of them liked the man, neither did they murder him. That was understood; killers rarely sighed, raised a hand and said, "Yeah, I did it, take me away." Their eagerness to supply alibis and steadfast denials of having anything to do with his death was not unexpected. Their personas, however...

The huge, bearded man in barbarian splendor, for example. Furry vest, baggy leather pants, purple silk shirt open halfway down his hairy chest, he looked ready to play a supernumerary in a production of "The Ring Cycle"; all he lacked was a horned helmet. His enormous medallion even boasted a double-bladed axe crossed with a crescent moon. It was oddly reminiscent of a labrys.

Apparently he was a Zodian, somehow connected with the women wearing rainbow layers of silk and flashy tween jewelry; she earnestly hoped he didn't have the same strange speaking pattern phyl'ta did. Although his Pennsylvania driver's license said his name was Larry Meinerling, his badge read LORD LAERTES.

"So, what do you hear from Hamlet these days?" Rebecca had offered in an attempt to find something light to say to such an imposing and weirdly dressed figure.

He'd blinked at her, confused for a moment and then shrugged with a grin. "People keep asking me about Hamlet," he rumbled, stroking his beard. "I've never actually seen it."

"Ah. Well. Laertes was his friend in the play."

"I picked it from a book on fantasy names," he admitted. "It sounded medieval. My girl tells me Mel Gibson was in a Hamlet movie; I should pick it up one day."

In fact, only two of the entire array of judges used the name on their government-issued IDs. One was a local college professor who wore a smirk along with her Hawaiian shirt. She seemed to find the entire situation amusing. The other was a Latino from Miami who had the title Señor Cuero; his proper name was George Santos. The tall drag queen with the giggle-inducing stage name Chava Nagilla was Alan Green; Master Zenu was an enormous red-haired Texan named Chester Vole.

And finally, she met the much-referenced Mistress Ravenfyre, Mack Steel's co-titleholder, a handsome, leggy woman in her midthirties with elegantly styled, long curly hair in a beautiful autumnal copper color that complemented her creamy complexion. A narrow nose was the only out-of-balance feature on her face, her green eyes too perfect to be natural.

Together, they repeated the same story she'd heard since her interviews began. Mack Steel had annoyed, angered or insulted half the bar the previous night and more than half of the entire kinky community during the previous year.

"He kept calling me *Mr. Jose Cuervo* and then pretending he made a mistake," said George Santos, his accent pure Miami. "What a racist douchebag."

But other than that, their story agreed with the general

timeline she had already sketched out. Steel left earlier than the rest of them did because of his tiff with Kevin McDonald, and no one saw him after that. Those who had partners and other potential alibis eagerly offered names and phone numbers to her; the remainder all looked at a young woman who made Rebecca do a double take, as she looked almost identical to the young man who had accompanied the contestants. Like some sort of human sheepdogs, she realized. Handlers. But both of them were small, slender, dark haired (with the same spiky short haircut) and they were even dressed alike.

Because lord knows, this event needs more people dressed alike, was her fleeting thought.

"Everyone here took the same shuttle back to the hotel," the girl-Jack-dressed-like-the-boy-Jack said. "Mack left on his own; he should have saved a cab receipt if he wanted to be reimbursed, but, um, he would have brought it this morning."

"Maybe Paul has it," suggested Chester "Zenu" Vole.

"No, don't you remember?" George Santos asked. "Paul was there afterward. I thought it was strange, that he didn't go with his master...er, boyfriend. With Mack."

Oh, *really*? Rebecca thought. Dammit, how had she missed getting an exact timeline? This was not like her; this case had thrown her off from the start. She looked at the colorfully dressed group and was about to ask where to find the group of egregiously offended people called bootblacks, when she suddenly noticed the strange shape of a sort of holster or scabbard on Mistress Ravenfyre's hip.

A sculpted handle protruded from the top, with a cap that looked like some sort of bird, but it was the holster itself that drew her attention. Instead of being a single sheath of a blade, as she'd already seen several times on other people, this one had *three* pockets.

A three-bladed knife?

"Ms. Schneider, may I see that knife you're carrying?"

Wendi/Ravenfyre looked down as if surprised to find it there and then handed it over with a slight smile. "Of course, Detective!"

The sheath had two narrow bands of leather that snapped over the hilt of the weapon, securing it in place. Rebecca put the knife down on the conference table, gloved up and drew the intricate toy from the scabbard. For this was a toy—no one would mistake it for something to bring to a knife fight. It was cheaply made— a little lightweight for the size, and garishly colored with paint and glass or plastic "gems." But it did indeed have three distinct, sharp blades, the one in the center longer than the two flanking it, engraved with RAVENFYRE in script. The handle was wrapped in thin, red leather of some soft texture, and the bird on the hilt might have been an eagle or some sort of hawk.

"I'm sure you will find it's never drawn blood," Ravenfyre said with a patient, helpful attitude. She affected a slight, indistinct accent, sometimes a little British, sometimes a little French, all of it colored with a genuine midwestern twang. "Please feel free to spray it with that...blue stuff. As long as it washes off!"

Luminol. Everyone was an expert on crime these days.

"It's a very interesting knife," Rebecca said, turning it from side to side. "I'm afraid I'll have to take it as potential evidence. But it will be returned to you when the lab is done, assuming it's clean."

"Wait—are you saying the Ravenfyre knife is the murder weapon?" All accents except for the real one vanished as Wendi's eyes went wide. She had been so calm and assured as she explained her complicated, polyamorous living arrangement-slash-alibi; apparently she had a husband *and* a female companion who was her slave and lived with them, and both of these people would swear to her whereabouts after the meet and greet. But now, with her face paling under well-applied makeup, she looked a little lost and frightened.

"There was a distinctive wound," Rebecca said, unwrapping an evidence bag.

Mickey Abraham laughed. "Oh, my God, Mack Steel was killed by the plus-five magical athame of dominance?" Wendi glared at her as the other judges looked at the now bagged knife, but Mickey kept laughing. "This is too rich! Better let the Detective know the bad news, Ravenfyre!"

"Bad news?"

"Well…you see…the knife was my sort of, um, talisman for my title year. And…um…" Wendi looked around and two of her fellow judges produced their own copies of the knife. The Zodian named Larry pulled one from behind his back while Master Zenu removed his from a black canvas bag with Bondage Bingo written on the side. Then the girl named Jack sighed and said, "I have one too, but it's in my room."

"Me, too," added George Santos.

Rebecca blinked and looked at the additional knives and then at Mistress Ravenfyre. "How many *are* there?"

"We had three hundred made," she said with a slight blush. "My year's done, so I only have about ten left; they're all back in my room. But, um. There might be a lot of them here. I gave them out to anyone who, you know…did me a service or was nice to me during the year."

Dr. Abraham was gasping for breath she was laughing so hard, wiping tears from her eyes. "So, given three thousand attendees this weekend, there might be over a hundred of those Chinese pigstickers here," she gasped. "Ha-ha! Looks like someone tried to frame you, Ravenfyre! With one of your own magical flaming raven-swords!"

"This is not funny!" Ravenfyre wailed.

And Rebecca could only agree. She picked up her phone to call for more help.

CHAPTER 14

THE NEWS THAT THE RAVENFYRE KNIFE MIGHT BE THE MURDER weapon swept the conference even faster than the news of the actual murder.

"I protest! I do not consent to the confiscation of my property!" shouted a bearded leatherman in a sash that read NEW MEXICO DADDY. Wisely, he made no move to reclaim his knife or stop the plainclothes officer from tagging and bagging it; Earl had sent word around to both request cooperation with the police and to make it clear that no one was to do anything that might make it seem like they were resisting or interfering with the investigation. Cooperation was uneven.

"Don't get your sash in a twist," snapped Slave Bitsy, helping to coordinate the knife collection at a table hastily set up near the Grand Ballroom space. "Just hand over the blade and keep moving!" She had already turned hers in, just to show how cooperative she was, and hearing the complaints of some of the attendees was wearing thin. The New Mexican titleholder gave a frustrated snort as he shouldered his way into the room where the opening ceremonies were about to take place.

"I'm never coming to this event again!" he yelled over his shoulder.

"I'll cry later!" Bitsy countered. "Why couldn't the killer take out a few more of those assholes?" She paused in her muttering to check her headset. "He's here? Fantastic. Send him right to the ballroom; shove his luggage somewhere safe, and we'll get it taken to his room." She clicked a few times to let the staff know that the elusive Dr. Julian Westfield had arrived at last.

"I don't *know* how many there will be," Rebecca explained for the tenth time. "I've got fifteen already. As many as a hundred. Yes, a hundred! No, I can't wait six weeks, these people are out of here in a couple of days...yes, I know it's the weekend...wait, don't put me on hold, wait!" She growled as the static-marbled easy-listening hold music came back on and slammed her phone down on the table. "Dammit!" Then she turned to Earl who was standing nearby, a look of dread on his face. He was wearing what looked like a silver leather tuxedo with a black shirt and bowtie; the look was somewhat marred by the presence of his walkie-talkie and cell phone holsters.

"I'm sorry, Detective, but I just can't release my registration records to you without a warrant," he said. "My lawyer was very specific! I'm responsible for the privacy of my attendees. I want to help, I really do, but if I made those lists available to you, no one would ever trust me again! The security of personal information is very important in this community! There are *reasons* people use scene names."

"I'm sure there are," she replied, glancing down at her list of people's real and fake names. "But the best reason I know why people use a false name is to commit a crime."

"It's not a crime to come to this contest or put a different name on a name tag," Earl insisted.

They were across from the knife wrangling, at two tables set up to form an L-shape against one of the walls. A box held the already-tagged knives, with a patrolman standing guard over it; the chain of evidence was going to be hellish for this little party.

What a long day! Struck by the complexity of this new turn of events, she'd called in her uniforms and Detective DeCosta and issued new marching orders. Find out who else at the event might have one of these knives and start rounding them up. Get images from the security tapes, and start checking alibis; ask Earl about finding this "Wolfboy" Paul mentioned. Five different calls to Eduardo and the lab geeks made up the first round of begging for answers to her various queries—fingerprints, criminal histories, anything they could get her by Sunday morning. She allowed the judges and contestants to continue their meetings, figuring she could pull Ferri out as soon as she had a free moment, but free moments had been scarce. The protein bar she'd scarfed down for lunch did nothing to increase her stamina or lift her mood. She was way past time for her workday to end, but who paid attention to minutia like that anyway?

Earl's sudden resistance to cooperation was frustrating. How many times did she have to explain that these people were not doing themselves any favors by hiding information she needed? The faster she could solve this, the faster they could go back to their private little lives, with their scene names and classes and dances and dungeons. Instead, the longer they drew it out, the greater time they'd have in the media spotlight. While the television people seemed to pop in and out as fast as the protestors who would no doubt be picturesquely featured on the evening news, there was at least one real newspaper reporter lurking, and incredibly, she'd gotten a pass or membership to the event.

Rebecca was doing her best to stay as far away from her as possible.

"So, you see, there's a *clear* difference between a slave, a sub, a boy or a girl, and a pup," Phedre said with a triumphant nod.

Nancy Nichols blinked and automatically responded, "Oh, yes, of course," while pondering how to get to first, the victim's bereaved boyfriend, secondly, Detective Feldblum, or ideally, both of them.

Cary had gotten her pretty far in terms of dirt and story fodder, but it wasn't until Phedre joined him and demanded *her* interview time that Nancy was able to score her renewed press pass. The big woman with the improbable nickname of Bitsy hadn't wanted to hand it over, but when both Cary and Phedre pleaded on her behalf, the producer, one Earl Stemple, had given in. She tried to interview him, but he was clearly distracted, talking into a headset while trying to text and hurrying off to some emergency.

She found a quiet spot at one point and dashed off not one, but two pieces, one on the murder and one on the subculture itself, and then added a sidebar with links just for added value. Vic was thrilled, both by the stories and the pictures, which although not bloody, did include people dressed in sexy costumes. "Aren't you glad I sent you there?" he insisted when she called him to let him know the stories were on the way. "Come on, you hated me yesterday. Now, you got two stories on the wires already! Do you need help? I can send Hector over for some more color pieces."

"I love ya like herpes," she told him. "I'll have the fashion piece for you later, and you keep Hector the *hell* away from my goddamn murder story."

Bastard. You'd think he came over and killed the pervert personally for her.

But she did appreciate her insider position for this gig—it sure beat covering a drugstore hold-up or even her much coveted crane collapse. However, her two stooges—or, rather, her two new BFFs—were fonts of way more information than she ever needed to know about this strange community, and they stuck to her like cheap concert posters on plywood. Thank goodness they had to tend their own little versions of media so she could maneuver her way to her real goals.

In fact, Phedre was turning to wave to someone; Nancy expected to see the black girl from the previous night, but this time it was a skinny, pink-cheeked little slip of a thing in a maroon, latex cheerleading uniform. She was holding the tiny video camera, though, and Phedre was putting herself together for broadcast.

"This is Fiona, my girl," Phedre said, re-pinning her hair back.

"I thought the girl from last night was your girlfriend?"

"Oh, she is. That was Dorcas, my primary! We're polyamorous. Fiona has a husband, so we're secondary relationships for each other. She's also a subby! Dorcas is definitely more a top-Daddy-type!"

Fiona giggled and made a sort of curtsy.

Nancy kept her mouth shut, even though every instinct screamed to ask for more information. I already have enough stories to last a year, she reminded herself firmly, including at least one on polyamory. "That's great," she said, trying to add something lifting and positive to her tone. Then she waited until the two women got into their filming and slipped closer to the tables where the detectives seemed to be conferring. There was a new guy on the scene, kinda young, African-American, looking awfully pretty and sharp in a chalk-striped suit. He had a netbook on the table and was pulling sheets of paper out of an envelope at the same time. Oh, yeah...multimedia potential! Nancy casually worked her way through the room.

Detective Dominick DeCosta was annoyingly proficient, Rebecca admitted to herself as he shared his intel with her. He'd not only helped go over the security camera footage, but he put together a complete set of stills for her as JPGs on a thumb drive, and even went to the hotel business center and printed out several frames he found to be worth investigating. This put him way ahead of Grant, her regular partner, who couldn't figure out how to send a text message from his cell phone or how to not hit REPLY ALL on email.

"These are all inside your estimated TOD window, and all dressed up like bikers, like your witness said," he explained. To her surprise, there weren't that many. "Turns out not too many got off on 20. And the costumes…well, if you get another witness who maybe saw someone dressed like a big damn baby, or some kinda vampire, I got pictures of them, too." He shook his head. "Disgusting stuff, some of it. Asses hanging out, *everything* hanging out. And some of these folks need to keep their regular bodies covered, let alone their junk."

"There's no need to be insulting," Earl said, stiffening.

"You don't think this is some crazy, sick stuff?" Dominick laughed. "I'm telling you there was a big fat guy dressed up like a goddamn *baby*, lollipop and diaper and all, and you think that's okay and normal?"

"We're all consenting adults, and we're not breaking any laws!"

"Murder ain't against the law 'round here?"

"Gentlemen," Rebecca interrupted. "Let's focus. Show me the potentials."

Dominick snorted and dropped the printouts on the table. "Here you go, one parade of perversion."

There were six, all shown getting out on the 20th floor between midnight and three A.M. All were dressed in black leather, five wearing the kind of hat Joshie had pointed out to her. Most of them were also carrying bags of one sort or another. She shuffled them and immediately pulled one out.

Well, well. It was Giuliano Ferri, the contestant who left

the meet and greet early. He looked positively cheerful and was carrying a black canvas bag over one shoulder.

Beside her, Earl gasped. "Do you recognize any of these other people?" she asked, fanning the pictures out for him. He opened his mouth and closed it again, obviously conflicted, and she lost her temper. "It's likely one of these people is the *murderer*," she snapped, slapping them onto the tabletop. "I'll hand out dozens of these pictures to a team of cops and have them going all through this event if that's what it takes, but it'll be much easier for us all if you could just give us a little help here, Mr. Stemple!"

That was when Bitsy reached the table; she glanced over the pictures and sighed. "That's Wally McPherson from Leather United, Metro Portland. That's, um, Slave...Mike-something, he's with Master Frank this year."

"Bitsy!" Earl said helplessly.

"Come on, Earl, you want everyone to pack up and leave? That's what'll happen if we have cops waving pictures at folks when they're trying to get into the fashion show! That's Giuliano Ferri, one of the contestants. That guy, I don't know, but I think he registered with two women. This one, I don't know her name, but she's from Los Angeles...Master Josephine knows her. And that's Dick Schneider, Ravenfyre's husband. Oh, and Westfield's on the way up, the stage crew says they can't work the spotlight, and the Headmaster wants an extra three minutes for his magic-school runway walk. He lost his music, though, and asked if we have any Enya or Danny Elfman." She elbowed her way back to her own table, command voice issuing directives to form a single line.

Oddly, Rebecca could hear, through the din of the crowds, something teasingly familiar. She frowned and shook her head, as whatever it was tugged at her memory and then vanished again. After she finished writing the names and references Bitsy had so easily recalled, she pulled out the pictures of Ferri and Schneider, noting that of the six, Schneider was the one not wearing a hat.

"Let's get them now," she said.

"Oh, jeez, really, now? It's our opening ceremony, and Mack's memorial! Can't it wait? I promise you, they are not going anywhere!"

"Are you crazy?" Dominick asked, looking down at Earl and shaking his head. Rebecca agreed with him in spirit, although she still tried to keep her tone civil.

"Earl, we need to talk to these people *now*. So, you call them or we will find them any way we can. I'm sorry your event is inconvenienced, but this takes precedence."

"Becca?" came a horrifyingly familiar voice. "Is that you?"

Rebecca looked up and saw the face and eyes that matched the laugh she'd caught just a moment before, that oh-so-memorable, warm laugh with the little hitch at the end that sounded almost like a hiccough. Those bright hazel/green eyes now behind dark, angular nerd-girl frames, devastatingly cute on an angular face with a slightly pointy chin. But instead of the loose, comfortable cotton trousers and canvas shoes and the worn linen shirts she kept finding at the bottom of drawers and in her closet long after the breakup, this woman was wearing Levi's jeans over heavy black boots, a black tank top with "Brat" stitched in pink over her rounded breasts and a leather vest festooned with a multitude of colorful pins. There was a black and red leather band on her right wrist and a Celtic armband tattooed over her shapely bicep.

Looks like she's working out, Rebecca thought with a weird disconnect. Her molasses-colored hair was no longer in wild ringlets and waves, but trimmed short over her ears. One hand half covered her mouth as she stopped short, staring at Rebecca.

"Trudy?" Rebecca said haltingly.

"Oh, my God, Becca, it *is* you!" The woman practically leapt over to the table and threw her arms around the detective, much to the shock of everyone else there.

Everyone, that is, excepting Nancy Nichols. "My, my, my,"

she murmured, surreptitiously taking a photo with her cell phone. "Detective Feldblum!" she said loudly, after slipping the phone out of sight. "Friend of yours?" But she already knew the answer. That was no *friend*. Nancy Nichols, keen observer of the human condition, knew an ex-lover when she saw one.

CHAPTER 15

A COMBINED MAJOR OF ENGLISH AND POLITICAL SCIENCE DID not turn out to be a hiring magnet when college was done. But the debt piled up attaining that degree was unalleviated by the dismal job prospects, and Rebecca Feldblum was severely underemployed for someone who wanted to live and work in New York City. Every day she put on what felt like a costume of skirt, low heels and sensible blouse and helped people open savings accounts and explained how to use ATM cards and order checks. Every night she sent her resume off to jobs that sounded as mind-numbing, if not more so, and dutifully went to networking events at the large LGBT community center. It seemed like half her income went to rent, and the other half to her student loans, leaving lots of generic cereal breakfasts, brown-bag lunches and the splendid options of rice and beans, mac and cheese or anything made with tuna for dinner. Her apartment was a fourth floor walk-up over two Brooklyn College dudes who seemed to smoke a lot of pot and play a lot of video games, loudly.

The only bright spot in her life was Trudy.

They'd met at a martial arts academy in Park Slope. Rebecca's mother and sister had given her a year's membership and classes as a graduation present, along with two uniforms and a book on Zen. That was her family, all right; never buy a *thing* when you can have an *experience*, her mother always said.

Rebecca had taken karate classes all through school and enjoyed the skill and challenge and feeling of strength and confidence she got while sparring. And since she would not have been able to afford the classes at the dojo, it was a timely, thoughtful and generous gift.

Trudy, on the other hand, came to the school looking for dates.

"Everyone said this place was a lesbian meat market," she admitted after their second post-dojo coffee together. "But wow, it's way too violent for me."

That was Trudy all over, as well. Full of half-thought-out plans and ambitions, lighthearted and playful, she was a bright foil to Rebecca's darker moments. She had majored in computer science in school, lucky her, and had a stable job in the IT department of a cable company. But instead of being the buttoned-down career-minded go-getter Rebecca associated with the whole computer field, Trudy was a food co-op member with an aging Volvo decorated with Greenpeace stickers and a closet full of natural fibers and pricey walking sandals.

They moved to an apartment together after three months of dating.

Making love with her was a revelation. The awkward safe sex negotiations and maneuvering around issues like who did what and when and whether sex toys entered the picture were replaced with ongoing flirtation. "I want you inside me," Trudy had whispered one night, while they were dancing at a tiny lesbian bar. "Any part of you. All of you. Your tongue, your fingers, anything you got..." Rebecca almost stumbled on the way out the narrow door, her entire body wanting exactly that, feeling like she'd

116

die if she didn't find a way to give Trudy what she craved.

Making out in the vestibule of Trudy's apartment, she slid her hand past the waistband of Trudy's jeans and tucked two fingers past the moist, hot tangle of soft hair into softer flesh, and Trudy gripped her shoulders and shuddered, her hips thrusting forward with such intensity they almost fell to the floor together.

But Rebecca held her up, almost impaled on her fingers, feeling the slick wetness of passion coating her knuckles and palm. It was difficult and clumsy, this standing posture with her hand jammed tight between flesh and cotton, working an impossible angle while exchanging gasping kisses and bites…but she wouldn't stop. Couldn't stop. She couldn't let her go for the minutes it would take to get out of clothing, to cross over to the battered futon. She rocked and twisted her hand, jammed her knee between Trudy's legs and used the extra pressure to force her fingers deeper into her body. Her mouth covered Trudy's soft lips, mingling tongues and moans echoing as they writhed together against the wall. Rebecca wanted at least two more hands, to run through Trudy's hair, to fondle her breasts, to cup her cute ass, to hold one hand over her head, pinning her above and below. Finally, that was her last choice; she pressed Trudy's right hand back against the wall and as their fingers locked, Trudy moaned into Rebecca's mouth and then bit her sharply as she came.

Gasping for breath, they looked at each other and gave weak laughs. "We should go inside," Rebecca had said.

"Hell, yeah," Trudy rasped. "I think it's time you met my battery-operated best friend."

That was Trudy.

Trudy took Rebecca to Connecticut to meet her family; Rebecca escorted Trudy up to Riverdale to return the favor. Rebecca got to eat a little better, although much of what Trudy made was vegetarian or even vegan. They talked about marriage and careers, about moving to Park Slope. They exchanged rings.

And then, on the last Sunday in June of that year, as they strolled through the vast festive chaos that was the annual gay pride parade, Rebecca picked up a recruitment flyer for the NYPD and slipped it into her bag of swag. The time started running out on their relationship before they even got on the train to go home.

That was Trudy, as well.

Surreal no longer seemed a sufficient description of this case.

Detective Dominick DeCosta stood at the back of the ballroom watching the unfolding evening with a chill around him so palpable even the busboys kept their distance. The room was packed with costumed freaks, mostly in black leather, latex and a few uniforms here and there, but with plenty of other weirdness to add color. Hundreds of them were seated at the banquet tables, nibbling on steam-tray appetizers and standing on line at the cash bar like some very strange corporate Christmas party.

It made him itch. Moving to New York was one thing; he'd known all along how different it would be from his Mama's home in Mississippi and even his Daddy's place in Virginia. That was why he came; a life of drunken hillbillies and trash and stupid homeboys looking for excitement did not suit his image of what a police officer—a *detective*—should be handling. He wanted not only a big city, but a huge one, millions of people, a place where a man could be reinvented and challenged. He'd come north knowing it would be completely unlike anything he'd ever known before going away to school. But this...was culture shock beyond what any reasonable soul could imagine.

Meeting *that* detective, then thrown into *this* freak show.

And then for Feldblum's...*friend*...to show up.

Awkward. The look of horror on her face as she was getting hugged was just cringe inducing. She grabbed the girl and pulled her away, calling out needless instructions for him to take over. Shortly after that, she returned and called it a day and told him she'd be there bright and early tomorrow morning to round up suspects. He was free to grab them from the opening ceremonies or knock off until 8 A.M., but she was *gone*, barring new discoveries requiring her attention.

He didn't blame her. It wasn't likely their suspects would leave, seeing as most of them were high-profile celebrities at this thing. And he was a full detective now; there was a part of him that felt real proud she had just casually left the investigation in his hands. Another part of him felt intimidated at the thought of conducting an interview on his own. There were so many ways to screw up a line of questioning, make a suspect switch from cooperative to stubborn, friendly to angry. Perhaps he would wait until the morning, when she came back. There was a good reason to wait— he was handicapped by the lack of information from the lab geeks and computer savants. The boxes of fantasy knives and the dead silence from the crime scene techs were like black holes, sucking potential from the investigation.

He continued to weigh the option of grabbing one of their suspects for questions or waiting until he had the more seasoned cop with him. In the meantime, he looked through the program he had grabbed and the bag of materials the big girl running registration had given him. His notes were already several pages long, and he knew he'd be up late researching on the Internet.

This was not exactly what he'd expected after the long wait before finally getting a bump to homicide. Vice cases, sure; he'd seen a lot of strange stuff while working vice, and some things he'd like to erase from his memory. But this bunch just gave him the creeps. It wasn't just their kinky clothing choices and bizarre sex games, although that was enough for any sane man. But over by another wall was a table where people could stash their bags— and there was a mountain of them. What were they carrying that needed so much luggage? What could be hidden in them?

Logic said he should have knocked off for home himself, but

the chance to even *observe* some of the potential suspects was too alluring. He wanted to not only look prepared for the interviews but also be ready to catch these crazy people in the tangles of the lies they no doubt told about themselves without even thinking. That, he knew without even saying a word to them. All he had to do was read their biographies in the program. If you believed them, everyone here had been born living some kind of kinky lifestyle, with special rules and titles and fancy made-up names. Every single one of them won awards, got prizes and were masters of some kinky shit. They had so many fancy terms for who they were and what they did, they made the habitual liars of the sex trade seem straightforward.

In the real world, a pimp might call himself a *manager*—here, if a guy had four girlfriends who all swore devotion to him, he was a *master*. There was even a class called "Four's Company: Managing Your Household Staff."

The women who hid their bruises and blinked as they swallowed tears and said, "It was my fault, I made him angry," they would probably have something to say to these ladies here who talked about something called *complete surrender of power*. The big-talking, twitchy bastards who were too fast with their fists? Maybe they were *sensation sadists*, like the people on the panel, "Make It Hurt So Good." The cheaters and the players, oh, lord, if they only knew they were *polyamorous*! And as for the Vikings...

He had no clue about the Vikings.

Oh, they dressed it up by saying "consensual" about as often as a TV preacher said, "donate," and probably with the same intent—to offer a sort of salvation. But they were obviously on the defensive, using words like real, natural, true, total, complete— anything to make sure everyone understood this wasn't just pretend play. Under it all, it was clear they knew what they really were.

Perverts. Freaks. Sickos dressing up their sickness while trying to celebrate it. Abusing themselves and each other and lying about it.

Case in point—the eulogy for the late, unlamented Mr. Mack Steel.

They got some doctor from California—of course—to get up and say nice things about the man. Apparently, this was a challenge. Dominick leaned against the wall shaking his head.

Dr. Julian Westfield was a tall man with a potbelly, bald at the top of his head but sporting elegantly silver hair along the sides with a silver beard flowing to his chest. He was wearing slightly baggy jeans under biker chaps, a blue chambray button-down shirt and a black leather vest; a patch on the back of the vest pictured two crossed whips inside a ring of linked handcuffs and the name PACIFIC COAST BDSM ALLIANCE. He got a good round of cheers when he was introduced and spent a little time looking somberly at the crowd before clearing his voice to speak.

"Even as we gather to celebrate our sacred sexuality," he began, his deep voice selling every word, "we are in the midst of tragedy. Real violence—the desecration of a human body and soul, the very antithesis of what we stand for. A star in our constellation has fallen, and we are all diminished by his loss. Mack Steel was a leatherman—a man of leather—a man who knew what he wanted and reached forth his hand to take it..."

Dominick swept his gaze through the audience. There was the grieving boyfriend, at a table near the podium, dressed all in black with a big black dog collar around his neck, looking out of proportion to his size. He looked like he was sobbing while the man next to him was awkwardly patting his shoulder. Could that be the mysterious "Wolfboy" who was his alibi? Maybe he'd go over later and ask if Paul could point him out.

And there were the contestants, all at one table, including the one pictured in the elevator, Ferri. He was staring at the speechifying doctor like he was searching for truth; but then, so were most of the others. One of the women seemed to be snoozing, her head dipping down toward her chest before she jerked awake and tried to look interested. One of the contestants was actually black, sitting there all in biker leathers. Really, my brother? Dominick thought. Way to represent. There was a distinct absence of darker skin tones here, but there were enough to make him wonder whether they also actually played the master/slave games.

Far away from the stage were tables where people were talking or even snickering; Dominick almost pitied the folks way up front who had to look as though they cared. The briefing he got from Feldblum and his own poking around made it clear that very few of these people were going to miss the man.

"Representing this prestigious title, Mack worked hard all year to spread the word about our leather lifestyle," the doctor was going on. "We'll never know how many lives he touched..."

"Or how many slaveboys," snickered someone from the nearest table.

"He touched a friend of mine, but he got a shot and it cleared up right away."

More laughter. Several tables away, people looked around for the source. The speaker went on, oblivious, his mannerisms theatrical, his voice quivering with emotion.

"Winner of Mr. Frisco Leather...two times winner of the Mr. Stud contest...Mack Steel traveled around our great nation spreading his sense of passion for our lifestyle and values. At times controversial, he was never at a loss for something to say..."

"Something nasty!"

"Or stupid..."

Dominick suppressed a slight smile as he picked up the responses and muttering.

"And yet who can deny he was a steadfast and loyal friend, a good lover and master to his partner..." He glanced down at his notecards, "Paul...who served him as his boy, with him throughout his leather journey..."

The whispers near Dominick continued, accompanied by giggles and snorts.

"Keeping him from making a fool of himself every other minute..."

"Making sure he didn't show up at the wrong place three hours late..."

"Distracting him away from the fresh meat..."

"Watering his drinks..."

Paul sobbed louder, and several of the people around him left their chairs to comfort him. Dr. Westfield paused, looked over the edge of his glasses and then shuffled his cards to continue.

One person from the judges' table edged her chair back and looked like she was excusing herself. It was the short woman, the college professor in the Hawaiian shirt. She unhurriedly meandered through the tables, glancing back to the stage from time to time, but it was clear she was heading out.

Dominick tracked her to one of the main doors and figured she was hitting the rest room, but the way she kept glancing back made him curious. He edged toward her direction on an intercepting trajectory and then paused as he saw her meet up with another woman who was also looking around as though making sure she was not being watched. The two of them left together.

Now, who was that other woman? He knew he'd seen her; was she on the elevator camera? In the program book? He slipped out of the room for another glimpse and quickly filed away the basic descriptors for the lady. Light brown hair, past her shoulders and straight, about five foot and three, maybe five inches in her heels, a little plump, say a hundred forty or fifty, light skinned, button nose, wearing a chain collar around her neck...

She and the judge turned a corner toward the elevators, but not before they paused and the judge grabbed her and gave her a very long and very intimate kiss, along with a blatant ass-grab. Then, they ran off together.

He found her in the main program book. There she was, on her knees, in some sort of corset thing and the same chain collar, beside a standing—and familiar looking—man wearing all black leather and a seated woman in a green latex gown. She was Slave Willow, who apparently belonged to Mistress Ravenfyre and her husband, Master Dick Schneider. Masters and slaves! Did they really have no idea how offensive that was?

And although he didn't know much about their weird mating/dating issues and styles, he was willing to bet that when someone takes a picture of you in a dog collar, on your knees with Person A, you better not be sneaking off for some kinky nooky with Person B. So, maybe it was a good idea to have stayed a little while longer. He would go back and listen to the rest of the speeches, watch the persons of interest, familiarize himself with their rituals and language. Then, maybe, he'd grab Ferri or Dick Schneider and lean on them a little. Now, which one? The man who also went missing about the time the dead guy left the bar, or the man whose wife had been victimized by the deceased? He weighed his options carefully, wanting to utilize what energy he had left and spend it on the best possible results. It would be nice to get some new information and make a good impression on his temporary and senior partner, especially since he got a strange feeling Feldblum didn't much like him. He couldn't imagine why, since they'd just met. He hoped she wasn't racist.

That would be ironic, though nothing new.

Then, his phone buzzed to let him know there was new information from the lab, and when he finished reviewing the report, he knew which lucky man was going to get his evening interrupted by the big, bad homicide detective.

8:36PM Soon u will b history
Reply 8:39PM Loser!!!!
8:59PM Ur past is ctchng up 2 u!

Reply 9:02PM Fuck u

9:15PM So long suka! I dance on ur grave!!!

Richard "Call me Dick" Schneider looked more embarrassed than guilty. He winced as Dominick read the messages Dick had exchanged with Mack Steel in a dispassionate voice, spelling out the texting abbreviations. Dominick looked up from the screen of his netbook and asked, as he leaned back, "You dancing now? Or did you save your dance for his room when you went there that night?" He slid over the frame from the security camera. The empty meeting room was still set up like a classroom, but they were seated across from each other at the table up front. A posterboard off to one side had what looked like a complicated diagram on it, depicting a human body with different areas shaded in different colors.

For a minute, Dick Schneider didn't say anything, only looked down at the picture on the table while he rubbed his forehead. Dominick watched him, the slight tremble in his fingers, and the loss of color in his already pale cheeks. His ID said he was forty-six, but his high, creased forehead and receding hairline could have belonged to a man ten years older. More than anything, he looked tired.

"Maybe I should call a lawyer," he finally said.

"Y'all go right ahead," Dominick said generously. "Why not text one? You can ask him about making death threats while you're at it."

"These aren't death threats! They're just...trash talk. I was happy to see him lose his title, that's all, and get into that stupid fight at the bar in front of everyone, instead of doing his nasty, shitty things where no one could see! The man got a full year of being held up as the epitome of our community, a leader, a hero, and if people really knew what a complete jerk he was, they'd have taken him down ages ago!" He flushed a little and rubbed his forehead again.

125

"What do you mean, where no one could see?" Dominick asked. "Almost everyone we've spoken to told us he wasn't exactly Mr. Personality."

"Popular is one thing. A decent human being is something else. You have no idea what he was capable of! He almost ruined my family, he cost Wendi—Ravenfyre—her job!"

"Really? Do tell."

"It was completely calculated, a deliberate act of *outing*, and no one held him accountable, ever! Even Earl—the producer of the contest—said he couldn't do anything. We just had to take it and suffer, and Wendi had to smile and pretend like nothing was wrong all year while he laughed at us!"

"What did he do?"

Dick took a deep breath. "I told you. He outed her. In the newspaper, our local newspaper. He wrote a letter congratulating her on winning the contest and they *published* it."

Dominick frowned. "But...didn't you want the publicity? This is some giant honor, right? You get to be superstars in the kinky world and all that? Why did she run if she didn't want people to know?"

"Well...yes, that is a point, but not everyone who has a title is out by their real name. I mean, obviously, her name isn't *Ravenfyre*. She chose that name so that she could have some distance between her scene identity and her real one. It's all well and good for a San Francisco gay man to be out as Mr. Leather-anything, but when you're a married woman living in the midwestern suburbs and working at a library, maybe you don't want your next-door neighbor to know everything about your sex life! He used her real name in the letter, like, ha-ha, joke's on you, and the very next day she was called into the director's office and told it would be best if she left her job. One of our neighbors stopped talking to us and even walks her damn kid across the street from our house to avoid just going on our sidewalk!"

126

"Mmm, that's pretty bad," Dominick admitted with a nod.

"And what's worse is that we couldn't even complain! People would say just what you did—that we were asking for it by her running for the title and all that. And let me tell you, she was nothing but *nice* to that mother—that son of a bitch. She was going to have his name on the other side of that knife, did you know that? Only he never answered her emails, so she went ahead without his name on them. She did make business cards with both their names on them, hell, we still have about five hundred of those. We had to redo them when we realized he was jerking her around behind her back. But like some kind of snake, he just kept slithering on, spitting hate and venom at her all year!"

"That must have made you pretty angry."

"Angry? Lemme tell you, I must have told Wendi a dozen times, it wasn't worth it. I mean, great, she got some clothes and some trips to places we've never been, but honestly, I could have lived without spending a weekend in a motel by the interstate while she judged Mr. and Ms. South Dakota Rubber. And, and all the people complaining that she's not gay, or she's a sell-out because we're married—for crying out loud, it's *normal* to be married! It's not our fault gay people can't get married! But sometimes people seem to act like it's our fault or something."

"Yeah, it must be pretty hard to be a famous pervert when you only want *some* people to know you're a famous pervert," Dominick drawled. "What do your neighbors say about your slavegirl? That's a normal part of your normal marriage, too?"

"We're consenting adults!" Dick said, looking slightly more embarrassed.

"Yeah? Did Steel threaten to send a letter to your paper congratulating you for bangin' two ladies?"

Dick's mouth dropped open and then snapped shut as the color on his face deepened. Dominick leaned forward and pressed, "Because from where I sit, it sounds like you got lots of reasons for goin' up to his room and stabbing him with one of the knives you got stockpiled. How many did you turn in tonight, anyway?"

"I...I don't know! Willow packed them. She brought them down...maybe eight or nine? How stupid would I have to be to kill the man with my wife's own signature knife?"

"Maybe you gave us nine clean ones and ditched the bloody one. Plenty of knives around means plenty of suspects; you could get away clear while we're buried in tons of false leads."

"But I didn't do anything!"

"You just sent him messages threatening to dance on his grave? And did you tell your slave to do that, too?"

"Willow? No! Did she? That was...I never told her to do any such thing! That was...wrong of her! Not what we'd like her to be doing at all!" He looked genuinely shocked. "Did she really?"

"I guess we'll be talkin' to her next," Dominick said. "See if *she* can explain what you were doing looking around up on Steel's floor."

"She has nothing to do with this! With any of it!"

"Then tell me what were you doing on the 20th floor."

Another rubbing of his forehead, as his eyes drifted left. He's about to lie, Dominick realized. "No, don't even try it," he cautioned. "Come on, I'm not stupid. Your room is on the opposite end of the building; you had no reason for being up there, unless you were goin' after Steel."

"I was seeing...someone else," he said.

The detective waited as he squirmed.

"It's kinda private."

"You screwing around, too?" Dominick asked.

"Too?" He looked confused and then his eyes narrowed. "No! I'm not cheating around on my wife! It was...business. And my wife knew exactly what I was doing, just ask her!"

"I guess we will," Dominick said casually. "But right now I'm asking *you*. Who did you meet?"

He compressed his lips. "I decline to say."

"Mr. Schneider, let me be really clear with you. Your wife was victimized by a man who was found murdered by a knife *she* made, and you were seen going up to his floor that night, within the window of opportunity, with no explanation for your presence. I'm going to have to ask for your clothing, a complete timeline of your evening, and I think it's time we searched your hotel room." Dominick rose, snapped his netbook closed and started gathering his papers.

"Wait, wait!" Dick cried. "Jeez...fine, search our room, whatever...but look. It's just *business*, I swear. I went nowhere near Steel's room!"

"Then what room did you go to?" Dominick demanded.

His eyes shifted back and forth and then down. "Dr. Abraham's," he admitted with a helpless sigh.

Dominick sat down. "Now tell me why," he said. Inwardly, he was grinning. What a story he would have for Feldblum in the morning! It just got weirder and weirder.

CHAPTER 16

IN MOVIES, RELATIONSHIP DISCUSSIONS ALWAYS SEEMED TO take place while the romantic couple strolled the Brooklyn Promenade or some other riverside park where the iconic skyline of Manhattan could be seen. There would be a sentimental '80s ballad or exciting, rising orchestral music to accompany them.

In reality, Rebecca thought, stirring milk into her white ceramic mug of overheated coffee, 99 percent of New Yorkers actually talk things over in a diner. And why not? Open twenty-four hours a day, a never-empty cup of coffee, and anything from disco fries to French toast, roast chicken to chocolate pudding, all sorts of comfort food available to soothe the heart. You had the safety of being in public, where causing a scene was less likely, but the near-privacy of a padded booth and a jukebox competing with the clatter of a huge kitchen staffed by people who were not paid or tipped well enough to make them care about little things like being quiet and unobtrusive.

Her coffee steamed and shimmered. Trudy stuck a straw into her milkshake and raised the enormous glass in a toast.

"It's good to see you, Becca. Wow, you look great!"

Rebecca sipped and burned her tongue. Grabbing Trudy and hissing, "Can I see you outside?" had been impulsive. But standing there in a crowd of kinky people with a judgmental partner while your ex leapt on you was surely enough to throw anyone into a deer-in-the-headlights freeze. Now, safely away, she didn't know what she wanted to say, ask, or do.

"I...it's good to see you, too," she said, knowing it sounded as awkward as she felt.

"I can't believe you are investigating this murder!" Trudy shook her head, leaning back against the bench. "I mean, wow. It's like karma. Do you know who did it?" She grinned. "I guess not, since you're here and not arresting someone, but do you have any clues?"

"No. I mean, yes, of course, but it's too early to say anything, and certainly not to a civilian," Rebecca said, her tone harsher than she really wanted it to be.

"Oh." Trudy deflated a little, but then perked again. "But I'm sure you'll solve it. You are the smartest woman I ever knew. I'm so glad it's you here and not some homophobic asshole guy treating us like freaks."

Like my new partner? Rebecca thought. Too late! But then, the unformed feelings Trudy's appearance produced rose up like steam, and she found herself blurting, "What the hell are *you* doing here?"

Trudy blinked, her green-flecked eyes widening. "You said you wanted to see me outside!"

"No, no, I mean...at this contest! What are you doing dressed like...that?" Rebecca waved her hand at the leather vest and BRAT shirt. "For God's sake, Trudy, you went to anti-porn rallies and said heterosexuality was the institutionalized justification for the subjugation of women! You...you left me because I was joining what *you* called a fascist, patriarchal system of oppression! And now you're into leather? BDSM?"

"Oh. Well..." Trudy showed her cute teeth in an embarrassed grin. "Well, I guess, um, things were a little more complicated than that."

"More complicated? You called me a *Nazi* when I came home with my uniform. A Nazi!"

Trudy stopped grinning and lowered her head. "Oh, God, I was such a jerk."

"Yes! You were." Rebecca drank her bitter coffee and banged the empty mug down onto the table. They sat there in silence as the waitress came over and refilled it, tossing more plastic milk containers onto the table at the same time.

"I'm sorry," Trudy said. "Really. That was a shitty thing to say."

"And it wasn't the only thing you called me, just the worst," Rebecca said. "Because I found myself a job I wanted to do, a good job. You said I was going to be protecting wife beaters and arresting demonstrators and supporting an abusive culture of violence." There were times in police work when a good memory was a blessing. Other times in life, not so much. "And then, you left me. Now, years later, you're into this bondage and spanking stuff? You're even a, a *sub*?"

Trudy's head sank further down as Rebecca purged some of the old pain. But she looked up at that last word and raised her eyebrows.

"You know what a sub is?"

"I've been here all day! I know more about this whole...scene... than I ever really wanted to!"

"Oh."

They both turned their attention to their drinks and then looked up again at the same time, which made them glance down again. Naturally that led to them both meeting eyes one more time, and that time, they laughed.

"I was wrong," Trudy finally said. "And stupid. I'm sorry.

Sometimes, I don't believe that was really me; I mean, I threw away the best thing that ever happened to me because I was repeating tired old leftist, feminist cant without even knowing I was kinky. I mean, maybe I knew, but I didn't want to think about it. I didn't know much about myself at all, really."

"So, you're not a feminist any more?"

"Of course I'm still a feminist! I'm just a *kinky* one." She laughed again, with that lilting hitch at the end, and scooped some whipped cream off the top of her milkshake. "And I dunno how submissive I really am, actually. I kinda suck at obedience and servitude! I am a bottom, though. Just not one of those 'yes ma'am, no ma'am' types." She pointed to the word Brat, all pink and glittery and grinned. "It's why I'm still single!"

Rebecca nodded more out of social habit than understanding. Her brain was just exhausted; too many threads of information, too many questions and things on her to-do list and frustration and exhaustion and hunger. (The french fries being delivered to the booth next to them smelled so good...) And overriding all of that was Trudy, still talking, still explaining and laughing at herself. Even with her exhaustion and distraction, though, Rebecca did hear that one line.

The best thing that ever happened to me.

Really? She still thought that?

And if so...was it crazy to imagine they could work something out again? They had been so good together until the break up, just so right. They sang along with the radio at the same time, read the same books, hungered for each other's company. Was it insane to want to recapture that magical time?

Oh, definitely. Stupid, too, and a distraction, and there was no way she wanted to get involved in this role-playing and BDSM and leather stuff. She drank her coffee and tried to listen to the words and not get caught up in those dancing little green flecks in Trudy's pretty eyes.

* * *

Somewhat to the amazement of everyone on staff, the Friday evening events recovered from the stumble of last minute changes. There was the horror of the hastily assembled chorus to warble *Wind Beneath My Wings,* and the inevitable breakdown of various emotionally vulnerable members of their community. But the dungeon play spaces in the hotel opened on time, and the taxi line did brisk business taking people down to the Shaft to enjoy the leather bar atmosphere. The Single Mingle got their snacks and party favors delivered, and at midnight, the popular Pajama and S'Mores party, for the people who liked to role-play like little kids, was packed. Down the hall, the Lipstick Leather Lesbians had their annual Lingerie Luau, and since both parties made judicious use of marshmallows and underwear, there was some accidental crossover. But for a change, this did not lead to angry shouting matches and accusations of invasion of privacy and safe space. Instead, they worked things out without alerting security, much to everyone's relief. The convention security was busy patrolling the lobby and the halls outside the playrooms, making sure no cameras or unfamiliar people got in.

Special prayers were offered for the repose of Mack Steel in the Free-Form Worship and Meditation room, and the stage crew had an emergency meeting to discuss the changeup in contest choreography. Should they still restage his winning tableau? Yes, was the final decision, with a memorial podium representing him. Someone volunteered to find the appropriate participants and make sure they were correctly costumed; others took over the responsibility for finding the music and doing the stage direction. Everyone avoided mentioning what a relief it was not to actually have him there.

Nancy Nichols stood stock still and found herself in a situation never experienced before.

She was completely without words.

Given her choices and stripped of her cameraman, Nancy Nichols went straight to the dungeon. Of course! She had to sign yet another agreement not to take photos or become stricken with remorse after having witnessed scenes of depravity. She swore by all things holy that she was an adult of sound mind who did in fact wish to see examples of bondage, sadomasochism, nudity, cosplay, suspension, whipping, spanking, role-playing, and an assortment of terms she would have looked up if she wasn't pretending to have left her smart phone somewhere else.

There were actually several dungeons, dungeon meaning "hotel ballroom with bad lighting, loud music and awkward furniture." Nancy chose the largest one, labeled PANSEXUAL.

"This is where the chefs from TV shows come and get their kink on?" she asked one of the two people standing rigidly by the door. He looked back at her in confusion, and checked her ID a second time. She considered prompting her own joke with an added clue—"PAN sexual, get it? Pots and pans?" but then she heard a cracking sound coming from inside the ballroom, so she just grinned and moved along.

Once past the doors, she had to pause and let her eyes become accustomed to the lighting. The few normal fluorescent panels on the ceiling were covered by colored sheeting in amber tones, and small lamps seemed to be clamped to tables and...structures... throughout the room. To one side stood a giant metal dome, like some oversized playground equipment, easily twelve feet at the top. The floor under the dome was padded with layers of mats, and Nancy could see why. Suspended from the network of girders was a woman wearing nothing but coils and coils of rope and a smile. Not just trussed up by her wrists like an illustration in a comic strip version of a dungeon, but her entire body wrapped in neatly arranged rope that was then looped over and through the bars of the dome at multiple points. She was facedown, with her arms spread wide, as though she had been caught in flight; below her, a man wearing a kilt and an expression of intense concentration was still running rope back and forth and making her even more secure.

It was...pretty, Nancy had to admit. Not her thing, to be sure—who had patience for all that knot tying and rope coiling? And what do you do with a woman suspended in midair above your head? Blow her kisses? It would have made for great photos, and her fingers itched to pull her camera out for just a few secret shots. No stupid signed agreement would keep any reporter from doing her work! But what good would that picture do? It had nothing to do with the murder and illustrated nothing except that the kilt-guy was probably an Eagle Scout.

And where was the good stuff, anyway? She wandered the room, taking in the minidramas happening from station to station and compiled her first impressions. Unlike the stereotypical image of an orgy, a tangle of bodies all jumbled together in one heaving mass, BDSM looked to be an activity one did on a piece of equipment with some room around it for voyeurs. She was not nearly the only one taking a tour of the place; more people were standing in small clumps and talking or wandering aimlessly than actually using the equipment and stations. She passed what looked like an authentic gynecologist table and snorted. What woman would happily climb into the stirrups in public? What kind of masochist...

Oh. Right. Nancy shook her head. What a weird world these people lived in.

Finally, she spotted something that seemed more like a whips-and-chains activity. A man wearing nothing but some kind of leather jockstrap and a pair of boots was bound inside a tall, square wooden frame. It was obviously very sturdy, because he was pulling at the thick leather cuffs around his wrists and ankles as the woman behind him lashed at his body with one of those

Zorro-style whips, long and black. This was the source of the cracking sounds—when not hitting him, the woman made a little flick of one wrist and the whip snapped in the air like a firecracker going off. Interestingly, it didn't make that sound when it actually hit the guy—and neither did it seem to leave the huge, bloody wounds often shown in pirate and gladiator movies.

Nancy moved in closer to watch. The woman with the whip in her hand was concentrating as much as Mr. Bondage-Kilt-Man. She would pop the whip against her slave's skin and then gather it up in both hands while he hissed and danced and struggled in his leather cuffs. Then, she would step in close and run the braided leather over his back or ass, and he'd lean back into her. It was hard to hear what they were saying, but it was clearly not some sort of "Take your punishment, you pathetic worm," kind of thing. In fact, she looked downright affectionate when she was next to him, one hand cupping his butt or reaching around him to playfully tweak a nipple. And when he wasn't wincing and giving an occasional yelp, he was glancing over his shoulder at her, looking eager and happy.

Definitely not a cartoon version of BDSM. The woman wasn't even in a leather corset and heels, but jeans and what looked like sensible boots. She wasn't wearing a shirt—only a leather vest over her decidedly non-perky breasts. When she concentrated, she frowned a little, and bit her lip. This was no Princess of Pain.

Of course, he was no sniveling, fat Wall Street banker type, either. He looked like a scruffy bike messenger, with long hair and a beaky nose. The leather jock seemed out of place on his skinny body, too bulky and macho for a man who would look much more at home ordering a Grande Soy Mochaccino with a shot of hazelnut and extra foam. The tattoos of manga-style babes who were wearing stereotypical dungeon mistress outfits only added to his overall sense of geekiness.

And yet, after yelping and jerking in his bondage after a few well-placed snaps of that whip, he sagged forward, gasping for breath, and his lady friend came up behind him again, stroking him, whispering in his ear. He pushed back against her, his ass rubbing her jeans, and she laughed and spanked one ass cheek so hard the sound almost resonated. He yelped more in play this time and then rocked his hips back and forth in a crude, teasing parody of sex.

Okay, it was cute. Nancy was going to move on; nothing much to see here. But then the mistress reached into one of the ubiquitous shoulder bags carried by an abundance of attendees and pulled out a very different looking whip. Nancy had heard of a cat-o'-nine-tails—this one must have had a hundred. It was a thick bundle of black tresses, each less than half an inch wide. She could tell because the mistress had to shake them out before using the thing. It looked like it should hurt—wouldn't getting hit by that much weight feel more like a punch than a little snap?

The mistress drew her fingers through the tresses one last time then pulled her arm back and forward in a neat motion. The man in bondage did not yelp, as he had with the single braided whip— no, this time he moaned.

And a good moan, too, not one of pain. It carried even through the crowd noises of the large room. Nancy took an involuntary step forward to see—and hear—better. Surely, he didn't like this better than that lightweight whip?

Oh, but he did. The second thump of this whip landed on his shoulders, the black tresses flattening against his pale skin. He gasped and *wiggled* in his bondage, his hips moving again, and he nodded happily, his eyes closed. Yep. Clearly, this fat bundle of leather was much more...pleasurable than the skinny whip.

This wasn't torture, unless you counted "being tortured with ecstasy."

Nancy watched the two as the mistress kept working that fat bundle of leather strands up and down her boyfriend's back, across his ass, against his thighs. He loved every stroke—arched himself back toward her to welcome them, breathed deeply in preparation for the heavy thud, groaned as his hips thrust at nothing. There was a certain rhythm to the beating, like a drumbeat of pleasure, punctuated by groans and whispered encouragement. The mistress laughed as she used the whip and said, "Good boy," and "That's my boy," in between strokes. Rather than sounding arch and strident and angry, she sounded downright affectionate.

This was not the average cartoon dominatrix scene at all. Where was the cringing, the humiliation, all that "you pathetic worm," dialog so loved by B-movie script writers? Nancy wished for a good camera, hell, a video camera, to document this, although where she'd sell the recording was a complete mystery. When the mistress/dominatrix/girlfriend seemed finished with the whip, she walked in close again and sensuously pressed her body against her boyfriend's back. She ran both hands across his chest, playfully tweaking his nipples, and his hips gyrated so violently it looked like he was about to explode right then and there. In fact, his animation was so complete, he seemed more like some sexual athlete than a victim of S/M torture.

An unwanted "why haven't I forgotten you yet?" memory intrusion of her last time with a potential new lover was unexpectedly sharp. He had talked a good game and sure had the eye-contact/noncreepy compliment combo down pat, but when it came to actual performance, he was lackluster and by-the-numbers. In fact, this man in bondage, waggling his hips and groaning, was porn-star material compared to Mr. Oh-did-I-lose-your-number. And she couldn't even see the extent of his hard-on, hidden behind that sturdy leather jock.

As the mistress started to unfasten the bondage, questions tumbled through Nancy's mind. Was this the extent of their sex play? How do you know when the S/M is over, without a handy barometer like orgasm? (Faked or genuine.) Did these people actually have real sex at all, or was it all performance, or was this dramatic stuff saved for weekend events and they screwed at home? Eager for more examples of this sort of thing—from a purely journalistic perspective, of course!—Nancy swept her eyes through the room for her next adventure in learning. It was going to be a late night, and apparently, she still had a lot to learn.

Across from her were three men about to start something involving two of them being bound together facing each other, completely naked. She could swear she saw the glint of something metallic and shiny where their cocks were being mashed together; could that be body jewelry? Were they fastened together that way? One of them was a stunning bodybuilder type; she could see the cute indent in his sculpted asscheeks as he shifted and rubbed against the man tied in front of him.

Oh, yes, this was an *excellent* educational opportunity.

All in all, the evening went on without any major screw-ups. Cooperation and mutual respect ruled the night, and the volunteers on staff breathed a sigh of relief. Perhaps, thought Earl, as he finally staggered to his room at 3 A.M., they could manage to get through the weekend with no more tragedy. The police would handle a quiet investigation and not come up with anything that would need anyone's attention. The contest could go on, and the parties, and then everyone would go home in peace.

Of course, this was a vain hope. Early on Saturday morning, Slave Bitsy, resplendent in a floor-length, dark grey gown with a silver brocade waist cincher enforcing her hourglass shape and keeping her breasts displayed to their very best advantage, was first at the registration desk. She unlocked the office behind the tables to bring out the laptops and label printer and get them started; by the time she went back for the lanyards and boxes of forms, one of the newest volunteer staff arrived with a cup of hot Earl Grey tea. (Bitsy trained her staff quite well in what it took to run a con, and the first order of business after "Don't Piss Off Slave Bitsy" was "Sucking Up to Slave Bitsy Is Never Wrong.")

This new guy overheard her complaining about the loss of labor and volunteered right on the spot, even though he'd paid full price for his ticket. She quickly sent around a text to her best friends asking about him, and no one said he was an asshole or a jerk or a congenital idiot, so she accepted him, gave him the twenty-minute training in five minutes and handed him a different colored badge. Much to her surprise, he actually turned out to be quite useful. She checked his badge to remind herself of his name, and murmured "Tom, Tom," under her breath.

She sent the skinny volunteer crawling under the table to plug the various electronic devices into the floor outlets and heard him ask, slightly muffled by the table drape, "What's this?"

"What's what?"

Tom crawled back out with a plastic bag in his hands. Bitsy sighed. "What do I have to do to people to make them stop leaving their garbage at my station? I swear, if I find out who left that here, I'll skin 'em and make myself a pair of gloves!"

He laughed heartily and tossed the bag onto the tabletop.

It clunked.

"Oh...fuck," Bitsy moaned. She prodded the outside of the bag and felt the hard, pointy metal edges, and then pulled her hand away. "Oh, fuck me *hard*." She pulled out her phone and found the card the police had left with her and completely missed the lingering glance of longing Tom gave her before continuing the set-up chores.

CHAPTER 17

THE WESTERN HARRISBURG ALLIANCE CHURCH OF OUR
Savior returned bright and early Saturday morning to hoist their
signage and resume their chants. This time they were joined by
a few more taciturn allies, including two dour, pudgy men in
monks' robes, one holding a staff with a cross on top and the
other a sign that read LEVITICUS 20:13.

Rebecca did not need her new partner to recognize the reference. She mentally tallied the new group of protestors. In addition to the monks were three women standing next to a tripod
upon which was a sign that read SAVE OUR CHILDREN FROM
PERVERSION! They were handing out flyers that had a lot of text
on them. Then there was the lone African American gentleman,
grey bearded and dreadlocked, standing on an actual wooden
crate, a boom box at his feet playing some sonorous chant that
did nothing to improve the awkward cadences of the Harrisburg
clan. He was holding a ragged leather-bound book that he raised
in both hands from time to time, as though imploring divine inter-
cession. All of these people were neatly corralled behind the metal

barriers kept for exactly such small crowd containment; nice work by the uniforms.

She kept her face masked as she brushed past them directly into the path of a reporter from New York's full-time television news station and the cameraman behind him.

"Detective! Detective! What can you tell us about the BDSM Killer?" the altogether-way-too-perky young man asked, his eyes bright and eager. "Will he strike again?"

Rebecca blinked, unable to even fully react to such nonsense. "Are you kidding me?"

He continued without pause. "Mothers United for Families says they are starting a nationwide boycott of the Sterling hotel chain and New York City for hosting the Global Leather event where children can see naked, homosexual sadomasochists on the street; do you have any comment on that?"

"What? No one—no one is naked anywhere on the street!"

"The practices of bondage and sadism actually amount to felony assault, Detective—do you anticipate mass arrests today?"

Rebecca's brain finally awakened, and she snapped, "No comment." She stepped to the side, swerving around them, and let the amused doorman get the front door of the hotel for her.

Grant was still on the disabled list. She'd been up way too late and didn't even have enough time for a coffee at home before her phone started ringing, her email flooded and the infuriatingly efficient and calm Dominick DeCosta informed her that not only one, but *two* more of these fantasy knives had been found abandoned overnight; he had interviewed Mr. Schneider and had all sorts of new information for her; and by the way, had she read the headline article on the murder in the *New York Record* and/or the sixteen pages of reports Eduardo had forwarded to them?

Oh, this day was starting out just *dandy*!

Ludivico called to ask why she hadn't brought in any suspects. "Just round up some of those weirdos, I'm getting hammered here with stupid questions! Get it off the news cycle!"

"As soon as the lab processes fifty knives and gets back to me with latents!"

"Hey, Feldblum, try *detecting*. Use the new guy, he has experience with sex crimes."

"Yeah, speaking of that, where did he come from?"

"Alabama, Mississippi, one of those places. Warwick at the 25th flew him over to us, swore he was an ace in uniform, great on vice investigations. But he wanted homicide assignments. You wanted help; you got it. So what if he's a little cherry? I got no time for chitchat, Detective. Wrap this one up fast before we wind up on TV, okay?"

Too late for that now. She flashed her badge to get past the hotel and then the contest security and found Dominick had commandeered a room for their use, down the hall from the rooms where the contestants and judges did their conferring.

Today he was wearing a three-button black and white checked sport coat over black trousers, a gold buckle on his belt and a mustard-colored shirt. Rebecca felt a little more than rumpled in her chocolate slacks and tan blazer, and she'd forgotten any jewelry other than her watch. No question, she decided. He is prettier and better put together. And, his efficiency, though annoying, did go some way to alleviate hearing his prejudices. The cup of take-out coffee he had on the table for her, along with a dizzying assortment of sweeteners, went even further.

He shrugged as she set them aside. "I figured milk was okay, but beyond that, I don't like to guess how sweet a lady likes her drink."

"You are thoughtfulness personified, Detective. Thanks for the updates, are there any highlights?"

"Mmm-hmm," he intoned, his nod matching the musical rise and fall of the assent. "I stayed a little longer yesterday and I saw some *strange* happenings that might impact on this investigation.

And I talked to Mr. Schneider—the man's got his secrets, but I don't think he's the number one suspect—but I got two follow-up interviews to do to check his story. *And,* it looks like some new information from the background checks and lab guys looks most promising. We got two more knives; one stuck in a hotel dry cleaning bag and left under the registration desk, the other was in a trash can on the second floor. I had a scene man come pick 'em up; they both had blood on 'em, so he says, and one had pretty clear prints on it. Should be back at the lab already with all the others. Other news is that our victim's mama did *not* give him that name."

"I know *I'm* shocked. Tell me he was Myron Finklestein or something."

He raised his eyebrows. "Close! Albert Clarence Stahl. And though he hails currently from California, seems he's a local boy, born and raised over in Jersey." He glanced down at his notes, flipped a page. "East Orange. And what do you know, the gentleman has a bit of paperwork with us." He pulled a printout from his stack and passed it to her, and continued. "Even more interesting is that the suspect I think we really want to lean on, this Newark Leather guy, has a *very* similar rap sheet. Here is what we got on Albert-slash-Mack."

Rebecca's eye skimmed over the suspended license for unpaid parking tickets and right to the misdemeanors. Petty theft, public intoxication, disorderly conduct, possession of marijuana, prostitution; mostly in New Jersey. Shore towns, weekend follies no doubt. But other than more tickets, including two moving violations, nothing from California.

"He moved west and cleaned up his act," she said.

"Yep, changed his name and left it all behind. But look at this." He passed her the Ferri sheet and she laid them side-by-side.

My, my. Not the same exact dates on *all* of the arrests, but there was a clear cluster of charges for both men in a window of about seven months of time. She looked up at Dominick, who looked pretty smug.

"And on top of that, I got kinky death threats on the vic's phone, one from *Mr.* Mistress Ravenfyre and one from the, uh, slavegirl who lives with them." He rolled his eyes. "And when we get to *her*, I got even more; seems some of these freaks don't even get enough at home! Like I said, I don't think Schneider is the one we want, but he does have a few strikes against him. I think I got the real name of the Wolfman...boy...whatever. Dan Wenzelo...member of the Wolftooth Clan, some gay orgy house, I kid you not. I called a number I found for him and left a message." He rolled his eyes.

"Fill me in on Schneider-Ravenfyre and then let's move on to Ferri," Rebecca said, putting the cup down. The coffee seemed more bitter all of a sudden.

The Jacks were slightly distressed at the arrival of the detectives, but neither one tried to actually stop them from entering the rooms. It did turn out, though, that Giuliano Ferri was in the judging room at that very moment; he would be out in less than fifteen minutes, would they care to wait?

"No, we'll just stand in the back," Rebecca said.

The distress level went up, and the two youthful volunteers looked at each other nervously. "But...you might make him nervous," offered the male Boy Jack. Today, they were both wearing white button-down shirts, black leather ties and leather vests with a patch on the back that read You Don't Know Jack! plus black leather jeans. Their baseball caps said Boi and Boy.

"That's not on my worry list," Rebecca said. "You know what is? That when I asked where everyone was, you said they were all in the bar until late. Then I find out Mr. Ferri wasn't. So, I have to wonder, sir, why you didn't tell me that."

Boi Jack hauled off and punched Boy Jack in the shoulder.

"Jesus!" she exclaimed. "You lied to the cops?"

Boy Jack yelped and grimaced at her. "No! I mean, yeah...but we didn't know for sure he was actually missing! Maybe he was tricking outside or something!" He sighed. "I didn't want to get him in trouble."

"Oh, Em Gee, Jack, that was so *stupid*," Boi Jack said through her teeth.

"Yes, it was," said Rebecca, slightly amused by their interplay. "But if you have anything else I need to know, it would be a great idea to come up with it now." But they both looked at her with helpless shrugs.

"Is there some kinda fetish thing about wanting to look like twins?" Dominick whispered as they walked over to the judging room.

"No idea."

"And what's a *hoi*?" He pronounced it boy-*ee*.

"It's pronounced just like 'boy'--some young lesbians who are more, um, masculine-identified call themselves that."

"Okay..."

The judges were seated at several banquet tables placed in a single row against the right-hand wall of the windowless room. They all had yellow legal pads, glasses of water and cans, bottles and take out containers of various beverages, and a large purple and black binder in front of them. Boxes of sharpened pencils added their grade-school scent to the closed atmosphere in the room. There was a tray of Danish crumbs and a few pieces of green melon still on one of the sideboards, and urns of coffee stood next to sweating pitchers of ice water.

Across from the judges was a single chair, but Giuliano Ferri was standing next to it. He was dressed in tight leather chaps with a yellow stripe down each leg, a black leather jockstrap, and a complex upper body harness that crossed his pectoral muscles and showed off a perfect T-shape of fine black hair on his torso.

He was wearing his title sash as well but had taken off the leather officer's cap and was holding it under one arm.

Master Zenu was asking something; he paused and looked at the door, and Rebecca merely slipped aside to stand by the wall, keeping silent. Boi Jack, who accompanied them into the room shrugged, and Zenu looked back at Ferri.

"Well. Like I was asking...what do you think are the most important characteristics of a Mr. or Ms. Global Leather?"

Ferri glanced at the detectives, then adjusted his stance. He took a deep breath, picked his head up and swept his gaze across all the judges. It looked calculated. "First of all, honesty. Integrity. To be a leatherman means to stand up for yourself and for your tribe, your community. You have to represent what is best about our world without feeling ashamed or embarrassed; stand strong. So strength, I guess. And, uh, whaddayoucallit, passion. You gotta have a passion for being who you are and where you are."

Master Zenu didn't have a follow-up question; instead, Dr. Abraham asked, without even looking up, "What was the last book you read that influenced your thinking on the scene?"

"Uh. The last book?"

"Yes. *Any* book. Not necessarily scene related, although that would be best. But any real book, a thing with words in it, either telling a story or describing a history or explaining a theory or asking questions or maybe on the mechanics of auto repair. Even a *comic* book, but anything requiring you to read words off a page or electronic device and figure out what they mean in relation to your identity or thoughts or feelings about being kinky, being a leatherman, being a titleholder." Now, she raised her head, and fixed him with a basilisk stare.

"Well...I read...last year I was kind of busy, I was on the road a lot representing my title...and you know, I don't read that much, I'm more of a visual guy..."

She stared at him and he tried the visual sweep of the other judges again. "How about the last book you remember reading, ever?" she asked, her voice deadpan. "*Treasure Island? Stuart Little? Hop on Pop?*"

There was a muffled snort from one of the other judges.

Ferri said, "I read *You're Kinky and That's Okay* a couple years ago."

Dead silence, except for the tapping of her pencil against the tabletop.

"Did you now? And what pearls of wisdom did you gain from that estimable tome of erudition?"

There was a dark bead of sweat now edging its way down the side of his throat. "Well...that...it's been a while...but basically, the book says that if you're kinky...it's okay."

The pencil in her fingers snapped and Dr. Abraham took a sharp breath.

"Oh, hey, that's time!" Boi Jack announced before the academic had time to say anything. "Thank you, Mr. Newark Leather! Judges, we're gonna take a five-minute pee break; make sure you are back in five minutes!"

The explosion of movement released the stale odors of people sitting still for too long. Every judge got up to exit, with George Santos patting Ferri awkwardly on the shoulder as he passed. Ferri looked deflated, and then shrank even more when Rebecca beckoned him over. "We have a few questions too."

"But don't worry," Dominick added. "They ain't about books."

"I knew you'd come after me eventually," the Jersey man said when they got back to the room Dominick had commandeered.

"You could have saved us some time, then," Rebecca said, waving him to a chair. "Tell me your story."

He sighed and nodded. "I knew Mack. I knew him from way back. We were kids together over the river. I don't mean like school, I mean club kids. We used to sneak out, use fake IDs go to the bars and dance clubs, hook up with guys...kid stuff. We stole some beers once in a while, smoked some weed, just, you know...stupid kid stuff!" He looked up at two impassive faces and suddenly laughed. "God! Judged all weekend, here!"

"Yeah, but this is more serious then boosting a few beers," Dominick said with a slight growl. "I don't care you went out clubbin' with the man when you was a kid..."

"But *they* would care! Here! If they knew we'd, uh, *known* each other, Mack might not be allowed to judge me..."

"You really think we care about whether your fellow freaks get to give you a freak sash?"

Rebecca raised a hand for peace and Dominick played neatly, subsiding back with a grunt. "Mr. Ferri, it's not just that you didn't tell me you *knew* Mack. It's this." She pulled out the picture of him in the elevator.

"Oh." He took a deep breath and pursed his lips.

"Yeah." Dominick tapped the paper and pushed it across the table. "So, this is what we got from you. You *don't* say you knew him, you *don't* say you left the party when he did, and you *don't* say you went up to his floor the night he was killed. Now you see why we're asking questions?"

"I know...it looks suspicious," he said, hanging his head. "But...I didn't kill him, I just...I went to see him...to...talk, that's all."

Rebecca waited and Dominick remained silent. Damn, she thought. He's good. Why does he have to be beautiful, a good cop and a prejudiced asshole all at the same time?

Suck it up, buttercup, she told herself. Grant's an ass and a lazy, lousy cop. Things could be a lot worse. Be professional.

"Look, it's against the rules for us to associate with the judges. That's why I didn't mention it, okay? I was cheating."

"By just talking? You couldn't talk to him in the bar?"

He gave a brief laugh. "He didn't even *recognize* me in the bar. He even forgot my real name. I mean, it wasn't that long ago, and I sure recognized him, but okay."

"What do you mean your real name?" Dominick frowned and pulled out the rap sheet. The arresting name was the same; under aliases was typed *Julie*. "Julie?"

"Hey, it's short for Giuliano! What can I tell ya? You try growing up with a name no one can spell. *Everyone* called me Julie. Oh! You know his real name isn't Mack Steel!" He slumped as the detectives looked at him with smiles. "You already know that, huh?"

"Oh, we know more. Like, you weren't just *friends*, you were little delinquent hustlers," Dominick said. "Was he your *boyfriend*? Did you work the hustle together, pick up johns for kinky threeways?"

Ferri shrugged. "Kind of. For a while. And some of those arrests were just bullshit! They'd pick *us* up, and let the guys from the suburbs in their minivans just drive on home. Find a joint in your pocket and ask who you're dealing to, just plain harassment. Cops would get bored and go pick up a few fags down on the boardwalk. I mean, look at that shit, it's really petty, most of it." He flushed, and ran his hands around the edges of his cap, stroking the leather.

"So you recognized him," Rebecca prompted.

"I...yeah. When I saw he won this contest, I knew I'd come and compete this year. Because Mack...okay, you already know he wasn't, um, the most likeable guy. Shit, people hated him! But not me!" He leaned forward. "I didn't even hate him after he left, 'cause really, what was here? Tricking and waiting tables? He got out, went to freakin' San Francisco, went all big-time homo, that's fine with me. But I figured, he'd do me a good turn for old times."

"When did you hook up with him and where, exactly?"

"He got into this stupid fight with Kevin at the bar—now, there's the guy you should be questioning, he has a temper on him!"

"We have him covered, please go on."

"Well...I saw him getting ready to leave, so I slipped out like I was going to smoke, and caught up with him down the block. I don't know what time it was. Maybe...ten? Ten thirty? I reminded him who I was, and he went all apeshit happy. We came back to the hotel, I went to my room to change, then up to see him. Then we talked, caught up, it was awesome. He said he'd vote for me and get the other judges to line up—if he wasn't disqualified. And then I went to bed. End of story."

"No, I don't think so," Rebecca said. "First—you did go into his room?"

He licked his lips. "No."

"So when we get the fingerprint report from the room, we're not going to find yours anywhere? No hairs? Nothing with your DNA on it?"

He opened his mouth and then deflated again. "Okay. Yeah. I went in."

Dominick pointed a finger at him. "You do not understand how much trouble you're in, Mr. Newark Freak! The man's dead and you were in his room!"

"I didn't kill him!"

"What was in the bag?"

"What...?"

Dominick tapped the elevator photo again. "The bag, what's in the bag? You got one of those fancy knives in there?"

"No! I never had one of those things; I only met that woman yesterday! I had toys in the bag. Toys and a clean shirt."

"What are you, Santa?"

Ferri folded his arms. "*Adult* toys. A couple of whips, some cuffs, some rope."

"So, you tied him up before you knifed him?"

152

"I didn't knife him!"

"But you *did* tie him up? Did you have sex with him first?"

"No! Wait! I...what do you mean *first*? We just talked! Do I need a lawyer?"

Rebecca leaned forward, elbowing slightly in front of Dominick. "I don't know, Mr. Ferri, do you? Is there something else you're not telling us? Honesty and integrity, you said before? How about some of that?"

He was really sweating now, droplets beading onto his leather harness, the scent off of him masculine and slightly rank. "I told you everything!"

"I don't think so," said Dominick, shaking his head. "I think you're lying. I think you went in there, partied with your old friend, and maybe he said he wasn't gonna make you Mr. Top Freak, so you caught him out and slammed your fancy cartoon knife into him!"

"And I told you I didn't even have one of those knives! I'm not even into knifeplay!"

"You use rubbers when you guys went to town, Ferri? 'Cause we got four down at the lab, getting tested right this minute."

Or, sometime in the next six weeks, Rebecca thought with a sigh. But at least TV crime shows made people believe DNA tests came back on the same day. Giuliano Ferri seemed to be one of those people.

"Oh, Jesus Christ," he moaned, cradling his head in his arms. "Fine! We fucked! But I swear, I did not kill him! I'd never kill him!" He raised his head and there were tears in his dark eyes. He dashed them away furiously. "I loved him. I loved him years ago, and I loved him even more when I saw him the other night, and oh, God, the minute he was back in my life some motherfucker murdered him!"

Rebecca leaned back for a moment, trying to word her next question; Dominick kept up the pressure.

"Back in *your* life? Steel had himself a boyfriend already, all domestic partnered in California. Were you trying to get them to break up?"

"No! I totally let Mack lead. It was his idea to, you know, get it on."

"Where was Paul?" Rebecca asked.

Ferri looked back and forth between them. "At the bar? I don't know."

"So he wasn't there when you were with Steel?"

"No. Absolutely not."

"So you and Steel used up *four* condoms, is that what you're saying?"

Ferri smiled just a little bit, and his eyes shifted in memory. "I told you. Me and Mack...we were good together. *Real* good."

"You sound sure about that. Maybe one of those was used with Paul?"

Ferri shook his head. "Nah, I remember...what we did. We hadda swap 'em out. If he fu- uh, had sex with Paul before we hooked up or after, maybe they didn't use 'em. Not everything we do requires a rubber you know." Now he looked a little more challenging, as if he was prepared to give examples. Rebecca didn't go there.

"Have you met Paul?"

Ferri shrugged as he rubbed his eyes. "No. I saw him at the bar, with Mack. But Mack left without him, came back here with me. He did text him, though, while I was in the room. He said he told him to go hang out with some other guys n' shit. He said Paul was his slave, he'd do what he was told, and that's, well, not only kinda normal for the scene, you know, the leather thing, but for Mack, too." He sighed. "Mack was good at getting guys to do what he wanted, even back before...all this leather stuff. When he wasn't pissing them off. But that...that was just the way he was."

"And you liked that?" Rebecca asked.

154

"Not like a slave, no. Not that there's anything wrong with that." He winced. "I mean...back when we were together, Mack was always the one who led, the one who decided things, moved first. Sometimes, he was a jerk about it, don't get me wrong. But he was good to me, with me. It made me feel like I was different in his life. Sometimes, with a guy like that, you just let shit go because mostly, it all works out for you and him and who cares about anyone else, know what I mean? I didn't know what was gonna happen when I went up to see him. Maybe we'd trick, maybe not. But we did, and I'm not sorry about it, and he was alive and very well when I left!"

"And what time would that have been?"

"I don't know. No, wait! When I got back to my room, I watched this show that just started on TV, so it had to be twelve thirty, exactly! Because when it was over I set a wake-up call and I saw it was already one, and I was thinking I had enough time for a good five hours of sleep with plenty of time to hit the gym in the morning." He folded his arms and looked pleased with himself for remembering.

Rebecca exchanged a quick glance with Dominick and felt his agreement. "Do you know anyone who can say they saw you that night? Pass anyone in the hall?"

He shook his head. "I'm sure I did, but I don't remember anyone I knew. I was pretty tired and nervous about the contest."

"Tired from *playing*?" Dominick asked, back on the attack. "Did you use your *toys* with the victim? Maybe go a little too far, let things get out of hand with the rough stuff?"

"No! As a matter of fact, no!"

"So they're not gonna have his blood on them or anything like that?"

This time, Ferri smirked. "I'll bring them down if you want. You can search my room! I got nothing to hide. I know there's nothing on the toys, 'cause I ain't even used them...in a long time.

And how many times do I gotta tell you? I don't *do* blood, I don't do knifeplay. It's the dykes...the *lesbians* who are all into that bloodsports shit."

Rebecca wrote down "knifeplay," and asked, "So Mack did agree to help you in the contest?"

The smirk instantly faded. "Yeah. I knew he would, that's the kinda guy he was."

And the kind of guy you are, she thought. "Why was it so important that you win?"

"Well...it's kind of a big deal. You win this title, and you get travel and professional photo shoots and they make videos and shit. It's a great way to punch up some modeling gigs, see the world. You get a whole freakin' wardrobe and a website, and everywhere you go, people give you stuff and you're a star. Mack, now, they gave him a lot of grief, he said his year was the pits and he couldn't wait to get out. But he said if I won, he could, you know. Travel with me. We could hook up again, he could show me around a lot."

"You mean you intended to get back together with him?"

He nodded. "Maybe. Like I said, he was real happy to see me. It was like we were never apart."

"But what about his boyfriend?" Dominick asked.

"His *submissive* boyfriend," Ferri corrected. "Mack was gonna set it up like we were co-masters, maybe, make sure he got plenty of attention; that's what the boys want anyway. I figured we'd work it out; if Mack said he'd be okay with it, then it was okay."

For a moment, both detectives were silent. Then Rebecca quickly said, "Mr. Ferri, you said when you and Mack...were together, you didn't use your toys. Why not, since you brought them?"

He gave a low, soft laugh. "Tell you the truth? We didn't need 'em. It was like...old times. It was just good sex."

"Can you tell me what you and Mack were wearing?"

"Nothing! Well, when I got there, I was all in leather, I thought he'd like that. He was, um…in a robe when I got there. I guess he took off all the stuff he had on in the bar. But we didn't get all dressed up in costumes or anything, just got to messing around after we talked a while, and then, you know. Regular sex."

"No whips and chains when you're not on stage?" Dominick asked with a slight sneer.

Ferri met his eyes easily. "Just 'cause I like it kinky don't mean I don't like it regular, too."

Rebecca gathered up the rap sheet and elevator shot. "Mr. Ferri, we'd like a DNA sample."

He eyed her. "Does it hurt? Do you have to pull my hair out or something?" He smoothed back some of his glossy short hair.

"Not at all," she assured him. "We'll have someone here in a few minutes."

"And then I can go?"

"For now," said Dominick, standing. "But I wouldn't go too far."

"I can't," he said with a sigh. "There's another interview after lunch, dress rehearsal at four, photo op at five thirty, dinner at six, the ball is at eight…lemme tell you, I will be here all freakin' day and night, and the contest ain't even 'til tomorrow."

"You believe him?" Dominick asked her when they were alone, dividing their chores and interviews.

"He's still lying about something. But I have to say; the story fits what we've heard of Mack's character. No mention of the panties, though."

He nodded, handing over copies of the lab reports. "Yeah. And I am not happy about *two* new knives—I asked security to see if we got any camera angles on the dump sites, but so far, no luck. Still, what's with both of 'em bloody? We gonna find another body, too? Some kind of kinky cult murder pact?"

"I actually suspect some of this blood has something to do with *knifeplay*," Rebecca said, turning back a page of the program and pointing. "I'm thinking that before we follow up on your Schneider interview with Dr. Abraham and, um, maybe Slave Willow, I am going to find someone named Cutter Hatfield and ask about this class called 'Glowing Like the Metal on the Edge of a Knife: The Romance of Knifeplay.' Then, you can find out why the people who get a charge out of polishing boots hated Mack so much and what the Wolfboy has to say about where the victim's slave was when the victim was being unethically swayed by a former lover."

Dominick shook his head. "Crazier by the minute."

CHAPTER 18

CUTTER HATFIELD, FIFTY-NINE YEARS OLD AND WIRY, STOOD slightly above five feet in her engineer boots, but the flame-colored arch of spiked hair that rose like a cockscomb added an impressive three inches to that. The sides of her head were razor-cut to the scalp and showed her natural color was white. She was in the typical all-black ensemble the majority of the conference-goers wore, but her vest was velvety soft deerskin and laced on the side with red thongs. Also red were the wrist sheaths for what she cheerfully explained were throwing knives.

"Years ago, everyone had to have an Aussie kangaroo single-tail," she said. "Then suddenly, it was medical equipment like scalpels and cauterizing pens. Then, hand-dyed hemp rope, then matching floggers for Florentine flogging—that's using one in each hand. Electrical play got really hot for a while—no pun intended—and everyone had to have a violet wand and a TENS unit and tons of accessories. There's always some new, trendy thing for play. I'm hoping for throwing knives next. I got a source that guarantees fast delivery in any color I want, real cheap."

"Don't you think throwing *knives* at people is a bit too dangerous to be called playing?" Rebecca asked, so glad she took on the vendor space without Dominick.

Cutter grinned, revealing tobacco-stained teeth. Her entire booth had the faint woodsy scent of the pipes and cigars she sold along with quite a wide collection of sharp implements. "It's all relative, Detective! In the hands of an amateur, a singletail whip can really hurt someone. But most people in the scene, they pick one up and practice with it for hours before even waving it at someone else. Same thing with knifeplay. When I was a kid, me and my girlfriends pierced each other's ears at a party one night. I promise you, we did more damage to each other than you'll see in a year's worth of knifeplay fanatics doing their worst." She tugged at one earlobe, weighed down with four rings.

Rebecca picked up a folding knife with a serrated edge. "You sell a lot of these?"

"The Spyderco? Not so much that one, but the whole line is a best seller. Quality pocket knives, they keep a beautiful edge. A lot of cops use 'em. I can give you a good deal on that one if you want it."

"So what would someone do with this for...play?"

"That would be used for two things—cutting rope in an emergency—you know, if you can't get the knots untied, or someone gets dizzy and you need them out fast? Or you can use it to scare or threaten someone. I guess if UPS delivers a package while you're playing, you could use this to open the box. But you don't want to use a serrated edge for actual skin cutting, and I advise people not to use folding knives for that, either. Too hard to keep clean."

Rebecca put the knife down. "So, knifeplay includes really cutting someone?"

"Oh, yeah!" The woman pushed up the sleeve of her black T-shirt to reveal an intricate raised scar depicting a double-bladed axe. It was not colored, like a tattoo, merely the raised, thin lines of old, healed cuts. It had a subtler, yet more disturbing quality to it. There was no hiding that this was done by slicing into the skin. It seemed primitive, atavistic. And then there was the subject of the body art. Rebecca quirked an eyebrow.

"A labrys? Like those Zodians wear? Are you a Zodian?"

Cutter exploded in laughter. "Me, one of the horned hat brigade? Hon, I lived on a real-life goddamn lesbian separatist *commune* in my salad days. Yeah, it's a labrys. Don't know how those patriarchal role-players got it into their heads they should be wearing them, but I sure get a laugh out of it when I see it. There's even a guy here wearing one crossed with a moon-sign. That was the symbol of this old newsletter we had back in the day, *Wimmen of Wisdom*, something like that. Met my second or third girlfriend through their personal ads."

So that was where she'd seen the labrys-plus-moon image, Rebecca thought with amusement. Funny.

"So, what kind of a knife is used for making a scar like that?" she asked.

"The *only* thing I recommend for cutting is a scalpel," Cutter said, indicating a line of boxes packed with individually wrapped implements. "They come out of the plastic already sterile. You use them once, and then throw the blade or the whole thing away. They're hella sharp, clean, and made to cut the skin, and the chance of a serious accident with a little blade like that, no weight on it…pretty slim. But I hear it wasn't a scalpel that did the job on Mack." She reached over to a knife that looked easily as fantasy-based as the Ravenfyre style, with multiple blades, one of which curled at an angle impractical for cutting anyone but whoever held it. She passed it to Rebecca.

It had the same strange, light heft of the Ravenfyre knife, with similar anodized colors in the handle and tang. This one was green and black, with little diamond designs on the longest blade.

"That's made by the same Chinese supplier Ravenfyre used. I

know, because I referred her. I could have probably made a few bucks handling the order myself, but you know, sisters in the scene and all that." She rolled her eyes. "Even though she's straight. Anyway, you don't want to use something like that for cutting. You get a knife like this, and it's just for theatrics. You run it along someone's skin, poke 'em a little, tell 'em you're gonna do awful things, you pretend you're a barbarian spacegirl, whatever. It's for display. It'll take an edge, but it won't hold it, and the balance is... well, feel it. These things don't *have* balance. I'm surprised anyone could get hurt on one. It must have been a quick, hard stab."

Rebecca put the knife down. "Why do you say that?"

"No way could that thing cut a throat. The outer blades are crappy. And it's not designed for cutting! If it was made of quality material, I'd call it a poniard, or a parrying dagger. The knife doesn't have any weight to it, so whoever killed Mack had to have slammed that sucker in fast and hard, like a punch. Probably just one lucky shot, because if you missed a vital organ or just poked someone with one of these toy knives, they'd probably be fighting back. I didn't know the guy, but he looked strong in his pictures. My guess is the killer was really lucky. And got him up here, or right here." She pointed at the base of her throat and then under her breast. "Am I right?"

Rebecca smiled. "Thinking of doing police work?"

Cutter laughed. "Nah. But I know knives! And the Ravenfyre knife would break on a rib or on the clavicle; I'd almost guarantee it. So, I'm thinking the central blade had to go through the neck or right into the heart, maybe through the aorta. A kidney shot would do it too, or up in the thigh and groin, if it hit exactly the right spot. People don't understand how hard it really is to kill someone with a knife; and when they do know, the last knife they'd choose is some piece of crap like that."

"Is that all part of 'the romance of knifeplay'?"

Cutter sobered. "No. Look, I travel around the country, got

my van parked out back right now. I do kinky shows, knife shows, fantasy and science fiction stuff, whatever I can find inventory for. Most of the people who buy from me are either complete newbies or they know exactly what they want. They're not the kind of folks who would ever actually use a knife in anger. You picked up one of the best pieces on the table, right away. You're a cop; you know quality. That knife? If I sell one this weekend, it would be amazing. People here, they want the fancy-ass showy blades for impressing the ladies, or they want something clean, sharp and safe, for making pretty pictures in skin. *That's* drama, the sense of danger, right? That's romance. Sexy." She sighed and put the fantasy knife back on its stand. "But, I gotta admit, since word got out the Ravenfyre knife did the deed?" She grinned sheepishly and threw up her hands. "I got three special orders for one. Go figure!"

The bootblacks seemed like cuttings from the same tree, all of them in black jeans and T-shirts revealing well-toned upper arms. Their leather accoutrements varied only slightly—chaps on one, suspenders on two, one in a chain collar, most with arm or wrist-bands. All smelled of a combination of sharp oils and pine soap. Three were male, one was female, or so Dominick assumed from a visual scan. Because who knows with this crowd, he thought. Certainly, last year's winner wasn't exactly helpful with first impressions; the badge read FERRAL, and the wheat-colored face under long, black hair tossed over dark, narrow eyes was ambiguous enough to star in a Calvin Klein ad. A husky voice that could be high for a guy or low for a girl completed the incomplete picture.

Global Bootblack Ferral was much more helpful concerning the murder, though.

"I knew you'd come around eventually," the bootblack said with an almost detached satisfaction. "We talked about it and

I don't think we got anything really interesting for you, unless you're looking for proof that the guy was an asshole."

The story of the meet and greet came out in pieces, with each competitor adding mostly inconsequential details, all of which fit the timeline of the evening. Yes, they had all seen the victim and his boyfriend early in the evening, right after the judges arrived, as several came by to get their footwear polished. Yes, he had been obnoxious to them, especially to one named Timmy, whose chair he'd sat in, and toward the single girl bootblack, a tall, buxom redhead with LeatherDreamz on her contestant badge. There were some elements to their stories that made the detective pause, until he finally stopped and had to ask.

"Okay, I get that you polish boots," he said. "But, why?"

Five pairs of eyes looked at him like he'd asked why ice cream was tasty.

"Because it's freakin' hot," LeatherDreamz said, tossing her hair back and revealing what looked like a strangely large hole in her ear, lined with some sort of metal rim. "You know, like leather is hot."

"It's more than leather," said Timmy. "It's the whole scene. The polish, getting your hands in it, working it in, making something shine..."

"It's doing it for a hot top," interrupted a short chubby man named Eddie, from Raleigh. "Especially a bear."

"A guy in a bear suit?" Dominick asked incredulously. The bootblacks laughed.

"No, a hairy guy," said LeatherDreamz. "Eddie is all about the bears. But I don't care if they're tops or not, all I want is hot shoes, you know? I want bitchin' Fluevogs, sleek-ass Dehners..."

"Gimme some old school Fryes and Carolinas."

"Nothing like a rare Doc Martens, though, keeps you on your toes, makes sure you have the right dyes and the wax for the stitches..."

"But come on, what about a pair of Wescos, smacked right down in front of your face, begging for some loving."

All of them drew in a breath and let it out in a whispered, "Wescos..."

Dominick took in a deep breath himself. "Okay, never mind why you do it in general. Why would you..." he looked at Timmy, "or anyone...shine shoes for this guy Mack? Sounds like he had a bad reputation way before he showed up Thursday night; don't you get to say no?"

Ferral sighed. "Technically, yeah, we can refuse anyone. But we don't get judged just by showing up and looking good in a *leather fantasy image*. We have to *work* for our title!"

"Yeah!"

"Damn right!"

"Word."

"See, we collect votes from people who sit in our chairs," Ferral explained. "We're rated on how many boots we do and how many people vote for us. Everyone you might turn away doesn't just cost you that vote, it could cost you every person *they* talk to. And though we know Mack's an entitled son of a bitch who thinks... um, thought...the world revolved around him, not everyone else knew that. He could seriously screw with your tally if he wanted to, and he was just vindictive enough to do that."

"Seriously. He told me if I didn't lick his boots when I was done he'd make sure I didn't get any customers for the rest of the weekend," Timmy spat.

"Lick his boots?" Dominick repeated in faint disgust.

"Right?" Timmy exploded. "I mean, he's hot looking. If I didn't know he was such a jerk, I'd *totally* be into that, but man, don't threaten me!"

They all nodded in agreement and Dominick pressed his lips together tightly to keep from asking what was wrong with them.

"And dude, don't let your boy do the threatening for you

either," laughed LeatherDreamz. "I don't know what was worse, Mack all puffed up and full of top's disease, or that so-called slaveboy of his offering his help and bragging how much better he does it while looking daggers at anyone who even went near his precious Daddy's boots. Like, come on. We know not to leave fingerprints on your lousy leather."

"His leather was fine," Timmy said. "But you know, not that well cared for. There were patches and cracks that looked like they'd never been treated, and loose threads that should have been trimmed and the buckles...!" He shook his head, making *tsking* sounds. "One had *water spots*."

"So maybe slaveboy was really watching to get pointers."

"He could use a few if he's been the one taking care of Mack's boots. There he was, ragging on me because it was taking so long, but if they'd been well-maintained to begin with, I could have been done in ten minutes, tops!"

"What kind of a slaveboy lets his master out in sloppy leather? Poseurs." LeatherDreamz rolled her eyes.

Dominick was thinking there was nothing new they could tell him about that night. What a waste of time to come and have to hear about this weirdo fetish for cleaning shoes! Only one of them even owned a Ravenfyre knife, and that was Ferral, who had left it home in Ohio. "Thing's a piece of crap," Ferral admitted. "I keep expecting my wife to throw it away when I'm on the road one weekend, and really, I wouldn't miss it. But she was a nice lady to give it to me, anyway. Do you want me to send it to you when I get home?" There was a hopeful look in the bootblack's eyes.

So Dominick was about to move on, but then something they were talking about sounded odd. He listened to them continuing to complain amongst themselves about Mack and Paul and then interrupted. "Wait a minute. Did you all get the feeling that Paul was...jealous maybe? Possessive of Mack?"

"Oh, duh!" exclaimed LeatherDreamz.

"Seriously," said Timmy.

"But...jealous because you were polishing his boots?" he repeated, just to make sure. "Like he couldn't drop them off for that at the train station for ten bucks?"

They all looked slightly scandalized. LeatherDreamz held up two fingers in the shape of a cross and made a comic hissing sound and they laughed.

"To us, this isn't like...a chore," Ferral said with some patience. "It's not like taking out the trash, or sweeping the kitchen."

"It's a *calling*," LeatherDreamz said. "It's a sacred relationship between humans and the first clothing they ever wore, like, on this planet."

"And you almost never polish empty boots in this scene," Timmy added. "Serious no-no, unless master has a dozen pairs or something."

"It's a fetish," insisted Eddie. "By nature, it's intimate. Think about it, what else does someone wear every day and stand on, rely on, but a good pair of shoes or boots? And when they're polished, they should be *on* you, man, so the guy doing the blacking is touching your feet. How many times do you want to let a stranger touch your feet? That's a really personal part of the body. A bootblack in the scene isn't seeing just the footwear—we see the whole person."

"Nothing makes someone look as sharp as a clean, polished pair of boots," said Ferral. "When we work, we're improving not only their look, but how they project themselves. Plus, leather care is a forgotten side of the leather culture. People just go out and buy their stuff and put it on and when they take it off, they throw it in the corner like a pair of jeans. They don't know how to take care of it, how to repair it, clean it, keep it looking good. We're the ones who do that, teach it. We're the *real* leather in the Global Leather title. Everyone else just...wears it."

Dominick resisted the urge to examine his own shoes, but couldn't help it. He'd just brushed them off yesterday, and they seemed fine to his eyes, but when he looked back up, the boot-blacks seemed to have decided, as a group, that his shoes needed work. They gave him an array of pitying looks, although LeatherDreamz *might* have licked the corner of her mouth just a little obviously. "Okay, now, let me get this right. You're saying Paul was jealous because you were...getting it on with his boyfriend? In some, um, kinky *leather* way?"

He got another round of looks suggesting he was being somewhat oblivious. "It's not just that, sir," LeatherDreamz said, sounding like a very patient kindergarten teacher. "We know he was a jealous little boy because we hear things."

Something clicked. "You're like bartenders," Dominick suggested. This earned him smiles and nods.

"Exactly," said Ferral in satisfaction. "Folks come to the chairs, they lean back, get some quality attention paid to something they value a lot—and they feel like they're on top of the world. In charge, in control. Top, bottom, doesn't matter here. They're in the chair; they're like a king. They relax and before you know it, they get to talking."

"I must have done boots for at least five guys who hooked up with Mack this year," said Eddie. "Everyone knows he played the field. I have no proof, but I think he even played with contestants he was judging!"

Dominick cocked his head and framed his question. "Okay. So, the man was a dog. But everyone else we've talked to said Paul was cool with that. Part of being into all that slave...stuff. You guys say different. What am I missing?"

They were all nodding at him again. Eddie said, "Well, if we're talking about tricking, sure, that's easy to excuse. They're just hookups, just sex."

"But what we're trying to tell you is that what we do is more intimate," offered Timmy.

"Than *sex*?"

"It's service," said LeatherDreamz. "Service isn't something you can, like, just do with a stranger and walk away, like getting a blow job in a bathroom."

"So you're saying Paul wouldn't have as much of a problem with someone having *sex* with his boyfriend because that's not personal, but polishing his *boots* is?" He couldn't help it; his voice scaled up. The bootblacks didn't seem to take offense. In fact, they looked even more animated and eager to help.

"This is one of the major reasons we're not like the vanillas," explained LeatherDreamz. "Sex doesn't begin and end between your legs, you know?"

"Intimacy is the point," said Timmy. "Mack was probably one of those guys who could go with a different guy every night, but he had no real connection with them."

"He didn't put a collar on any of them."

"He didn't get his picture taken with one of them at his feet."

"So, no biggie if he got his rocks off. But take care of his leathers? That's something his boy should be doing."

Dominick looked at Timmy. "But you said his boots weren't all that well cared for. And Paul kept watching you and offering suggestions and acting possessive?"

The bootblacks exchanged meaningful looks and nodded at each other. "Wow, I never put that all together," Timmy said, clicking his tongue. "Guess I might have been more charitable."

"Put what together?"

Ferral looked at Dominick and shook his head. "You said it, sir. The boots were sloppy, but the boy was possessive anyway. Trouble at home, for sure." There were nods all around.

It was completely incomprehensible. Dominick sighed and shook his head. "Whatever y'all say," he muttered.

Ferral grinned suddenly, shaking the hair out of those dark eyes. "Yeah, well. No one gets the bootblacks."

CHAPTER 19

REBECCA CHECKED HER EMAIL AFTER SHE LEFT THE VENDOR area, averting her eyes from the rack of rainbow-hued dildos and butt plugs in more styles, sizes and shapes than she ever imagined. She tried not to puzzle over the table of horns, fangs and gloves with talons stuck at the ends of the fingers, all displayed on mounds of what looked like rabbit fur. She also passed at least four booths that seemed to carry the same identical array of clothing so popular among the leather crowd—vests, leather pants, jackets, shirts, skirts and kilts, the vast majority in black. Several times, she thought she saw Trudy out of the corner of her eye, but there was no shortage of short-haired girls in glasses wearing T-shirts and leather vests.

Not that she was sure what she'd say or do if she did run into her.

So instead, she firmly turned her attention to some of the reports crawling in from the crime lab. Eduardo had gotten some help to start scanning the Ravenfyre knives and several had come back positive for blood, although they were all minute, trace amounts. They had processed the request for a DNA profile on the contents of the condoms found in the trash, and separated out three distinct hairs from the bedclothes so far, one of which belonged to the victim. There were no defensive wounds or indicators of anything contributing to the cause of death other than the stab wound, which the M.E. agreed had been accomplished in a single upward thrust, the wound opened wider when the killer levered the knife to pull it out. It was highly likely the murderer had been splattered; if the detective found some clothing, they sure could make an identity.

No kidding, Rebecca marveled. And if I found a guy holding a knife dripping blood *and* wearing those clothes, I bet they could make *that* identity, too.

But that did raise a question—what did happen to the bloody clothing? If one of the newly abandoned knives turned out to have been dumped by the killer, where did he dump his black leather clothing, all covered in blood?

A quick call to the hotel manager's office confirmed that no bags of clothing, leather or not, had been found in the trash or stuffed into a hotel laundry cart. She asked them to re-examine any large bins or places that would not be emptied until Monday. He sounded offended; apparently this was not his first experience with a suspicious death in the hotel. He did promise to go over everything one more time. The team she had yesterday should have covered all the obvious places, but it was a big hotel.

She finally got to her newest mail, which Eduardo had tagged helpfully with several exclamation marks. She had to read through the text twice to understand it; the first reading made no sense at all. Then, she sighed and headed back to the room where she expected to meet a master and slave or a wolfboy or, if she was in luck, all three.

Earl groaned as Aphrodite Turner called his name. He turned as the dark skinned, dreadlocked woman called out again, knowing that eventually, she'd take him down, much like a lioness upon a gazelle. She was just about as tall as he was, with a classic hourglass figure draped in an oversized T-shirt that read TWISTED, KINKY & SOBER over gold leggings and calf-high stomping boots; topping that ensemble was a thin, black leather trench coat with a huge logo embroidered on the back, depicting a multitude of hands raising a heart that streamed lines in black, blue and red.

Earl always thought, somewhat sacrilegiously, that it looked as though the hands were heaving the heart around like a child in the middle of a blanket toss. He never said that aloud.

"Earl! You have to stop them! They're *harming* people!"

He groaned with a mighty, internal *what now?* He had a dozen new vital, important, emergency, last minute situations requiring his immediate and complete attention, many of which involved tonight's Global Leather Fetish Ball, the event that garnered more attendance and money than the actual contest.

"Who? What?" he demanded, feeling surly and on the verge of not caring who knew it.

"Them! The master-slave fanatics! Isn't it bad enough that you're still making money by exploiting addictive behavior with your damn cash bars? Those manipulative whack-jobs are holding some kind of *healing circle* or whatever-have-you for people who lost partners in the Mohawk Room!" Her deep brown eyes were narrowed in sharp intense passion; there were few things Aphrodite bothered to involve herself in which did not earn her impressive energy for confrontation. And no people were more deserving of such scrutiny, so it seemed, than her fellow members of the leather/BDSM/kink/fetish/poly/pansexual community.

"So? I'd've thought you'd approve of that."

"Excuse me? They're doing it all *wrong*! Dr. Westfield will be leading the real recovery workshop for grieving at three, *in the same room*! How is he supposed to help people if they get all off-tracked by some weird energy-sharing ritual led by some guy called National Daddy Sir or Lord Bear-crap or whatever they call themselves?" She rolled her eyes in exasperation. "The recovery movements are not fodder for any so-called *master* to hijack. And how is something sponsored by the ICO/oC supposed to be inclusive, anyway, since they're a bunch of racist elitists?"

Aphrodite had some issues with the ownership/slavery community.

"Anyone who asked could get access to the healing room, and they asked," Earl snapped. "Westfield's thing can be more inclusive. There's space for everyone; no one's getting harmed."

"Oh, my lord, Earl, do you hear what you're saying? Of course people are being harmed! They're being tricked into thinking some crazy-ass ceremony with a sash prince or some tin-plated dictator with delusions of mastery will actually help them heal, when in fact..." She took a deep breath, amber highlights showing on the planes of her face, "the energy they're experiencing could be as *toxic* as reliving their traumas all over again! They're just asking for PTSD or whatever-have-you! You gotta cancel their event now!"

"No way, Aphrodite. You don't wanna go, don't go. But they're entitled to their space same as you."

"I'm going to post that to KinkyNet!"

"You do that! And be sure to tell anyone who cares that I said if anyone *wants* toxic energy, their kink is okay by me!"

They both stormed off.

"Frankly, I feel betrayed!" Cary Gordon said. His eyes narrowed as he clutched his briefcase to his chest. "BDSM Killer! You might as well just throw us to the wolves! I can't believe I trusted you!"

"Cary, Cary!" Nancy wheedled, following him through the

lobby. "You know the writer doesn't choose the headline! Was that phrase anywhere in the article? Didn't I quote you correctly? Didn't I put in that whole *paragraph* about safe and sane stuff?"

He sniffed. "After a page of suggesting that one of *us* did it!"

"That's not my fault, Cary, that's what the police think! He was killed by someone with a fantasy knife that his own, um, co-title-person made! How can that not lead? You know the rules of journalism!"

Of course, she wasn't quite sure he did, and it really didn't matter that much any more. She had her story; she had her foot inside this kinky extravaganza. She even had her ticket to the ball just in case they tried to pull her press pass again. She certainly didn't *need* Cary or Phedre to continue educating her about the ways of their community. But she was also far too thrifty to throw away a source, even a whiny one.

"Well, I'm going to be blamed for even talking to you! No one will trust me!"

Nancy quickly shifted gears. "Really? That sucks!" She opened her eyes wide with what she thought would look like genuine concern.

Sure enough, it stopped him in his tracks. "You have no idea! This is a very suspicious community sometimes! Especially when it comes to confidentiality."

"Yeah, that's what you were telling me yesterday. But they can't blame you, Cary! You're their, um, herald! Their voice. How else will they ever understand the greater issues at stake here?" She tried in desperation to come up with one, but luckily, Cary came through for her.

"Don't you think I know that?" he whined, relaxing his death grip on the briefcase long enough to sling it over his shoulder. "Journalistic integrity means the world to me! But I rely on volunteer writers and photographers; even my web page manager is a volunteer! The few dollars we get from bars and leather stores and porn sites go entirely for printing costs; I don't even get a salary. If one of my advertisers pulls, or two of my staff, I'm crippled, just like that!" He snapped his fingers.

"So you need to toe the party line. I get it," Nancy said with all the sympathy she could muster. "Don't you understand my editor wanted something more sensational from me? I told him all about the workshops and the safety classes and the, uh, meetings and stuff, but all he wanted to hear about was how much blood was splattered across the room."

Cary's eyes widened. "There was blood splattered across the room?"

"See? You can't avoid it, my friend. It bleeds, it leads. That's what the public wants to know about. I have zero control over what they actually print once I hit SEND. Believe you me, I had a thousand more words in that piece, all gone now! Including some really nice sections about how safe all the, uh, play was in the dungeon last night. But the public doesn't want to read about nice, safe things. Or at least my editor doesn't." Luckily, she was already thinking of reworking her dungeon observations into a quick and dirty piece for a risqué website catering to frustrated housewives. She sighed and shook her head sadly, the very image of a writer plundered of her best prose.

"Oh." He sighed. "It's a harsh business, journalism."

Bingo.

"You said it, buddy. Look, can I buy you a coffee? Or, a bite? I bet you don't have much of an expense account. And I'd like to know more about these owner-owned, mistress-master-slave relationships. Maybe you could introduce me to Steel's boyfriend, I'm sure he has some special memories he'd like to share, or maybe just a chance to ask for help in solving the murder."

Cary looked around nervously and brushed back a length of stringy hair. "Well...I don't know. Although, it is true, I have no budget for sundries like food on these trips! But I doubt Paul will want to talk. The poor boy's almost in seclusion. He couldn't handle the singing last night—wasn't it awful? And there will be another tribute tonight and still another tomorrow at the contest! I think he might be considering just checking out and going home."

"And he lives..."

"In San Francisco, with Mack. They were domestic partners, you know. Poor guy, I hope he can afford to keep their apartment...oh, dear..." He glanced to one side and Nancy looked around to see the source of his distress. Lumbering upon them from behind her left shoulder was one of those Zodian fellows, giant furry boots on his feet and a voluminous black suede shirt covering his huge belly and exposing more chest hair than really necessary. He was followed by a waif in fabulously colored layers of chiffon and silk, carrying a bulky leather trench coat in her arms. She had straight, dark brown hair styled in a Bettie Page bob and two large gold rings in each ear lobe.

"Gordon! I have a bone to pick with you! What's with identifying Zodians as potential suspects in this murder?" He had a deep voice and the movements of a man used to being able to take up a lot of space.

Cary immediately threw his hands up. "It wasn't me! It was her editor!" he cried, pushing Nancy neatly and thoroughly under the bus.

But it ain't my first time dodging treadmarks, she thought, smiling broadly. "You must be Lord Laertes!" she said, sticking her hand out. "What an honor!"

He stopped in his tracks, so suddenly that his lady friend almost collided with him. She immediately adjusted herself to stand behind him two paces, on his right. His mouth gaped open for a moment as he examined Nancy's hand, and then he shook it gravely. He seemed both pleased that she knew him and unaware that his name was clearly displayed on the badge pinned to his furry vest.

"Thank you," he said cautiously. "I take it you are the reporter who wrote that story in the *Record* this morning?"

"Well, I wrote a version of it," she said easily. "But it's amazing how things can change once the editorial spin sets in motion. I never said a single word about suspecting any Zodians. In fact, I've been trying to find a Zodian to interview!"

"About what?" he narrowed his eyes, squinting down at her as he folded his arms.

"About your lifestyle, of course! It's completely fascinating. And how your, er, people, are reacting to this horrible murder."

"We are shocked and dismayed, of course!" he pronounced. "As part of the leather/BDSM/kinky/poly/pansexual/Zodian community, we denounce the villain who infiltrated our sacred boundaries and spilt blood on our honored traditions!"

"Do you have any suspicions about who the killer might be?"

"A rogue! Not a man of our clan or people, that's for sure. We only draw our knives in defense, never to cowardly murder a man in his bed!"

"But you do carry knives."

He looked proud as he drew a short, leaf-shaped blade from a scabbard strapped to his thigh. "This is a Zodian Honor Blade! Not some woo-woo three-bladed fantasy knife no one would possibly use in defense of his home or women. Not that I have anything against Mistress Ravenfyre. She earned her title and served it well, with honor. But we Zodians don't believe women should carry knives; they should be defended and cherished, not brainwashed into thinking they should be warriors."

Nancy was about to ask what he thought of women carrying *guns*, like the detective investigating the murder, when she was interrupted.

"Besides, if a Zodian had done it, you'd find b'bo shit strewn around the bed." An acerbic voice offered this from Nancy's right side; she could hear an angry snort from Lord Laertes as she turned to see the new addition to her little group. Cary was also groaning again from behind her shoulder.

"What's a b'bo?" Nancy asked.

The newcomer was a short woman with tired eyes behind thick glasses, her salted dark hair trimmed up around her ears, looked slightly more animated as she gave Laertes a sardonic bow. Oddly in this mostly-black-clothing crowd, she was wearing a bright Hawaiian shirt under a leather vest. "Ah," she said brightly, looking at Nancy, "You see, Zodians ride small *dinosaurs* into battle, and on their endless quests for under-dressed, large-breasted babes who haven't been brainwashed into thinking they shouldn't be subject to kidnapping, gang rape and lifelong slavery. A Zodian is nothing without his loyal b'bo! What other creature would offer blood for him to drink before the Moon Dance begins? What else would he sling said babes across while transporting them back to his Sacred Land? No b'bo shit; no Zodians. Oh, wait...there are no such things as Zodians! Some mental defective with mommy and penis issues made them up back in the eighties! I keep forgetting that." She grinned at the two Zodians before abruptly turning away and crying out, over her shoulder, "But don't let that stop you from sharing some grilled toh'f steaks and hot Chjam herbal wine with larry'ta and Larry!"

"That's laer'ta!" called out the silk-dressed woman with a tilt of her dainty nose.

The retreating woman said, "Look up false consciousness, princess, and cut back on the patchouli. Seriously, it's supposed to be dabbed on, not showered in."

Lord Laertes slammed his knife back into its sheath and cried "Hah! At least *our* books get read!" at her back. He turned back to Nancy and said, "See? That's the sort of nonsense we have to deal with all the time! People making fun of our ways, thinking we've lost our grip on reality! Dinosaurs! I have a Jeep Cherokee, myself. And notice how well she knows the Zod books? She's a sub, deep inside and hates knowing it. It's the radical feminists like Abraham and their anti-sex whipped dogs of the media who hate us and would like to blame a pointless act like killing Steel on us."

Ah, so that was Dr. Mickey Abraham. A radical feminist judging this contest? How curious. She'd have to track her down later. But for now, she looked up at Larry/Laertes and asked, "Why do you think it was pointless?" Even Cary, who had been wringing his hands throughout the confrontation, paused and looked at Laertes to hear what he had to say.

"Well...the man was done with his year! He had no rivals, he had nothing to defend. I heard his slaveboy wasn't even with him that night, not that a man depends on a slave, even a man slave, for defense. And I have nothing but the highest respect for the gays—gay men have been some of the best warriors in history! But what was there to be gained by killing him? Nothing in our Code would suggest killing a man as he gives up the highest honor he can attain." He laughed and shrugged. "Not that, we, uh, kill people, really."

"Right." Nancy nodded. "So who do you think did it, then? And why?"

"It might have been a man brainwashed into thinking that Steel represented the best of what our community had to offer. So, by defeating him, he would then be the better, stronger man. Or, perhaps a rival who wanted his boy." He nodded, lost in thought for a moment and then immediately added, "But Zodians are straight. The males."

"You don't say. Hey, Lord Laertes...how about some lunch? My treat. You can bring your, er..."

"Girl," whispered Cary, as a suggestion.

"Slave," said Laertes.

"Wife," said the slight women behind him.

"Well, yes," the Khan of the Eastern Kingdoms said.

179

"Seven years this June," laer'ta added with a smile.

"That's great!" Nancy said, ushering them toward the lobby restaurant. Oh, this next story was gonna be worth six pages in a glossy monthly, or she'd eat…grilled toh'f. Whatever that was. She hoped it went well with ketchup.

CHAPTER 20

THE DETECTIVES FOUND DR. ABRAHAM PICKING MOROSELY at a tuna melt in the hotel restaurant. She was only too happy to accompany them back to their commandeered interview room where she laughed out loud when Rebecca asked her why she met with Dick Schneider, and why her fingerprints were found on the Ravenfyre knife that was discovered under the registration desk.

Because that was the subject of Eduardo's last email—Abraham's fingerprints were in the system from a series of arrests for disturbing the peace, loitering and other offenses familiar to anyone with experience in civil disobedience. And they came up quite clearly on one of the knives that also tested positive for the presence of blood. Rinsed off, Eduardo reported. Smudged a lot and mingled with other prints as well. But there were enough matching points of similarity to make the ID clear. This plus her strange late-night meeting with Mr. Schneider bumped her up on the persons of interest list.

She seemed more tickled by the questions than intimidated. "Betrayed! Betrayed by my flirtation with radical politics and slutty slavegirls!" She almost giggled and shook her head, clearly not distressed in the slightest.

"You think this is funny?" Dominick demanded in his bad cop role.

"Why yes, I do, Detective DeCosta—any relation to the Arthur Avenue DeCostas? No? Best Eggplant Parmesan in the city. Well, I think it's ridiculously, fabulously, wonderfully funny, possibly the funniest thing to happen all weekend, so I thank you from the bottom of my heart. My completely non-leather heart, that is. I am sure my leather heart is supremely offended. Leather hearts are always offended about something, when they're not bothering people with their leather emotions and leather palpitations." Instead of taking a chair, she perched on the end of the table. "Are mine the only fingerprints to be found on *all* of those magical knives? I'm amazed. But then, maybe not. You can find mine quickly because of ACT UP, I'm assuming. Or, the university system. And people in the scene these days wouldn't participate in a protest march if it didn't take place on Twitter. Too much focus and effort required. The thought of these people bestirring themselves to commit actual crimes seems somewhat farfetched, as they are far too busy typing bad grammar to each other online. Which also accounts for no fingerprints on file from employment in some form of higher education."

Dominick darted a quick glance at Rebecca who took over. "Your fingerprints did pop up right away due to your arrest record. But let's face facts; they are on a knife and the knife also tests positive for blood. You have been identified as someone who had contempt for the victim…"

Another laugh, this one harsher. "I have contempt for most of the scene! If anything, Mack Steel and I shared a mutual disdain for the tourists and weirdos who have seemingly taken over what used to be a fairly quiet, secret-obsessed little subculture of mostly queer kinky people looking to be left alone into an international display of tacky clothing and antiseptic pseudo-sexual behavior with a near complete lack of coitus. Not that I thought highly of the man; he was an idiot and an impolite buffoon who couldn't form a complete sentence without the help of his boy, a dictionary application and someone holding up cue cards." She rolled her eyes and removed her glasses to wipe them on the tails of her Hawaiian shirt, this one decorated with images of dogs drinking beer and dancing the hula. "But kill him? I couldn't be bothered. If I killed everyone like that in the scene, I'd be on the FBI Most Wanted List, not up for tenure. Although, maybe that sort of publicity might just ensure the tenure. I'll be sure to consider it if they pass me over again."

"So, whose blood is on the knife?" Rebecca asked. "Why did you dispose of it? And why were you meeting Mr. Schneider?"

Mickey sighed and replaced the glasses on her nose. "That is a long and tawdry tale, Detective Feldblum. Complicated, as these things tend to be and sad in the greater scheme of things, I assure you. But the blood is not that of Mr. Steel, I did not dispose of the knife—I assure you, if I had, it wouldn't have been dumped in the one place most likely to be found immediately the next day—and I was meeting with Master *Dick* on some personal and petty business." She shook her head. "Left at the registration desk, with fingerprints and blood intact! If anything, this would point away from me. Twenty years of watching *Law and Order* reruns might have informed the densest of would-be criminals how to clean off and dispose of a murder weapon, let alone a few thousand written murder mysteries, which I also enjoy from time to time."

"So you've thought of how to dispose of murder weapons?"

The professor looked at Dominick in amused surprise. "Don't you find that most people do? When they watch their crime scene TV shows or they're streaming their pirated movies, don't you think they are all thinking, 'I'd never get caught; I'd clean everything in bleach, I'd use a disposable phone, I'd be smarter!'? But the fact is, criminals tend to be mostly very dumb—that's why they're criminals, and not, oh, overeducated, wise-ass college professors. They can't remember how to enter the inventory numbers, so they steal from the shelves instead. They sleep through the alarm and get fired from Taco Hell, so they shove a jogger over for their smart phone, and then they take a picture of the scene and post it on the Internet. Real murderers don't clean everything and dispose of things neatly—that's why you *find* them. Isn't it usually the idiot sitting there with a gun in his pants and blood on his shoes? Unfortunately, stupid people also exist throughout the law-abiding portion of society as well." She spread her arms.

Rebecca almost smiled, because she was mostly right. But instead, she pressed, "So, again, whose blood was it, and why were you meeting Mr. Schneider? And if you didn't dispose of it, who did?"

Dr. Abraham sighed again and then shrugged. "The blood belongs to Willow—oh, pardon me, *Slave Willow*. Possibly in lower case, although I can't be sure about that. I gave the knife back to her after she asked me to use it on her in a consensually negotiated act of adult carnality, the first, I might add, that she has experienced in over eight months. I was meeting with *Dick* because he wants me to figure out a way to get his wife's book published."

"Are you a publisher?"

The woman gasped and clutched at her heart. "Why…no! I am not! You, upon your first conversation with me have discerned this vital morsel of information! And yet these provincial putzes seem to think I, with four academic textbooks and over a hundred professional articles in sociology, anthropology, sexuality and various and sundry topics you couldn't possibly be interested in, will find them a high-level, traditional media publisher for her barely literate collection of pointless essays, speeches and assorted online discharges on the subject of being a *dahm-ay*. A publisher,

184

mind you, who will give her an advance, cash money upfront, and send her on book tours." She laughed again, this time punctuated with snorts of derision.

"So, you said no."

"I have been saying no! And yet they have persisted. Did I mention that stupidity is not limited to the criminal element? How this woman got an undergraduate degree, let alone a job at a library, astounds me. Thus, when I noticed their neglected little slavegirl, I did take it upon my marginally misanthropic self to seduce her just for spite. Serves me right that the silly bitch wanted me to do what she's been begging the Grand Mistress Lady Raven-wendi or Lord Master Dick to do to her for over a year now."

"And what is that?" Dominick asked.

"*Fuck her.* At knifepoint, if you please, but sheer, primal sexual pleasure, for the purpose of orgasm, thank you very much. Not being flogged at some public event while being used as a demo bottom, not merely sitting at their feet gazing up at them adoringly. The poor thing hadn't had sex since before Madame won her title, and even then, apparently it was only rarely that she actually got, hm. How shall I put it? Rode hard and put away wet will have to serve, I think." The professor grinned with a flash of teeth, and shook her head. "I could get more graphic and descriptive if you really want me to, but basically the poor thing's been horny for a year while living with two people who swear they're all-kinky-all-the-time. Pure bi-sub syndrome. If only she'd read my book! Or anything I'd ever written. Or, the threads and threads of other bi-subs complaining about their lot in life on KinkyNet."

"So, you're saying she brought you the knife and asked you to stab her and then took it away and hid it?" Rebecca asked.

"That is what I am saying, ma'am, and so it happened." She sighed, pulled her shirt down and smoothed it out and then looked at them with a shrug. "Not that I stabbed her, mind you. I *cut* her, and very lightly at that, on her cute, rounded buttocks, until I realized that the knife was an unsafe piece of shite and shouldn't be used to section a soft cheese. I am guilty of shagging someone else's property, but only because they left the poor thing chained outside all night, and her howling was audible to any dyke passing by. Plus, by taking their non-lawfully-recognized, polyamorous third, I symbolically pissed all over their lawn."

"The blood will be tested, you know."

"Oh, I'm sure! And you'll find it's hers. Unless she stabbed Mack on her way back to her sleeping bag at the foot of Dick and Wendi's bed. Which, frankly, I wouldn't put way past her, as she hated his guts from sheer loyalty, despite her neglectful treatment by her presumed owners. On the other hand, if she didn't have the ovaries to pick herself up and leave domestic servitude when she wasn't getting laid, why would she bother with murder? That's the trouble with kids in the scene these days. So *lazy*."

CHAPTER 21

Dᴏᴍɪɴɪᴄᴋ ᴏᴘᴇɴᴇᴅ ᴜᴘ ᴛʜᴇɪʀ ʟɪsᴛ ᴏꜰ sᴜsᴘᴇᴄᴛs ᴀɴᴅ ᴛʜᴇ timeline and the latest emails from the lab as the two detectives took their lunch break in the coffee shop down the block from the hotel. The protestors had grown by a few, but the media seemed to be staying away. Little favors seemed a blessing.

Rebecca ordered the garden salad with grilled chicken, and Dominick the bacon cheeseburger deluxe; when her coffee and his iced tea were delivered, they quietly scanned the new reports. The other knife found that morning had trace amounts of blood but had been wiped with something that cleaned a lot of the surface and eliminated or obscured even the tiniest of prints. Eduardo guessed alcohol or window cleaner or both; it would have to be dismantled to examine the parts under the cheap leather hilt wrapping to see if less degraded blood samples might be there. And although DNA test results might be back next month, they did have the blood types for Mack, Paul, and Giuliano Ferri and hair samples from all three as well.

"So, Steel is in his room by, let's say ten thirty, leaving his boyfriend at the bar. We know Dick was texting him right after the confrontation with Kevin. Kevin's wife swears they got in between one and two A.M., and he was in the room all night, for whatever that's worth, but we have no other evidence he was anywhere near Steel's room, and he did not own a Ravenfyre knife. Giuliano Ferri leaves the bar slightly after Steel, and is on the elevator at eleven, with his *toybag*. We got a new image of someone who *might* be Ferri in the elevator getting off on the 12th floor, where his room is, at about midnight, which fits his story.

"Dick and Ravenfyre and Willow get to their room, according to Dick, at around one in the morning; Dick is out of the room, according to the time stamp on the security camera, by one fifteen, to meet with Abraham at her room down the hall from Steel, who might already be dead. I asked for more security footage from their tower, to see if we can catch him coming and going from that room. She says she remembers him coming by sometime after one."

Rebecca nodded at the summary. "What we still don't know is when Paul got back to the hotel, where he went at what time, and if anyone can vouch for his presence."

"What we do know, though, is there's no way he'd have one of those knives, unless he stole one."

"Yeah, I don't see the Schneiders giving him one," Rebecca agreed.

"And I'm all over this guy... Dan Wenzelo, Wolfboy of Wolftooth or whatever he calls himself. I got him coming by to meet me at three. He's been hard to pin, but once I made it clear I'd come get him in front of his people if necessary, he got very cooperative."

"Good. Once we have a firm timeline for Paul, we can look deeper or eliminate him from the suspects. Here's something to think about—I read through the preliminary M.E. report and that knife wound was one hard thrust upward." She moved her fist to demonstrate. "Steel was six foot one; Paul is five-eight, Dick is five-nine."

"Yeah and Dr. Abraham is about five-four, but you don't have to be short to stab up. What if the killer was bending or kneeling?" Dominick snorted. "Kneeling is popular with these people, right? And then up with the knife by surprise, because Steel thinks they're all slaving at him or something."

"So you're leaning toward Paul then?"

"Or Ferri. He's about five-ten, and strong enough for a powerful thrust."

"But no knife again. Joshie thinks the guy he saw was between five-six and nine."

"Yeah, and we all know how reliable people are when it comes to that sort of thing. Especially at two in the morning. For all we know, whoever that guy saw was completely innocent, and the real killer was a Viking guy in horns."

They paused while the food was served and they doctored it with dressings and condiments. Dominick favored mustard and ketchup on his burger; Rebecca used oil and vinegar while wishing for chunky blue cheese.

"The thing about these knives is that we'll never know how many of them were here. Who knows how many are still up in rooms because people were afraid to bring them in? Or how many have been doused in rubbing alcohol or dumped in a trash can three blocks away? Even the Ravenfyres don't know how many they brought with them, and any of them could have slipped one to a suspect and just neglected to mention it to us." Rebecca nibbled at the salad.

"That is one strange little threeway. The missus and hubby got themselves a girl to share but they don't sex it up with her for a year? But she's so loyal she sends..." He slid a finger across the touchpad and continued, "a message that reads 'u dont dserv air 2 brethe or lthr,' to a guy her...partners...don't get along with. But at the same time, she sneaks off to boogie with the professor who also doesn't think too kindly on 'em. What's bi-sub syndrome, anyway?"

"Don't know. I tried to look up some of Dr. Abraham's work and found something titled 'The Evolution of Hierarchical Behavior Expressed Through Chthonic Fetishization,' and gave up after that. I don't speak academic fluently enough."

Dominick laughed. "The what-what now?"

Rebecca eyed him suspiciously. "What's with the vanishing and reappearing accent?"

He grinned and popped some fries into his mouth. "Oh, dag, caught out! Yeah, I can put it on for some extra charm or menace. You gots to use what the good Lord gave you in this job, *knamean?* If someone thinks I'm all tame and cuddly because I sound soft-spoken and back-country, they open up. Or when they think I'm a big scary black dude gonna get all ghetto on their ass, what do you know? They open up. Or, I put on my college style and hey, look at that."

"They open up."

"'Zackly. Different strokes and all that. You're a damn good cop, by the way. You sound nice as my Aunt Yolanda the preacher, talking to the elderly ladies all patient and understanding, even when they're sitting there in their kinky costumes talkin' about their kinky threeways and all that." He nodded with approval. "When I was talkin' to those bootpeople, I swear I kept wanting to ask 'em why they weren't at Grand Central at least getting some tips while they get their freaky jollies on."

Rebecca made a noncommittal noise and returned to the time-line so they could split up their interviews and get as much done before the big event that night—the Global Leather Fetish Ball. Having ducked out on last night's ceremonies, she was tempted to return for this. It would provide her with a way of looking over the majority of attendees all at once. But more importantly, it might provide a look at their suspects in a public space. Mickey Abraham was right; a lot of criminals were pretty dumb, a fact for which many cops gave earnest thanks. And often, a killer could not resist peeking in at the aftermath of their violence and temerity. In a community of people who thought they looked dangerous because of how they dressed, the mannerisms of an actual murderer might be patently obvious.

The thought of seeing Trudy again hardly entered her mind at all, really.

"Since you stayed around last night, I thought I'd come back here after dinner and catch the show," she said idly.

"The ball? What, and maybe miss the sight of some big, hairy dude dressed like Cinderella? This is gonna be the highlight of my week. Possibly my year! Wouldn't miss it."

Outstanding. Well, you're not here to see Trudy anyway, she reminded herself.

Ten minutes later, after more discussion and the steady ingestion of food common to anyone who worked insane hours, their phones buzzed simultaneously. One minute after that, they were tossing bills down onto the table and running back to the hotel.

CHAPTER 22

THE VENDOR SPACE FOR THE EVENT WAS LOCATED ON THE third floor, in two sections of a three-sectioned convention space. The third partition was set up with a few round tables and some chairs designed for ad hoc meetings and places to connect outside of the classrooms, play spaces and private rooms. A long table against one wall was piled high with flyers, postcards, samples, business cards and other ephemera for attendees to collect; there was a flip chart set up in one corner covered in scrawled messages and Post-It Notes relaying messages unlikely to garner timely responses.

And in the middle of this space, separated by two uniformed officers and ringed by contest security was Cutter Hatfield, the blade and cigar vendor, her eyes squinting over little granny-style glasses and her arms folded over her chest, and a little balding man dressed in black leather who was shouting loudly for a lawyer. While there had been some effort at crowd control before the detectives arrived, the room was packed with contest staff members, vendors and gawkers, all loudly asking questions and demanding attention. Earl Stemple was arriving at the same time, from another door, Bitsy right on his tail.

"I'll sue you all! I want a lawyer! How dare you touch me, you filthy witch?" shouted the balding man, shaking his fist at Cutter.

"That's *Wiccan* you pointy headed closet case!" Cutter shouted back. "How dare *you* try to shoplift from my table? Try again and I'll wring your scrawny little neck!"

"You all heard! She threatened me!" he cried, his voice rising in pitch. "That was a threat!"

"How the hell did you get in here, you slimeball?" demanded Bitsy.

"Yeah!" angrily demanded Tom, right behind her and shaking a fist in support.

"This is a place of public accommodation!" the infiltrator yelled. "You lesbian man-haters can't keep me from spreading the word about your perversion!"

"I'm probably straighter than you, you sneaky, mouth-breathing whack-job!" Bitsy snarled. "Where are the cops? Arrest him! He's a thief! He's trespassing!"

"Yeah! Arrest him!" repeated her volunteer.

Around them, several people started to chant "Arrest him! Arrest him!" and Rebecca elbowed Dominick lightly. He nodded grimly and pressed his way into the center of the room.

"Okay, let's clear some people outta here now! Nothing to see!"

"He was trying to steal from my table!" reported Cutter. "One of my fantasy knives!"

"She assaulted me!" he screamed back, his lips curled in contempt.

"He probably killed Mack!" cried a voice from the crowd. There was a sudden ripple and then cell phone cameras began clicking on all sides.

"No cameras!" yelled Bitsy and Earl, but chaos had been loosed. A contest volunteer shoved one of the people holding a phone, and someone else screamed as they lost balance and dropped theirs and someone else stepped on it. Someone screamed, "Don't touch me!" as people surged either to see what was going on in the center of the room or to try and dash for one of the two exits.

Rebecca sighed and waded in to help sort things out.

He was Woodrow Gallia, and Rebecca immediately recognized his name from many hysterical articles she'd read over the years, detailing the sins, perversions and dangers of the "homosexual lifestyle." He ran or belonged to an organization called the Families for America, but she could never recall ever seeing another spokesperson for them, or any suggestion of how big a membership they actually boasted.

She'd seen him on TV one night when she was up with a bad cough and had no better company than late-night talk shows. He'd brought photos and wobbly videos of drag queens and leathermen with certain parts blocked off with black bars, helping to draw attention to places where a penis might have been. He was dressed in a rumpled suit and narrow tie, a pedantic lecturer whose material was far more provocative than his delivery. She remembered getting annoyed and switching the channel to an infomercial.

Now, he was dressed in thin, ill-fitting biker chaps over low, black dress boots, and a cheap pleather jacket with more zippers than actual closures would require. It was also draped in thin, silvery chains. The badge he wore was a decent copy of the official version for the event and identified him as MASTER HANK. With his thin, pale face and scalp, his oversized glasses and beady grey eyes he resembled nothing more than an anemic ferret.

"I want to press charges!" said Earl, as the police and hotel security helped clear the room and convince most of the near-brawling attendees to disperse peacefully. The few remaining were volunteers or potential witnesses.

"So do I!" said Cutter.

"Just try it! I'll sue you both!" sneered Woodrow.

"Shut up, all of you," growled Dominick. He shook his head with a rolling of his eyes as Rebecca pondered what, if anything, they should do about this.

As far as their shouted accusations could explain, Woodrow had entered the event without a membership; that *did* count as trespassing. Cutter swore she caught him in the act of removing a knife from her table and trying to spirit it away. He claimed he was merely looking at it. But she had grabbed him; a lot of people saw her, and she admitted it freely.

"I'm not going to let some skinny little sneaky-ass homophobe steal from me," she said proudly. "I've chased down real gang members, I'm not afraid of this pissant."

"He's done this before!" announced Bitsy with a growl. "He took videos at the Ms. Annapolis Fetish contest and said they were abusing the hotel maids by leaving underwear on the floor."

"Covered in filthy disease germs!" Woodrow snarled back.

"He took descriptions of classes from Together in Leather Forever in Miami and posted them on his website. They lost their host hotel and had to relocate. I know he's contacted the management here, too!" Earl added. "He probably called those crazy people with the signs yesterday."

"When you have men forcing their arms unto another man's bottom and calling it love, the public deserves to know! How many of these hotel rooms have you spread with AIDS?"

"Hey, did I tell you all to shut up?" Dominick turned to Woodrow. "You are trespassing. That's one count we're gonna book you on. Now, what about the knife?"

Cutter produced a garish fantasy blade in the same family

as the one she'd shown Rebecca. "He was putting this into his bag!"

"Fine. I'll take it. Did anyone else see this?"

"Of course no one else saw it, I wasn't stealing anything! Why would I steal one of their satanic ritual knives?" His eyes were wide and nostrils flaring; he would have fit in well with the Western Harrisburg church folk in that moment. "I was examining it!"

It turned out that no one near the table had actually seen him try to steal the knife, but there was a moment of silence when Rebecca asked to see the bag he had been carrying. The crusader blinked at her and kept uncharacteristically quiet, and then a plastic conference bag was produced by one of the patrolmen called to the scene. It contained nothing more than the standard swag, and Cutter was shaking her head. "Not that bag. He had a black nylon bag, like a computer case."

"No, I didn't," he said quickly.

She squinted at him. "Oh, yes you did!"

It was quickly found under one of the tables, marked with two dusty boot prints, probably kicked in the near-melee. Rebecca picked it up and held it out to Woodrow. "Is this yours?"

"No!" he insisted, licking his lips. "I never saw that before!"

"Huh. Then I guess I can look inside," she said, glancing into the unzipped top.

"No—wait!" he started to protest, reaching for her. Dominick blocked him easily and shoved him back a step as Rebecca overturned the bag. Out slid a pile of loose papers, a mini voice recorder, a separate tiny video camera and a bundle of flyers wrapped in a rubber band. A few loose sheets of paper fluttered to table; some fell to the floor.

"What the hell?" Rebecca dropped the empty bag onto the table and picked up one of the loose papers. It was a picture of Mack Steel and it looked like it had come from the collection Paul had shown her. He was posed against a giant X-shaped cross, leaning against it with his arms folded and a sarcastic smirk curling his lips, wearing only tall, lace-up boots and a leather jockstrap. But someone had doctored the photo by adding strange occult artwork over his chest and on his cheeks, and planted a picture of a large dagger thrust into the middle of his stomach. Over his head, now decorated with cut-and-paste clip-art horns, was a banner headline reading, "Satanic Sacrifice at Homo Torture Orgy."

Bitsy and Earl both gasped; Cutter's jaw dropped. Rebecca blinked and shuffled through some of the other pages—there were several copies of this and two variations with different alterations made to the picture. But in every one, Mack Steel was depicted with a knife through his body. She grabbed the video camera and turned it on, flipping the switch to memory. She quickly scanned a few shaky shots of the lobby of the hotel and the vendor room and kept returning to the menu, seeking older files. When she got to Thursday night, she watched quietly for a moment and then showed the small screen to Dominick.

DeCosta watched a few seconds and then grabbed Woodrow by one arm, turned him around and said, "You are under arrest, sir. You have the right to remain silent..."

"Oh, my God," Bitsy whispered to the still shocked Earl. "That is so *hot*."

CHAPTER 23

WOODROW GALLIA LAWYERED UP IMMEDIATELY. HIS HIGH-profile legal advisor was on the way, and the anti-gay activist was not saying a word to anyone. He wouldn't even answer questions about possibly seeing someone *else* stalking Mack Steel. And he certainly had nothing to say about the fliers depicting the man as stabbed.

Probably his best bet, Rebecca thought, as she hammered out the inventory of seized items at her desk. Dominick vowed his report would echo hers—the briefcase was in plain view, the suspect had insisted it wasn't his; the objects inside were not obstructed from casual examination.

And the contents were dynamite.

The videos went back to Thursday evening, and some were as innocuous as brief shots of various leather-clad people arriving for the meet and greet at the Shaft. But the two clips from late that night showed Mack Steel, and in situations removed from crowd scenes.

The first shot of him was outside, in his bar leathers and sash, arm up as he hailed a cab—and right behind him, fuzzy in the tiny screen but clearer when uploaded onto her computer and blown up on the monitor, was Giuliano Ferri, who was grabbing Mack's ass and laughing. The two men clowned around with touches and kisses until the camera stopped.

The second shot, though, was Mack alone, walking down a hotel corridor and unlocking a door. At the last minute, the shaky, low-held shot wavered and Mack turned to look toward the videographer, his mouth opening. Then, the shot wobbled and bobbled and went to black.

Of course, this was proof of nothing but weird, obsessive stalker behavior. But it did serve to fulfill the command to "bring in one of those weirdos," didn't it? And a creepy stalker was a good suspect by any measure, especially one with a fascination for knives.

Still.

She saved the arrest report and sent it to print and leaned back in her excellent chair. The Midtown East Precinct was in the tenth year of a three-year renovation project, which meant little outside the lobby, Lieutenant's office and secure cells was in any shape to support teams of detectives and squads of uniforms. Her desk was an old, steel monstrosity without access holes for computer cables; the cheap lamp to her right, she bought at IKEA. But her chair...ah, it was perfect. An ancient oak teacher's chair with a bowed back and carved arms, she had found it in a warehouse in Pennsylvania during a brief attempt at a relationship with a lawyer into antiquing. It cost forty dollars and a far-too-lengthy argument about how much better off she'd be if she left behind this idealistic lifestyle of imagining she enacted justice and learned to trade stocks and write contracts instead.

Forty dollars for the chair had been a steal.

The others in the precinct knew better than to "borrow" it. Once, someone had scrawled "dyke" in black magic marker across the top bar on the chair back. She saw it, took a deep breath and asked, loudly, for the girlymen in the office to stop leaving their little love notes to each other on her chair. The mostly male coterie about fell over, laughing, and she cleaned it off with some Windex. She never tried to find out who did it, and the next day someone left a somewhat squashed but still fresh cheese Danish on her blotter, wrapped in wax paper. That was cop-world for you.

Still.

She'd left DeCosta back at the hotel while she escorted Woodrow in and filed the paperwork. "No sense in letting our investigation completely stop," she'd said, while he nodded.

"And besides, you know the procedure better," he added with a slight twitch of his mouth. "You know this is a new assignment for me."

"You could have told me. But I'm not bitter. Just find this damn Wolfboy and make sure our bereaved slave isn't really a depraved slasher."

That was part of her unease. She still didn't have a complete picture of everything that happened on Thursday night, including little nagging details like *exactly* when Steel told Paul to go off in search of his own entertainment. Why did Paul stay at the bar? Was he instructed to stay away from their room all night? She poked around her email messages for the reports on messages pulled from Steel's cell phone, and asked to see *all* the texts he sent and received that night.

She knew Ferri hadn't told Dominick the complete truth, either. He shifted his story repeatedly, and now they had actual video that suggested he and Steel did more than just renew their acquaintance outside the bar. Hell, that did not look like two old friends meeting for the first time in years—it looked like two long-time lovers. This morning, she'd been impressed by Dominick's interview report on Ferri, but had it been a mistake to let him conduct it on his own? Perhaps if she hadn't been so unprofessional as to dash off just because she ran into an ex, she might have caught Ferri in some of these lies. That story about Steel not recognizing him in the bar was a big one; what else was untrue? She would have to be there when they spoke to him again.

Her thoughts turned to the most immediate situation. Trespassing, disturbing the peace, loitering; more charges familiar to civil disobedience, and none of them sufficient to hold the weaselly Woody Gallia for a more than a few minutes past his lawyer arranging bail. The shoplifting accusation was barely worth applying, although she threw it in there because Cutter insisted on pressing charges. Lieutenant Ludivico had called, annoyed that she'd arrested a Christian activist. But even he had to admit stalking videos and pictures of the deceased with knives sticking in him were fairly suspicious. Someone was going to blow up all his images and videos and put together a complete timeline of his activities and send it to her. She put in a request for some credit card records so she could find out where he was staying and perhaps find a computer that might have more of his videos and reports.

Why did it seem Gallia had some sort of obsession with Mack Steel and Satan and stabbing? His website had plenty of outrageous photos and videos on it, but a quick scan revealed nothing more than a few shots of Steel with other leatherpeople in the San Francisco Pride march, and even there he wasn't singled out, merely listed as part of the "Annual Pervert Parade." How did he get that photo of Steel, and when did he make the alterations to it? When downloaded to her desktop, it had a last revision time stamp of Friday afternoon, which could mean that it had been worked on then, or merely saved or scanned.

And of the pictures she quickly flipped through on his site, none were done up with this particular theme of ritual slaying, horns, pentagrams and other weird symbols. Maybe it was all just a weird coincidence that Woody happened to make his little satanic ritual pictures for the first time and stalk the man on video the very night he was murdered.

Although weirdness did seem to be the one thing this case had in abundance and coincidences were known to occur from time to time, it was a bit too much to expect this was all just happenstance.

She downloaded the background reports she'd requested on her other persons of interest so she could read them in nice, large print on her monitor before heading back out. Aware of time slipping away, she scrutinized every word for a potential clue, hoping Detective DeCosta wasn't calling *everyone* he met a freak, and feeling like she was missing something very obvious.

After the boot polishers and the somewhat mature lady with the red Mohawk talking about being a witch—excuse me, ma'am, *Wiccan*—and the general fun-house atmosphere of costumes and role-playing, it was only natural that Wolfboy of the Wolftooth Clan was dressed in blue jeans and army boots and a plain black T-shirt with a small logo on the chest supporting a wildlife refuge. He was thirty-four, with long, straight dirty blond hair he kept in a ponytail. The kinkiest thing about him was an aversion to meet Dominick's eyes. It could be social anxiety, the detective thought. It could be one of those mental things, like autism.

Or, it could be the guy was just twitchy.

"I'm sorry I couldn't, uh, get back to you," he started out stammering, as soon as he met Dominick in the makeshift interview room. "I'm busy. This is a big event for me, I'm teaching classes, and I have meetings…"

"Yeah? What do you teach?"

The man cleared his throat and cracked his neck, looking away for a moment. "Well, I teach, uh, sort of sex classes. This time, I'm teaching…I taught….uh…is this relevant?"

Now it sure was. Dominick nodded, perversely needing to hear him say it out loud. "Lemme have it."

"I taught 'Wild Things: Bringing Out Your Inner Animal.' It's, um, about acting like animals, sort of. For fun. That was yesterday. And, um, today I was on...a panel discussion. And, I have to go soon because I'm helping...a special event soon." Shifting his eyes, he studied the carpet patterns.

"The Puppy Show," said Dominick.

Dan Wenzelo, Wolfboy of Clan Wolftooth, sighed and offered half a grin. "Yeah. I'm into the whole puppy thing."

What "the whole puppy thing" might embrace was a tempting question to ask, but Dominick merely nodded. He knew the schedule because he'd threatened to arrive at the Puppy and Pet Show to ask Wolfboy his questions right there if the man couldn't make an effort to come see him privately. "Great. I'm more interested in what you were doing Thursday night, though, and who you saw."

"I went to the meet and greet," the man said with a slight hesitation, thinking back. "It was downtown, at the Shaft. My whole clan...my friends...were all there, so they can vouch for me."

"When did you come back here?"

He returned sometime around eleven thirty, after the furor over the Mack Steel incident. "Everyone was just shouting over and over again about what happened and what was going to happen to the judging and whose fault it was...I was done! I had to teach the next day, and I always have a party...I mean, uh, I have some friends over to my room." He already had a cooler full of water, beer and soda—he called it pop—stashed in his room. And he didn't return alone.

"My friend Carson came back with me; and we had some friends drop by. But never more than four at the same time!"

Dominick frowned. "Okay. So, who were these other friends?"

"There was this guy Rubio or Romeo or something. He

brought his boyfriend Andy. My clan brother, Midnight—uh, Mike. He's also with someone else, but his, Master...um, partner wasn't feeling well, so he came to my party. Room! He came to my room. It wasn't really a party."

Ah! Now Dominick got it. "I don't care that the hotel don't want more than five in the room. And I don't care what you *did* in the room. What I care about is who was there."

"Oh!" Wolfboy gave a nervous laugh. "So, well, you know about Paul, then."

"Paul Helms was there?"

"Oh, yeah, he shared a cab with us from the bar."

At last! Dominick added that to his timeline. "Around eleven thirty?"

"Yeah, more or less. Then we put on some, um, movies. And this guy Rubio, he said he had a friend with a portable sling, and did we want it, so he left for a while with some other guys to get it. And while they were gone, me and Mike texted some other guys we met—and they came by, too. I don't remember their names, but they were in the vendor space today selling electrical toys. They brought one to the party and it was weird." He laughed and started to look a little more relaxed. "We all had to try it."

"How long was Paul in your room?"

Wolfboy thought, his eyes shifting again. "All night?"

"You sure about that?"

"No." He tapped his lips nervously and returned to examining the floor. "I sort of got distracted from time to time. But I am pretty sure he was there most of the time, and he spent the night with me. With, um, us. In the room."

"Do you have any memory of when he might have left or come back to the party before morning?"

Another evasive look. Damn! I should have tracked you down earlier, Dominick thought.

"Honestly, I didn't notice," Wolfboy finally said, gnawing

halfheartedly on a thumbnail. "He's a nice guy. I'm pretty sure he was there most of the time. But I got, um, distracted. And I did have guys coming, um, in and out. So to speak." He blushed and shook his head.

"You say he arrived with you. Did you see him when…Rubio left to get the…thing you said they got?"

It took careful prodding and a lot of specific questions, but after an interminable fifteen minutes or so, Dominick had sketched out additions to his master timeline. It was clear that without further verification, Paul Helms was effectively without an alibi from between approximately twelve forty-five and four A.M., when Wolfboy admitted he remembered cuddling in his bed with two guys and seeing Paul on the foldout couch with someone else.

"What was he wearing?"

"Nothing."

"I meant, before he want to sleep, or earlier in the evening?"

That took more thought and prods. It was the sort of questioning that drove rookies crazy, made the short-tempered officers slam their fists and shout and sometimes made them break the law. But Dominick kept his cool, listened and probed and finally not only got the information, but actually got to see that Wolfboy's eyes were a light brown.

"You're really nice," Wolfboy said nervously, checking his watch. Dominick could hear the "for a cop," and shrugged it off, using the moment of goodwill instead.

"Just one more thing. What would you say was Paul's mood that night?" he asked, leaning back.

"He was okay."

"How did he wind up going to your party? You said he shared your cab from the bar; have you been friends for a while?"

Wolfboy shook his head. "Nah. I mean, we knew each other. Seen each other around for a year or so, I guess, mostly at things like this. It was weird to see him without Mack, though, and when he was sort of on his own at the bar, I just asked him if he wanted to hang out."

"Did he tell you why he was on his own?"

The man shrugged. "Sometimes, it's like that, especially when your boyfriend is, um, famous. Like my friend, Midnight? His partner is this guy named Master Frank, and he's a big, uh, teacher, I guess. He comes to these things and he's got boys all over him, so he goes to the dungeon and does his fancy bungee cord suspension stuff and Midnight gets to come hang out with me."

"Did Paul tell you it was like that with Mack?"

"Everyone knew Mack was like that." He seemed very sure about that, nodding.

"So, did you think Paul was lonely, or sad? Or more happy to be out for a night on his own?"

"Dunno."

"Well, did he have fun at your party? Did he seem to be having a good time when you saw him? Play with the…electrical thing? Did he hook up with anyone?"

Wolfboy sighed and checked his watch again. "Honestly…no. I just invite guys; it's up to them to have the fun. He was mostly watching the videos when I saw him. Maybe he was tired. Uh, I really gotta go. This contest…I mean, show…we're, trying to make it a Global Leather title, you know, Global Pet maybe, and I need to be there."

"Just two more things," Dominick said. "Did Paul take a shower in your room? And did any of your friends lose anything overnight? Or wind up with something extra in their…toy bags?"

"Oh, yeah, he showered before we all went to sleep. I remember, because we ran out of towels." He smiled faintly. "But I don't think anyone lost anything or wound up with more stuff. Although, that happens a lot. I mean, you get six, eight guys all dressed in black T-shirts from the same events, all wearing jeans and boots and belts and jocks, and then they all wind up on the floor. Once

I came home with an extra vest, I mean, that was weird. So, uh, maybe it happened? But no one's come to complain to me about it. Is it important? Are you looking for something in particular?"

"No, just checking up on a possible clue. Thanks for your help. Let me know if you find anything missing or added in your own stuff," Dominick said, letting the evasive man go off to do his puppy nonsense.

He looked at his notes of new information and pondered how meaningful it was. Then, as he added the details to his master timeline, he wondered how Feldblum was doing back at the precinct with Woody the Anti-Gay Crusader.

Goodness, but this event was a magnet for people who liked to be on the TV preaching about one thing and one thing only. His Aunt Yolanda would have a choice word or two for those who never seemed to read anything else in the Good Book. And for those who committed acts of cruelty, hatred and violence in the name of the lord? Words would not suffice, and she was a big lady. He smiled, hearing her voice and smelling the peach cobbler in her kitchen as she told him all boys were born with the devil in them, but his was surely the most *creative* devil of them all...

Just then, his phone buzzed. The text message read, "What else is Ferri lying about? omw back. Don't forget to 63." Good, she was on her way back.

Speaking of Aunt Yolanda, there was Feldblum reminding him to eat. He supposed that meant she did like him after all. As for her question about Ferri? "That's just exactly what I was wondering," he said softly, as he got up. There had been a moment when he watched her head off with Woody and wondered if she was the kind of cop who would go in, process some papers and then call it a day—bringing in a suspect was always a nice way to justify your time sheet entries. But although this guy was a very tempting suspect, what with the video stalking and the weird sex pictures with satanic nonsense drawn on 'em and all that—

(please, child, does a murder suspect get any better?)—there was something missing.

Like a motive. Or any objective proof. And absolute certainty they had the actual murder weapon. Oh, and some physical evidence might be sweet, too. Instead, what they had were a couple of squirrelly gentlemen who might or might not have some missing hours to account for, and a couple of stories with very loose ends.

Detective Dominick DeCosta—oh, how he liked the sound of that, especially when teamed with the homicide assignment—checked the schedules to see where he would find the Global Leather contestants and what they might be doing. He would also look in at the front desk to make sure Paul Helms and Giuliano Ferri had not checked out yet. Then he'd take his 63—a meal break—and get ready for this Fetish Ball.

The *New York Record* website was the first paper to have a picture of Woodrow Gallia being taken away in handcuffs and the *only* place to find a picture of the incriminating "Satanic Ritual Murder" flyer, which the enterprising Phedre had pocketed while everyone else was staring at the sexy black cop arresting the Christian activist.

"Can you believe this *shit*?" she cried to Nancy, her veneer of video activist/gossip queen and news talent so-slightly chipped. "This is what makes it so hard for us to just peacefully live our lives! This is what the vanilla world thinks we do! But instead, it's what they do to us!"

"It's horrible," Nancy managed to say, trying to keep from salivating. "Monstrous! The world needs to see such....naked bigotry! I'll give you a hundred bucks for it."

Done and done. The associate editor who pulled her cell phone picture of it out of the editorial inbox called Vic at home immediately, and he almost creamed his khakis when he saw it. Nancy hit the hotel business center, scanned it and sent that for a higher-resolution version. Then she typed like mad, her little netbook propped onto a window ledge at the end of a hallway. And when she finished her on-the-scene update and hit SEND, she attached a request for reimbursement for "freelance photography," which she figured would cover her payout to Phedre. Then, she revised her proposal for a several-part story designed for a news and culture website, humming happily to herself and considering a weekend at some posh spa, preferably in a warm and sunny location. The Mayan Riviera always sounded nice.

Donny was on his way with his newly approved press pass to the Fetish Ball, she had *five* byline pieces, all of which were now getting re-sold into multiple markets, her Twitter feed picked up hundreds of new followers, and she still hadn't gotten to one of her high-profile potential stories, like an interview with one of the principles in the murder investigation. Once she did, this could be award-winning stuff right here. And all this from a candy-ass look-at-the-freaks story! This was one of her best assignments, *ever.*

Bitsy held an emergency meeting of most of the security staff while Earl left to put a cold towel on his forehead, swallow some antacids and squeeze into his leather Royal Canadian Mounted Police uniform.

"Okay, this is serious, folks, we need to be on our toes tonight! This is the biggest event we do, and we got people coming in by the thousands! We're surrounded by wackos and protestors and cops and every kind of annoying media whore, and you're all I got to help keep everyone here safe."

She looked around the room at the array of nervous volunteers and the four off-duty cops the event hired on a per-night basis. They were the only ones who didn't look like they were ready to puke. Well, not completely true. The new guy, Tom, looked like he was ready to take on any number of fundamentalists, armed or not. His little pointy jaw was thrust forward, and his eyes were narrowed in a fierce sort of intensity.

Heh. Cute. Like a ferocious corgi. She remembered his instant fury at Woody the Infiltrator and almost cracked a smile.

She returned to business.

"People coming in just for the ball are going to be routed through the garage entrance if they want to avoid any press around the front door. So we now have *three* different access points to the ballroom. And tonight, we need to check not only badges and wristbands, but actual IDs." She shook her head at the groans and protests that rose. "Can it! It's that, or risk letting in another guy like Woody the Weasel! You wanna explain how another one of our titleholders got killed 'cause we didn't check a lousy ID? If anyone complains, send 'em right to me, I'll explain it in simple language!"

"Did he really kill Mack?" someone asked.

Bitsy looked at her over the rim of her glasses. "I don't know, maybe he had some *other* reason to carry around pictures of Mack with a dagger through him! Sure, he did it! That bastard's had access to our event since before we opened, with a fake badge and everything! Because our security dropped the ball! This is unacceptable!"

There were quick nods of agreement.

"So I want two sets of eyes on every mother-humper who walks in tonight, and I don't care if they're with *your* mother. I want IDs, or no access! If Grand-Master Poo-Bah of the House of Leather Asses walks in, you get his ID! If Mistress Mommy-ma'am and her dancing slavegirls come sashaying through, check every goddamn toe-tapper! If *I* walk past a station, I want you to check *my* ID! And if I try to tell you no, I want you to *tackle* my ass! Do you all understand?"

"Yes, Slave Bitsy!" many of them chorused, now with all of them nodding.

"Good! So grab some protein and take your piss break now, while I get dressed! I need someone to lace me up! Jacquie, you know how, right? Come with me!" She jerked her thumb toward the door and a slight, butch woman grinned and followed her. Bitsy completely missed the look of longing on Tom's face.

CHAPTER 24

"RACIST, SEXIST, ANTI-GAY! LEATHER HATERS, GO AWAY!"

As chants went, it wasn't the worst she'd ever heard, but it sure wasn't poetry. Night had fallen, and the carnival of activists and protestors now outside the Grand Sterling Hotel was brightly illuminated by streetlights and a few media rigs. Rebecca paused to tally them; the Western Harrisburg crew had expanded to their maximum of five members, and the Mothers United for Families had brought out a spokesmom in a red suit and some professionally printed signs decrying perversion and featuring Keane-eyed waifs. The African-American gentleman and his soapbox were gone, but the counter-demonstrators filled the void quite admirably.

One cluster seemed to be from some organizations following the standard media-appropriate guideline of neatly dressed, camera-ready representation. About a dozen individuals, some passing out pamphlets, others holding posters with simple messages like FREEDOM FOR ALL, and STOP PERSECUTION OF SEXUAL MINORITIES. They were mostly white and older than thirty.

The chanters, however, had not gotten the memo on looking mainstream. A somewhat smaller but much louder collection of mixed gender, mixed color folks, most under thirty, not counting the one man with a long, scraggly grey beard, wearing a wedding dress under a motorcycle jacket. Their signs were not all media friendly, one of them a large, foam raised middle finger that the bearer kept shaking toward the Western Harrisburg clan. But the curvy lady in the pink and black bustier, fishnets and impossibly spiked heels; the fully outfitted leatherman, complete with a sash proclaiming him to be St. Louis Sir Leather; and the skinny youth in latex shorts, a chest harness and large black wings strapped to his back were certainly getting their pictures taken as they chanted. The three of them held a banner that read Queers United in Malediction. Someone in a brown suit kept trying to put himself in front of them, blocking them from cameras, but it looked like the half-dozen stoic uniforms present kept the various factions from truly interfering with each other.

Some cabs occasionally pulled up in front of the hotel's main entrance to disgorge passengers who didn't seem to care about the various protestors or media; others were directed elsewhere. There was one woman dressed in a white leather jumpsuit suggesting a kinky, cross-dressed Elvis, being filmed by the main doors of the hotel; Rebecca assumed she was the official media for the event.

Rebecca walked between the barriers; everyone knew she was on this one already, and she maintained her silence in the face of a few peppered questions, comments and chants.

"Detective! Did Woodrow Gallia kill Mr. Global Leather? Was he a closeted kinky gay man?" shouted one reporter, extending a microphone toward her.

"Sending a *lesbian* to investigate this homosexual murder is a blatant miscarriage of justice!" cried the spokesmom, raising one arm with a finger pointed heavenward. "The Mayor is trying to blame this on good Christians while the homosexuals slaughter each other in disgusting pagan rituals in a hotel frequented by families with *children*!"

"Hey-hey! Ho-ho! Leatherphobia's got to go!" chanted the Maledictory Queers.

Leatherphobia? Rebecca sighed, steeled herself and plunged back into the Global Leather empire. To her right, just as she walked by, she could hear the woman being filmed saying, "And after this, will anyone ever want to be Mr. or Ms. Global Leather, ever, again? This is Phedre Lysande, at the opening of the Global Leather Fetish Ball."

"You left out the bootblacks," said the camerawoman. "Again."

"Dammit! Okay, one more time…"

Two security lines snaked down the hallway from the main ballroom as hundreds of attendees wrestled tight fetishwear, tiny handbags and inaccessible pockets for their identification. Huge posters forbade cameras, cell phones and recording devices; the coat check line was doubled with people wanting to check their electronic devices along with the cover-ups that made them street legal.

He was insane for going through with this, Earl thought, surreptitiously adjusting his leather breeches. They had gotten tighter again; unless he cut back on the donuts and meatball sandwiches, he'd need a new fancy dress outfit for next year. The red leather tunic had a few more bulges and bumps than he'd ever remembered seeing before; he sucked in his stomach and wondered if he could just do without breathing much all night. Nope. He would need to lose the weight or get something new.

He'd just seen some hot fireman-style trousers made in garment weight lambskin. A steal at only six hundred dollars. If he bought them out of his profit for this fiasco, he'd have enough left for… nothing. This was a complete loss. He let out his breath and his stomach and sighed.

Cancellations were the least of his worries; dealers were reporting lackluster sales and vowing not to return. The buzz on KinkyNet was devastating, predicting the death of the contest, the title, even the entire title system. The yellow wristbands for those not wishing to be photographed outnumbered the silver and black style for the more exhibitionist sorts, and photos of the fashions on display were a major part of what drew people to the ball.

Instead, the pictures people had were of the protestors with their stupid signs and vile insinuations and that bizarre picture of Mack all devilled up. Part of his brain was relieved; it *had* been some crazed anti-sex bastard who killed poor Mack, and not someone in the community. But the story didn't end there— what people would remember was a titleholder died, targeted by a nutcase who got into *his* event. They'd remember waiting for an hour to get into a ballroom, they'd remember interminable tributes and mean-spirited celebrations, and they'd remember it was at Mr. and Ms. Global Leather. And Bootblack.

He carefully straightened the Sam Browne belt crossing his torso; he never felt less sexy in one of his all-leather getups. Instead, he felt the heat of the crowded corridors and the vague itchiness of spots where sweat had already dripped and dried. He almost envied the barely clad trio of Zodian ladies in their pastel lingerie, giggling behind lavender lace veils. Of course, he couldn't carry off the jeweled loincloth and bikini-top look, but at least his skin could breathe.

On the other hand, it could be worse; he could be into rubber. An entire rubber club did show up, marching proudly past the media at the front door and saluting the protestors with a united *bras d'honneur*. Earl hadn't seen it, of course, being called away for the tenth emergency of the night, but it was quickly relayed over the security radios, and would probably be the front page of some newspaper the next day.

More great publicity. Sometimes, he didn't know whether he

loved his community or hated it. But for better and worse, the Rubberfolk United Together were present, in their rubber skirts and trousers, tunics and blazers, jockstraps and chest harnesses, jumpsuits and chaps; one even had an entire Mets uniform (away game version) done in rubber.

There was a masochist for you.

Walking past them was like passing a balloon factory, with a slight undertone of sweat and Armor-All. Mingled with the musky-spicy signature scent of the Zodian girls, it was downright sacrilegious; maybe he could mention that to the religious people downstairs, so they could have something new to protest. Then he remembered the petition to make the Global Leather Contest a "scent-free" event and decided he had enough protestors.

How do you ban scent, anyway? With sniffers at the security check?

"Do you know who I am?" thundered one of his more famous instructors for the weekend, a talented singletail whip trickster who could snap tossed items out of the air and other nifty, crowd-pleasing tricks.

"Yeah, you're in the way," snapped one of the gender-blending trio behind him, all dressed in tuxedos with red leather bowties and cummerbunds.

"Wear the wristband or take a walk," said one of the security staff.

"Earl will hear about this!"

"Earl just heard. Wristbands for *everyone* tonight and tomorrow," Earl said, showing his own banded wrist.

The Famous Whip Instructor growled and extended one arm. "Loosely!" he cautioned. "I have carpal tunnel."

The Southwestern Association of Submissives/Slaves had set up a table just before the main ballroom doors, and the staffing members were giving out black ribbons hastily wound into the familiar loop of all charity/awareness ribbons; they were suggesting

216

a donation in Mack's memory for the benefit of...something. Earl forgot already whether it was supposed to be for Paul, or to get Mack's body home to San Francisco, or to cover funeral costs, or just because for a certain percentage of the community, the first instinct after a crisis was to raise money for something. Already shaken down for identification, some people blocked the doors trying to find singles. Others, long accustomed to picking up anything left on a table, grabbed a ribbon like they were going to be rare items one day.

The sound of Madonna came through the open doors and two drag queens on the arms of formal leather escorts sighed dramatically. The one with the florescent beehive whined, "Oh, my gawd, are we never going to hear something *new* at one of these things?"

The one in the sequined McQueen knockoff tittered and said, "The eighties called and they want their music back!"

"I am totally tweeting that when I get my phone back."

"What do you mean we can't go in? I showed you his driver's license!" The woman holding her slave's leash scowled with imperious displeasure. She was in a black nun's habit and platform heels. He was wearing latex shorts, tall, lace-up boots, and a gasmask with obscured eyepieces.

"We have to...see what he looks like..." said the volunteer with a helpless shrug.

"But that ruins the *scene*!" the woman cried.

Hated them. Earl decided he definitely hated them all. Why did he do this? Never again. Let the title die along with Mack. Someone else could handle this nonsense. He stormed off into the restricted corridor, his treasured Strathcona boots giving him blisters.

CHAPTER 25

Rebecca found Detective DeCosta in the hallway outside the rooms designated for use of the Boys Jack and their charges and all the special acts and varied celebrities. He was watching a group of six people all wearing masks with muzzles and ears, little mitts on their hands, collars around their necks and kneepads. He was humming "Who Let the Dogs Out?" while they seemed to be organizing themselves into some sort of order.

"You project the appearance of a man completely at ease in his surroundings," Rebecca said, as they met. "Find something you like?"

"No, I like hound dogs, myself, and I don't know what sort of mutts these folks are supposed to be." He led her away from the busy hallway and brought her up to date on his revised timeline.

"So, this is what I'm thinking. Tonight, our two real suspects are here. Ferri has to walk in with the rest of the contestants for some kind of show. They're bringing Helms up on stage later on to talk about Steel. But other than that, it's a party; they got no commitments. I say we hit them both on their stories."

"Hit the grieving boyfriend when he's about to make a eulogy and the contestant before he does his little song and dance?" Rebecca raised an eyebrow.

"Or after. Emotions will be up either way; probably better for us to grab them after."

She nodded. Cruelty was something cops and sadomasochists had in common, although she assumed the kinky people slept better after inflicting their preferred painful actions. "You don't like Woody for the murder."

"Nah. He is definitely obsessed. And no question, everyone *here* thinks he done it. But how would he get one of those knives? And why would he do it? And is there enough of a window of opportunity for him to do it between all those pictures and videos we ain't gone though yet?"

"He's in the body size range of the mysterious person Joshie saw. Maybe he had a past with Steel, saw he was coming to town and just snapped." She eyed him steadily. "A lot of homophobes turn out to be gay, you know. Sometimes, it's the ones with the worst things to say. Self-hating and guilt-ridden, just the type to keep it all inside and then...snap."

He nodded somberly. "Yeah, I heard that. But I got to say..." He shrugged and spread his arms. "And I got no *reason* to..."

Rebecca nodded, not sure if she was disappointed at his not taking up the bait, or pleased at how he managed it. "No, I get it. Me, too. It's just not fitting together. If they find his prints in Mack's room or some pictures of the crime scene on his camera or a thousand frustrated love letters on his personal computer, I'll be the first one to bring him down. In the meantime...yeah. The two *real* suspects, even if no one here wants to believe it. Plus, I'm still not too sure Dick Schneider is in the clear. Just because the professor can vouch for him for fifteen minutes doesn't mean he didn't have the rest of the night to saunter back there and dispatch the man who got his wife fired and made their life a mess."

"Yeah, I gotta tell you there's something going on there I don't like either, with their slavegirl running off on 'em and all that. Maybe I need to check some things with her."

The detectives entered the ballroom, and Trudy came to Rebecca's mind again. She had a sudden memory of dancing with Trudy at some bar up in Provincetown, and how good she felt in her arms.

But of course, Trudy was kinky now. And into being over-powered or dominated in some way, although Rebecca couldn't remember her ever being passive about *anything*, let alone sex. In fact, she'd been quite the aggressor and instigator, which had suited them just fine...

Focus, Feldblum, focus.

The array of black leather didn't seem to take up a smaller percentage of the fashion choices in the crowd at the ball, but the style of clothing did change. Instead of T-shirts and vests, long and short sleeved leather and latex shirts appeared, along with elaborate fetishy gowns and uniforms of all nations and services, from cops and firefighters to members of various armed forces to a trio of what appeared to be adult male Girl Scouts. It was surprising how many people were there in actual formal attire, all dressed up as for any evening event, mingling with the more exotically garbed attendees.

Of course, some fetishes seemed better suited for a ball atmosphere than others. The ponies looked oddly appropriate, harnessed and belled and haltered; the puppies somewhat less so. The...pack?—Rebecca wondered, as she watched, if they called themselves a pack—of dog-humans she'd seen in the hall were scampering amid the attendees, some of them on all fours, two on their feet, being patted or scratched or sent off with waved hands. One of them seemed to be wearing a sash; how nice for him. And then there was the tall person dressed like a giant dog—a fox terrier maybe, or even a fox, it was hard to tell—who sported a large bowtie around the costume neck and a cummerbund and jacket over the furry upper body.

No trousers, though. Probably hard to fit over the costume legs.

A group of Zodians *danced* their way into the room, and not just the ladies. The girls were in harem-style outfits, still sporting layers of silk and satin and gauze in rainbow colors and draped with ropes of glittering jewelry; but now most of them also wore veils in different shades of purple. One would have expected a sort of belly dance from them, and certainly their inspired wiggling, shaking and slinking had that charm of an activity joyously engaged in, if not especially well done. But the men who followed them in were also doing some sort of dance, or stylized march; they, too had changed their barbarian splendor just a bit. All of them now sported headgear, from a knotted bandana on one to a fully horned Ride-of-the-Valkyries Kill-the-Wabbit Viking helmet. One gentleman wore a Japanese-style helmet with dramatic wing-shaped cheek pieces. And as they followed their dancing girls, they clashed leaf-shaped sheathed daggers against little truncheons or batons and stamped their boots down in a steady rhythm. Every once in a while, they grunted in unison, or cried out a word in some language other than English.

Some people giggled; others applauded.

"What the...what are they doing?" Dominick asked, aghast. "I mean...what is that?"

"That is the Zodian Master's Moon Dance," said a sardonic voice from behind them. They had stationed themselves out of the way, on the far side of the lighting and sound station. It provided a clear view of most of the room without being in anyone's way, and had the convenient bonus of being partly shielded from view. Rebecca had changed into a spare black blazer she kept at the precinct, but there was no way either of them looked like they'd fit into this crowd tonight. Out of the way was best.

The speaker was a familiar face; Rebecca knew this was the reporter from the *New York Record*. She had a citywide interest, but seemed especially likely to catch disaster and crime stories, or perhaps those were her primary specialties.

"The moon dance," Dominick echoed.

"You bet your ass; drunk on hot Chjam herbal wine mixed with b'bo blood, the Masters of Zod dance beneath the ring of moons to gather warrior energy and cry their pain to the uncaring skies. Thus, they emerge newly clean and strong and ready for battle, or for the love furs."

Dominick looked at her and then at Rebecca, who pressed her lips together tightly.

"The love furs."

The reporter grinned and nodded. "Do you believe that happy crappy? I know more about those guys now than anyone, *ever*, should know. About a dozen books, or one book written twelve times, back in the eighties. Some kind of dungeons-and-dragons thing for geeky, horny teen boys. Some guy with serious issues wrote 'em, retired, and is probably sitting on some private island gloating over the royalty checks from the continued sales of the series to people who think they can live it out. Hello, Detective Feldblum! How about an interview?"

Rebecca remembered her name. "Nancy," she said. "Nancy Nichols from the *Record*; this is Detective DeCosta. And we have no comments about any of this."

Dominick stifled a laugh and shook his head, looking back at the Zodian parade. "My lordy-lord. When I think I seen it all, they come up with something new. Blood drinking, moon-dancing... and love furs. Where are those PETA people when you need 'em? Protest the damn Vikings and their *love furs*."

"That's still no comment," Rebecca said firmly.

"You're breaking my heart! What are you doing here anyway?

Didn't you catch the guy earlier?" Nancy looked at them both and smiled wider. "Ah, you don't think Woody the Wanker did it, huh? It does seem a little too movie-of-the-week, doesn't it? And the deceased had *so* many people who hated him so very much. How about a trade, Detective? I'll show you mine if you tell me something I don't know..." She waggled the shoulder case for her netbook. "You would not believe the dish and dirt people have given me. I was thinking a few feature articles, maybe a series. Now, I'm thinking a whole book!"

"If you have anything to help this investigation, we'd be delighted to hear about it. But my answer remains no comment."

A squawk from the sound system caught their attention as Earl took the stage to introduce the evening's MC and thank the attendees. While he spoke, Nancy thumbed her phone impatiently. "Jesus, this is such a *garrulous* community. They act all shy on you for about a nanosecond, guarding the Ancient Secrets of their Sacred Old Guard Brotherhood of Kinky Hoo-ha, but the minute you give them time to breathe they're telling you not only their life story, but the story of the guy next to them and what everyone did in the dungeon last night. Then they run and post pictures of it on KinkyNet and complain they have no privacy. Speaking of pictures, Detective, this look familiar?"

She flashed the screen of her phone toward Rebecca and showed a reproduction of the photo used in Woodrow's satanic flyer, minus the additions. "Where did you get that?" Rebecca asked.

"Funny story. You'd think I got it off MGL_MackSteel dot com, but it's not there. I actually found it on this right-wing anti-gay place—and *not* the one hosted by Mr. Gallia, either. Then I found it on another one, same theme, different group. My assistant says he's tracked down eighteen different websites with this picture on them and more are popping up by the minute. Gallia's version is doing the rounds, with his story, but the plain picture is being used just to talk about how Sodom on the Hudson is welcoming sex perverts."

Rebecca frowned.

"Yeah, kinda odd, isn't it? If only I knew *one* thing, I think I might be able to help you a little."

Dominick snorted. "And what's that?"

"What was Mr. Global Leather gonna do next?"

"What do you mean?"

Nancy looked at Dominick with a raised eyebrow and some pity. "Seriously, handsome?"

"Shh!" said the man behind the soundboard. Rebecca looked up at the stage and saw that one of the contestants was walking out to much applause. But she didn't hear what was being said; she was furiously running through her memory and considering Nancy's question.

Nancy got more text messages from her nineteen-year-old nephew, who was at home in Scarsdale and searching the Internet for her (and the football tickets she promised to score for him). Perhaps *assistant* was a grandiose word for who he was, but definitely not for what he was doing. She waited patiently, knowing Feldblum would come through with something in exchange for the prompt. When someone came by offering raffle tickets to benefit a free-speech organization, Nancy cheerfully bought a dozen. Free speech was something she could always get behind.

Kelly Manning, the former Ms. Global Leather, came out in a black leather kilt, a white, linen ruffled shirt and a classic Montrose doublet also in leather. The silver buttons gleamed under the stage lighting, and the fur on his sporran waved gently as he strutted, banded in the leather pride colors with a heart dangling like a charm over the white bar in the center. He waved as he strode out acknowledging the cheers and then stopped to do a neat catwalk turn before continuing to the microphone stand.

The MC opened an envelope and read, "Does size matter? Explain."

There was a ripple of laughter from the audience as Kelly grinned and considered. Then, he took a deep breath and said, "Yes. Absolutely. So many people have told me size is the most important thing, the first thing they look for, and after my own personal experiences in life, I am forced to agree." He paused, looked down toward his sporran and then back up, his face resolute. "But of course, I'm not talking about personal endowments! I'm talking about community size."

"What the hell is this now?" Dominick asked. "I thought they were going to sing or dance or something, like Miss America."

"Pop questions. They're random, and each contestant has two minutes to answer one." Nancy shook her head. "That guy used to be a girl, can you believe it?"

"Seriously?"

"Would I lie to you, Detective Gorgeous?"

"DeCosta," he murmured, folding his arms. Scanning the room, he caught sight of the lady who had recognized Feldblum the night before. What was her name? Judy? No, Trudy. She was wearing one of those fancy corsets with a brocade pattern on it, over a long shimmering skirt. Funny, he'd thought of her as a little tomboyish last night, but not so much tonight. She didn't seem to be with anyone in particular, but mixed with the crowd, sipping from a tall glass and swishing that swirl of black fabric as she walked. He wondered what it would be like to find one of his exes at this event and shuddered, then turned his attention back to the stage. He decided not to draw Feldblum's attention to Trudy's presence; he looked away so as not to alert the reporter, either. She'd been eager to know who Trudy was, and he saw no reason to evoke her curiosity again.

"And that's why it's imperative that we all get out and vote in every election, and keep ourselves informed and aware and active in our ever-growing community," Kelly finished up, just before a buzzer rang.

The applause was far more enthusiastic than Nancy thought the little speech deserved, but the reason why became clear when the next contestant, Jason Asada, got the question, "If you were a superhero, what would your powers be?" He froze under the spotlight and weakly offered, "Batman?"

"There's a guy who never has to worry about the burden of intellectualism," said Nancy, shaking her head.

"I'm going to find Paul," Rebecca said to Dominick in a low voice.

Dominick nodded. "You want me to keep an eye on Ferri or come with?"

"Would I steal you away from all this? No, watch for Ferri and the Ravenfyre family. I want to know if the husband or the slave go off for more secret meetings tonight."

"You got it." He turned to Nancy and asked, "So, what's with the puppies and horsies and stuff? You know that, too?"

Nancy grinned. "You have no idea how much I've learned. Like I said—a book. A whole freaking book."

Backstage was a space defined by moveable panels making a corridor to an exit door leading to the rear hallway, which then lead to the prep rooms. The harried stage manager and her team of volunteers leapt over cables and wove between contestants, handlers, the MC's girlfriend and wandering security people trying to look authoritative. Boy Jack kept one hand on his headset control box as he ushered his charges back and forth, his waves frantically echoed by volunteers needing to look busy.

"Jack, is Paul with your guys?" came Boi Jack's voice over the headset.

"No! Why would he be?" Jack whispered back.

"We showed him his saved seat at the judges' table and he was here a minute ago, but he's gone now and I can't find him!"

"Chill. Maybe he went to pee."

"I got a bad *feeling*, Jack. Look for him, please?"

Jack scanned the area, then grabbed a volunteer and told him to go back to the prep room and check for Paul. Then he grabbed Blade, who was walking in the wrong direction, and shoved her toward the stage. Should he alert Earl? Or text Bitsy and have her people start looking for Paul? Or just concentrate on his job, which was getting this particular group of people to the stage without any of them falling down the stairs?

Thinking of his leather sibling made him sigh. Jack did have good instincts about trouble; that's why she was such a good handler. He pulled his phone out and started texting.

"Imagine that you have been invited to come and address the Global Leather contest twenty-five years from now...when you look out into the audience, what do you see?"

Angelina Swiderski frowned for a moment and smoothed down the side of her latex poodle skirt; she would have fit right into some alternate universe sock-hop, down to the anklets and saddle shoes and the large pink bow in her hair. "Wow, that's a great question!" she said, with temporizing pauses. "What a terrific question, really. Thank you for that question. I guess I see all my NuKnk brothers and sisters all grown up! Because in twenty-five years, we'll be the elders in the community, right? And we'd probably think everyone younger was annoying. But I guess I'd look out and see lots of little cameras instead of all these people, because in twenty-five years, no one will be going out except to hook up, I mean we're heading that way right now. My speech will go out line by line to anyone who wants to hear it, and no one would have to travel to New York to come to this...I guess. But, uh, we would, anyway! Because the community is more than hooking up. It's being together as a tribe..."

"Great answer," Ravenfyre said with disgust, making notes on her scoring sheet. "In twenty-five years, there won't be a community. Just keep backpedaling, girl."

"Except she's probably right," snickered Mickey Abraham. "Perverts are early adapters to technology; when we can all stay home and wait until our phones tell us the perfect orgasm facilitator is ten yards away, or just sit at the computer and watch it live, why bother to get all dressed up and endure the company of our fellows?"

"She's pretty well spoken for twenty-three. And her blog gets more hits than you can count. She does a lot to promote events nationwide—it's not her fault clubs are closing and the scene is changing. The leather/BDSM community will always survive in some way," said Master Zenu.

"Now that the police have all the Ravenfyre knives, you might be right, Zenu. I know it makes it harder to commit *my* satanic rituals, personally. Luckily, I still have my Zodian Honor Blade!"

Mistress Ravenfyre and Lord Laertes both leveled icy glares at Mickey and then turned their attention pointedly back to the stage.

Paul Helms was not in the hallway between the ballroom and the dressing room, nor did anyone see him enter or leave bathrooms on that floor. One of the professional security guards nodded when Rebecca described him, and pointed her down toward the main stairs leading to the lobby.

Since the ballroom was filled with people, it was odd to see the lobby also busy. Screens blocked an easy view from outside the hotel, but once past them, attendees milled around, or gathered in conversational clumps around sofas and armchairs. Some did not seem dressed for the ball, in casual or street wear; others were perhaps in no great hurry to attend the pop question portion of the evening. Apparently there were awards to be presented and performance art on the schedule for later on, and somewhere in there people might actually dance.

Rebecca walked around the perimeter of the lobby, her eyes scanning each group of people, looking for Paul's slight frame. He was a body conscious young man; she remembered his tight jeans during her first interview with him. This was one of the things that kept nagging at her, too.

The murderer had most likely been sprayed with blood, but they had no clothing and barely any evidence of a cleanup, just a few footprints leading to the bathroom and one missing washcloth from the room inventory. Dominick told her he'd asked about Paul showering in Wolfboy's room, but it was so late in that evening, it couldn't have been to wash off blood—he'd have to pass a room full of other men to get into the shower anyway. No matter how distracted they might have been, blood was messy. Plus, they knew Paul had been scantily clad at the bar before coming back to the hotel; did he change into full leather after killing his lover?

Reconstructing possibilities showed more gaps in their time line. For Paul to come back to the hotel, show up and sleep in Wolfboy's room and appear the next morning in jeans and a T-shirt, where was his bar outfit from the night before? Did he come back to the room he shared with Mack to pick up clothing? He said he hadn't been there at all, but if that was the case, did he go to the bar with the clothing he was wearing the morning they discovered the body?

Giuliano Ferri was in his full leather clothing on the surveillance camera, plus he had carried a bag large enough to put more clothing in. However, he'd eagerly handed over that black leather bag, complete with a collection of sex toys; Rebecca had it forwarded to the crime lab for swabbing. On first glance, it seemed pretty clean—no smell of anything but leather. The whip, paddle, handcuffs, rope and assorted little metal clamps that looked painful were almost pristine; there was even a butt plug still in its shrinkwrap.

That seemed weird, too. He had protested he still liked "regular sex" even though he was kinky—but so much about him seemed brand new to all of this. How does a new guy wind up running for a title?

Her phone buzzed and she quickly glanced down at it. There were no further incriminating videos or pictures on Woodrow's cameras; in fact, there were shots of people in the lobby of the hotel within fifteen minutes of his video outside Mack's room. Well, that seemed pretty clear.

The transcripts for Steel's phone usage had come through at last. With one quick glance around to make sure she still didn't see Paul, she thumbed the file open, found the text messages and started scrolling through them. At last, she found a thread between Steel and Paul. Reading them backward according to time stamps, she reconstructed them in proper chronological order. Paul had said Steel told him to take the night for himself; Ferri said Steel *texted* Paul with this instruction.

There were at least a hundred text messages from Thursday, half of them one or two message exchanges and many of them variations on "See you at the bar tonight." There were the weird threats and taunts from Mr. Ravenfyre and slave Willow Ravenfyre. And, last in a string of pretty mundane partner-style texts— (Steel: Xtra mayo and prot bars. Paul: OKAY SIR!)—there it was. Eleven-fifteen P.M., Steel to Paul: "Trkng in rm. Take off. C u l8r."

How romantic and charming. Paul's response was a quick "OKAY SIR!" Sent at eleven-twenty-two, with no followup whatsoever.

See you later, in text-speak, not "come back tomorrow," or "see you in the morning." So, how did Paul know not to come back?

Out of the corner of her eye, she saw him at last, right by the lobby bar, hunched over against the wall in a position guaranteed to be ignored by the tenders. He wasn't alone; she approached without drawing attention to herself, to take a look at his companion. He was a blond guy with a long, shaggy ponytail wearing black jeans and tall, lace-up boots and a black shirt and tie; his leather vest had a back patch with a snarling wolf on it and a top rocker patch that read "Wolftooth Clan." And he was handing over a plastic bag with something in it.

"Are you sure?" The blond man was saying, shifting from one foot to the other.

"Yes!" Paul snapped,

"But...um...I'm really kinda sure this is yours..."

"Hello, Paul," Rebecca said, coming up behind the two. "Lose something?"

"Oh! Uh. Hi, Detective. No. I mean, no, I didn't lose anything." He looked flustered, and drank quickly from the tall glass in front of him. He was having cola and something; the glass sparked with bubbles and ice. For the ball, he was dressed in a black long-sleeved shirt under a plain black vest. The shirt was open at the throat to display a chain collar with a lock on it. He had tight blue jeans under soft black leather chaps, and a cap on his head; the cap looked a little large, and he kept adjusting it back slightly to keep the brim from slipping down his forehead.

Rebecca introduced herself to the blond man with the bag and the ponytail, and he shook her hand while his eyes wandered everywhere but her own. "I guess I'll, um, go then," he said nervously.

"What's in the bag?" Rebecca asked.

"Nothing," said Paul.

"It's a T-shirt," said Wolfboy. "The other cop, the, um, African-American guy with the Southern accent? He asked if anyone lost or found anything in my room, so, after the pet show I asked around. And my buddy lost a pair of jeans and this other guy lost a jock but wound up with extra socks, but no one claimed the socks yet..."

"I didn't lose anything," Paul insisted.

"Yeah, but, um. You're the only guy except for Midnight who wears small, and he found two of these in his bag..." Wolfboy pulled a contest T-shirt out of the plastic bag. "He said it was wet, too. And he can't find his pants, heh. And I think I might have lost a T-shirt, but I don't care, I got a million, so I thought this might be mine...but I wear a medium."

"It's not mine, okay?" Paul sucked in the remainder of his drink and started waving for the bartender.

"May I see it?"

Wolfboy handed it to Rebecca, who shook it out. It was from last year's contest, obviously worn and washed many times. It was dry and badly wrinkled and had a faint, sharp odor on it.

"I guess I'll take it to the lost and found," Wolfboy muttered.

"I'll be happy to take care of it," Rebecca said.

"Really? Well. Okay." He handed her the bag. "Do you guys still want to know if anyone found extra stuff or lost stuff?"

"Yes, we do," she said, slipping the shirt into the bag and handing him a card. "Thank you."

"Um. Okay." He ducked his head and hustled away. Rebecca turned to Paul, who had not captured anyone's attention for a refill.

"Are you sure this isn't yours?" she asked.

"Yes! I didn't lose anything. Except Mack." He sniffed suddenly and shook his head. "I wish I could get five minutes with that asshole you caught!" Then he blinked and looked at her curiously. "But...you did catch him! So...why are you here?"

"There are some loose ends, Paul." She lifted the bag with the T-shirt. "Like...what were you doing between one and four A.M. that night? You said you went to different room parties, but so far we haven't found anyone else who saw you."

He laughed suddenly and rubbed at his eyes. "Oh, God. See, if only I actually had one steady guy on the side, it would look better, right? Fucked because I don't have a fuckbuddy! Ha-ha!" His shoulders shook and she realized he probably had at least two other drinks before this one. Looking into his eyes and smelling his breath, she adjusted her estimate upward. He'd been drinking for some time. And he was going to have to make a speech?

"Paul!" cried Boi Jack, bursting upon them in a flurry of wild-eyed near-hysteria and a rattle of papers clutched in her hands. "Where have you been? You're almost up!"

"What? Oh." He looked down at his watch and sighed. "Okay. Let's do this."

"Excuse me!" Boi Jack said to Rebecca, somewhat belatedly. "But we have to go!" She thumbed her headset controls. "I got him! We're on our way back!"

"I'll come with you," Rebecca said. "Paul, quick question—how did you know Mack wanted you to stay out all night?"

Paul looked puzzled for a moment and then shrugged. "He told me."

"How and when?"

"He...I..." He fumbled in the pockets of his skintight jeans and pulled out some crumpled bills, peeling a few off and placing them on the bar. "He sent me a text!"

"The text says he'd see you later."

Boi Jack stared at them in anguish. "Do you need to do this now? Because he's up after the pop questions! And that's like... now, almost!"

"We'll walk and talk, unless you'd prefer to come with me for a few minutes while we clear things up, Paul?"

"There's nothing to clear up! He told me to take off, and I did!" He looked nervously at Boi Jack. "I gotta go."

Rebecca swept her arm indicating the direction to the elevators. "Let's go. You know, Paul, you did a lot for Mack; everyone we've spoken to says you were…very good for him."

The three of them started walking away from the bar together. Rebecca continued, "In fact, some people said you were one of the reasons why Mack could do everything he did during his title year, that you organized things for him, kept him on time, supported his appearances. It sounds like a lot of work."

He nodded eagerly. "It was! Hard work. You have no idea how complicated things can get; I had to plan his travel and book…the planes. Flights and hotels and all that. And, and keep track of all the programs he was a member of to get points. So annoying! I knew all of his passwords for every website and all his membership numbers…God, so much. And I had to handle all the contact with the producers and idiots who run the events, and I had to manage his web page and email and…"

Boi Jack shot him a brief glare when he used the word "idiots." He didn't seem to notice.

"And *then* I had to make sure he brought all his title stuff, the belt and vest and medallion, and knew where he's going and what he was expected to do. And, and, I also wrote his speeches…" Through his slurred words, she could clearly hear the desperation to be appreciated for his role in Mack's life.

"See, that's what I'm talking about," Rebecca said. "You did all that for a year—"

"*More* than a year! I helped him win Frisco Stud! *Twice*! No, that was Mr. Stud. Leather. Whatever."

"Impressive. But I have to ask, Paul. With all of that to do, and this being his last weekend with the title…why weren't you there in the morning to wake him up and get him to the judges' room on time?"

Paul stopped and raised a hand over his eyes, squeezing them tightly shut. "I…I should have! But I…I failed, okay? I had my phone turned off because I thought I'd just wake up early like normal, and I failed him when he needed me the most!" With a harsh profanity, he broke into a dash up the stairs instead of waiting for the elevator.

"Oh, jeez," Boi Jack muttered. "That's all we need." She thumbed her headset controls. "Stage, Paul is heading up and he's a little upset. Like, epic upset, and he's had a few, know what I mean? Maybe we should cancel his speech?" She looked at Rebecca. "I'm sorry, but wow, it woulda been better if that coulda waited until tomorrow. Or even better, Monday!"

"Believe me, there's little I like about the timing of this weekend myself."

"It *is* kinda weird, though."

"What?"

"Paul *did* usually get Mack up and at stuff on time. That's why, when I didn't see Mack at breakfast, Paul was the first one I called. I must have left, like, a dozen messages for him, text and voice." She shrugged as the elevator arrived. "I guess he really did screw up, badly. That's gotta suck."

CHAPTER 26

"You're stranded on a desert island with the judges of this contest. Who will be doing what job to help you survive or get rescued and who becomes your special friend?"

The audience laughed, at least those still paying attention. On stage, dressed in rubber breeches and tall boots and a black rubber bowling shirt with a dark green stripe down the sides, was Maurice, Mr. Palm Springs Rubber. He shook his head and smiled.

"This is a question?" he asked as he stepped up to the microphone. "Who will get the coconuts, who will make the fire, who will build the grass hut, like that? And who becomes my boyfriend? This is not a question, this is *mishegoss*...that's nonsense, for you people who don't know from Yiddish. And what does that have to do with leather? Or rubber, even? Nothing! I think we have better things to think about, maybe? Like, how do we keep the modern Nazis, those *schtunks* outside, with their signs and their fear and their hate, away from us? How do we keep from fighting each other when there are guys like that *mamzer* who came in here and killed one of us, guys who really want to hurt us, not just wave their signs and call names?"

He paused, shaking his head, and the audience quieted a little. With a mighty sigh, he continued. "I don't know. Maybe I'm too old, lived too long. But this craziness we do—leather here, rubber there, the masters and slaves over there, Old Guard and the new kid-kinksters, whatever they call themselves, over there, the bears and the people with the animal play over there..." He gestured to the corners of the room, "and then there's the Zods..."

"Zodians!" came a few shouts.

"Zodians, Zodsters, whatever you like, Mr. Big-shot-got-horns-on-your-hat; hey, I kid, I kid. But you know, back in my day, it wasn't all different little pockets of guys all doing their own thing and making faces at the other guys. I think maybe we got something right back then, even though we weren't nice to the ladies and we sure didn't hang out with the straight people. But we depended on each other—who else could we depend on? When you had just one bar, of course the drag queens and the leather boys and the every-day-I'm-just-gay guys would all drink together, and what was wrong with that? I hear all you young kids talking tribe this, family that—you know what a tribe is? People who know the rest of the world don't want them to exist. You know what a family is? It's a mish-mash of people who got one place they always know they can go, and like the poet says, they gotta let you in. And like it or not, everyone who is your family... you're stuck with 'em. Your *mishpoche*, that's everyone, from your buddies who look just like you to the lady you don't even know if she's from your planet—they're still family. You gotta let 'em in; they gotta let you in.

"Some *mamzer* killed one of us here this weekend. Murdered! You think in the big picture it matters how I tell you who gets the coconuts on a made-up island? Of course not! What matters is, are we good to each other? Are we kind to each other? Do we get along even when we don't understand why some *alter kocker* is dressed up like some guy who got lost in a rubber factory? Are you a *mensch*—a good human? Or some kind of *schmuck* who wants his own treehouse on the made-up island?" He straightened the collar of his shirt. "That's what I think matters, not that what I think matters. And, in conclusion, George, you're a nice guy, and Zenu, you're my type, except for the red hair—my mother told me never date a redhead. So, since I always went for the burly, hairy fellows, I'd say it would have to be Mr. Laertes who I'd get over to my hut on the made-up island. He wouldn't be the first heterosexual fellow I'd brought over to our side, you know."

The audience applauded and laughed with glee as Laertes straightened in his chair and reddened. Mickey Abraham doubled over in laughter with Chava Nagilla. Maurice seemed a little surprised by the sustained applause and paused to wave once more before leaving the stage.

"Can I vote for him?" Dominick asked. "I didn't get half of what he was saying, but it sounded funny."

"Nah, only the judges get to pick the winners." Nancy was getting good and bored already. The questions were either dull or downright juvenile. The clothing was interesting up to a point, but there were just so many pictures of leather bustiers and assless chaps Donny would take before he rolled his eyes and started taking artsy pictures of window reflections. One turn around the room netted zero interesting interview subjects. No one had anything new to say about the murder, although she had plenty of quotes about how safe they all were and how it was only a matter of time before the leather/kink-phobic right-wing lunatics started mowing them down or carting them off to camps. The most inflammatory statement she'd gotten was from a woman who was starting some sort of organization for kinky gun owners.

"If Mack had been properly armed, no one with a knife could have gotten near him," she said with the conviction of any gun nut out there in the regular world. Fortified, United Leather Lifesty-lers Armed Ultimately Together Operation will serve as an educational and advocacy group..."

"United and together sort of mean the same thing."

The woman sighed. "I tried to come up with something else, but nothing fit, exactly."

"And there's nothing in the name that's really about guns. Fortified sounds like you take vitamins, and armed could be anything. Half of you guys are already armed with your Zodian knives and whips and things. How about Shoot Assholes First, Thank You."

The woman paused, considered, mouthed the words. Then, she shook her head. "I bet we'd have trouble with the word 'assholes' in the name. But wow, that was fast, and only one letter missing!"

Nancy couldn't believe she'd actually considered it.

But that was it so far, for interesting subjects. The Zodian girl was up on stage now.

"This slave thanks the producers and volunteers of the Global Leather Contest and Ball for the opportunity of allowing this slave to speak to such an illustrious group. This slave does not deserve honors; this slave is only a tool for her owner and community to use..."

"Somewhere, Gloria Steinem is getting nauseated and doesn't know why," Nancy muttered.

"Yeah, I don't get that," Dominick said, looking up from his cell phone. "This master and slave stuff is so offensive in so many ways, but man, is this what someone wants their daughter to be doin'? Standing up there in harem-girl clothes calling herself a tool to be used? Damn." He shook his head.

"Ah, so in addition to being good looking, you're a sensitive kinda guy, huh, DeCosta?"

"I don't know if I'm sensitive or not, but I do know there's nothing sexy about a woman who calls herself a damn tool. I see way too many women being used by their men to like the sound of that. Hell, I been there." He shoved the phone away and folded his arms. "It ain't right."

Nancy examined him in speculation. "Where are you from, Detective? Georgia?"

"Mississippi by way of Virginia and Maryland. How 'bout you, Ms. Nichols?"

"Me? I'm New York City born and bred; I get nosebleeds in Westchester and the bends when I hit Jersey. So, tell me. If you don't think Woody the Wanker did it, who did? Was it Mack's title-partner, Ravenfyre? He did do some serious, real world damage to her."

"Yeah, we know. Why do you call him that?"

"Woody? He makes a habit of going to these kink conventions, all disguised. Then he takes pictures or buys some toys and videos and shows 'em on cable TV or his website and raises more money to send him to another kinky thing. You know he's got a hard-on for this stuff; he's just using outrage to fund his travels. Probably doing the nasty to himself right now in a jail cell, thinking about wearing ladies underwear..." She stopped when Dominick leveled his eyes on her.

"Oh? What's up with ladies underwear?" she asked.

"Nothing," he said quickly.

"Oh, no, you can't sell me that," she said. "There's something about ladies undies in this case. Was the killer wearing them? Was Woody? Or, wait, were they shoved in the victim's mouth?" Her eyes widened with delight.

Dominick looked at her in confusion. "Why would they be in his mouth?"

"Oh, my God, Detective, you should read what these people write about. There's so much about shoving things in mouths, you know they're all still orally fixated. Well, except for the anal fanatics. But the whole panties-in-the-mouth thing is *very* popular

240

with the straight guys, although the Zodians probably call it loin-clothing or something. Why did it raise your eyebrows?"

"No comment," Dominick muttered. He pulled out his phone again and started texting.

"And finally, we have Giuliano Ferri, Mr. Newark Leather!"

Polite applause mingled with the sound of a crowd ready to move on, just a little bit too enthusiastic for a short amount of time. Ferri was wearing a long-sleeved leather shirt tucked into tight leather jodhpurs plus his sash over that.

"The last question of the evening is...Mac, or PC, and please explain?"

There was a ripple of laughter and then some cries of surprise; someone yelled out, "Too soon!" Ferri looked around in puzzlement and some of the judges looked slightly uncomfortable; Mickey Abraham collapsed across the table in very unscholarly giggles.

Ferri drew himself up and stepped to the microphone, removing his cap. He took a deep breath and started, "I guess we're talking computers here, and I'm kinda, waddayoucallit, computer illegitimate..."

More laughter erupted and he looked a bit more confused. He was about to continue when one of the screens marking the stage area suddenly wobbled and rocked on its feet; he looked off stage left and his fingers tightened around the brim of his hat. Paul Helms, his upper body flushed and sweaty, his hair disarrayed, half stumbled onto the stage, with both Boys Jack behind him. He stared at Ferri while the Boys seemed to be momentarily stunned by the situation.

The MC desperately tried to maintain control. "Er...please continue!"

Ferri glanced at Paul, looked back at the audience and tried another deep breath. "As I was saying...I don't know much about computers. But I do know that having…being…I mean, being into leather is…" He stopped, closed his eyes for a second and then shook his head. "I don't know where I was going with that. Sorry. I, uh…"

Dead silence ruled the room, as Boi Jack whispered to Paul and tried to get him to leave the stage. Paul swayed slightly but didn't move. Giuliano Ferri eyed Paul again and then sighed.

"I can't do this. I'm done with this BS. Let him talk." And then he jammed his cap back onto his head and exited stage right to a flurry of movement and whispered questions and exclamations into phones and headsets.

Dr. Abraham clapped and whistled in appreciation. Nancy Nichols snickered as she made her own notes. Dominick DeCosta started moving.

Not waiting for an invitation, Paul strode to the microphone stand. The Boys Jack melted back; their place was not on stage and no one expected them to physically manhandle someone. Volunteer security stood on their toes, uneasy and unable to figure out what they should be doing while the stage manager furiously consulted with Earl. When the stage manager shrugged and gave a thumbs-up, the microphone stayed live. Apparently, Earl was okay with the defection of the contestant and the early arrival of Mack's surviving partner. That, or he'd thrown up his own arms and given in to fate.

Paul grabbed the microphone and angled it down, fumbling slightly. He cleared his throat loudly, and some people in the ballroom jumped.

"You think it's funny," he said in a low voice. "You think it's funny that the question was Mac or PC, and Mack is dead. You know what? That's not fucking funny!" His voice cracked and he squeezed his temples with one hand, trying to regain control. "You hated him…you were jealous of him, and you know why? Because Mack wasn't PC! Ha-ha! Because Mack said what he thought and did what he said and didn't ap-apologize...for anything...to anyone! He didn't sing 'Kumbaya' with all of you in your fancy clothes and costumes! He lived...the life. The leatherman's lifestyle, not some damn suburb-living kinda thing where you get dressed up on weekends and think you're so hot. You're not! Mack...was hot. Mack was real. And he didn't need any of you, and you hated him for it and now he's dead and you're making...jokes."

He paused and Boi Jack started tiptoeing out onto the stage to try and walk him off, but then he raised his head again and she scampered back.

"Lemme tell you something about Mack! He was...the best master, the best daddy...ever. He was tough, but he knew what was right! He didn't take shit from *anyone*. All you guys talk about is Old Guard and fancy manners and stupid Zod crap, but he was *real* leather, *real* SM, a *real* dominant. He was tough! Strong! He didn't care what names he got called, 'cause it didn't matter to him. That's what a leatherman is! None of you know anything about it! Just a bunch of poseurs and fakes, drag queens and role-players and, and newbies who don't know anything! Taking classes and *talking* all the time and never doing anything, that's what you are! Mack didn't need classes! He was nat...naturally dominant...

"And Mack was so...hot...so beautiful...you just don't know... the best top, the best master...a real man. Not some pansy...fairy... fake!" His voice cracked and tears streamed down his cheeks; his narrow chest heaved as he breathed heavily into the microphone. Both of the Jacks came out, one on each side, and tried to pry him away. "Let me talk! You don't understand! Bunch of fucking *fakes*! You're not leather! You're just *clothes*! Talk! No one like Mack, ever!" he insisted, shrugging against them. "And no one understood him but me!"

More security volunteers were peeking around the edges of

the standing screens or through cracked doors; in the back of the room, Earl ran a finger across his throat over and over until Slave Bitsy Olmstead strode out on stage, elbowed Boi Jack aside and wrapped an arm around Paul's shoulders.

"Come on, kiddo, time for a nap," she growled softly into his ear, and he burst into louder sobs, but allowed her to pull him off the microphone. The Jacks scampered in two different directions as the MC reclaimed the microphone and said, "Let's hear it for Mack Steel! Uh—and Paul! We're gonna take...a five...ten minute break!" The deejay hit the sound system fast, and thumping music drowned out the first wave of confused applause, loud conversation, arguments and exclamations of surprise, horror or glee.

"This...this is the best leather contest *ever*!" gasped Mickey Abraham, tears of laughter coating the inside of her glasses. "We should kill one of the contestants every year!"

CHAPTER 27

THE TWO SUSPECTS EXITED FROM TWO DIFFERENT SIDES OF the stage, but they both had to go to the same destination, the conference rooms set aside for costume changes and prepping the various contestants and other stage personalities. Dominick, following Ferri, got there before the frustrated contestant did; one of the helpful volunteers told him the man had rushed off to the bathroom.

There were two public bathrooms down the hall, but the gender designations for each had been covered with paper signs reading GENDER NEUTRAL BATHROOM.

"Really?" Dominick muttered as he picked the one on the right and pushed the door open. "Ferri? You in there?"

"Go away. I'm done. I quit."

"I'll pass that on to the powers that be," Dominick said, walking in. A quick glance showed it to be the men's room. Giuliano Ferri was leaning over one of the sinks, his face and hair wet, splatters on his leather shirt. He turned his head toward the door and groaned.

"I have nothing to say," he said, shaking his head and spraying water. With both hands, he squeezed droplets from his hair and then shook again.

"That's your right," Dominick conceded. "But I still have questions. Like, what was *that* all about? You said you never met Paul Helms, but that was some staring contest you two had on stage back there before you ran off. And then there's the little issue of you saying that you and Mack hooked up outside the bar on Thursday night, but now we have some video showing the two of you actin' all lovey-dovey before coming back to the hotel. You just got reacquainted and you're hanging on him like some teen girl? Time for some truth here, Ferri. Come on, 'fess up. You were in contact with Steel before this weekend. *And* you got something going on about Paul. Did you have some kinda freaky threeway with him and Steel that night?"

"No," the man said, reaching for paper towels to wipe his face and shirtfront. "I mean...no, we didn't have a threeway. I told you, Mack texted Paul and told him to stay away."

"All night?"

"How the hell would I know? Maybe."

"And you were okay with that? A man sends away his boyfriend—his domestic partner—and you stick around for play-time? That didn't feel weird to you? You were just fine being a little fling for one night?"

"Sure! I mean...it was fine. I wanted to hook-up, even if it was just for one night. *He* was the one saying we should get back together!"

"Yeah? Even though his partner is probably out there now crying his eyes out? You don't feel even a little guilty?"

Ferri angrily tossed the wadded up towels into the trash. "That's not my fault! Look, if Mack had kept him there, I woulda had no problem with that!"

"So, you'd let him do you, too, huh? Just like that, because Mack said so?"

"That's how it is in this community," Ferri snapped. "The master gets to pick who does what and when. It's just...what they do."

"What *they* do, but not you?"

"I got more interests than BDSM, sure. But I have the same right to be here as anyone else. Or, at least I did. I'm done with it now. This is all bullshit."

"Like the story you gave us about Mack not recognizing you in the bar? And how Mack was all in charge of the little kinky sex games with you? You were in charge, weren't you? *You* were the master."

Ferri opened his mouth in what seemed to be authentic shock. "I...no! I wasn't...I mean, this is personal! What we did has nothing to do with...anything!"

"How personal? Like, sharing underwear?"

The contestant shuddered and his shoulders collapsed. He tried to say something, but no sound came out and he wiped at the water drops on his shirt, flicking them onto the floor.

A man dressed like a World War One British aviator pushed the door open and saw them both standing there and hesitated before heading to one of the urinals.

"How about you and me go talk somewhere else?" Dominick said. "Someplace more private. And then you can tell me the truth."

"Okay. Fine," Ferri said softly. "I can explain. Let me grab my stuff and get rid of this contest crap." He unpinned the contestant badge and threw it into the trash. Dominick got the door for him knowing that this was going to settle a lot of questions.

In the aftermath of Paul's speech, the fluster and fussing of the ballroom crowd refused to settle down as people recounted what they remembered and offered genuine or feigned sympathy for him, for Giuliano Ferri, and even, occasionally, for Earl and his volunteer staff. Torn from Internet access for too long, several bloggers, tweeters, and other social media addicts ran back to hotel rooms and to the lobby to share their observations with the world. Cary Gordon listed every other drug- or alcohol-fueled speech or performance he could remember, carefully hiding the actual names and years of the events but providing just enough information for those in the know to tell whom he was writing about. Phedre Lysande stood in the hallway, breathlessly describing the chaos on stage for her vlog and then smoothly segued into a recounting of the various outfits and uniforms worn by the contestants. Her carefully arranged pompadour was falling down around her ears as her hair resumed its natural curl, but she didn't care. Her view numbers would skyrocket after tonight!

Nancy Nichols left the ballroom, fairly sure that this was no real story. No one outside this community would care who was or wasn't running for the title; no one would care that the grief-stricken lover of a murdered man behaved badly in public. It was good, juicy stuff for one of her future lifestyle stories on this population, but not news.

However, the *way* Ferri dropped the ball and left the stage—and more importantly, how Detective Delicious DeCosta left immediately after him? That had potential. Was Ferri a suspect? Did he know Paul Helms? Waiting long enough to not be on DeCosta's heels, she followed him far enough to see him go into the bathroom. That was okay. She could wait. She ducked back down the hall where she could keep an eye on the bathrooms and the comings and goings between the main ballroom doors and the green room corridor.

Earl Stemple's headset and phone earpiece were turned way down, so he could think. Their incessant beeping and clicking and buzzing showed how his carefully orchestrated evening was coming apart, with staff members unsure about what to do or where to go or whether their standing orders had been changed. Everyone wanted an executive decision on what to do next, from whether to let the contestants and judges take the rest of the evening off to what sort of music to play next to whether there should be extra safe-space rooms made available tonight for anyone traumatized by what they'd seen.

Plus, one of the featured performers canceled, saying there was too much "negative energy" at the event and she had to go; the judges were demanding to know whether Ferri was in or out; the Puppy/Pet show hosts were annoyed that the blowup on stage ruined their planned spotlight on the winner, and the staffers in the hospitality suite were upset that the Boys Jack had "stolen" a case of juice boxes and some pretzels and cookies to feed the contestants and judges who were using the green room.

It was enough to make a leatherman cry. He delegated as much as he could, but still had to make a dozen executive decisions, and quickly. Luckily, Bitsy showed up, looking literally sewn into a black leather fishtail gown, laced up the back with gold cords, her shapely calves peeking demurely while she strode confidently on three-inch heels. Above her showcased bosom, she wore a band of deep purple leather with a gold lock dangling open in the front, a nice, tantalizing invitation to the right master, if he existed.

But dressed to the nines or not, she was his best volunteer and he was thrilled to see her. She'd been the one to take action and get Paul off the stage, and she miraculously took over half the decision making with ease and her typical charm and tact.

"Get the judges another round of drinks and tell 'em to keep judging Ferri until we tell 'em otherwise! Get fresh coffee to the green room, and a lot of it, and tell the contestants they're still coming out for the final formal leather photo, so keep their damn jockstraps on! You! Text or call Master Frank and ask him if he wants to do his fancy rope/bungee thing tonight instead of Empress Snake Eater, and if he says he needs demo bottoms, tell Tufiya and Boy Bixby I'll let them off a shift of dungeon monitoring."

"Do you think we can do without two DMs?" Earl asked, signing an agreement for extra coffee and tea setups.

"Earl, do you really think all these people are gonna head to the dungeons tonight? They're all gonna be on KinkyNet busting your balls over this."

Earl closed his eyes for a moment and nodded.

"Excuse me, Slave Bitsy?" asked one of the volunteers. She turned and glared; it was useful Tom. Not bad at all for a late addition to her staff; she was beginning to like him. He looked a little nervous in his formal leather breeches, tucked into tall boots, his grey eyes appearing darker because of the silver-brimmed leather cap he wore.

"What?" she snapped.

"I was wondering…thinking…that perhaps…when you're done here…" He swallowed and shifted his shoulders back. "Maybe you'd like to dance?"

Earl glanced over at the man. Bitsy outweighed him and his leathers by a good hundred pounds, and in her heels was significantly taller as well. Fat chance, buddy, he thought, before scrolling through his phone messages.

"Dance? Do you see the chaos happening here? I got idiots running around like headless baby chickens, and I got people asking stupid questions, and I got a ton of things to do!"

Tom nodded and swallowed. "Yes. And I'm glad to help. But you *will* be done, eventually. There's only so much you can do in a night. And…I'm a good dancer."

Earl almost snorted. But to his shock, there was silence from Bitsy. He glanced up and over to her and saw her cocking her head to one side as she considered the slender little man dressed all in leather.

"Sure," she said.

The man smiled and brought a hand from behind his back. He had a corsage consisting of a single plum-colored rose, arrayed with a tiny spray of baby's breath and dark green leaves. "This is for you. I'll go check that the coffee is being set up and find out about Mr. Ferri. And then I will see you later for that dance."

Bitsy and Earl stared after him as he marched off. For a moment, surrounded by questions, comments and demands from humans in front of them and on various communication devices, they were both speechless.

Rebecca heard Paul's entire little explosion and watched the struggles to get him off the stage with some curiosity. It seemed that no one wanted to interfere with the plainly out-of-control man, even though it was best for them all if he was quietly led away. Well, dealing with the bereaved was always a challenge. Add too many drinks and an emotionally charged atmosphere and an inopportune question...

There was no denying his grief seemed legitimate, but that was no proof of innocence. She'd been at more than one crime scene where the killer was holding the body of their victim and crying their eyes out in genuine sorrow.

Was she going to get much out of him if she tried more questions? Overwrought was a state not known to support clear thinking, which could work in her favor.

From her position by the doors used by the stage crew, performers and guests, she saw Bitsy turn Paul over to the two young people named Jack, who each grabbed one arm and "helped" him out of the ballroom. Paul was still sobbing, alternating between despairing mumbles to himself and loud insistence that he could walk "just fine!"

She peered out from behind the standing screen to see the ballroom was still packed; the lighting had changed from simply illuminating the stage to the waving and bobbing colors and flashes of disco lights; she could hear a much louder than usual swell of crowd noise as very few people danced. Most were shouting over the music and probably still discussing the onstage meltdown. Across from her she could see the judges' table; all of them seemed to be there, although it was hard to tell with most of them dressed in all black, surrounded by more people in all black.

The music was anonymous and thudding, something vaguely modern without lyrics or character. As she ran her gaze around the room, she could almost think it was any dance club she'd ever been to, except for the strong smell of leather and the occasional strange silhouette, like the tall gentleman with the horns on his helmet or the woman in a kimono, and the innumerable military-style leather caps.

Also called Daddy hats, according to Joshie, which suggested that only masters or doms wore them…but what about the keys? And the colorful hankies spilling out of some people's back pockets—Rebecca had heard about a "hanky code," with the colors signifying what the wearer was into, but she didn't know what any of the colors meant.

But all the different pins? What did it all mean? What did any of this nonsense mean?

What a headache this case was. With a sigh, she turned back into the corridor. Maybe Paul could manage to answer one more question or two and then she'd go home and to sleep, and maybe tomorrow things would be clearer, or they'd have more finger-print reports or blood on one of the knives. Or maybe DeCosta was pinning Ferri to the wall right now and getting a confession. She'd gotten a couple of texts from him keeping her apprised of his movements, some clearer than others, but the last one said he was going to grab Ferri. She'd be fine with his discovering Ferri did it, fine even with losing the collar herself, if she could just put this behind her.

Collar. Cap. Something tugged at her again and she paused,

252

trying to make the connections. She was startled out of her reverie by an actual tap on her arm and almost jumped.

Trudy was standing next to her, looking a little sheepish, but pleased. She leaned in and articulated carefully, "Hi, Becca! What are you still doing here? Did you come for the party?"

"Oh. Yes, well, no. I'm still working," Rebecca said, loud enough to be heard.

"Oh, bummer! Do you need more proof? Are you looking for clues? Can I help?" She looked positively eager and for a moment, Rebecca felt confused. That was not the attitude of a woman who left her because she was going to be a cop! But then, look at her now, in some sort of fancy, femmy costume, her curly hair free, eyes dancing behind her nerdy glasses in the disco lighting.

"Actually," Rebecca said. "Can I talk to you for a few minutes and maybe ask some questions?"

"Of course! Anything for you!"

She decided the eagerness in Trudy's voice was a product of needing to shout to be heard. Rebecca led her out the back door, past contest security, who let them through, now used to Rebecca's presence. Down the hall, she could see one of the Jacks was holding a leather cap while Paul coughed and sputtered over a trash can. How attractive. Well, obviously she couldn't question him while he was tossing his cookies.

She took Trudy in the opposite direction, toward the main ballroom doors, and then down the stairs to the other floor containing conference rooms. It was quiet down there, with a sign in the middle of the hallway depicting the master schedule and a few draped tables piled high with brochures, samples, CDs, flyers and business cards. The silence alone was mood enhancing.

"I'm sorry to take you away from the party," Rebecca began.

"Oh, please, I think we just saw the highlight of the party." Trudy rolled her eyes. "They're going to be talking about this for years! Crazy fundie kills a titleholder with the other titleholder's own signature dagger, and then a contestant and the dead guy's slave both go ballistic on stage? No one's going to be thinking about who won the Pet Show or the Scarf Dance, I'll tell you that."

Rebecca shrugged. "Well, then I'm sorry to take you away from the gossip. But I can be quick, I just need a few concepts explained and then you can go back to...the ball." She was about to say 'your friends' but paused; was Trudy there with anyone? She had said she was still single.

Focus, Feldblum.

"You got it; what's unclear? Although, I have to warn you, sometimes the definitions of concepts in the scene are kind of, well, shaky."

"Let's start with the leather hat. I saw mostly men wearing them, but some women. I was told it is sometimes called a cover, or a Daddy cap? Is it only the masters who wear them?"

Trudy grinned. "According to some people, yeah, that hat or sometimes, *any* headgear is only worn by tops. But you have to understand, there's no fashion police out there checking what's on your mind or in your pants when you come into the scene, so pretty much anyone wears whatever they want to wear. You'll get some old fogies and people who seem to have protocols as their fetish saying only tops can wear the hat or only boys wear shorts, but what are they gonna do if someone shows up wearing whatever they like? Gnash their teeth and write about it online, I guess."

"Mack Steel wore one."

"Sure. And now his boy has it."

Rebecca looked at Trudy in amazement. "That's why it didn't fit," she mused.

"Yeah, and if you look at their publicity shots, Paul didn't wear one before, at least not in any I've seen. They were probably trying for the old guard image, and don't even get me started on that stuff. It's what some people imagine it was like to belong to a gay biker gang. We could be here all night talking about how controversial that is!"

"No, I don't think I'm ready to go into that." That cap should have been inventoried with the rest of Mack's effects, Rebecca thought furiously. What else did Paul keep? She'd let him remove most of his possessions after a quick glance through them; there was no blood or mysterious tears on anything. In fact, most of it was still packed in a suitcase; he said he hadn't had the time to fully unpack yet.

Trudy giggled suddenly. "You think Paul killed him for his Daddy cap?"

"How about another question? I've seen Paul in two different collars, chain and leather. But there's a lock on the collar. That means he has the key. Is that odd?"

"Oh, hell no. I mean, these days they practically strip-search you at airports. I know a ton of bottoms who hold the keys to their collars so they can take them off when they go to work."

"And is there any significance to whether it's chain or leather?"

Trudy shook her head. "No, it's all style or fashion. Some people think a chain the bottom can't unlock is more committed, but come on. Just because you can take a wedding ring off doesn't mean a marriage doesn't exist. And how many people get tattoos with someone's name and then break up anyway? It's all symbolism. One of the judges is this woman Mickey Abraham. She wrote this great paper about semiotics in the scene. It's really dense in some spots, but pretty complete in discussing how symbolism works and shifts among the kinksters. I guess you don't have time to read up on it, though."

"No, not really." Rebecca sifted through a dozen other things she wanted to ask, and started discarding questions that were more about her curiosity. Then she remembered a cryptic text from Dominick; he'd sent her a note that read "Panties = not manly?"

"The whole leatherman image is about masculinity, right?"

"Sure. I mean, of course there are leatherwomen, too—and they can take on that whole look of chaps and vest and jacket. And some even take on masculine titles and roles—I have a couple of friends who are into Daddy/boy play. Any kinky dyke might call herself a leatherwoman; I have, even though it's not the leather that turns me on, per se. But then, there are also some leatherwomen who take all that and turn it over and embrace a more feminine image—I mean, look at Ravenfyre; she's a high femme if you ever saw one. All her leather is girly. I don't know if I've ever even seen her in pants."

Pondering how to inquire about the panties without mentioning them, Rebecca carefully asked, "Is there any reason why a leatherman might wear or play with women's clothing?"

Trudy thought about that for a moment. "Well…I guess for humiliation play. Make his boy wear a dress? Although I've never seen that, anywhere. Of course lots of guys will do drag once in a while, but I don't know I've seen much of that in a leather context either. Usually the two don't mix, except drag queens do entertainment at leather things. And, at a drag ball you'll see guys in full leather escorting the drag queens. Honestly, most of those guys seem to be playing dress up, too. Drag balls are just another planet!"

Rebecca couldn't help but laugh. After a moment, Trudy laughed too.

"Right, like who am I to talk? Considering the party I just walked out of and how I'm dressed."

Rebecca took in Trudy's whole outfit. The shiny black skirt consisted of layers of black chiffon and satin, and the green brocade corset was embroidered with a subtle diamond pattern. Her skin was pale and soft under the hall lighting, and her shorter hair showed off her pretty throat and narrow but strong shoulders. "You look very…nice," Rebecca said hesitantly.

"Thank you!" Trudy beamed and whirled around once, making the skirt flare. "I got this last year and this is the first opportunity I had to wear it. To think I used to not even like skirts!"

"It looks good on you."

"Thanks! You look pretty good yourself."

They looked at each other for another long moment, and then Rebecca cleared her throat and gathered her thoughts. "Okay... so doing *drag* isn't necessarily forbidden in the leather or BDSM culture."

"No...but drag is a different identity. Like Chava, she's another judge? In boy drag his name is Alan; he's very nice. Chava's a bit of a bitch. Anyway. The fact that there's a drag queen on the panel is very old fashioned. These days, you'll rarely find a bar where drag and leather both hang out, and the guys who do both generally don't take one to visit the other. Usually. Remember what I said about concepts being kind of fuzzy? Personally, I think most people don't care; hey, we're all queer, we're all kinky one way or another. Probably half the guys here have done drag at least once. But if you find a guy in a dress *here*, he's more likely to be straight than gay, and probably a sub, too. Maybe that's why gay guys don't do drag at kinky events, actually! To avoid being mistaken for a straight, submissive cross-dresser." She considered this, chewing absently on her bottom lip and nodding. "Never thought of it that way! Well, it's like what Mr. Rubber said on stage tonight: we need to all just stick together, especially when there are assholes like those protesting outside and the guy you arrested."

Rebecca nodded, although she wasn't sure about what anyone said on stage; maybe she missed a speech about everyone getting along? "You think most people wouldn't care if a gay leatherman did drag. But what about using women's clothes for...sexual play? Not just to perform. Would anyone care about that? Or might someone into that...want to hide it?"

"Hey, when a lot of your image is invested in masculinity, some-

257

times you don't want people to know you also like to, I dunno, crochet or bake cookies. Doing drag or cross-dressing might seem counter to what it means to be a man, even among guys who should know better. There are macho jerks everywhere, after all. And just think of all those homophobes who they keep catching picking up guys in bars and bathrooms, right? They're all hating on the queers until we find out they've been getting it on the side for years from other guys. But they hide it with all their manly posturing." Trudy rolled her eyes. "It's getting so the more some guy on TV talks about how gays are disgusting, you should start a countdown until they find him on his knees behind a glory hole." Her eyes widened. "Was Woody really one of those? Did he meet Mack to have sex? Was he a secret crossdresser, too?"

"No, no," Rebecca said quickly. "There's no evidence of that at all. But...thank you. Those were things I needed to know."

Trudy beamed again, flashing her teeth. "Excellent. I'm glad! I'd be happy to tell you anything you want to know, or find someone who knows more, if you need it. Here, let me give you my number." She sorted through one of the swag tables and found a pen from a lube company and wrote a number on the back of a flyer for an event called Fists of Fury: Erotic Boxing. Rebecca fumbled for a moment and handed Trudy one of her cards. Their fingers met as they made the exchange, and they acknowledged this by looking away at the same time.

"I have to find my partner and call it a night," Rebecca said.

"Yeah, I might turn in early myself. Long day tomorrow, with the contest and all that. Will you be back here for it?"

"Maybe. Probably. Not for the contest specifically. But there might be more to look at here, a few more interviews."

"I hope I see you." Trudy smiled and swirled her skirt again. "I really do. You should wear your uniform."

And to that, Rebecca found she had no answer. Her uniform, which Trudy once called an emblem of oppression? She smiled a little awkwardly and they walked back up the stairs to the main ballroom area. Just as she was lost in the thought of how the green in the corset picked up the green in Trudy's eyes, Trudy stopped, turned around and kissed her on the side of her mouth. Then, she leaned in forward and whispered, "You could bring your hand-cuffs, too. Are you seeing anyone these days?"

And with a giggle and a wink, Trudy lifted the front of her skirt a little and swept her way back to the ballroom. Rebecca stood stock still for a moment, smelling the faint, flowery scent of Trudy's perfume and feeling heat on the spot at the edge of her mouth. It took her several minutes to organize her thoughts enough to go looking for Dominick, especially since what she really wanted to do was chase after her ex-girlfriend.

CHAPTER 28

"Tell me about the underwear," Dominick said, sliding his hip onto one of the tables in the empty conference room.

Giuliano Ferri was sprawled in a chair, looking uncomfortable in his leather outfit. He wrestled with his sash and pulled it over his head, knocking his hat off, then tossed the sash onto the floor.

"I don't understand what it has to do with anything!" He kicked the hat away from him and unsnapped the top snaps on his shirt.

"And yet I'm asking. Tell me about the frilly yellow panties."

The former contestant sighed and lowered his head almost between his knees with a groan. "Okay, okay. They were his."

Dominick was glad the man wasn't looking at him, because he was completely surprised. They were Steel's?

"Uh-huh," he said. "Do go on."

"They were from years ago, back when we were...friends. And I kept them as sort of a...souvenir. Kinda. So, when I knew I was going to see him again, I brought them like a gag."

"A gag...for his mouth?" Damn, I'm gonna owe that reporter dinner or something, Dominick thought. But Ferri looked up with an annoyed expression.

"No, I mean, like a joke! Like, ha-ha, see what we were doing when we were young and stupid."

"Uh-huh. So, why don't you start back then for me. You were young and stupid and boosting beers and hustling on the side..."

"Aw, it wasn't any big deal. We never even spent the night in custody, it was all desk tickets and harassment." He flushed anyway, and took a deep breath. "Anyway, we also did a little dancing at the bars and clubs when we could get the gigs. I mean, we weren't that good. But tips were tips, and a bunch of horny guys throwing money at you inside a building sure beat checking out some asshole in a car or a minivan and hoping he wasn't dangerous. But I didn't know what I was doing; I was fresh meat when we met. He taught me how to wrangle a date; he hooked me up with condoms and told me where to go to find the right kinds of guys. So, when he said, come on, let's do drag, I went and got myself panties."

He leaned back in the chair and laughed, shaking his head. "I mean, how stupid could a guy get? I didn't know you didn't, you know, get *all* dressed in girl clothes. So, I show up the first time and I got these little undies on and he laughs and laughs..."

"You're not supposed to wear them?" Dominick asked, confused now.

"No; we weren't, you know, trannies or anything. We were doing *drag*. You wear a really tight jock, or special underwear that sort of hides your junk. I mean some of that looks like girl panties, but I just grabbed this frilly pair I found at some dollar store. Man, he laughed so hard I got angry! So I told him, man, I'm gonna score more tips than you, and I wore 'em anyway." He smiled a little, remembering. "And I did, too. So after that, he started wearing them, too. Some of the guys really liked it; hell, I had mine bought right off my ass once or twice. The manager of the bar that used to hire me liked my drag name better, too. I was Julie Box—like jewelry box? Al…Mack…called me JB."

Dominick wasn't sure what any of this had to do with anything, but the man was talking. He would steer him to the present day. "When—and how—did you guys reconnect?"

Ferri nodded and pushed himself up in the chair. "A couple months ago. I was looking at this hookup site and there he was. I recognized him right away, even though when we was kids, he was skinny like I used to be, and he didn't have no mustache. And he had this porno name now, Mack Steel, and I just laughed. So, I wrote to him and he told me all about how he was all big into the leather scene now and how hot it was with guys wanting to, um, get with him. All his fans. And so, I kind of looked into it; it's not like I stuck with drag. I can dance a little, but that whole lip-synching and all the work you have to do to make up acts…that was just too much.

"I went to this leather bar a few times, and the scene was sort of hot, so I got a vest and some chaps and a whip and started fooling around with guys. And meanwhile he was, like, coaching me, like he did back in the day, only with email and sometimes I'd call him. It just felt right. I started sending him pics, he sent me some…"

"Wait, wait. We have someone looking through his email, I didn't see anything that sounded like this in it."

"I didn't use his *public* email! I used the account he uses for tricking and stuff. We were actually sending messages to each other at the bar! That's how he told me when he was leaving."

Dominick felt his stomach tighten. Damn! Another email account? And there they were going through all his other avenues of social media, web pages and discussion boards and Twitter feeds and KinkyNet…what else were they missing?

"Can I get the email address you used for him? And yours, so I can check out your story?" he asked, trying to sound casual. "I want to make sure we're covering all the bases."

"Well...look." Ferri leaned forward again with a sigh, bracing his hands on his knees. "I don't care that you know I was cheating with the contest and all that, it was gonna come out anyway. But...I get the feeling now...maybe Mack *didn't* want his boy to know about some things."

"Really." Dominick kept his face neutral. "That's not what you said before. And Paul told us he wasn't jealous, that Mack only hooked up for a night and that was it."

"He ought to know, I guess. Maybe I'm wrong. It wouldn't be the first time, know what I mean? But Mack kind of suggested that there might be more for us. To me, at least. And I thought he worked it out with his boy and all that, but you made me, you know. Kinda curious about it. Maybe he wasn't that clear?"

"So, you had an online flirtation with Mack for a few months before this contest?"

"Yeah. He was the one who told me to enter Mr. Newark Leather. Shit, easiest thing I ever did. Put on the right clothes, sneer and strut, say the right things and boom, you're in. I think he had this idea that I'd win this, then next year we'd enter his boy or someone else who hooked up with us, and sort of take over the contest? And then we'd be on easy street—make money putting on leather and sex shows and party and travel and screw around and have guys just licking the floor to get to know us." He got a faraway look in his eyes and then looked sad. "It sure sounded sweet. I didn't know if it was ever gonna happen, but I thought just seeing him and getting with him one more time would be hot. So, I brought the panties and some other stuff for a laugh, and he did laugh! And then we messed around, had great sex. Used all his condoms." He smirked.

Dominick looked skeptical. "You were barely there an hour by your admission."

"Hey, he only had a couple, and we did a lot. We were always, waddayoucallit, versatile! I told him I'd bring more than one next time."

"And did he wear the panties? That night?"

Ferri looked shocked and then offended. "Hell, no! You think we pranced around like faggots wearing girl clothes? Just because you do drag doesn't mean you get all into cross-dressing for the kinky parts."

Dominick raised an eyebrow. "I did not say that or use that word."

"Hmph." Ferri subsided a little. "No. He didn't and I didn't. He said he hadn't done drag in years, anyway, not since he became Mack Steel, Secret Agent Freakin' Leatherman. I laughed at him; said what the hell, I still do drag sometimes, for parties, just for fun. It don't bother me or anyone around here. So he says, Mr. Global Leather don't do drag. But when he steps down, he can do whatever he wants. Whatever. I just brought them, like I said, for old times. To make him laugh. Because...I still had them, you know?"

"Sounds like you were serious about him. Like maybe you wanted more than just a one-night fling. And maybe once he did his thing with you, he was gonna shove you off. That could be a hell of a reason to get real mad with him."

Ferri met the detective's eyes and shook his head. "Mack was the first guy I really loved. He could be a giant douchebag, yeah. He was all ego and testosterone and not too big on long-term plans. But I...loved him anyway. Since him, there ain't been a single other guy I wanted as much. If he said, wow, that was hot, see you next year, I woulda been happy. If he said come back to San Francisco with me, I woulda packed on Monday."

"And where would Paul fit in with that? Did you get the feeling Mack told him about the good old days with you?"

"I dunno. I didn't ask. But honestly, I guess I didn't care. Mack was never what you'd call a one-man man." He raked a hand through his hair, looking a little defiant. "I figured we'd work things out. But okay. It was kinda weird that he wanted to make sure his boy didn't see us together. When he showed up on stage tonight, man, I just couldn't deal. Like, what does any of this matter, now that Mack's dead? But I felt kinda bad anyway."

"And when you left his room, you didn't go back at all that night?"

"No. I got back to my room, watched a little TV and conked out. I had to wake up in time to get to the gym and have breakfast with the other contestants and do all that crap. And then we found out he was dead." The two men sat in silence for a moment while Dominick thought about what he'd learned.

"You think...Paul killed him? Not that nutcase from the TV?"

Dominick shook his head. "As far as I'm concerned, *you're* not totally in the clear, Mr. Ferri. Seems that every time we go back to you, you got a different story. What else are you hiding?"

"Nothing! Now you know everything!"

"Can we have the clothes you wore that night? To test them for blood?" They didn't have a warrant, but he could always ask.

Ferri nodded and started popping the rest of the snaps on his shirt. "You can have all of it. I am *done* with this leather crap."

Dominick held up one hand. "Let's get you your street clothes first. Are you planning on checking out tonight?"

"I...I dunno. I didn't think that far yet. I guess I could. Nah, why bother? It's late, and a long train ride home. I'll check out tomorrow, the room's paid for. Besides—you know where to find me. Back in Jersey, where people aren't crazy with all this contest crap."

The two detectives met in the lobby, past the still crowded bar and social areas. Rebecca had the bag with the T-shirt; Dominick had several plastic bags stuffed with a steer's worth of black leather clothing.

"These guys bring enough costume changes to go on a week-long freak vacation," he said, hefting them. "I'll get these to the station for the lab to pick up. I got more information, and some theories, but man, I am beat and you look about ready to fall over yourself."

Rebecca nodded with a weary expression. "Take this too— it's an extra shirt from Wolfboy's little party. There's a strange chemical smell on it; I think it might have been washed in something strong, so who knows if it might be useful. I'll be going to the station in the morning; I want to go through some of the transcripts and inventories. Did you find out anything about the panties?"

"Yeah, I got the whole story on that. I'll send you a copy when I write it up. If he was telling the truth, we got a whole new twist to this crazy case. And I'm gonna chase down a new email account Ferri gave me and see what else Steel was hiding. What about Helms?"

"Sick as a dog and barely able to walk. So, I'll be back here at some time tomorrow. Listen, if you're due a day off, you can take it. Unless the lab geeks come up with something new and definitive, it's going to be 'he said/he said' for a while. I'm thinking this will not resolve before these people start heading for the hills."

"No, we *got* this, I just feel it. Let's meet tomorrow, after some sleep. I'll bring my revised notes, and we can make sure we got it all covered." He noticed a slight, pink smudge on her cheek and coughed. "And, uh…I'll see you tomorrow, then. I'll try not to call before nine." He left quickly, taking long strides.

Later, her bathroom mirror showed her what Dominick had seen, and she groaned before wiping the lipstick off. But when she collapsed into her welcoming bed, the image in her mind was of Trudy, asking to be handcuffed. And she could hear the clicks of the ratcheting mechanism as she ran the cuff open in one hand…

It took a while to fall asleep.

CHAPTER 29

MISTRESS RAVENFYRE PROPPED HER FEET UP ON A CHAIR and allowed one of her submissive fans to rub them; the classic patent leather four-inch lace-up boots were beautiful and showed her legs to their best advantage, but they were barely made for wearing, let alone standing and dancing. She kept back a deep, loud groan of pleasure, allowing a gentle sigh to escape instead. Now that the music had switched from techno-dance to some sort of Afro-Cuban mix, it seemed the sound level and number of dancers had both decreased. The buzz of conversation never ceased, even as tides of people came in and out in order to see one of the performances or get introductions to lesser title winners.

The animal play community had managed to gather quite the cheering section for their Pet of the Year award, despite the distraction of the Helms Eulogy. Personally, Wendi Schneider couldn't have imagined a better farewell to that prick if she tried. A drunken rant by an unhinged submissive seemed the *perfect* way to remember the man who ruined her title year and cost her a job. Now that there'd be much less money coming in from appearances, she really needed to sell her brand to the community to keep up any sort of income.

She looked around the room and didn't spot Dr. Abraham. Damn the snotty, bitter little egghead anyway! Sitting there snarking for days about the contestants, the other judges, everything in the scene! Why anyone cared what she thought was a mystery. So she'd written a few books—no one read them! She didn't write things that regular people could enjoy and understand, let alone afford. Not like her own essays and speeches, which always got a ton of "likes" whenever she posted them.

Dick came up next to her. "Ready to go, hon? I checked, and we're all done for the night."

"Thank God. Okay, Stefan, that's enough. Thank you so very much, that was exactly what I wanted." She waved a gracious hand at the man, who looked up and nodded with a blush. She bent down to pick up her boots and decided not to put them back on. Screw her image. No one would care tonight.

"Where's Willow?" she asked Dick, as he gave her an arm.

He frowned. "I thought you dismissed her."

She stared back at him. "She said *you* told her to take a break earlier."

"I did, about an hour ago! I didn't say she wasn't supposed to come back."

Wendi shook her head. More annoyances! What had gotten into that slave all of a sudden? First, she couldn't remember how many knives she'd packed, making them look foolish when the police asked about them; she kept vanishing during what should have been short errands; then she'd gone monosyllabic several times when questioned about what was wrong. And Dick had said something about the police discovering Willow had sent text messages or something to Mack before he died, making them all look even more suspicious, if not just showing what poor slave owners they were. It was like she saved some dysfunctions *just* for this last weekend for Mistress Ravenfyre to look like the zenith of dominance and the leather/BDSM lifestyle! Good thing this wasn't a relationship title. Not that she could recall the last time they played much; perhaps she would schedule a nice, elaborate play night when they all got home. Even a lifestyle slave had some needs, she supposed. Beyond the need to serve and all that.

But when they got back to their room and Willow wasn't there either, Wendi and Dick both checked their cell phones for any messages. Nothing. Wendi called her and got bumped right to voicemail. That was worrisome.

Wendi sighed, slid her feet back into her boots and they went back down to the ballroom, where they questioned security staff and mutual friends, but no one had seen Willow in some time.

"Oh, my God," Wendi said gazing at Dick in horror. "Oh, my God, what if another of those maniacs has her? Where could she be?"

"Maybe she just went out for…something to eat," Dick offered.

"Did you check the dungeons?" suggested a leatherdyke wearing a security badge.

"She wouldn't go to the dungeon without us!"

The security volunteer shrugged. "Maybe she just went to watch. Do you want me to radio around for people to look for her?"

Wendi and Dick looked at each other and shook their heads. "We'll keep looking," Wendi said. They went straight to the dungeon space.

The floor above the main ballroom had several conference rooms that could be divided up into different configurations. During the day, some were sectioned off for classes in physical techniques and others remained open for casual playdates. But at night, the center rooms were opened up for the mixed-gender space, and the two end rooms labeled for men or women only. The couple went into the larger playroom and walked the perimeter, looking through the various knots of voyeurs and those waiting for the special equipment, like frames strong enough for suspension. They skirted hazards like beginners with long whips and piles of toy bags shoved up against posts or piled around the tables of water and safe-sex supplies. No sign of her, although there was a crowd watching four or five of those people in furry costumes rubbing up against each other and spanking big paws over furry asses and thighs. "Damn, it's gonna be a *fur pile* soon," one of the spectators said, as the couple passed.

"Okay, we'll go back to the room and try calling her again," Dick said. "Was there a pool party tonight? Maybe she went to that?"

Wendi nodded absently, wondering what a fur pile was. They skirted a knot of Zodians doing a whipping scene with their girls, a muscular leather daddy type putting his boy over his knee, and a couple of women testing the structural integrity of a bondage frame, and then something tugged Wendi's thoughts away from furries and their culture. She paused to look at the two women gently rocking the heavy wooden frame and tapped one manicured nail against her upper lip.

"Hon? I'm going to check the women's space."

Dick waited politely outside the door while Wendi poked her head in. An old Sinéad O'Connor song was playing, and the lighting was made deliberately lower than the main play space. Against one wall, a woman in leather pants and a sports bra was doing a slow, teasing warm up with a large, puffy looking flogger; the woman she was beating was tied to a frame, twisting her body and moaning as the thick bundle of tresses delicately fell across her back. Three women were conferring in a corner, one on her knees, the other two caressing her while they spoke in low tones. And across from the door was a sling; it was in use. Wendi could see two feet in the stirrups and the back of a short woman standing between the spread legs of the occupant. She almost backed out of the room immediately but then heard a very familiar series of gasps and cries of "Oh, yeah, oh yeah, oh yeah!"

"Willow!" she cried out, pulling the door open so wide it slammed against the wall.

Dr. Mickey Abraham looked backward over her shoulder and raised an eyebrow. "Ravenfyre!" she exclaimed.

"Mistress?" gasped Willow, lifting her head from the sling pillow.

"Wendi?" called Dick from outside the door.

"Rocky!" quoted one of the leatherdykes from the trio in negotiation. "Dr. Scott!" cried the other. They started giggling, the bottom between them covering her own mouth. The woman with the flogger turned around to issue a stern "Shh!"

"Well," said Mickey, pulling a glove off one hand with a snapping sound. "Isn't *this* awkward?"

Downstairs, in the ballroom, Boi Jack and Bitsy both got security alerts. Boi Jack groaned and considered ignoring hers. The judges had been dismissed, all of the special guests and performers were done for the night, and her responsibilities should have been finished. She hadn't seen Skylar since day one, but they had texted back and forth about possibly hooking up tonight after the dance. Her leather brother Jack was already on his date with his longtime fuckbuddy. Why hadn't she turned in her headset and declared herself off duty? She toggled the talk switch with ill will and barked, "What?"

"It's Ravenfyre! And Master Dick and Mickey Abraham and slave Willow!"

"What about 'em?" Jack asked wearily.

"They're, like, all up in each other's faces! What do we do? Should I call Earl?" In the background, past the static of the radio, Jack could hear what did indeed sound like a melee.

"I'm coming," she said, pushing herself to her feet.

271

On the dance floor, Bitsy discovered that Tom was an *excellent* dancer and knew how to salsa. He brought her close after a turn into a secure hold, looking up into her eyes, and led her into another turn. She liked the way his hips moved. She also liked how he didn't seem hesitant about touching and leading her; in fact, he was downright...dominant. The man knew how to lead a dance, that was for sure. It was just so easy and natural to follow and enjoy the rhythm of the music and the alternating moments of intimacy and freedom that came in the seductive dance. She was glad she switched her glasses for contact lenses tonight and that she'd spent a little extra time on her hair earlier.

"You are the most beautiful woman I've ever seen," said Tom, as he pulled her into a clutch before leading her out again.

She kept dancing with him while her radio and cell phone sat on a table, buzzing and blinking away.

The corridor outside the playrooms was now packed with people shouting and trying to shush each other and volunteers desperately attempting to keep the hallway clear and not disturb the people still playing. Just as Boi Jack skidded to a halt outside the knot of people surrounding the Ravenfyre family and the academic contest judge, one of the off duty police officers stepped between the combatants and gave a short and harsh, "Quiddit!"

"My God, Willow, how could you?" Mistress Ravenfyre raged.

Willow showed her teeth nervously, wrapped a large towel tighter around her half-naked body and tried to hide behind Dr. Abraham, a failed attempt since the professor was smaller.

"What, did you specifically instruct her *not* to get herself shagged?" Mickey asked, seemingly unperturbed by the confrontation. A bottle of lube poked out of one of her vest pockets; another glove dangled from the other. "Because you know, many so-called dominants fail to successfully communicate their preferences and commands to their submissives, leading to *tragic* misunderstandings. Hey you know what? Westfield's a life coach, maybe you should book a few sessions with him. You'll be, ah, *okay*, in no time!"

"You bitch!" Ravenfyre spat at her.

"Hey, now, I told you all to pipe down," said the police officer.

"Don't you call her a bitch!" shrieked Willow. "She's a better dom than you are!"

Mickey Abraham pursed her lips and half covered her mouth, completely failing to hide a smirk. "Oh, now, honeybunch, maybe this isn't the time or place to discuss the failings of your owners…"

"They're *not* my owners! They just say that when all I ever do is clean their house and run their errands, and they don't even play with me! Ever!" Willow stamped one bare foot against the carpet in the hallway and pointed at Dick. "He hasn't even done *anything* with me since our third playdate, and even though he calls himself a master, he's really a bottom!"

"I'm shocked. You don't say. Oh, my goodness," Mickey intoned solemnly.

"Willow!" said Dick, holding his hands up as though warding off a blow. "What are you doing? What are you saying? What has she done to you?"

"Got me off, which is more than *you* ever did!" Behind her, the women who had come out of the women-only playspace started cheering.

"You go, girl," said the woman with the flogger.

"How dare you?" Ravenfyre said, drawing herself up. "We collared you! Gave your life structure! We took you into our home!"

"And took me for a ride! All year, dragging me around to look good for you, but did you play with me at all? Like, ever? No!"

Willow looked around, seeing a few nods and a lot of eyes on the scene. "No!" she repeated. "All you did was tell me what I did wrong and promise me more play later and later and later, and then you'd forget, or say I didn't earn it, and *he* couldn't even get it *up* any more!"

"Ooh," chorused some of the spectators. One or two dashed back into the dungeons and brought back friends. The crowd in the hallway grew enough to slow the attempts of newcomers to get through the doors.

"That's cold," commented the police officer, trying not to grin. His shoulders were shaking. "Day-umn!"

Willow looked at him and nodded passionately. "Cold like my bed, on the floor! And, and they wouldn't even let me have a *vibrator*! And meanwhile I'm doing *everything* for them, including writing half of *her* columns for KinkyNet!"

Ravenfyre paled. Mickey laughed. "I've heard of ghostwriters, but this is the first time I've met a *slave* writer; were you planning to even mention her in the dedication, Ravenfyre?"

"What the hell is going on out here?" thundered Lord Laertes, coming out of the mixed gender space. He had removed his shirt and was wearing his furry vest and medallion over his bare, hairy chest. He was a little sweaty, holding a thick, heavy whip in one hand. Behind him were some more Zodians, including his petite wife, who was wearing nothing but a sheet and looking very annoyed.

"There is nothing going on; these people were just about to head out of here, weren't they?" said the police officer. Boi Jack finally got through the ring of people around the combatants.

"Yeah, what a great idea, let's all just go back to our rooms, it's late," she said. "Come on, Mistress Ravenfyre, Master Dick, I'm sure we can all work this out tomorrow..."

"Seriously?" the cop asked. "Your name is *Master Dick*?"

"Oh, hey, Wendifyre, maybe you should take the advice

from your column on, what did you call it? Complete Surrender of Power? And call upon Willow's slave soul to answer to your dominant heart. Or, was it pancreas? I suck at gross anatomy; so many of the internal organs look similar. I do, however, know a vagina from a vulva, something you frequently confuse in your own writing—or did Willow write those columns, too?" Mickey half turned toward Willow. "Perhaps *you* should write a book."

"You mean like the books you wrote, Dr. Abraham? The books you don't want anyone to know about?" Dick snarled. "You want to talk about bad writing? Then let the world know that *you* wrote the goddamn Zod books!"

For a moment, there was a startled silence. Mickey pursed her lips tightly and covered her mouth with one hand. Ravenfyre stood stock still, her hand raised as if to stop her husband; Willow turned to look at Mickey in amazement.

"Wha-what?" asked Lord Laertes, his eyes wide in horror. "What? *Her*? She wrote *our* books?"

Mickey shook her head and then started laughing. After a moment, she looked up at the shocked crowd around her and shrugged.

"Busted!"

The hallway erupted in fresh bedlam.

Downstairs, Bitsy and Tom were rocking together, moving sensuously to the Moroccan music mix the deejay had switched to. When the music segued into another selection, Tom took both Bitsy's hands in his and said, earnestly, "You are an enchanting woman. I would love to get to know you better. If you find me at all interesting, I know you'll need to check me out with your friends in the scene. And then I'd love to have some long, delicious conversations about what you like and what you're curious about and to tell you anything you'd like to know about me. I would love to earn your trust, and maybe your respect. And see where that might go."

Bitsy looked into his eyes and tightened her hands in his. "I just want to know one thing, Tom."

"What's that?" He smiled up at her.

"Instead of going to yours, do you want to come back to my room? I have a Jacuzzi suite."

He blinked, opened and shut his mouth and then nodded firmly. "I'd love to. Let's go get my toy bag."

Bitsy gathered her communication devices, turned her cell phone off without checking messages and handed her radio to the head of the overnight volunteer staff, who had been trying to figure out what the hell was happening on the dungeon floor and what he should do about it.

"I might be late tomorrow!" she called over her shoulder, as Tom took her arm.

"But...Bitsy! There's some kind of fight..."

"She's off duty right now," Tom said. "I'm sure you all can handle something without her for one night. Tonight, she's mine."

"Oh, yes sir," Bitsy purred.

CHAPTER 30

MACK STEEL USED THE SAME PASSWORD FOR HIS SECONDARY email address as he did for the primary—ASSword1.

He was not a creative man. Nor a very literate one, even allowing for online message styles. But "dog" did not even begin to describe his sexual adventures. The man wasn't just an occasional chaser of erotic opportunities; he was practically a sexual athlete.

"Good God Almighty," Dominick muttered as he added another hash mark to his tally. "That's sixteen...dates...he had in the last month! How the hell did he find the time?"

"I doubt they were dates in any social sense of the word," Rebecca said, shuffling through printed reports.

"Got that right," Dominick said. "And on top, he's romancin' Ferri from California and planning to meet him here and maybe bring him back. Or not. I'm not seeing anything that promises more than hooking up here and coaching him on how to win."

"Maybe Ferri was reading between the lines."

"Maybe he was imagining the whole thing, and when he found out the truth..." Dominick made a stabbing motion.

"Here it is!" Rebecca produced the full list of clothing items taken from Steel's room. She started putting marks next to certain items.

Dominick looked up and rotated his head to crack his stiff neck. Since he was only here temporarily, he didn't even have a desk assigned to him. Rather than use Grant's desk, which was across the room, he had plugged in his own little notebook computer across the desk from her, so they could share the printed records of the case back and forth.

"What are you looking for? We know his boyfriend took the hat. But nothing else would fit him, right? Steel was a much bigger guy."

Rebecca nodded. "I'm looking for the clothing Joshie saw in the hallway. Leather pants and jacket...I see we picked up chaps, and I see blue jeans...no cap, no jacket, no pants. There's a rubber T-shirt, but no leather shirt." She tapped the back of her pen against the side of her monitor.

"What are you thinking, the killer took the victim's own clothes? Ferri could have worn them; his legs are about the same length. The shirt might have been a little loose on him; he doesn't have the shoulders and chest Steel did. In fact, he could have worn that T-shirt. It would have been tight, but a lot of these people dress in tight clothes. But the thing is, we got a picture of him in his own leather suit coming *up* to the room."

Rebecca rocked back in her chair, making the springs creak. "Let's say you killed someone while you were dressed in jeans and a T-shirt. Blood gets all over you. You need to be able to walk out of there, so you grab what clothing fits you and put it over your own. Clothing that makes you anonymous in that setting. Later on, you ditch it, after you've gotten cleaned off."

Dominick shook his head. "Then we'd have *two* sets of missing clothing."

"Well, maybe the killer wore very little." Rebecca clicked

around and pointed at her screen. "Like maybe just tiny little shorts and some kind of straps across the chest. To hide any splatter, just wipe off the blood with a washcloth, then cover everything with a leather shirt, pants, a jacket, anything that lets you blend in. Pocket the washcloth and walk away."

Dominick leaned forward and pulled the computer screen so he could see the picture. It was a shot of Paul Helms and Mack together, at the Shaft. Mack was in an outfit that could be described perfectly as leather pants, shirt and jacket, and Paul seemed barely dressed in tight little shorts and a harness.

"You said Paul turned up at Wolfboy's party in...street clothes?"

They compared notes. Paul Helms took a cab with Wolfboy from the bar, wearing a T-shirt and jeans; Wolfboy didn't remember a bag, but couldn't swear there *hadn't* been one, either. At some time during the night, Paul had been wearing nothing but his leather shorts—"The kind without real pockets, you could really see his, uh, body," Wolfboy recalled. And at some point, Paul was naked—after his shower, before bed, and then as they slept late in the morning, everyone pretty much got into street-legal clothing to run back to their regular rooms or to start their day of classes, workshops and vending.

"No leather pants or jacket in there," said Dominick. "But you say Wolfboy found an extra T-shirt...what, do you think Paul ditched his shirt in the room? Why? Because it was bloody?"

"Let's say it was bloody. Because look—the shirt Wolfboy had was size small. When I saw Paul for the first time, he was wearing skin tight jeans and a *baggy* contest T-shirt." She looked up at Dominick.

"So, he grabbed the wrong T-shirt; Wolfboy said that happened a lot."

"There's more. When I met Paul, he was also wearing a *chain* collar." She tapped the image on her computer screen again. In it,

Paul was clearly wearing a thin leather collar.

"But maybe is was all some kinda freak code or something? Like, dog chain at the hotel and leather at the bar?"

Rebecca sighed. "You don't like Paul for this?"

"No, I like him fine. He sure had some words to say about how *manly* Mack was and how he wasn't no girl and stuff like that; that sounds to me like he might have been a little sensitive about the whole panties thing. And I know we got no other evidence to say so, but the boot people said they thought he was jealous and there was trouble between him and Mack. And I sure don't like this whole hidden email account Mack had. But we got no proof Paul ever returned to the room that night, and we still got no bloody clothes anywhere. And it's possible the killer just took the clothes as a trophy or something. Kill the man, take his leather." He paused, and then shuffled through his notes. "You know…Paul was wearing a leather collar on Friday night. But…it was much bigger than that one in the picture. How many collars does a dude need, anyway?"

"As you said, maybe it's a code of some kind. As far as I discovered, there is no special distinction between whether a collar is made of one material or another, just a fashion choice. So, we got nothing clear on that. And no more lab reports until tomorrow at best." Rebecca brought breakfast this morning. She opened a paper bag and offered Dominick a bagel and a plastic knife. He considered the choice and made a happy exclamation when he found the bialy.

"Unless you were saving it?" he asked.

"No, you can have it. Where did a Southern gentleman find out about bialys?" She grabbed an everything bagel for herself.

"Virginia," he said, poking around to find butter. "Quantico. Long story, but there was a guy I knew there, terrorism expert from up here. He used to fly down with a couple dozen of these every once in a while."

"You have hidden depths, Detective. You have FBI contacts? You got anti-terrorism training?"

"Dom. Or, Dominick, since I think I will *never* ask someone to call me Dom again, ever." He rolled his eyes. "And I took a few trainings, yeah. Nothing special."

"Right. Well, I think we have to assume any bloody clothing has been removed from the hotel, except for this T-shirt, which smells kind of funky, like it was rinsed in bleach, even though it's black."

"Bleach? Where do you get bleach in a hotel? Housekeeping?"

"No, I checked; they use nonbleach cleansers on their carts. The laundry all goes out; the only machines they have in-house are for small items, and guests don't have access."

The two of them sat in silence and nibbled on their breakfast, sipping coffee. Rebecca pondered where to bring a whole outfit made of leather. She'd had the vendor space and the green room and the hospitality suite all checked for abandoned bags and extra outfits and nothing had turned up. But the entire event had places for the bags people carried with them whether toy bags or knapsacks and shoulder bags for whatever they bought from the vendors. You could temporarily stash a bag almost anywhere for a while; but eventually it would have to live somewhere private. Surely, if Ferri or Paul had handed a bag of clothing to someone else to hold, they would have been suspicious? Would a third party really hide such a thing from the police to protect their community? She asked that out loud.

"Hell yeah," Dominick said. "These people got secrets. They're kinky, they got extra partners, they're sneaking around on the side of those extra partners...none of them want publicity or attention, except those crazy people out in the street, protesting about their rights to be freaky. Most of these folks don't want the headlines about all their secret kinky playtime."

"They got it anyway."

Not only did they have the headlines about the murder itself, which might have passed without further comment over the weekend news cycle, but now they had the satanic murder angle as well.

Woodrow hadn't even spent the night in custody. He was on the Internet already, decrying the police brutality that had him arrested and chained while real homosexual perverts chained and murdered each other in a ritzy New York City hotel. He was going to sue everyone. Oh, and he claimed that because of his ministry, thousands of deluded perverts would convert to a normal life-style, too. He had a follow-up report about that.

Seeing as there was only so much craziness Rebecca could deal with before her second coffee, she hadn't bothered to watch the follow-up. She was glad her Lieutenant was taking Sunday off, so all she had from Ludivico were phone messages and an angry email demanding more tact and better results.

"And what about those pictures Woody had?" she asked, pulling the flyer out. "Paul had prints of these shots in a folder. He said they were for a calendar."

"And Nancy said she was finding them all on these Christian websites all of a sudden, but they weren't on Steel's own website."

"So..how did they get out?"

"Is that relevant?" Then, Dominick frowned and clicked away at his keyboard. "Watch me do some heavy duty tongue biting. Yes, it surely is. Because Steel mailed one of these to Ferri, just last week."

"What?"

"Yeah, they sent lots of pictures back and forth, some pretty hardcore porno, some just cell-phone-in-the-mirror crap. But man, I can't believe I missed this..." He turned the screen to her; neatly framed was the exact photo doctored by Woodrow for his flyer, minus the alterations. "Now what does *that* mean?" Dominick cried. "Why would anyone send this to someone bound to misuse it?"

Rebecca shook her head. "To distract us? It worked. It brought Woody to the scene, with his protestors, made Mack look like a victim of a smear campaign, if not a hate crime. It changed the headlines from a gay man being killed at a leather contest to him being part of some satanic cult, which no thinking person would believe. Still, some people *would* find it easy to believe he was killed by a fanatic for some inexplicable reason having to do with mixed up religious messages and...I don't know, insanity. Like, maybe Woody thought Mack was the devil and that's why he killed him? Frankly, he doesn't come across as *that* crazy. Did Steel send that picture to anyone else?"

"I'm looking...looking..." He tapped and opened message after message, sometimes grunting and shaking his head as many different images flashed by. "Damn, how could a man have so many pictures of himself bareass? It's like he did nothing but take pictures, find hookups and go slutting around..."

"I'm finding it hard to believe Paul was really as content with that as he's said. No matter what sort of relationship they had."

"Mmm-hmm. Though I've known all sorts of women who don't mind that their men go 'round town now and again so long as they come on home with their paycheck and take care of the family business. So far, all I see is that picture to Ferri and no one else."

"So, Ferri or Paul could have sent that picture to the anti-gay websites somehow, to throw up a distraction."

"It might have worked, if only *both* those guys didn't have holes in their stories and plenty of reasons why they might not be happy with Mack." He dropped the little computer back down on the desk and swore gently. "Day-umn! Now either one could have sent this picture out! Are these guys workin' together to just mess this up? Maybe they *both* done it!"

The two of them looked at each other over the tops of their monitors. Rebecca put her bagel down.

"Both?" they said together.

"Back to Global Leather," Rebecca said, sorting the reports and pictures into folders.

"Lemme have another bagel, first. You got garlic? Maybe it'll ward off the vampire freaks."

Sleep deprivation, stress and a weekend diet of hospitality suite snacks had taken its toll on the volunteer staff, and the morning business at the registration and information desks showed the strain. The revised schedule for Sunday was transported in short stacks from the business center as they were copied, and snatched as soon as they arrived.

The final contestant interviews were re-scheduled, delayed by the continual interruptions caused by police interviews and searches and various vapors and chill-out requirements from the participants. So many people crowded Master Bearclaw's class, "When Daddy Goes Away: Surviving the Loss of Your Dominant Partner" on Saturday that he was doing it again today, and it had to be housed in one of the dungeon play spaces immediately after the Keynote Breakfast.

Wolfboy had told everyone he met that the police were looking for lost or found clothing and a large tangle of T-shirts, stockings, hankies, socks and various undergarments were collecting at one end of the registration table, occasionally mistaken for a clothing drive.

The passel of dungeon-goers who demanded partial refunds because of the disrupted playtime the previous night were supplemented by those who missed the entire episode and wanted updates. More attendees checked out early, saying there was far too much media attention or toxic energy. Replacing them, however, were waves of new folks who had not purchased tickets for the weekend who *now* wanted to attend the contest, since the entire kinky community was talking about nothing else. Dozens of people crowded around the tables wanting service, information, or just someone else to tell their stories to.

The anti-gay and anti-kink protestor crowds had swollen outside, so fewer people wanted to venture out of the hotel. Therefore, the lobby snack bar was packed with those not going to the Keynote Breakfast, but trying to get something to eat. The hotel sit-down restaurant had a one-hour wait, and the revolving doors emitted a steady stream of delivery boys from local diners, meeting people in an area already overcrowded. The din was immeasurable, the chaos completely insane.

And in the center of this maelstrom, Earl Stemple tried desperately to maintain some sense of order. He should be at the Keynote Breakfast, but instead he was personally handling one miniature crisis after another. With the Boys Jack trying to keep the judges and contestants sane and orderly and Bitsy missing—missing!—he was being drawn steadily under. Of all the times for Bitsy to abandon him!

And yet, as he half listened to a polyamorous family of six complain that their sacred flogging circle had been utterly ruined by the fracas outside the dungeon, as he allowed Aphrodite to take an additional room for the recovery community since so many of them had been additionally triggered by Paul's alcohol-fueled explosion of grief and fury, as he signed an order for more chairs to be set up in the ballroom/contest location and decided, finally, to cancel the proposed memorial tableau for Mack on stage this afternoon, he forgave Bitsy Olmstead.

She, at least, was getting laid. Which was more than he got at any Global Leather event.

At the same moment, Maureen "Bitsy" Olmstead was thinking almost the same thing. It had been far too long since she'd gotten so thoroughly, completely, deliciously used and abused. Until she felt not only sated, but gloriously wasted, languid, as her romantic BDSM novels would put it.

She had given Tom her room number so he could dash back to his own and pack his toys. She'd felt a combination of hope, lust and caution all at once. One-night stands were definitely not to her taste or her ethics, and she'd never even met this guy before, or vetted him past a casual ask-around. And even that was more about whether he'd show up for his volunteer assignments, not what sort of player he was, or what he was into, or whether he had a string of sixteen KinkyNet girlfriends all waiting for their one date a year or even a wife and five kids somewhere.

And sure, he might be safe, he might have the right clothes and the right toys, but he could be *boring*. One might be tempted to think toys and a willingness to use them were enough to make any playdate fun, but Bitsy had gotten more and more discerning over the years. In her twenties, it had been fun and entertaining to date any number of masters and dominants and would-be dominants, all equipped like some kinky Ken doll with any number of accessories. She even remembered some of them more for what they had or did as their specialty than for their personalities. Japanese bondage guy, who mumbled things about not wanting to have to catch her if his knots didn't hold. Electrical play dude, who had every shiny, buzzing, beeping, clicking toy known to the world but mostly used them to substitute for the touch of skin to skin. I-Control-Everything Buttwipe, who actually wanted her to record her entire day in an online journal, down to the portion sizes of food she ate and TV shows she watched and websites she visited.

Now, she didn't leap into playing on the first date. Hell, that she usually required dates at all made it challenging for a lot of men. But she had to know more about them than whether they were kinky. She liked a dominant man as well as any other submissive lady, but there was no way on earth she was going to go all Zodian and give up her good job to live in some doublewide wearing silk scarves and speaking like a lunatic. She was a tough, adult, independent woman who liked a sexually dominant man who wasn't a control freak, a loser, a fantasy role-player or a collector of a ton of girls whom he played with on a rotating schedule. And it took time to learn these things about someone! To break her own loose rule made her feel a little foolish and chagrined. But she got to her suite, brushed her teeth and turned up the heat and decided any man who knew how to dance was at least self-disciplined enough to know a thing or three about leading, and a sense of rhythm wasn't a bad place to start when having sex.

She'd expected Tom to show up with a huge bag stuffed with toys; quantity was quality to so many kinksters these days. But he had a modest bag, neatly packed. She saw this as he laid out a suede flogger, and then a black one in velvety soft deerskin, then a little nasty one made of loops of rubber. He also brought a rattan cane, a set of black leather cuffs padded and lined in red, and he set them onto the coffee table in the room and looked at her with a smile. "You know," he said, pushing the bondage materials to one side, "I don't know why I didn't leave these in my room, except that I've been thinking just how damn...pretty...you'd look in bondage. But I understand if you'd rather pass on bondage, since we barely know each other."

"I like bondage," Bitsy said, disbelieving her honesty even as she spoke. "I like it a lot. I like to pull at something. But the rubber thing...I don't like, I can tell you that right away."

Tom picked the little stingy whip up and dropped it swiftly into the bag. "Is there anything else you want to tell me? Should we just sit here on the couch and talk a while about things we like?"

Bitsy dropped neatly onto the couch next to him, her hip rubbing against his in a mating of leather gown to breeches. "I like the couch part," she said, her voice slightly low. "Maybe you can show me what you like?"

He reached for her waist with one hand and cupped the other around one of her well-supported breasts, and their lips met with such violence it hurt. But he climbed up against her, onto one knee on the couch, pushing her back and following her relaxation into the stiff cushions with possessive, hungry hands and an exploring mouth and dancing tongue.

As negotiations went, it sure beat checklists of kinks.

He insisted upon stripping her, unlacing her gown and the corset under it, scratching her pale, creased skin to get rid of every possible pinching and itch and feeling of compression. He expertly ran his hands over her naked body, stopping here and there along his ministrations to inquire about a tattoo of a butterfly on her heel, an old scar on her hip from an accident, a tightness in her right shoulder from typing too much. He kissed her with hunger and passion and a luxurious, frustrating lack of urgency. Night turned into morning as he bumped up the room heating again and flogged Bitsy at last, bound to her king-sized bed, her ass upturned for him while she wiggled and pulled with joy at the restraints.

His slight weight on her back as he whispered in her ear, "What's your safeword?" had been almost as funny as the question.

"Listen, Tom. If I don't like something or I got something you need to know, I speak English, I'll let you know," she said, flushed with too much pleasure to even put some ironic sting into the words. Instead, they felt like lines spoken in a dream, unreal.

"I'm glad to hear that, Bitsy. But shouldn't you be calling me something like sir?" He slapped one hand down against her hip, and she both yelped and laughed.

"Yes, sir! More, sir!"

"That's a girl. Now you get whatever you want. Isn't that easy?"

Oh, and it was easy. What's more, it was...fun! And just pushy enough to be interesting without getting creepy; just friendly enough to be intimate without feeling pressured. She taught him what made her orgasm; he learned fast. And the sole negotiation for fucking came when he asked whether she really cared whether the condom was ribbed or not. Before she was able to even think of how nice it was not to have to insist on one herself, he was inside her and she lost all critical thought processes except oh, oh, how good it felt to have a burning hot ass and a cock inside her and a voice telling her what a good, good girl she was.

"You're amazing," he murmured to her after he dropped the cuffs and whips and other toys off the side of the bed and curled an arm around her. "I'd like to stay."

"That's good," she murmured back. "Because I'd tackle you if you tried to leave."

"You could try," he said with a good nature. And then it was later in the morning and light was coming in through the open blinds, and Bitsy felt the light go away again as he slipped the blindfold over her eyes.

"Surprise," he whispered. "Up for a little morning fun?"

Answer her phone? Go wrangle irate, whining attendees and volunteers, listen to Earl drone on gloom and doom, deal with murder and right-wing nutjobs and drunk boys and who knows what else?

"Good morning, sir!" she said cheerfully. And wiggled her ample backside against him. "Is that a whip you have pointing at my ass, or...oh! Oh! Oh, yes, yes, that's the way...oh, *master*, yes!"

In the hallway between the rooms for the judges and the contestants, furious arguments had been underway since the first meet-up at nine A.M. The Zodians, in the person of Lord Laertes, had lodged a formal request that Mickey Abraham be removed from the panel because she was *obviously* prejudiced against Zodians. Various LGBT groups demanded she be removed because she would *obviously* favor the mostly heterosexual Zodians. It was clear that the lobbying and complaints would continue through most of the day, even though the judges had to make a unified appearance at the Keynote Breakfast.

The professor herself was somewhat less amused by the revelation in the harsh morning after, and was uncharacteristically monosyllabic and subdued. Even her black silk shirt featuring pictures of half-naked Hawaiian ladies bearing cocktail glasses didn't seem to elevate the aura of gloom around her. She did insist, however, upon staying until told otherwise. "I never really wanted tenure anyway," she said with a shrug, after her second large latte. "Might as well stick with this gig until the bitter, bitter end." She refused interviews with either Phedre or Cary, but did have a few choice words for the book vendor who angrily demanded she come and sign the Zod books instead of her academic volumes.

Meanwhile, both the Pansexual Institute for Sexual Studies and the American Sexuality Society found a rare moment in which they not only agreed, but issued nearly identical statements. Both groups called for Mistress Ravenfyre to be reprimanded for the outing of Dr. Mickey Abraham as the author of the controversial Zod books. "Confidentiality is one of our community's greatest values," read one of the statements. "Isn't it time to change Safe, Sane and Consensual to Safe, Sane, Consensual and Confidential?" suggested the other. Neither one paid the least bit of attention to the fact that it was actually Master Dick who did the outing; Mistress Ravenfyre was, after all, the titleholder.

The Zodians were, as Maurice put it, completely *verklempt*. Some Confederations reported cries for book burnings and the public repudiation of the newly revealed author. Others refused to believe it and claimed it was all some bizarre publicity stunt—by whom and for what, they did not explain. Online discussion groups exploded in angst, recriminations and theories. "Was Abraham misused by a dishonorable Zodian in her youth?" someone asked, completely unaware of the impossibility of abuse from a follower of a culture she had herself created.

And it was laer'ta who was sent to the contestant room to deliver the word from the Nevada Zodian Confederation to phyl'ta.

"You do not have to continue competing," laer'ta said gently, taking phyl'ta's hand. "We are behind you one hundred percent whichever way you choose. But if you think this is too much to handle, you are welcome to back out right now and go back to Master Phyl just as proud as any slave!"

"This girl thanks you," phyl'ta said. "But this one will stay and continue to compete."

When laer'ta left, Jazz Dean rolled her eyes and swore. "Jesus, do you really talk like that all the time?" For her final day of judgment, she was in leather jeans, motocross boots and a leather shirt that had been cunningly designed to look like the sleeves had been torn off at the shoulder seam. Her bare biceps sported a few old tattoos of mermaids and ocean waves, and she had seven-inch leather wristbands buckled on her forearms.

"It's really weird," said Mr. Shaft, Jason Asada.

"I keep thinking, like...*which* girl," laughed Blade Guthrie, yawning. "This girl says, this slave wants, whatever. Why not, like, just say, like...me. I'll, you know. Do whatever."

Lennon looked at Blade in amazement. "How did you win your title?"

Jazz stage whispered, "Idaho. She was the only contestant."

Blade snorted and nodded.

"It's certainly...an interesting culture," said Mr. Alberta Leather, examining the Canadian flag patch sewn onto his leather jacket. He removed a loose thread. "I've learned *so much* about it this weekend."

"If by 'interesting' you mean 'weird,' then I'm with you, bro," laughed Chevalier Franklin.

"Especially now that we know it was made up by a lesbian," said Kelly Manning. "I mean, who could have seen that coming?"

Jazz shuddered. "I don't know what was in her mind to come up with that misogynist crap. All women need to be slaves? All men are savage brutes?"

"But we are," Kevin McDonald laughed.

"Speak for yourself, dude, I'm a sensitive mofo, myself," Kelly said.

"Look, the real point is, no matter who made it up, it's fantasy! It's a fairy tale; there is no Zodian lifestyle! You might as well talk about the vampire lifestyle…"

"Well, actually, we do," interrupted Angelina. "The Nightwalker Family does bloodplay, and half of them say they're vampires. I interviewed them last year for my blog."

Jazz sighed and shook her head. "Fine, although they're nuts, too. What I meant was…look, phyl'ta—I mean, that's not even your name, it's your boyfriend's name with a 'tuh' sound on the end! How much more can you erase a woman's identity? And you're doing it all because someone wrote this half-assed fantasy twenty years ago? I mean, seriously, get a life!"

A few of the other contestants raised hands or fingers to try and stop the tirade, but no one actually said anything. All eyes turned to plump little phyl'ta, who was smiling an enigmatic smile as she adjusted her slave chiffons. For her final appearance, her blonde hair was swept into a complicated updo, and threaded with black chains glittering with different colored beads. Her fingernails glittered with tiny stick-on gems, all in shades of purple.

"Would the honored free women like to know why this slave lives this way?" she said lightly. When the folds had been arranged to her liking, she crossed her legs and said, "Because this one is happy to explain!"

"Yeah, cool, let her explain," Blade said, nodding.

Jazz shrugged and phyl'ta bowed her head for a moment. When she looked back up, the aspect of simple, smiling passivity was gone from her face.

"I'll tell you why I do it," she said, no longer keeping her voice in the upper registers. Several eyes widened at the change in her tone and style of speaking. "And you know what? I don't care if that old...*lesbian* wrote it for a joke or protest or whatever. Because I'm not doing it for her and I'm not doing it for any of you, and I sure am not doing 'cause I think it's some mystical, magical truth."

"Whoa," Kelly exclaimed. "Okay?"

"Look, I grew up in L.A.," phyl'ta said. "Do you have any idea what it's like to be short and fat in the land of tall and skinny? To burn like a potato chip in the shade when everyone else is tan? To be told over and over, my whole life, how ugly I am and how sad it must be to be me?"

"You're not ugly!" Kevin McDonald said.

"Maybe not to you—and not in the BDSM scene! I didn't feel *pretty* until the first time I got all dressed up in a fancy corset and stockings because my first master bought them for me." She sniffed a little. "I mean, not that he was much of a master, but I liked him and he thought I was hot, because I was a damn sexy submissive; I love getting beaten and caned and tied up and used really hard! He loved me because I was hot to him, all of me, and he didn't even have to say things like, I was sexy *despite* being fat, like some guys do."

Angelina nodded. "Yeah, well, the scene is more welcoming to lots of body types."

"So, fine, I could get laid, I could get played with. But I'm an old-fashioned girl! I like the idea of being a stay-at-home mom, I want a man who thinks he's my champion and my hero, who wants to take care of me. I want a man who responds to me when I want him, and someone who I can read, too.

"And you know what? My man likes the Zod books. Big fucking deal! He could like *Star Trek* or football or some stupid game online, but he likes Zod stuff. And when I talk this way and dress like this and say certain things and kneel a certain way, guess what? He goes crazy wanting me! He thinks I'm the hottest thing walking! It makes him happy and proud, and it makes him feel like he's a stud, too." She grinned suddenly. "Know why I do this? Because last night, while the rest of the Zodians were getting all upset in the dungeons, we were back in our room getting it *on*. Because last night, I came six times! Six! Because he thinks it's his duty as a Zodian master to make me 'weak in the love furs,' and so he figures that means getting me off so much I have to beg him to stop.

"So, if getting that from Phil means dressing up like this once in a while and doing a hoochie-coochie dance and talking like I'm retarded, guess what? That sure isn't much different from wearing high heels and miniskirts and a ton of makeup and pretending to care who wins the Super Bowl or the World Series, and millions of women do that. And because I go along with it, and let me be clear, I am *perfectly* happy to, Phil will be happy when I get pregnant and quit my job and we settle down together the way I always wanted. Because he's not just my boyfriend, he's my *fiancé*. So, yeah, that's why I do it. The lifestyle I want, the man I love, and a ton of screaming, sweaty, panting, oh-my-God it hurts so good orgasms."

There was silence in the room as they all digested her speech.

"Can't beat that shit," Blade said slowly, with a nod.

"Word," agreed Franklin.

"*Gay gezunt*!" pronounced Maurice.

Even Jazz had to nod.

"This slave thanks the honored free people for their kind attention," phyl'ta simpered. The room broke up in laughter just as Boy Jack came to escort them to the Keynote Breakfast.

CHAPTER 31

THE CROWDS IN THE LOBBY FROM THE MORNING HAD NOT subsided by the time the two detectives arrived. In fact, the line to buy tickets for the contest threaded from the registration desk almost to the front doors.

"Nothing like a little scandal to make an event more interesting, I guess," Rebecca said to Earl Stemple, once she and Dominick had made their way to his office/conference room.

Earl sighed and sank down into a chair at the overburdened table. He reached for one of his coffee cups, glanced down into the dried, dark residue at the bottom and shook his head. He placed the cup behind him on a counter already filled with them. and rubbed his unshaven jaw. "You have no idea. Last night, Giuliano Ferri walked off the stage during his speech, and Paul got up, completely drunk..."

"We saw that," Rebecca said.

"You did? Well, let me tell you, my nightmare didn't end there! Later on, it came out that Mistress Ravenfyre's slave was having an affair with—of all people!—Mickey Abraham!"

Dominick tried to head off a smirk. "You don't say?"

"It's unbelievable! And on top of that, this came out in a knockdown fight outside the, er, playrooms...completely legal and cleared by the hotel management and compliant with New York City safe-sex codes, I might add..."

"I'm sure they are," assured Rebecca.

"Well...right outside the doors! A screaming match...accusations on all sides and including some very personal, ah, attacks on the people involved."

"Sorry we missed it."

Earl shook his head. "But that wasn't the end of it. We then found out that Abraham is actually the author of the Zod books. I know this must sound like complete nonsense to you, but this is big, big news in the community."

Rebecca and Dominick eyed each other in surprise, and Dominick laughed.

"Wait now...that little professor wrote the books the Vikings base their, uh, lifestyle on? Damn, that's funny."

Earl shrugged helplessly. "I'll find it funny tomorrow. Right now, all I know is I thought it was bad when Mack was killed, but now it's just all worse. Not to say that this is more important than a murder! I mean, really..." He paused, looked around to make sure the door was closed and continued, "Who *cares*? It was always just a bunch of silly little fantasy books. I don't know why the Zodians grabbed them and based a whole...as you say, lifestyle...on them, but they're not hurting anyone and frankly, they add some color to our events. I was *glad* when one of them signed up to run for the title. After losing Giuliano last night, I thought we'd lose phyl'ta today, but for some reason, he's back and she's staying, and we've already sold a hundred new tickets for the contest." He sighed again. "Anyway, I'm babbling. What can I do for you, Detectives?"

"Ferri is back in the contest?" Dominick asked. "How's he

going to compete when he gave me all his leather last night?"

"He did? Huh! He talked to me this morning in the gym; I was trying to walk off some of my anxiety on the treadmill. I lasted all of about ten minutes before my heart started to pound." He patted his chest. "So out of shape. And this event gives me *agita*. Seems his sponsoring bar insisted he compete, even though he has almost no chance of winning now. Especially without something to wear on stage for his last appearance! Although, odder things have happened. Now we have more people interested in who's going to win than we ever had before. Someone even wants to stream the contest on the web, live." He looked at them curiously. "What do you think?"

"I think given the chance something else unexpected might happen, I'd skip the live broadcast," Rebecca said. "And I'd like to let you get back to work; would you mind a few more questions?"

"Of course not; I should thank you for the break time." He ostentatiously switched off his radio and muted his phone.

"Earl, this is sensitive, and I am going to have to ask you not to discuss the content of these questions with anyone else right now. To the best of your knowledge, did Mack Steel cross-dress, or perform in drag?"

His eyebrows flew up in surprise. "Mack? No, not to my knowledge! And given his general hostility toward women...well, okay, some drag queens do seem to have issues about women now and then. But to your question, no, never. He always was one hundred percent into the whole leatherman image."

"Would it have mattered to you if he did?"

Earl snorted and shook his head. "Please. So many men do drag, or at least try it once or twice. I didn't...I just thought I'd be so hideous, why even try? But probably half of the Mr. Globals have either done it as a pure gag or when they were skinny and pretty." He smiled. "There's an old joke that you do drag until your hair gets shaggy and you grow a potbelly, and then suddenly, boom—instant leather daddy!"

"So, you wouldn't have dropped him if someone revealed he wore lady clothes?" Dominick pressed.

"I didn't drop him when he lost the sponsorship of three leather clubs in the greater San Francisco area. I didn't drop him when he alienated the two other titleholders of his year. Maybe I should have! But believe me, if he pranced around in a tutu sprinkling fairy dust on people, he would've still been Mr. Global Leather to the bitter end." He eyed them. "So, he dabbled in women's clothing? Weird, I never would have guessed it. Not because I honestly bought into the whole manly-man thing, but because it would have revealed some actual depth of character."

The two detectives glanced at each other with mild looks of confusion. Then Rebecca asked, "Earl, did you ever get the sense that Paul was jealous of Mack's other...conquests?"

He thought about that, poking around the table for a mug that still had coffee in it. "No, not really. He always came across as very secure, in fact, kind of emotionally...empty. Like all he was, he invested in being Mack's boy. He echoed him in a lot of ways, laughed when he did, got angry when he did. In a way, they seemed like the perfect D/S couple—in public! Like I said before, I have no idea what they were like in private. Last night was very out of character for him, I've never heard of him drinking to excess or acting out like that. I can't risk another scene like that tonight; we canceled the memorial to Mack. We were going to stage his winning fantasy from last year; it's a tableau with a few men representing stages in his life, closeted kid, young leatherman man just coming out, and then a podium and a pair of boots with his cap on them representing him. I think Paul had it in mind to be the young man? But now...I think it's best we just let that go."

Rebecca nodded thoughtfully. "Did Mack ever discuss his

plans for what to do after his year ended? What does a former Mr. Global Leather usually do next?"

Earl laughed. "Take a vacation? Get therapy? Declare bankruptcy? You name the reaction, and we've had it, from dropping out of the community entirely to getting a sex change. Most of the past winners leave feeling pretty good about their year— they bring their sash or vest out at other events, get speaking or teaching gigs, if they have any skill at it. A lot continue to travel, raise money for their charities, give back to the community. Mack never said a word to me about his plans, except maybe a threat to expose me for unethical business practices." He rolled his eyes. "I assumed he'd try to cash in on his image more—maybe make some porn, or do some modeling for the soft-core market. I know he was approached to use his image to help sell leather gear a couple of times, but you can't do that during your title year. It's in the contract I have them sign. So, if he kept those contacts, he might have been ready to get some paying work immediately after stepping down."

"And that would be all right with you?"

"Frankly, anything he did that took him far away from me would have made me happy. I heard on the news this morning that Woody Gallia was released; does that mean there's not enough proof he did it? Because that flyer was pretty explicit to me!"

"We're continuing the investigation," Rebecca said. "Believe me, we have our eye on him."

"And he has his eyes on us! He was saying something crazy about how the leather community was going to be brought down by converts already inside. We're double- and triple-checking IDs, but who knows whether some of these people coming in to get tickets today are with us or not? It's not like we can take the time to look them up on the Internet." He shook his head and glanced at his continuously vibrating phone.

Rebecca nodded. "Thanks for your help, Earl. I'll make sure

we have some extra people around here to watch for suspicious behavior, okay? Good luck with the contest later."

The look he shot her was part gratitude and part dread.

"So, how do we find out if Ferri and Helms both did it if we got no clothes, no weapon? Neither one of them would have had access to a Ravenfyre knife."

"We're *assuming* neither one did, but we have no proof of that. I'm thinking it's time we talked to Wendi and Willow. I put in requests for Paul and Guiliano's email—let me add a note to look for more hidden accounts. If Mack had one, why not them? Cell phone usage, too, I asked for two weeks worth. Did Mack call Ferri, or vice versa?"

Dominick nodded. "Yeah, I got calls to Ferri on his cell, about a dozen over three months. Looks like they might have done most of their flirtation by email and texting...hey, wait." He stopped walking and frowned. "Come to think of it, I'm wondering if there are some messages *missing* in the email."

Rebecca looked at him. "Why?"

"Because it was so shallow! Mostly pictures and 'man, you're hot' and 'I want you so bad' stuff. But if they're only talkin' on the phone once a week or so, and there's nothing in the emails about what Ferri was saying—all that stuff about Mack coachin' him and maybe taking him to California and all..." He paused, ran his thoughts through and shook his head. "Damn. Nothing's fitting. If it was shallow, then Ferri either imagined it, or is trying to get one over on us. But if there was something there..."

"I follow your thoughts, except for one thing. Why would Mack delete emails in a *secret* account?"

Dominick thought about that. "Well, if I could get into it, why not someone else? Maybe he thought Paul was on to him?"

"But why hide only some of the communication with Ferri?" Her eyes narrowed. "Because..."

"It was *too* serious? Not like the others, the one-night stands and all this party/orgy lifestyle? But maybe Ferri was a special case? Maybe no matter how kinky Paul was, he wasn't going for no threeway."

Rebecca shook her head as she considered the options. No matter how they looked at it, it always seemed like either man had plenty of reasons to kill Mack. But two mysteries remained the same—where did the weapon come from, and where did at least one, possibly two sets of bloody clothing wind up? If Dominick was right about this community, it was possible that tonight and tomorrow, hundreds of people could file right by them, including one with a suitcase full of evidence, and there wouldn't be a thing they could do about it. Would someone be that blind to justice, to allow a murderer to stay hidden among them?

As they got to the grand staircase leading up to the conference room floors, she edged out of the way of two very tall women leading another in a full leather bodysuit, with massive buckles and locks all over it. Zippers and snaps showed where openings could be made over the breasts and genitals, but the entire garment was formfitting enough to seem almost shrinkwrapped to her fashion model-style proportions. She was also wearing a mask that covered her mouth and eyes, but a long, cherrywood-colored ponytail came out of the top of it in a stylized fashion, like an iconic photo from an old fetish magazine. She walked carefully, raising each knee slowly, while the two escorts guided her with touches from riding crops. Taking the opportunity to pass this trio, two more women dashed by, wearing shorts over bathing suits, each one carrying a towel as they headed toward the gym.

"Good lord, it never ends," muttered Dominick. "Can't these people just keep their perversion at home?"

Rebecca breathed out from her nose, hard, and ground her teeth as they walked up the stairs. Then, she turned, so quickly Dominick almost ran into her. In a low voice, she hissed, "Look,

Detective...just back off on all your freak this and pervert that, okay? It's unprofessional, it's rude, it's obnoxious and I am sick and tired of it. You don't want to work with me, fine, but until you're reassigned, just try to keep your language civil...*Dom.*"

"What?" he protested, his jaw dropping. "What do you mean—"

"Oh, my God," Rebecca said, looking after the two women heading for the gym. "What was I thinking?" She started back down the stairs, taking them two at a time, leaving Dominick to look after her for a moment in shock before he followed her.

"Girl, I didn't know he was a dom," whispered one of the women leading the leather-clad bottom.

"Clearly not a good one if she can talk to him like that," whispered back the other. "And in those suits, I thought they were vanillas."

"You never can tell."

The bottom between them nodded, and they continued their careful promenade.

CHAPTER 32

"I THINK THE LOCKERS WERE ALL CHECKED ON FRIDAY," SAID Roger, the manager on duty. "We had complaints from a few of the guests who saw one of the cops going through them, until they heard it was a murder investigation. I know he went through the laundry cart; our people did, too."

"But what about the lockers for people who were using the gym at the time?" Rebecca asked. "If they were locked, did someone open them for the patrolman?"

"Well, I don't think so, no," Roger admitted. "They didn't get the master key from the front desk." He slid it through the access port behind the door in the housekeeping closet. "But every locker opens automatically every night; we remove anything left behind and sanitize the interior. The policy is even posted on the wall. No one would have left something here all weekend knowing we were going to open the locker eventually!"

"They wouldn't have to," Rebecca said. "All they need is a place to move the items to when the cleaning crew comes through. And the gym is open extra late for this event, right?"

"Hell, some of these people are maniacs for the gym. We close it between three and four A.M. and still get complaints."

"And the dungeons are open until five A.M.," Rebecca said, "So, someone could stash something down here, take it out and toss it in a pile of bags upstairs for awhile and take it right back here, where it sits locked up and safe all day."

Roger clicked his tongue and shook his head. "Devious. But possible. They're all yours, Detective. Er...perhaps *you* should check the men's lockers?" He smiled at Dominick.

Rebecca shrugged. "Go ahead, I'll be on the other side."

The two women who had preceded them to the gym were already in the pool, along with half a dozen others. The little Jacuzzi at the far end was packed with a circle of hairy men of some girth and bulk, apparently quite comfortable with close contact. In the glass-framed workout room adjoining the pool were a few people on treadmills and one muscular man on a weight bench. The smell of pine disinfectant and chlorine fought with an industrial-strength filtering fan, but the rooms were still faintly clammy and musky. The locker rooms were narrow and contained nothing but the wall of lockers and one bench running alongside them; doors on each end led to showers and bathrooms or into the gym.

Rebecca dutifully checked each locker, but had only reached the seventh when she heard Dominick calling her.

A large pile of crumpled black leather was stuffed into locker 06 on the men's side, with a plastic event bag and a cheap, black tote bag stuffed on top. Dominick was taking pictures of the pile with his cell phone.

Rebecca pulled gloves out of the pocket of her blazer and removed the plastic bag first, which she slid into an evidence bag. Roger shook his head, impressed.

"How did you figure that out?" he asked.

"Every day I've seen people going to the gym. It got me to

wondering how long your lockers stay locked and whether using one leaves a record of which key opened it."

"Sadly, no. You just need the same key to open it, or the master. In fact, we've had keys from another Grand Sterling work on these. I'll be sure to write a memo requesting better security on them."

"And what's the story on cameras down here?"

He gave her a helpless smile. "Once, a staff member released some images taken from a security camera at one of our gym locker rooms; naked people, oh boy! We were sued, got a lot of pressure from consumer rights people, how dare we photograph people without their permission, yadda, yadda. The central office had all of them pulled after that. There's an exterior camera in the hallway, but I don't think they'll have images from Thursday night any more; it'll have been recorded over by now."

Why hadn't she thought of this on Friday? Rebecca removed the black bag, which had a Global Leather logo on it, and then the garments, one at a time. There was a long-sleeved shirt with snaps, a pair of jeans with a button fly, like Levi's 501s, and a motorcycle-style jacket. All in black leather. She sniffed at the shirt as she shook it out, then draped it over one arm as she spread the front panels open. A rub of one gloved finger came back with a dusting of rust-colored flakes.

"Inside," she said with a small feeling of triumph. "The killer put these clothes on over his own, to cover himself as he got away." The shirt had a label inside the collar, crediting Skinz4Real as the tailor.

How coincidental that this was one of the companies represented in the vendor room. "I'll take these," Rebecca said. "And go ask the people who made this a few questions. Will you take care of finding the others we need to talk to? After you check the rest of the lockers to see if there's anything else?"

Dominick nodded at her. "Sure thing. I'll let you know where

I wind up." He took a breath, considering how to address her recent outburst, but she had already turned to Roger.

"Thank you for your help."

"Nothing like a little murder to spice up a leather and bondage sex weekend," he replied.

As she walked out of the locker room with her armful of evidence, the party of bears leaving the Jacuzzi all trooped in; some of them crossed beefy hands over their crotches or chests. She rolled her eyes. "I've seen it all before, gentlemen," she said when they passed each other.

"Yeah, but I'm used to getting tips!" one laughed behind her.

Apryl Chin, owner, designer and head seamstress of Skinz4Real Leathers nodded when Rebecca showed her the shirt. "Sure, that's one of mine. You can tell because I always double stitch the pockets and provide the badge bar." She pointed a calloused finger at a patch of leather on the left side of the shirtfront. "See, it unsnaps. That way, you can clip or pin ID badges to it instead of ruining the shirt. I usually throw in an extra patch for any custom order, or sell 'em for fifteen bucks later."

"Can you tell me who you sold this one to?"

Apryl laughed and pointed at the racks behind her. Someone was trying on a pair of leather overalls and turning to look at them in the mirror; they were surrounded by walls of black leather. "Sorry, but probably not. It has a size on the label—that means it wasn't custom-made. I sell about two, three hundred of those a year, at these events and through my website."

"Did you ever sell one to Mack Steel?"

She shook her head. "Not that I know of, but I did donate a couple for the prize baskets last year, so he *might* have had one."

Further questioning revealed that she'd never sold one to Paul or Giuliano, either, unless they'd bought one online. But she had sold a short-sleeved shirt to Dick Schneider. "I kept trying to tell him he should get long sleeves," she said wistfully. "The poor man's got such skinny, pale arms. I mean, he already looks like a clerk playing dress-up, why remind people? Pictures of him wearing my shirt just aren't very sexy. I don't tell people it's mine, but you can tell because it's got the badge patch." She sighed and went to help a customer examining a rack of discounted miniskirts.

Now that Giuliano Ferri was back in the contest, it was easy to track his movements. Dominick called Dick Schneider and hit voicemail, and then checked the program. Ah, that was why he was busy—he and Slave Willow were teaching a class called "Sharing Is Caring: When a Dom Couple Shares Submissives."

That must be awkward, he thought, as he went to find the room. Maybe they didn't intend to share quite so *much* of their mutually "owned" girlfriend. Before he got to the location listed in the program, he spotted a familiar face in another room, and stopped to look through the door to make sure. Yes—that was Paul Helms, sitting in a large, ragged circle of people, a short, chubby man walking around in the center and making speechifying gestures. There was a tired looking man outside the door who looked up from his novel when Dominick paused. His T-shirt read, IF I SAID YOU HAD A BEAUTIFUL BODY, WOULD YOU SLAP MY FACE AND TEACH ME MANNERS?

"It's a repeat of 'When Daddy Goes Away,' " he said each word deeply colored with ennui. "All about what it's like to lose your dom. They're almost finished, though."

Willow first, or Paul? Paul was the suspect, but Willow was the one who handled the inventory of Ravenfyre knives. Rebecca won points figuring out where the leather clothes were; what could he find out to clinch this?

Thinking of her reminded him of her outburst and once again he shook his head, trying to put that aside. He'd ask her later, after he figured out who might have had that knife or something even more incriminating. As he was thinking, he could see Paul crying again; did the waterworks never stop on him?

He opened the door slowly and slid in to listen. The door watcher shrugged and returned to his book.

"Without your dom, or master or mistress, where would you go for support? Where could you turn to find a shoulder to cry on, an arm to lean on, words of wisdom from someone who understands that this was more than your *girlfriend*, more than your *boyfriend*?" The chubby man with the goatee was walking the interior of the circled chairs.

"Another dom?" ventured a woman off to one side.

"No, another sub," insisted another. "We understand each other."

"You're both right!" exclaimed goatee, whose badge read MASTER BEARCLAW. "You go to your community! You go to your people, your D/S tribe, because we know your pain. We share it! We are your shelter against the storms of grief, the loss of direction and purpose."

"Mack was my purpose," Paul sniffed. "He was everything to me!" On all sides of him, people reached out to pat him, clasp his shoulder.

"Stay strong," cried a man across the circle from him.

"You are not alone," assured Master Bearclaw. "Paul, your submissive brothers and sisters are with you. And the good dominants in this community will watch out for you and protect you."

Protect him from what? Dominick wondered.

"I just feel so alone," Paul continued, his voice low. "What am I going to do? Mack made the decisions...he led the way for me. What am I gonna do without him? Everything was his...I have nothing now. I feel like nothing. Those crazy people murdered him and they're saying he was a Satanist..."

"Aren't they saying Satanists killed him?" whispered one of the people near to Dominick. "Was he really a Satanist?"

"Shh."

"He was truly a martyr," Bearclaw intoned, to many nods of agreement. "Murdered, sacrificed because he was a leatherman! A master! You need to find strength in your memories of him, Slave Paul. Look to us as your family. We will support you. Look at how many people support you already. Although we can never replace the special relationship you had with Master Mack, we can at least make sure you aren't left with no resources."

That soon evolved into a lot of people volunteering help; a flight attendant swore that Paul would get first-class upgrades whenever he could swing it. Two women reported that the Southwestern Association of Submissives/Slaves had raised almost two thousand dollars already for Paul, and intended to do an online auction to raise more. Members of other groups promised to figure out ways to help him directly and indirectly, ranging from a promise of legal advice when he got back to California to the dedication of an upcoming book on dominance and submission to Mack's memory.

Dominick wasn't impressed. He'd seen over ten thousand dollars raised quietly on a Sunday afternoon to help a young widow keep her home after her husband died suddenly of an undiagnosed heart ailment. And the local community made sure that house was filled with food and love and company for weeks afterward, and her two babies were cared for while she looked for work. And that was in a town of about five thousand souls all told, none of them what you'd call wealthy.

The door behind Dominick creaked open and the reader poked his head in, caught Master Bearclaw's eyes and tapped his watch. Bearclaw said, "Well, that's our five-minute warning, friends. I think anyone who wants to talk to Paul should probably do it somewhere else, as there might be another class in here. Thank you all for coming and contributing to our dialog about this vital but unspoken part of our lifestyle! I'll take any last questions…"

But many of them were already gathering their things and getting ready to leave. Dominick noticed now how many carried bags—most of them large enough to put a whole leather outfit in. Rebecca was right—just pop the incriminating clothing into one of those bags and drop it anywhere. As long as it wasn't the only one in any given location, no one would notice anything. And if you want to make sure the bag couldn't be in your room, leave it locked up in that gym, with people going in and out at all hours, working out, enjoying the pool...

Chlorine. Not bleach, but *chlorine*. That was the smell on the T-shirt! Would a quick splash in a pool clean the blood off a shirt? He pulled out his phone and dashed off a quick message to Feldblum.

Paul was one of the last to leave the room. Lots of people wanted to hug him, pat him, say supportive things. When he shuffled to the door, Dominick stepped in front of him. "Mr. Helms? I'm Detective DeCosta. I'm working with Detective Feldblum on Mack's case."

Paul looked confused. "But...you caught the guy, didn't you? That whack-job. Wait. No, she said something about that last night." He shook his head and blinked. "I'm sorry. Last night was...bad for me."

"I'm very sorry. It's clear Mr. Steel was very important to you. You mind if I ask you a few questions? There are a couple of odd things going on that you might be able to help us with."

Paul sighed and shrugged. "Sure. I guess." He looked around the room. "Here? Someone's coming in maybe?"

"Nah," said the bookish room monitor. "The room's closed for now, I have to find people to get the play equipment back in here." He waved at them and Dominick sat down in one of the chairs. Paul sat back down and put his hands between his knees.

"Paul, do you know Giuliano Ferri?" Dominick started.

"No." It came out solid and firm, with no eye contact. Instead, he seemed to be examining his gleaming army boots. Dominick tried not to look at his own shoeshine, something of a new obsession for him. Paul's boots were mirror bright, and Dominick could smell the polish on them.

"Really? He's one of the contestants."

"I know that. But I don't know him."

"Were you aware that Mack knew him?"

Paul shrugged. "Mack knew a lot of guys. He was...always a stud, I guess. And he woulda met him on Thursday night, I guess."

Dominick cocked his head. "He did more than meet him, Paul. He invited him back to your room."

That made the young leatherman look up sharply. "He did? That guy was Mack's trick? Did he see the guy who did it? Did *he* do it?"

Dominick didn't say anything. He crossed one leg over the other and looked steadily at Paul for a few moments, until the young man started to squirm.

"What?" Paul asked in frustration.

"You're not foolin' me," Dominick said, calmly. "You knew they were hookin' up, didn't you? How'd you find out? Snooping through Mack's email?"

"I didn't need to snoop! I handled Mack's email! I did his website!" He colored and took fast breaths. "I didn't know anything about who he was...*using* that night, he just told me to take off, so I did! Just like I told the lady cop!"

"Yeah, you took off so well, you didn't show up the next morning when you should've been getting him out of bed and off to do his judge thing. Isn't that kinda funny when one of the first things people say about what you did for Mack is you got him places on time?"

Paul tightened his hands into fists. "I fucked up! Jesus! It happens! Don't you think I wish I had been there? Maybe I could have saved him!"

"Come on, Paul, you went back to the room, didn't you? Maybe you waited for Ferri to leave, then went right on in and killed the guy who was intending to make you the real low man on his totem pole."

Paul shook his head furiously. "No. No! I never went back there!"

"And then you conveniently slept late, with your phone conveniently off."

Paul sat there mute, his lips pressed tight together. Dominick waited for a few moments and then nodded. "Okay, maybe you didn't. Tell me this. Did you handle *all* of Mack's email accounts?"

"Yes! I mean...he had only one."

Dominick smiled. "You mean not counting the one he used to hook up with other guys."

" I didn't...what do you mean? There wasn't another email!" He looked down again. "I don't like this. Why are you asking me these things?"

"Because there *was* another email account, and it was full of him making dates with other guys, gettin' hit up from online ads and such, sending a lot of sexed-up pictures back and forth. And you say you didn't know he had it? So, he was sneaking around on you, even though you say it was perfectly all right with you when he hooked up with other guys?"

Paul swallowed hard and shook his head. "No. I didn't know. But...fine. Whatever. He didn't have to tell me everything. Because I *didn't* care when he tricked. It meant nothing. Those guys were nothing to him. I loved Mack! I'd never do anything to hurt him!"

"Not even if you thought he was gonna invite some other man into his life? Some guy he knew a long time ago, who also loved him? Some dude who wasn't just a trick? Maybe Ferri was a lot more than *nothing* to Mack, and that worried you."

"You think Mack was going to get all romantic with some

312

lousy Mr. *Newark?*" Paul laughed and shifted in his seat. "Mr. Newark? Some scumbag hustler out of nowhere in borrowed leather?" He shook his head furiously. "No. No way. If that guy thinks Mack loved him, he's...he's crazy! Like, crazy enough to kill him!"

"So when you were staring at him on stage last night, you had no idea he'd been with Mack on Thursday?"

"I...no. No." He continued shaking his head.

"You just charged out on stage givin' him the hairy eyeball because..."

Paul shrugged again and blinked rapidly. "I...I drank a little. I was upset! I wasn't thinking. And they asked this stupid-ass question, and that dyke was laughing like some crazy bitch, and I just...went off."

This time, Dominick shook his head. "I don't believe you."

"Believe what you want. I didn't know him, the fake greaseball. No way could he have won Global Leather! He probably wasn't even *into* leather. All his stuff is new! He's a complete fake!"

"But Mack was writing to him for months. Sending him pictures and all, sayin' he couldn't wait until they saw each other again, how much he missed him, how they was gonna be just like old times. They were making *plans.*"

"No. No. That's not true. Completely not true! Mack was solid with me. I knew he tricked! He didn't have to hide anything from me. I was his partner, I knew him better than anyone! Better than some *goombah* who can't even, like, speak English right. *No way.* He's lying if he told you that! Crazy!" He panted and shook in his anger, voice rising, pounding one fist against his leg.

"Okay, okay," said Dominick. "Then lemme ask this. The picture of Mack that we found on Woodrow Gallia...how did he get the original? I understand you have proofs from the photo shoots, but they're not on Steel's website anywhere. So, how did Woodrow get one?"

"I don't know. How should I know?"

"How many people have copies?"

He sat there for a moment, thinking, his eyes darting back and forth. "I don't know. I mean, um, we had copies. And the photographer. Maybe the photographer was hacked or something."

"Mmm-hmm. Mack sent a copy of that one out recently, along with his pictures all bareass and all. Did you know he did that?"

"No. Sent them to who? One of his tricks? *Julie?*" he sneered. "Well, there you go, maybe Mr. Newark sent them out!"

"How'd you know that was his nickname, Paul?"

"I...who? I mean...his name is like, Giuliani, right? Julie! Whatever! I didn't know, I thought...I thought maybe...it's a joke! Jesus!" He panted again and stood up. "I don't want to answer any more questions."

"That's too bad, because I am still asking them," Dominick said, rising himself. He towered over Paul, who shrank back. "For instance, Paul, you go to the gym while you were here?"

"No. Yes! Yes...a couple of times. Why?" Now his eyes widened further.

"You go swimming maybe? In your T-shirt? Late Thursday night? We're looking at tapes right now."

"No! What the hell are you talking about? I mean...yes, I went to the gym, lots of guys go! I bet that Newark guy did, too! Why?"

"Thursday night? When you were gone from Wolfboy's party, did you just happen to decide to go work out? Get in a little swim?"

The young man shook his head.

"And you were wearing Mack's *hat* last night," Dominick continued, stepping forward. "How many other pieces of his clothing did you keep when we asked for everything? Don't you know that's interfering with an investigation?"

"No! I didn't...what would his cap do for you? I...I can give it to you now!" He took a step back.

"And what about his other clothes?"

"I gave you all his clothes!"

"Yeah? Then where's his jacket? And his leather shirt and pants? Somehow you forgot to tell us they were missing!" Dominick moved closer again.

"I didn't know! I was upset!" Paul shook angrily and wiped his hands against his hips; there were actually marks from his short nails in his palms.

"Didn't know the man's motorcycle jacket was gone? You didn't notice? You askin' me to believe that when you're all about what a good slave you were and all that crap?"

"Screw you!" Paul shrieked. "I was a *great* slave! His best boy! If you want his hat, fine, I'll give it to you, but I didn't do *anything* to him! And he didn't love anyone but me! He didn't care about that Newark guy! And that's probably why he killed him, and sent that picture out to people who would...make fun of him! Make him into a joke!" He kicked out violently, knocking one chair into the two behind it. "He probably stole Mack's clothes, too, so he could jack off on them and wish he was a real man!"

"Maybe," said Dominick, stepping back. "Let's go get that hat, shall we?"

CHAPTER 33

SLAVE WILLOW WAS NOT A HAPPY SLAVE. YOU'D THINK SHE was the one who lost a partner this weekend, Rebecca thought. Oh, she immediately reflected. Perhaps she's lost two.

Rebecca had left the vendor's room and met the uniform she'd asked to take the evidence bags from her. "See if someone can get these out to the lab as soon as possible," she instructed him.

"I'll take 'em myself, I'm off in twenty," he said eagerly. Oh, yes; now she remembered him. He had been the first one on the scene.

"Thank you, Officer Wright. I appreciate all your help in this." He went off glowing and she wondered why she ever thought of him as annoying. He was just a rookie. Compared to DeCosta, his joke about Mack possibly being lubricated seemed awfully tame.

She was still furious about DeCosta. Furious with him for his relentless loathing of this world of alternative sexualities, and angry with herself for letting it get to her. She was supposed to be way past that. Maybe she was a little sensitive because last night she'd gone to sleep having very, very non-politically correct fantasies about Trudy, but dammit!

In the meantime, she had suspects to grab and persons of interest to question. Since she knew where Ferri would be, she went straight to look for Willow, hoping DeCosta was making short work of Paul.

She found Willow co-teaching some sort of relationship workshop with Dick Schneider. Neither one looked happy about it, and the audience for it was small. She waited for it to end and then walked in as the two of them were packing up their flip charts and pointers and piles of undistributed handouts.

In the program, she was listed as Slave Willow Featherstone. In reality, she was actually a Willow, but her last name was Smith. She had just turned thirty, and her shoulder length straight hair was an unremarkable shade of brown. It was also tangled and haphazardly parted; she was not wearing makeup or jewelry, other than a chain collar. She looked sad and a little numb when Rebecca walked up to her and introduced herself. When she looked up, the expression on her face just spelled exhaustion and a woman close to the edge.

"I thought...I told you people everything!" Dick sputtered. "There's no reason to question her!"

Rebecca looked at him and raised an eyebrow. "You might think that because you have this master and slave relationship that you can act as a guardian for her, Mr. Schneider. But Willow is actually an independent adult, and I can ask her any question I need to concerning this investigation."

Willow tugged at a lock of hair and then snorted in derision. "You bet your ass I'm independent. As soon as I can line up a place to crash, I am so out of his house."

"And you know what? It can't be fast enough," snapped Dick. "Go ahead, say whatever you want! As though you didn't say enough last night!"

"Then you can carry your own shit back to the room!" she cried, pushing over the flip chart stand.

"Okay, okay, you both need to chill out," Rebecca said. "Willow, let's just calm down, and I'll ask you a few questions. Mr. Schneider, if I need you, I'll call you."

"Fine!" He grabbed the stand and the chart and left in as great a huff as he seemed to be able to manage.

"What was I thinking?" Willow said out loud. "It's always like that! You give them everything you have, and they give nothing back, like it's an honor to do all their chores and wear a collar and pretend everything's all right."

"Well, it must have worked once," Rebecca said.

"Yeah, or maybe I just told myself that this time, it was gonna work, unlike the last three times." She sighed and sank down into a chair. Then, with a slight look of surprise, she looked up. "Um... what do you want to ask me about? Mack?"

"I want to know how many Ravenfyre knives you brought with you to this weekend."

"Ten," she said without hesitation. "There were eleven left. I figured I'd leave one at home as a backup in case Wendi's broke. They break pretty easily, 'cause they're cheap crap. Wendi was always swapping the one she wore with a new one, because the plastic jewels would pop off or the hilt would get tarnished."

"That was quick. I got the feeling that Wendi and Dick didn't know how many were brought."

Willow laughed. "Why should they? They could leave it all to their loyal slave! No, there were ten." She sighed. "Wendi was gonna give them all away later, at the contest, including three to the winners."

"So, the two of them not knowing how many there were made it easy for you to give one to Dr. Abraham."

The slave blushed and shook her head. "Yeah. Kinda dumb, huh? Maybe I was just ready to move on and wasn't ready to face it. All I could think was, here's this totally hot woman who is just…above all this. She laughs at it, makes fun of it, but at the same time, she's just so dedicated to what we do and who we are. And smart! She wrote all those books and she can talk about anything. You know what an evening at the Ravenfyre house is like? Reality TV shows and sitcoms and being too tired to play, ever." Her head sank and she looked suddenly younger and more vulnerable. "And then I got here and Mickey hit me with this cruise of death and I just thought…why don't I get some, too? It's not like Dick and Wendi haven't played with other people!"

"And giving her the knife?"

She rolled her eyes. "Well, that was just how *stupid* I can be. I just thought it would be hot to actually *feel* that knife before the last of them was gone. I figured we'd play with it, I'd slip it back in with the others and it would be gone. But she still had it when Wendi said I had to turn in all the knives! I had to get it later." She frowned. "How did you know? Did Mickey tell you?"

"There was evidence on it."

"Oh. Well, it wasn't my best thought out plan, I guess. I'm sorry if it ruined anything for your investigation. I should have just turned it in, but I panicked." She turned her soft eyes up and looked genuinely sorry; Rebecca couldn't help but feel a little better that someone didn't seem to want to toss obstacles in her way.

"It'll all work out," Rebecca said reassuringly. "In the meantime, I'd like to find out a couple of things. We know Dick was out of the room for a while on Thursday; do you know how long he was gone?"

"Oh, sure! He was out of there a little after one, I think? But back by one thirty. Past my 'bedtime' but I had to stay up so he wouldn't walk into a dark room." Another eye roll. "That was when he went to try and get Mickey to help get Wendi's book published. Like *that's* going to happen."

"So you don't think he murdered Mack?"

"Dick? Murder anyone? Oh, heck no. I know he texted him, though, at the bar. That's about how brave he is, he can thumb a really mean message in text!"

"So, why did *you* do it?"

She had the decency to look embarrassed. "Pathetic, right? What can I say? We were out and all dressed up and Ravenfyre—Wendi—was feeling all toppish and I was into the moment. At a big event, it's easy to pretend you feel like this all the time. So, I chimed in, too. I still had his number on my phone from when they won last year and everyone was all friendly acting." She sighed. "I really need to be more selective next time I answer a KinkyNet ad. But no, Dick couldn't ever really kill anyone. I mean, he couldn't even get Mickey to give him the name of a single editor or anything."

"Why didn't Raven...uh, Wendi...go speak to Dr. Abraham?"

"She was in the gym. She's always sending me or Dick out to take care of her stuff. Like, forget her actually doing her own work, right?"

Rebecca swallowed her next question and almost shook her head to clear it. "In the gym? At one in the morning?"

"Oh, yeah. Wendi's a *freak* when it comes to exercise, and she loves to swim. When they keep the gym open all night at these things, you can always find her down there working out or in the pool, even when she works all day." Willow looked up at Rebecca. "Crazy, right? But she's been down there a couple of times every day."

"When did she return to the room that night? Were you still awake?"

"No, she only told me to stay up for Dick. Once he came in, my head hit the pillow and I was out. That was a really long day for me. Thank God Wendi didn't make me go to the gym with her, right?"

Rebecca nodded as she gathered her thoughts and mentally

pictured the timeline of the murder. "Just out of curiosity, have you noticed any clothing missing from what you packed?"

"Oh, my God, how did you know?" Her eyes went wide. "We're missing a leather jacket! Wendi said someone stole it from her locker at the gym, which is just so her. I mean, who wears their leather to the gym? But she doesn't want to be seen in the halls in, like, regular clothes..."

"What sort of jacket?"

"It was red, and short, like it buttoned above her waist?" Willow indicated the length. "She lost it the first night. I had to complain to the management in the morning. She wasn't going to wear it again this weekend, but that must have been an expensive piece." She shook her head. "Are you going to investigate that, too?"

"Possibly." Rebecca tried to focus on remembering the rest of her questions. Did Ravenfyre actually do it? What did they miss about the relationship between the two titleholders? Was there something more recent between them that might have pushed her over the edge? Could there be any proof of communication between them? She would have to have someone go through the elevator camera footage again, dammit! But she also had to make sure she covered the questions she came in with. Oh, yes, now she had it. "Do you know if Wendi ever met Giuliano Ferri before this week?"

A blank look. "Who? Oh! Mr. New Jersey Leather or something, one of the contestants? No. She's not too impressed by him. Says he comes up with answers to questions that sound like he memorized things."

"So, she wouldn't have given *him* one of these knives?"

"Oh, no! You had to do something for her to hand over the knife. Like, pick her up at the airport and take her to dinner, or comp us all into an event or be some other big-shot titleholder she wanted to suck up to." Her laugh after this was harsh. "I don't even have one. Which I'm kind of glad about, actually. Who needs more reminders of a bad relationship? Imagine how weird Paul feels right now."

"Weird about what?"

"Well, he has to go home and find that knife in Mack's stuff, right? Eww. That's going to be creepy."

Rebecca stared at her. "*Mack* had one?"

"Of course! Wendi sent one to him and to Ferral as soon as she had them made! Her sash family, right? She was trying to get them to all pose for a picture together holding them. But by the time they were all together in the same space, she'd found out that Mack was dishing her since the beginning. Wow, was she mad! He even sent her this picture of Paul cutting bananas with it and some dumb caption about what a perfect slave knife it was or something. I'm sorry he's dead and everything, but he was a real asshole."

"Thank you," Rebecca said quickly. Now, she genuinely felt dizzy. "You've been very helpful."

"I have?" Her eyebrows flew up and she smiled, genuinely. "You know, believe it or not, I really like being helpful. It's a shame I can't seem to leverage that into a decent full-time slave position."

"Well...good luck with that, then."

In the hallway, she read the text from Dominick and sent back one of her own, saying that they needed to talk. She now had far more to communicate than a text could convey. But she liked what he told her. Chlorine, of course; that would at least hide blood on a T-shirt, if not eradicate it. But now she had two pieces of information that could change the whole focus of the case! Mack *did* in fact own a Ravenfyre knife. But would he have traveled with it? Perhaps to use it one last time to taunt Ravenfyre? Did she go to see him that night thinking to get it back? Somehow this led to murder and blood on her leather jacket, which she had to lose somewhere...

Was she strong enough to stab a taller, heavier man? An upward thrust required some power behind it. But if she did it, then she could have simply kept the knife that was *not* bloodied while dumping the other one. Which could be why she could so confidently pass it over and tell Rebecca it could be sprayed with luminol.

And that leather shirt with the blood on the inside—was it large enough for Ravenfyre to put on over a different leather jacket? Covered up in several layers, tall in her high heels, her hair tucked under a cap, she might pass as masculine, at least to a tired man at two in the morning.

But *Paul* had the cap.

What a headache. She made sure to write down her thoughts and what Willow told her exactly. Then, she called Eduardo at his private number and told him about the chlorine and the pile of more leather clothing on the way to the lab in Queens. He admitted that a bloodstain might be compromised by chlorine but promised they'd tag the shirt so the lab techs would examine the seams. "It's possible just a light rinsing didn't do anything more than make it harder to see," he explained. "Don't worry, if there's blood on it, we'll find it. And a plastic bag is perfect for finger-prints! Maybe the cuffs of the shirt or the fly and waistband of the pants might turn some up. I'm off, but I'll call Park; she's over at the lab today. How come you didn't solve it already? Wasn't it the construction worker or the Indian?"

"Thank you, Eduardo," she said, hanging up. Then, she left messages with two more friends in the department who might be able to get action on those warrants for her. She needed those credit card and phone records! She checked her watch. Lunch time—the contestants would be free now, until the contest later. She wondered how often Giuliano Ferri went to the gym.

CHAPTER 34

Dr. Mickey Abraham slipped into the O'Neal's Irish Pub down the block from the hotel and ordered the steak tips and a double Jameson. A woman hopped onto the stool next to her, and Mickey looked at her over the frame of her glasses.

"Hello, Doc!" Nancy said cheerfully. "What an exciting weekend, huh?"

"You're the reporter," Mickey said with a nod. "Go away. I only read the *Times*."

"Nancy Nichols. Is that what *all* the radical lesbian feminists on Zod read?" Nancy waved over the bartender. "I'll have an Irish coffee, please, and don't skimp on the cream. That hotel coffee is terrible, isn't it? Almost as bad as that speech at break-fast. Which was almost as bad as the petrified scrambled eggs, but not nearly as bad as not having the option to get a Bloody Mary. Put the professor's drink on my tab, will you? Maybe it'll make up for that lack."

"You're persuading me not to throw said drink in your face."

"I'm charming that way. Hey, don't be so glum! Imagine how

your sales are going to skyrocket after this. Now, everyone's going to want to read those books. You'll make tons. Screw the University if they don't like it...speaking of which, have you been contacted by anyone in your department yet?"

Mickey groaned and pressed fingertips to her temples. "No. And sales of those books were never a problem for me." She laughed. "They sold like popcorn! Like candy-coated breakfast cereals, rotting the minds of the *kinky menschen* instead of their teeth. Why do you think I wrote so many of them? They sold! I need to revise my textbooks every other year or so in order to eke out a few extra bucks out of them. My *good* books barely earn enough to cover my membership in various academic self-congratulatory societies, all of which are necessary to my continued employment. But this mental excrescence, this blight upon literature, this insult to the good name of pulp fiction—I can *retire* on those royalty checks!" She shook her head and slammed back her drink.

"You know, most authors would be, uh, kind of happy to be able to say that." Nancy got her drink and admired the thick layer of cream floating on the top. "You want one of these? Minus the whiskey, maybe?"

"No. Actually, yes! Why not stay awake while I get completely wrecked? It's the only way I'm getting through the last part of this farce."

"You could just walk away."

"No, that would mean the terrorists have won. Or, something. No retreat, no surrender!"

"So, tell me, Doc—why did a radical feminist write a whole series of books about muscle-bound barbarian men enslaving gorgeous women who like to be slaves? I understand why you hid it. Probably not the best way to get dates, right? But why write it at all? For the money?" Nancy switched her recorder on while she pretended to rummage for her wallet. She left the bag on the bar.

Mickey mumbled something, and watched the bartender whisk up a little more heavy cream.

"What was that?"

"It was a joke!" Mickey turned on her bar stool. "A stupid *joke*! I was in school and working long hours at the bookstore and doing tutoring and a little illicit paper writing on the side. I was struggling to get by and facing a career in a field not known for its economic security. I had no social life to speak of, except for one part-time lover whose life looked quite similar to mine. Other than banging our brains out, one of the only things we enjoyed was the cheap fiction we harvested from the coverless books the store was supposed to be throwing away when they returned the covers for credits." She shook her head with a harsh laugh. "We read it all. Romances, mysteries, cowboy books, you name it. It was free and it wasn't academic. In fact, the cheaper it was, the better we liked it. We used to read choice sections to each other, laughing at the awful writing and ridiculous plots and stilted dialog."

"Hey, sometimes, something like that is what you need to clear your brain. I like an occasional bodice ripper myself."

Mickey nodded graciously and swept a hand up in acknowledgement. "And next door, you may purchase any number of bodices to be ripped at your leisure."

"Maybe I will. Anyway..."

"One early summer night, we ran out of new material. This was not rare. But instead of resorting to the usual alternative distraction to our bleak lives, we instead conceived of a competition. We would each write our own trashy novel, including some of the worst tropes we had learned to adore. We would do this in six weeks—at ten thousand words a week, that was roughly what we wrote when in the spring semester, and our course load was much lighter in the summer. Then, we would submit them to publishers, sending them at the same time, and collect the rejection letters. The first one to get even the slightest letter of encouragement would win. Plus, we had to swear we'd not screw the pooch by riddling the manuscripts with bad spelling and grammar. To that end, we acted as each other's copy editor."

She sighed and accepted her Irish coffee. "You do not look congenitally stupid. You may proceed to fill in the blanks."

"You won the bet."

"Sterling, Nancy, simply sterling. For a lousy five hundred dollars against five percent royalties, I arranged to mortgage my soul. I won the bet, and paid the rent when the check cleared and went on with my life."

Nancy nodded. "And then the book sold."

"They slapped a cover on that embarrassment featuring a physically improbable man in a loincloth standing on a cragged rock with a physically *impossible* woman clinging to his leg. The angle of her pose hid her nipples, but not her gravity-defying gazongas. In the background, three moons hung suspended in a purple sky, over the silhouette of a sort of giant, horned iguana. With fangs. I remember laughing when I saw it." She sipped cautiously, and wiped cream from her nose.

"Did you laugh when the check came in?"

"No, although I did when the editor called and asked for three more. I honestly though it was Deidre playing a prank on me. I hung up on him twice. Finally, he sent a note on the publishing house letterhead, upping his initial offer significantly." Her lunch came and she stared at the plate, and then returned to the coffee.

"So you wrote 'em for the money! I'm sure you know what Samuel Johnson had to say about that."

"Indeed!" Mickey nodded, looking slightly impressed. "No man save a blockhead ever wrote, except for money. Which makes all of my academic kin blockheads, I suppose. Yes, he offered me more money and a greater share and he wanted three more books." She picked up a french fry and dipped it into the ketchup. "And I took it. That advance was my rent for *half a year*. It meant

I could give up tutoring moronic basketball players and writing their papers on 'Iago: Prankster or Demon?' And the books were so easy to write, I could just bang out a couple of chapters a night, when I had the time."

Nancy nodded encouragingly and signaled for another round.

"You have to understand, I didn't just say, oh, I'll write a pulp fantasy opera. I deliberately designed my whole world to be a poke in the eye of the genre! Yet, over all these years, none of these morons ever noticed how goddamn queer it was!"

"Queer? A story about he-men on their dinosaurs, kidnapping harem girls?"

"No, no, don't be obtuse. That's the plausible diversion, although frankly, if you read the men as stone butches, it works. But...just read the damn things! If you can bear to. Look at all the cultural signifiers I put in there! The girls wear *rainbow* silks, and lavender veils. The sigil of the greatest of the clans is a fucking *labrys* crossed with a crescent moon! They eat tons of goddamned..."

"Tofu," Nancy said, wonderingly.

"Yes! Grilled tofu! And in one book, they even get food poisoning from it, an actual historic event well known in the *why-mins* community." She giggled and ate another fry. "I can't even begin to tell you how much I planted in there. For every trope I thought would appeal to an adolescent boy or a grown man with arrested development—rideable dinosaurs and biddable women being the primary bits there—I tossed in a nod to the dykes. They sit around and pass chamomile tea with their tofu and dab a touch of patchouli behind their ears. The men get grumpy, then dance naked and drink blood once every twenty-eight days! Their dinosaurs are named after a major lesbian pulp character. Hell, I think I slipped in about a dozen famous dykes by chopping their names up and adding superfluous accents and apostrophes. What else did I have to do, take out ads saying, look here, it's a clumsy pastiche of mythic archetypes mingled with haphazard satire?"

Around the bar, a few people looked over at the two women. Nancy pushed her bag closer to Mickey. "So your formula actually worked. You should be pleased that you read the audience for it so well!"

"Pleased? I'm horrified! I've been out as a dyke, out as a leatherwoman, since the sex wars. I've struggled for the recognition of the serious study of alternative sexualities as something other than a mental defect or emotional pathology! I've written thousands of pages of research and theory, and I've consulted with international scholars and done everything in my limited power to make our community worthy of thought and consideration, to advance the way we think of ourselves, develop the language we use, and the concepts we pursue. But no one reads *those* books—unless I assign them. Instead, *my people* read the craptastic pulp I produced on a drunken bet! That's what they choose to celebrate! They dress up and act like lunatics because of me!"

"And all these years, no one ever noticed all the gay stuff you put in there?"

"Once. One woman noticed. Grad student at Ann Arbor. Wrote a paper that pretty much captured every reference. Her professor gave her a B. I found it online last year; almost every comment on it found her theory that a lesbian actually wrote the books to be patently ridiculous. I think later on someone else tried to build on it with actual suggestions as to who the culprit was, but I lost interest." She drank down the rest of the Irish coffee and shoved the glass across the bar. "This glass is *defective*," she announced.

The bartender nodded and started to brew a fresh pot of coffee.

"Well, that student is about to be vindicated," Mickey

continued. "And I am about to be pilloried. Ah, well, it was a good ride. You're probably right; the books will continue to sell. Most people don't read much, and when they do, they don't retain much, so this will get out, there will be six thousand comments on KinkyNet, mostly between the same ten people, and then everyone just might forget it. I'll keep a low profile and see what my department intends to do *vis á vis* my job and the tenure I felt sure was going to be offered to me this year."

"I have a different idea," Nancy said. "Why not embrace it?"

Mickey leveled a stare at her. "Now, why would I do that? You think I want to hang out with Lord Larry and his clan of overweight male chauvinists who think they're being radical?"

"Why not? Because you know who's with Lord Larry? His wife, or his girlfriend. You've been making fun of 'em for years, right? But this is your chance to stand up and make 'em look really bad unless they acknowledge that a woman—a gay woman—designed their sex life." Nancy's eyes glittered as she leaned forward.

"So?"

"So, use it! Make them admit you're the real dom of doms! And then, in simple language they'll understand, write their *rulebook* for them."

Mickey blinked slowly and squinted. "What do you mean?"

"Hey, they're all passionate about living the Zodian lifestyle, right? They fill up their web pages about it, they have their own cons, they write a ton of fan fiction...they *want* a rulebook. Well, write one! Only put the stuff in there that matters to you. The official Zodian creator says do this, bucko. So, put up, or go cosplay in someone else's universe." She sat back and spread her hands as the bartender delivered fresh coffees.

"That's crazy."

"So are they. But you can tell them how to treat their ladies right and they'd have to listen!" Nancy shrugged. "And you know what they say about psychiatrists, right? Collect the rent on the Zodian yurts they've built on your imagination. Milk that b'bo for all it's worth."

Mickey laughed. "You, I like," she said, shoving her plate over. "Have some fries."

CHAPTER 35

"LORD, LORD, LORD," DOMINICK CHANTED, WHEN REBECCA finished filling him in on what she'd discovered. "Now we got another suspect?"

"I don't know. I'm not thinking clearly. I was so focused on the people who were dressed like the person Joshie saw that I didn't even really consider those who might have arrived wearing one thing and left wearing Mack's own clothing. I artificially shrank my own suspect pool and now the whole case is contaminated."

They were back at the diner again; by the time they converged at the green room area, the contestants and the judges had scattered for their last chance at privacy and food before the contest. Rebecca didn't even mind. She was so upset by her incompetence she couldn't even think to order lunch. Dominick ordered her another salad and coffee while she flipped through her notebook with increasing annoyance.

"I called the station and told them to get someone looking through the footage you copied on Friday and look for Wendi; I also asked Roger for whatever images he *does* have from the camera outside the gym, so we can see if any of our suspects actually regularly go there, and what sorts of bags they carry when they do. I've called about those phone and credit card records twice, but of course no one's around to release them. It's just a computer file, what's their damn problem?" She checked her phone again and dropped it onto the table in frustration.

"Whoa now," Dominick said, raising a hand. "Nothing's contaminated, and we've been doin' the best with what we got. We just got a lot more information today, that's all."

The waitress came by with their drinks and Rebecca waited until she was gone to level her gaze at him. "Don't try your shifting accent with me, Detective, I am not some easily bamboozled suspect. We're screwed, and it's my fault. All our suspects will cross state lines tonight or tomorrow, making the investigation that much harder, and it'll probably get back shelved for months until DNA evidence comes back, by which time you'll be back at the 25th and won't have to worry about working with *freaks* any more."

He shook his head. "I hope I am not back at the 25th, actually. And if we gotta wait, we wait, all happens in its time. But if you think I'm going to magically enter a sector of police work where there ain't no freaks, I want to know where that place is!"

Was he that dense? "I meant you won't have one as a partner," she said.

Dominick did a physical double take, his head jerking back in surprise. "Excuse me?"

"Look, you don't think I've gotten plenty of that crap over the years? The lesbian centerfold slid into my locker, the naughty words written on my chair? Hell, when I was on patrol, I came back from the toilet one day to find my nightstick had been labeled OFFICER DYKE'S DICK. *That* was charming. And personally, I don't care if you're motivated by juvenile frat house humor, an actual terror of gay people or religious belief, but if you can't keep it inside, could you at least try to use more creative language?"

His brow knotted. "What are you talking about?"

Now she completely lost it. "Jesus Christ, DeCosta! You've been riding me since you showed up, with *freak* this and *pervert* that, and why can't they keep it covered, or closeted..."

"Wait, wait, wait one minute now!" he interrupted. "I haven't been saying that about you! Why...I mean, *are* you one of those people?"

"Yes, DeCosta! I know you just got to my precinct, but you really didn't know I was gay?"

He shook his head, and then nodded. "Of course I knew! I just didn't know you were into all that...stuff." He looked down and adjusted his tie as his voice lowered as well. "So, excuse me."

"Wait." Now Rebecca held her hand up. "Didn't know I was into *what*?"

"That leather...thing. The BDSM..."

"I'm not!"

They stared at each other, frozen in misunderstanding.

"Then what do you mean?" they both said simultaneously.

"You first," Rebecca demanded.

He nodded, and leaned back against the booth, looking at her skeptically. "What does being *gay* have to do with being a fetish-freak? I know plenty of gay folks who're just the same as everyone else; they got good lives, they get hitched, they make a home, they have jobs, have babies and such. I'm no illiterate thug who thinks gay equals sick and twisted."

Rebecca frowned. "But..."

"Look, Feldblum. If I had something against gay people, I'd have a very serious issue in my life. Like, the next time I went home for Thanksgiving or Christmas and asked my Aunt Yolanda to pass the buttered peas, she'd drop the pot over my head." He gave a short laugh, envisioning it. "And that would be before her, uh, life partner, my Auntie Claire, slapped me *upside* my head so hard the peas would just pass through my skull like buckshot through tar paper."

"Your aunt...the pastor?"

"Of the Zion Community Baptist Church, a welcoming and affirming congregation sharing in the love of our lord Jesus Christ, to be precise," Dominick intoned, laying a hand over his heart. "Yolanda and Claire took me in when I was a boy; raised me with love, real Bible truths, good food and the understanding that they were as deserving of God's grace as anyone else in the world, and truthfully, I feel much more deserving than most."

Rebecca stared at him, suddenly feeling dizzy again. "Then... you knew I was..."

"I knew who you was before I came here," he said earnestly, leaning forward again. "Dag, you know you're famous an' all dat!"

"Stop it," she warned.

"Right. But seriously, Detective. You got a sixty-nine percent solve rate all by yourself, and that's with the, uh, challenges you got being who you are and all that. Soon as I got my shield, I wanted to come down here and see what you do, learn from you. I figured, Southern, black boy from outta town, why not hook up with another outsider? We could cover each other's backs, work some new angles. That was my thinking, anyway. I couldn't swing the permanent transfer, and maybe you don't want me to now, anyway. But hell, yeah, I wanted to come work with you. I'm about as opposite from prejudiced as you're gonna find, unless you bring up another gay cop." He looked up at his arriving Reuben sandwich and spread a napkin over the shiny iron-grey tie he was wearing over a darker grey shirt. As he tucked the napkin in around his collar, he looked across the table at her.

"Yeah, so I'm sorry if I sounded harsh. I can get carried away. Comes from years of hearing my Aunts called all sorts of names, I suppose." He sighed. "But the truth is, it's *not* normal what they do over there. If some couple play their little games in the bedroom and don't disturb the neighbors, who cares? But to dress up and parade it around, scream out to the world, *look at us, we're different!*—what does that do, except make it harder for people who just want to be left alone like everyone else? And some of that stuff is just…wrong. Dangerous to the body and the spirit. Look at all the troubles people are having over there with their polyamory and their master/slave games. They spend all this time talking about how to beat each other up the right way, but not how to treat each other like good people. It's a wonder they don't have more killings going on, 'cause they sure are hurting each other."

"For most of them, I bet it's nothing more than another way to spice up their sex lives," Rebecca said carefully. "And if we can stand it when people paint themselves up for football games, role-play that they're superheroes at comic book conventions and dance half-naked down the street in New Orleans during Mardi Gras, I don't see that these folks are much different. In fact, most of them would rather not make a nuisance of themselves in public—look at how much trouble they go to in order to keep themselves hidden from the street! And how every time you talk to them…"

"It's *consensual* this and *safe* that," Dominick said. "Yeah, they sure talk it up. But the fact is, behind the talk, we got people lying and cheating on each other and one dead guy that everyone hated but no one actually did anything about. In fact, they gave him an award, and made him a star, mostly because, what? He looked good?"

Rebecca nodded. "Sure. And if I turn the TV on tonight and watch some reality shows, am I going to see many better examples of humanity?"

He made a harrumphing sound and addressed his sandwich with complete focus. Rebecca picked at her salad. After a few moments, they both looked up and gave half smiles.

"Truce?" Dominick said. "I'm sorry I was so out there. I'll tone it way, way back. You won't hear me say 'freak' no more. Are we good?"

"Sure. And I'm sorry I came down on you. That was out of line. I'm a big girl, I should have just moved on."

"No, no, I'm glad you got it out! 'Cause if you hadn't, you would be just waiting for the first moment to cut me free instead of lobbying your Loo to let me come down and join y'all." He added more dressing to his sandwich; the sweet smell of the corned beef and the sharp sauerkraut finally triggered some hunger in Rebecca. She chased a few tomatoes around her salad.

"I'm not among his favorite people right now, and not likely to be there once this event ends, and I don't have a serious arrest other than a whack-job who can walk away with a trespassing fine." Her phone buzzed, and she glanced at it. "Dammit. I'm thinking there's no chance of getting into anyone's phone or computer or credit card records today. The city might never sleep, but the bureaucrats do."

"Well, then we need to figure out what we need to figure out in the next couple hours and get it done."

Rebecca almost laughed at how cool and confident Dominick sounded. She shook her head, but pulled out her notepad and started making a new list.

Ravenfyre—where was she on Thursday night? Did she go to the gym, and if so, did she stop by Mack's room first? And was there a reason for her to be angry enough to kill him? Could she have been strong enough to stab a larger, heavier man, and cool enough to walk away dressed in his clothes?

Ferri—was there any proof of this relationship he claimed to be rebuilding with Steel? He had no alibi for the time of death, and so far, no proof that he had been anything but a quick date trying to get Steel to judge him favorably in the contest. "But now that it's possible there was a knife in the room already, we don't have to wonder where he got one," Dominick pointed out. "If he went there looking for love and got treated like some hooker, he still coulda killed the man."

And Paul—still no alibi, plus this strange behavior around Mack's missing clothing. "You can't tell me he gets all emotional over a hat but just forgot a jacket! Damn, even *I* know the jacket's more important."

"And we still don't know who sent the picture out on the Internet, or why. And what the yellow panties mean, including whether Steel put them on himself voluntarily, under duress, or even if someone put them on him after he was dead, although positioning didn't suggest that to me." Rebecca jotted those two notes down as well. "All we know is that Ferri brought them over, and Paul thinks they were there to shame the vic."

They looked at the list together.

"I'll put money down it's Ferri," Dominick said. "The only one big enough to punch that cheap knife in deep enough to kill. He sends out the picture, saying, my ex-boyfriend is Satan. He puts the panties on him, like saying, this is who you were back in the day, sucker."

"Lunch says it's Paul," Rebecca said, putting down her credit card. "Because hell hath no fury like a slaveboy scorned."

"Detective, you are on. Now, tell me again what Slave Willow said, exactly, just in case it was Ravenfyre all along and we're both wrong."

CHAPTER 36

THE VENDOR ROOM WAS PACKED BEYOND CAPACITY; LINES of shoppers waited in the adjoining rooms while security let them in one at a time, as others left with their purchases. Astonished but thrilled crafters and resellers swiped credit cards and wrote receipts and measured strangers who had not been to the event before this day for custom leather, latex and period clothing. Cutter Hatfield was completely sold out of fantasy knives; periodically she got on her cell phone to try and find someone who could bring her more from a warehouse just over the George Washington Bridge in Jersey, and do it within two hours. Two men in BDUs argued over who was going to buy her last Ka-Bar. Half the vendors demanded to stay open during the contest, and were petitioning Earl to extend their hours after it as well.

Also sold out was every single copy of a Zod book and every serious sociology text by Mickey Abraham, even the one copy of *The Paradox of Power Exchange and The Materiality of Semiotic Forms* at $75. "Will she be here later to sign it?" the buyer asked eagerly, her eyes wide and thrilled at the possibility. Dr.

Westfield even did a brisk business in *You're Kinky, and That's Okay*, happy to explain to anyone who would listen that it was *fine* for lesbians to have fantasies of male domination. In fact, it was healthy and normal. He intended to teach a class on that, this coming summer, at Kink Au Natural Environments, the annual kinky, nudist campfest. "I'm thinking of calling it, *When You Think the Unthinkable*," he said to a lady in a Wonder Woman costume, complete with a very realistic golden lasso. "What do you think?"

They reached the capacity for the ballroom and stopped ticket sales, causing a mini-riot in the hotel lobby that had to be quelled with security ranging from event volunteers to actual uniformed patrol officers stationed to watch for troublemakers. Two Christian activists almost got as far as the elevators before their Crocs gave them away; they were issued loitering and trespassing tickets and warned to stay far from the doors of the hotel, with the wavering crowd of protestors. The Queers United In Malediction jeered at them as they were escorted out, singing, "All we are sayyying…is give kink a chance!"

The mainstream media was noticeably absent; with no real developments in the case and a steady stream of pieces from Nancy Nichols being farmed out to various newswires, there was little that needed fresh photos. But Phedre and Cary were joined by members of the minor press, bloggers and freelancers for alternative and bar papers, all of whom got passes.

"Why not?" shrugged Slave Bitsy Olmstead, from her spot behind the main desk. "We sure got nothing to hide now! We'll just sell more tickets next year."

Bitsy arrived at the Breakfast Keynote in a Victorian gown done in a wine-colored satin jacquard. She floated across the room on the arm of Master Tom, who was dressed in his all-black-leather ensemble and looked about as pleased as a man could, his eyes bright and head erect. Any member of the contest staff who had it in mind to scold Bitsy for skipping out on the early shift immediately bit their tongue and said a cheerful good morning instead. Certain things just trumped, that's all.

But after breakfast was over, people shook each other awake after Dr. Westfield's stirring call for unity in the community, as everyone celebrated their unique specialness, remembering with sadness the losses of our past and rejoicing in the pleasures to come. Bitsy kissed Tom on the cheek and swept back into her leadership position in the lobby. He also went back to work, occasionally standing away from the table and gazing at her in open admiration.

Earl slipped next to her at one point and asked, "How was it?"

"Oh, Earl, I think this is the one, I can feel it," she purred back. "And he's only three hours away from me! We can actually *date*. And did I mention he has a real job? He's an electrical contractor! He wants to take me *shopping* later."

Earl nodded in satisfaction and decided to check the guy out using his own network. Bitsy in love was fabulous. Bitsy with a broken heart was a tragedy.

And he took care of his own.

Rebecca and Dominick made their way through the lobby only to be stopped by a hesitant, familiar voice. The formerly elusive Wolfboy waved at them awkwardly and they paused. He was standing with a knot of people all wearing vests with the same snarling wolf logo on the back. "Uh. Hi. Uh, you said you were interested in lost and found clothes, right? So, uh, there's some at the desk. Me and my...clan...we asked around." He looked sideways at them in his awkward way and pointed at the information table. "Was that, uh...good?" His clan members gathered behind him with earnestly helpful looks on their faces as well.

"Sure. Thank you, sir," Dominick said with a nod. "While you're here, were any of the rest of you at the party Thursday night? Does anyone remember when Paul Helms left or came back?" They conferred and talked over each other, but no new information was produced. They shrugged and looked disappointed when he simply nodded. Dominick thought for a second and then said, "You've been very helpful. Thank you, all." They all beamed and nodded back and walked off together. Dominick turned to Rebecca with one eyebrow raised.

"*Weird* is acceptable," she murmured, digging into her pocket for more gloves and then going to investigate the pile of clothing. Five minutes later, she put down the third pair of panties and looked over at Dominick who was separating out the T-shirts. "How can people lose so much clothing in just a couple of days?"

"It's *weird*," he said with a small measure of satisfaction. Then, he pulled a pair of jeans out of the box and looked at them thoughtfully. "Has anyone come by looking for stuff?" he asked the volunteer behind the table.

"Sure," the young woman said. She produced a handwritten list. "These are things people *lost*, and where they thought they lost them. On the other side are things people *found* and where they found them—that's what's in the box, although I don't think everyone actually listened when we told them to write stuff down. Wolfboy said you might be looking for something for the case, so we didn't let people pick up stuff they said was theirs. We said they could come by later, though. Is that all right?"

"Yes, ma'am, thank you. May I see that?" He took the list and scanned it until he reached one entry. "Well, I'm betting some Wolftooth Clan member named Midnight wants these jeans." He turned them over in his gloved hands and shook them out; they looked clean and unmarked and completely unremarkable in every way. "Wolfboy said he wore a small size, but he must have long legs."

Rebecca nodded. "He was at the party with Paul? You think Paul might have borrowed those? They'd be...long on him." She dropped a string tank top that read I'VE BEEN A NAUGHTY GIRL, TAKE ME TO YOUR ROOM into the box. "So, he'd have to wear them cuffed at the ankle." She took one leg of the jeans and held it up; there was a faint crease in the material.

"I need more evidence bags," she muttered. "The guys at the lab are going to think we're sending them a whole store."

"I got some," Dominick assured her. "Isn't that...*weird*?"

She could tell he was going to have fun with that. But right now, she didn't mind at all. Paul had been wearing jeans cuffed at the ankles when she first saw him. It was possible these had some trace on or in them, and they were closer to reconstructing the complete timeline with every additional piece of evidence.

"Ah, Detectives!" said Roger the hotel manager, coming from the front desk. "I have the files you requested. I hope they're helpful. Please don't hesitate to call me if you need anything else." He extended a little thumb drive with the hotel name on it, and Dominick took it with a smile.

"I'll go take a look at this," he said to Rebecca. "And I'll call someone to pick up the jeans. How's about you grab Ravenfyre and figure out if we can eliminate her?"

Oh, yes, Rebecca thought, as she nodded. Maybe they would close this one after all.

"For the last time, the judges' panel stays as it is!" Earl announced to the room, fixing them with his Big, Bad Producer Glare. "Zenu, *I'll* break a tie, if any, and that is the end of discussion! And Larry, if you want to walk off, you do that, but Mickey stays!"

"I protest!" thundered Lord Laertes.

"You've been protesting all morning; has it gotten you anywhere? Your choice is take it or leave it. And I don't want any craziness from you guys when you're out there, okay? I think we've had enough this weekend. Let's try to get through this with some dignity and integrity intact? Please?"

"Then you'd better make sure we don't get any drink tickets," snickered Mickey Abraham.

"You are cut off, Mickey. I mean, seriously. Is there any coffee coming?" He turned to Boi Jack who nodded as she tried to tie her bowtie. She and Boy Jack were in black tuxedo shirts under their leather vests, with red silk bowties and matching red cufflinks shaped like handcuffs.

"I sent out for *real* coffee, Earl. We're getting a whole box of it."

"Get two, and keep it flowing. Now, what's the next crisis?"

"Uh, it's Paul...he's kind of freaking out again? He's waiting down the hall, I got someone to go get him a soda or something."

Earl muttered a blasphemy and headed out to deal with that. There was an awkward silence as he left. Boi Jack said, "I'll see if that coffee's here yet," and edged out the door.

Every titleholder on the judges' panel had with them their full panoply of awards, medallions, sashes, belts, vests and anything else given to them as marks of distinction. They also seemed far more occupied in choosing which ones to wear and how to wear them than normally expected. But it was clear a pall had slammed down over their camaraderie.

It was easy to focus on the conflict between Laertes and Mickey and Earl, especially since no one even wanted to *discuss* the situation concerning Mistress Ravenfyre. That Mickey was outed was one thing. How it happened was another.

And Ravenfyre knew it. She had to send for a volunteer to lace her corset and help adjust the tiny velvet hat she was wearing pinned in her updo for the contest, since her own slave was... resigning? What did one call a slave who left? The sheer unfairness of it all was galling. It was her *husband* who'd uttered the unacceptable words, yet she had to take the blame! It was her *slave* who cheated on her, but now she looked like a bad mistress!

And all because she discovered that the nasty little dyke had actually written those barbarian porno books the true weirdos in the scene loved so much.

It wasn't her fault at all. She'd just been looking up some scene history stuff for the speech she was going to make to help her win her first title. She thought it would look good to talk about famous women in the scene, and Mickey Abraham had been one. Discussions on a forum about her work were so complicated and dense, and it was hard to figure out what exactly she wrote about. Wendi had her job at the library, though, so she asked one of the people with an actual degree in library science, since hers was in physical education. If people assumed she was a librarian, what was the harm in that?

Much to her surprise, the librarian not only explained some of Abraham's writings but told her there was a pretty good chance she'd also written the Zod books! Her explanation of how she found this out was far too long and complicated to follow, but eventually she got to the point by saying a few people thought those books were written by one of a small group of possible authors and one of them was Mickey Abraham. Talk about a shocker! There Wendi had been, thinking of a lesbian writer from New York as some kind of magical person who never had actual sex with men, but she'd written up some pretty graphic stories all about women submitting to them!

She didn't mention it to anyone else until people started talking about putting her essays in a book, and she wondered out loud to Dick whether she could be as famous as that Zod professor and he asked her what the hell she was talking about.

Oh, and for Willow to just out and tell everyone that she helped write some of those essays! It was enough to give her a migraine! But no one was yelling at *Willow* for outing her Mistress!

Although, she was right about Dick. Poor man. But at least he wasn't a public figure like she was!

Well, soon, this would all be over. She could pack her things, go home and let Willow go try and find some other owner who would take her in and teach her valuable lessons—because what is an assignment to write a few essays now and then but *teaching*? Everyone else in the scene was all about how mistresses and masters had to teach and mentor and all that stuff. Perhaps they would find a new slave, a better one. One who knew how to make e-books. And maybe one who gave manicures...

She realized the room had gone completely silent and looked up. Boi Jack was holding the door open with one hand while hefting a cardboard box of coffee in the other. With her was a woman in a totally vanilla black pantsuit, but a nicely tailored one. She looked through the room and smiled at Wendi directly.

"I'm Detective Feldblum, Ms. Schneider. Would you mind answering a few questions for me?"

Oh...crapola. Her carefully and precariously constructed façade crumbled and she burst into tears. "Oh, my lord," she cried softly. "I knew this was going to happen! I didn't mean for it to turn out that way at all, you have to understand that!"

Everyone in the room exchanged looks of confusion; Mickey Abraham opened her eyes and lowered her glasses down her nose a bit.

Rebecca stepped in and lowered herself easily so she was level with the seated titleholder. "What didn't you mean?"

"I didn't mean for him to *die*!" she burst out.

"Holy shit," Mickey said.

"Madre de Dios! What is going on here?" cried George Santos.

"Oh. Em. F'n Gee," gasped Boi Jack.

Master Zenu sat down heavily, in shock. Then, suddenly, he laughed. "Well, at least we'll have an odd number again!"

CHAPTER 37

DOMINICK RAN THROUGH THE FILES ON THE DRIVE ROGER
had given him, and kept his eyes on the little notebook screen.
How detectives did fieldwork before these things was a mystery
to him. But it was tiring to watch the little flicking images, and
hard to really discern details. As Roger had predicted, the camera
file had been recorded over since Thursday night. And he was also
correct about the number of people who used the gym; there was
a constant stream of people going in and out, most carrying bags.
And indeed, some were still dressed up in their fetish costumes
when they went in!

A mental image of someone in one of those gimp hoods riding
a stationary bike made him almost laugh out loud.

"Hi, Detective DeCosta," said a light voice from his right.
He'd found a relatively quiet spot to sit down, past the privacy
barriers set up in the lobby, but not too close to the front doors.
He looked around and saw Global Bootblack Ferral. He hit PAUSE
and nodded politely, his eyes taking in the amazing boots Ferral
was wearing.

They were tall, up to Ferral's knee, with thick soles but a sensuous curve all the way up the calf. And they were pristine! In fact, boots fresh out of a box shouldn't look as good as those were. Ferral grinned. "Custom-made. Like 'em?"

"They're very nice," Dominick admitted. Then he paused, and looked at them again.

"They're really expensive," Ferral started to say, sheepishly. "But I can see if I could get you a discount with the company that makes them, I'm sure they'd be happy to—"

"I got a question," Dominick said. "When did you polish those?"

"Polish? Yesterday. This morning I just ran a buffing cloth over them to make them shine."

"But they don't *smell* like shoe polish."

Ferral looked offended. "Of course not. When properly cared for, a boot should smell like its owner—but not too much—and what it's made of. If you smell soap or polish, or edge dressing, then the bootblack hasn't buffed it out enough, or the boot is so fresh off the stand it's still warm. Leather absorbs, yeah, but it shouldn't make you walk around all day smelling like turpentine."

Dominick nodded. "Would *anyone* who does boots know that?"

"They should, but they won't. A lot of people like the smell of turpentine, I guess. But it takes a long time and some elbow grease to really make a pair pop like this. Most people would be just as happy if they were just clean, so they stop buffing too early, or they don't treat the leather afterwards...you'd be amazed at the variables."

Dominick looked into Ferral's eyes and said, sincerely, "Thank you. I needed to know that."

"Any time, Detective. In fact, come by the chairs and I'll be happy to give your Oxfords a treat. You keep 'em really nice, but I can make 'em better."

Before Dominick could respond, his phone buzzed. "Thank you," he repeated, as he thumbed the screen. Ferral waved and walked off and Dominick read the message twice. "Well, damn," he said, as he shut his notebook and stuffed it into the case. "Now we both lost the bet?"

An array of differently colored bandanas had been proffered to help Mistress Ravenfyre stem her tears; Rebecca could see black, grey and red among them. But when the other judges cleared the room and left her alone with Ms. Global Leather, Wendi found her purse and used plain tissues.

"It...it was just supposed to be a j-joke," she stammered, wiping her tears and shaking her head at the blotches of makeup that came away onto the tissue. "I thought after he did all those awful things to me all year—you have no idea what that man did to me, he ruined my life!—that I'd just give him a taste of what that feels like."

Hurry up and get here, Dom, Rebecca thought, as she patted Wendi on the shoulder. "Just try to calm down, Ms. Schneider. I'm sure it'll be all right. Just take a few deep breaths, then you can tell me whatever you'd like to say."

She looked up sharply. "But I don't have to! I have the right to remain silent!"

"Absolutely," Rebecca assured her. "If I arrest you. But I'm not arresting you now, we're just talking. You were saying you didn't mean anything. So, I'm willing to hear whatever you have to say, if you have something to explain."

"You have to understand, I didn't know that horrible man was going to run over here like that," she said. "I didn't think anything would happen for days! And even then, maybe a few nasty comments on a few websites, but not killing!"

Rebecca pulled up a chair and sat down.

"I know Mack was cruel to you," she said. "I know he outed you in your hometown, and cost you your job."

"He did! Really! And said the most terrible, stupid things about me, to me—made fun of me whenever he could! So...you can understand why I felt so hurt and angry!"

Rebecca nodded sympathetically. "Of course. So, on Thursday night..."

"Thursday night, he was so hateful to that nice man Kevin in the bar, and then he left and we all thought we'd never see him again. Oh, and we didn't!" She gasped and wiped her eyes again. "I meant that he'd *leave*, though! Not die!"

"I understand. So, what happened Thursday?"

The door opened and Dominick stuck his head in. "Mistress Ravenfyre was about to tell me of a *terrible misunderstanding*, I think," Rebecca quickly said.

"Well," she sniffed and then blew her nose as delicately as possible. "I didn't mean for it to turn out the way it did. It's...mitigating circumstances!"

"Really?" Dominick said quickly. "I'm sure it was."

"See, I go to the gym late at night. I know, it's crazy, but if I don't get in my exercise, I just puff up like a balloon. And on Thursday, I was at the gym late and it was just horrible because I couldn't even get my regular workout. Why? Because a damn contestant was in there!"

The two detectives exchanged glances. "Which one?" Rebecca asked.

"The Italian from New Jersey."

"You don't say?" said Dominick.

"I know. How hard would it be to just stay away from places the judges might be going to? But he was right down there and I didn't even notice until I got into the room all changed. Oh! And, and then by the time I went back to the lockers, I had a jacket missing, um, stolen! It was a horrible, sucky night!" She looked up at them and sniffed.

"Was that when you went to see Mack?" Rebecca asked.

"Go see him? The last guy on earth I wanted to see was *him*! No, I went all the way back to my room and got on the Internet because I was just too angry to sleep. And then, I got the email with the picture."

Rebecca was starting to feel like Alice down the rabbit hole. Nothing was turning out anywhere near what they'd supposed! "The email," she prompted.

"It was from someone I didn't know, and it said something like, kinky gay man caught in sex orgy. I don't even know why I opened it, but there was this picture of *that man*...in my email! I mean, who would send that to me? It was like he was laughing at me! So...I forwarded it." She looked down and shredded a tissue in her hands. "With a note."

"Mmm-hmm?" Dominick encouraged her with his rising and falling intonation.

"Well, I knew that Woody guy had come to leather events before! He was at one I did in Minnesota, and one in...oh, one of the Carolinas, I think. And he's really easy to find online, and when I was looking for him I found all these other weirdos who have nothing better to do...So, I sent them *all* the picture...and sort of said...Mack was..."

"A Satanist?" Rebecca offered.

Wendi nodded and dabbed at her tears again. "It was the worst thing I could think of! Except for molesting children, that is, and I wouldn't *ever* joke about that. I just thought...maybe someone would do a story on the Internet some day. Not come down immediately and *kill* him!"

"Let's go back for a second here. You didn't know who sent that picture to you?"

"No, they weren't on my friends list."

"Do you remember the email name?"

She frowned and shook her head. "No; but I'm sure I can find it in my old mail."

"We'd like to get that from you, please. And when you sent out your, ah, note, what email address did you use?"

Mistress Ravenfyre blinked, surprised. "Mine? I just opened a new file and put all the addresses I found in the CC box and attached the picture..."

Rebecca pressed her lips together and nodded encouragingly. "So...you used your own email account to send them out to the Christian websites."

"Well, it's not like they're going to know who I am," she said, just a bit defensively. "Besides, it was a spur of the moment thing! I didn't plan to do it, I just...did."

The door slammed open and Dick charged in. "What's this... Wendi! What is going on here? I just heard you said you killed Mack!?"

She started to say something but coughed and sobbed again and he rushed to throw an arm around her. "We want a lawyer!" he immediately said. "Right now!"

"You don't need one," Rebecca said, rising. "What your wife did was not a crime."

"See! I told you!" She looked up, her eyes wide. "It wasn't my fault!"

"Ma'am, it wasn't your fault because Woodrow probably didn't get the email and immediately run over to the room to kill the man," Dominick explained. "He followed Mack from the bar to his room, but got chased away when Mack noticed him. Then he went and filmed some other people in the lobby. We got it all time stamped; it's highly unlikely he killed the man."

"Oh? Oh!" She swallowed and sniffed again. "Then it wasn't my fault?"

"It wasn't a nice thing to do," Rebecca said, looking down at her. "But Mack was probably already dead when Woodrow's version of the picture was created, and definitely long gone by the time the unedited version started popping up at different websites. However, I do want to make sure I heard you right about something else—you're positive you saw Giuliano Ferri in the gym that night?"

She nodded, wiping her nose. "Yes! Absolutely."

"And do you know exactly what time that was?"

"Ah...no. Not exactly." Suddenly, she needed to search for her purse and more tissues.

"And did you see Paul Helms there at any time?"

She shook her head furiously, the corner of her mouth twisting. "No, thank goodness. He gives me the creeps! Always following Mack around and doing all his work and sneering at people... ugh!"

"And what time did you say you left the gym?"

"I...don't really recall," she said, smiling as she pulled out her tissue pack. But it was empty, and she crumpled it in one hand, looking a little lost.

Rebecca said, cheerfully, "Then let's get some cold water on your face so you can go take care of your responsibilities. I am so regretful this had to happen right before you need to go be public. I'll come with you."

Dominick pursed his lips and opened the door for the ladies. He spied the box sitting on a nearby table and smiled at Master Dick. "Coffee?"

"Thanks for getting me away from Dick," Wendi said after she splashed water on her face. "He's a dear, but..."

"No worries. *Now* you can tell me when you saw Ferri?"

"About a quarter after one? Maybe a little later."

"Mm. And we know Dick got back to your room by one thirty, and you much later. So...where'd you go?"

"Actually, I stayed at the gym for a while. In the locker room.

With a friend." She leaned against the sink for a moment and then patted her face dry. "Do you need to know who she was? Really?"

Rebecca shook her head. "Not at this time. Did you see any other contestants or judges down at the gym that night?"

She nodded and searched through her purse for makeup. "George was down there using one of the machines. He didn't leave, but you know, people need to handle their contact with contestants in their own way. They say we should never be alone with them—I count a tiny little hotel gym as close enough!"

"Very wise. Thank you, Ms. Schneider."

Wendi expertly applied lipstick in two quick sweeps and blotted her lips neatly. She turned back to Rebecca and asked, somewhat sheepishly, "And there's no need to tell Dick I was... chatting with a friend, is there? This is a hard enough weekend for him already."

"I can see why. If you can get me the email address that sent you the picture, I'll let you get back to judging the contest. But don't be surprised if you find your email full of letters from the religious people you contacted, all eager for you to come on their shows and websites and tell them how you're rising out of this sinful lifestyle. You outed *yourself* to them, and I think Woody is right now boasting about how you will lead people away from the BDSM world."

Wendi paled again and drew in a deep breath. "But...I didn't mean..."

"And next time you decide to give a...*friend*...a present like your nice red leather jacket, try not to tell other people it was stolen? If the hotel had filed a police report, you or your friend could find yourselves in a bit of trouble when the jacket showed up."

She had the decency to sheepishly blush a little more while she nodded.

"Don't even say it," Rebecca said, as she and Dominick walked over to the contestant room.

"You know, my Aunt Yolanda would say, you should dance with the one what brung ya. Is *anyone* doing that here? At all?"

"I'm *warning* you, Detective."

CHAPTER 38

ONCE AGAIN, THE SECURITY LINES WERE SET AND THE audience members surrendered cell phones at the coat check or ran back to cars and hotel rooms to deposit them. A clear, sunny Sunday afternoon and a greater-than-usual number of same-day ticket sales meant a larger percentage of those waiting on line were not in fetish finery, although many had at least sprung for basic black. After doing this for the Fetish Ball and the Breakfast Keynote, the volunteers were smoother and better at managing mini freak-outs. One more protestor tried to get in, waving a Bible in one hand and screaming "Repent!" at the top of her voice. The uniforms quickly hustled her away to more cheers. All in all, the atmosphere was light and excited, with dozens of people scattered throughout the lobby chatting, texting and predicting the contest outcomes. It was T-minus ninety minutes for the largest Global Leather Contest audience, ever.

Behind the scenes, chaos reigned.

"Where's Ravenfyre?" called the stage manager.

Boi Jack shrugged. "The cops took her away!"

"Well, when is she gonna be back? We need to rehearse the walk-on!"

"I don't *know*, Dusty!"

"For crying out loud, it's *walking*; we'll make sure she understands what direction to go in," said Lord Zenu.

"As the leading titleholder, she's supposed to be first," Dusty said in exasperation.

Bitsy stormed over, grabbed Ferral by the arm and plopped the bootblack down in position one. "There's your lead titleholder," she snapped.

Ferral grinned and waved fingers at Dusty, who sighed. "Okay, fine. Ferral, you start out from this mark, and cross to this beat, one-two, one-two..."

Tom, placing programs on the seats, looked up at the stage and gave a love-struck sigh. He leaned over to the woman straightening out the end folding chairs and said, "See that lady? I am gonna make her mine."

She looked up at Bitsy, back at Tom and nodded, impressed. "Good luck with that," she said.

"I *am* lucky."

There were four stage crew tasked to changing the furnishings and scenery, and they were poring over the master script, which was spiked with different colored Post-It Notes, and supplemented by extra loose sheets of paper. The sound system was being tested in the background; speakers on one side of the room stubbornly refused to work, and the MC's headset microphone kept making mysterious buzzing sounds. The props for the Leather Fantasy Image performances were unpacked and set up in the crossover behind the scrim. Large numbers were printed on white paper and taped above each set of props, some with diagrams. The spot operator hadn't shown up yet, but that was fine, since the extension cords still needed taping.

Two people assembled an overengineered standing bondage

frame that would stay on the stage at all times; they kept referring to the plans that came with it while around them, strips of tape were being measured and placed. Discs and thumb drives of music were sitting at the soundboard waiting for the engineer to finish fixing the speakers, and the side drapes fluttered a full six inches too short.

A typical setup, in other words.

Outside the theatre and down the hall, contestants unpacked costumes and greeted their supporting role friends and loved ones and waited to be told in which order they would be introduced and enact their Leather Fantasy Image. Kelly Manning was assembling what looked like several sets of antlers, and had a tube of Krazy Glue in one hand. Maurice was carefully sorting what looked like a pile of differently colored squares of rubber; opposite him phyl'ta did the same with beaded chiffon scarves. Kevin McDonald went over staging with his wife and her two best friends, and the three women practiced turning together. Giuliano Ferri sat against one wall with two shopping bags at his feet. He was wearing jeans and an old Asbury Park pullover sweatshirt, and he looked distracted. Ferri wasn't alone in not fussing over costumes, props or gear—Blade Guthrie was asleep in one corner, dressed in full, old-fashioned biker leathers that looked completely authentic, down to reinforced patches and the scars of road rash.

Bottles of water were stacked in one corner, with granola bars, honey sticks and breath mints. Nervous sweat and the exhaustion of the weekend colored and scented the air as they waited for the final stage of the competition. When the door opened, they all looked up, expecting Boy Jack with their assignments. Instead, it was the two homicide detectives.

Ferri looked at them, and then down to the floor. With a heavy sigh, he pushed himself erect and walked out without saying anything.

"Sorry to bother y'all," Dominick said, closing the door again.

"What was that all about?" Kelly asked, holding an antler tine in place while the glue dried.

"I bet he's *disqualified*!" said Len Munro with triumph in his voice. "I knew you just couldn't quit one night and come back the next!"

"No, Paul, it's out," said Earl, hating himself as he said the words. "Look, I did two tributes and a memorial service to Mack already. It's the contest now, time for them to be able to shine."

"That's fucked up!" Paul cried. He was in his version of full leather—his shorts and army boots, a short-sleeved leather shirt, wristbands, and his narrow formal collar. "That's just not right. They'll have all year to be stars! Think of everything Mack did for you!"

Like leave me in debt with his corpse coloring any future event I do? Earl thought uncharitably. Oh, how he hated this feeling! How could he turn down a young man grieving for his master? Then he remembered why.

He put a hand on Paul's shoulder, glad they were in private, down the hall from the dressing and green rooms. "Look, Paul, do you even remember what happened last night?"

Paul shrugged the hand off and half turned away, his face flushed. "That was a mistake. I admit it. I was upset! I am totally not drinking tonight. I can have one mistake, can't I? Look, this is important! It's Mack's image! And I was supposed to be the Young Leatherman and now..." He cut himself off and looked so sad.

I'm such a sucker, Earl thought, as he thumbed his radio switch. Click. "Dusty! I'm coming in, can we make one more change?"

"No, absolutely not! Are you crazy?" Something fell with a loud crash. "I'll see what I can do," he said to Paul. And the boy beamed at him like a goddamn kid at Christmas and once again, Earl knew why he never made any real money from these things. He was just a soft touch.

CHAPTER 39

"WHAT?" GUILIANO FERRI ASKED, FOLDING HIS ARMS. "I told you everything already!"

"Oh, no, actually you didn't," Rebecca snapped. "You went down to the gym on Thursday night after your little date with Mack."

"Jesus Christ! Who cares! So I went to the gym!" His nostrils flared as his lips parted. "I didn't have to tell you every move I made all night!"

"And yeah, actually you did," Dominick said. "Because once again, you swore you told me the whole truth, but it turns out you were lyin'! This don't make you very trustworthy, does it? And let me tell you something else—there's no sign of any romance in any of the notes or messages to you from Mack's email and whatnot. So, I'm thinking hey, I guess he was lying about that, too!"

He shrugged and eyed the ceiling. "Believe whatever you want. I got my own email stuff, I got proof if you wanna see it, but I don't have my computer here." He paused and then dug in his pocket. "But I got my phone! Look!" He started thumbing at the small device.

"Tell us about why you were in the gym, Mr. Ferri. And in what time frame; when you got there and when you left," Rebecca said. "*And* why you didn't tell us before."

He sighed as he navigated menu options and started looking through his messages. "I...look, I can tell you I went there to work out, and whatever, I did, a little. But you know why I didn't tell you I went? Because it didn't have nothing to do with me seeing Mack! Even though he told me...here. Here, look at this..." He adjusted the tiny screen and read, "Yo bro. Can't wait to see you and get off. Let's be like Anna and JB again for evs. Love, Anna."

"Anna?"

He looked at Rebecca and rocked his head back and forth, rolling his eyes again. "His stupid drag name. Anita Spanking. I was all like, I Need A Spanking is INAS, and he said, like, no, Anita with a 'a' like Anna, and it stuck. We were just kids, it sounds so stupid now."

"So...he was a sub?" Rebecca asked, now further confused.

"Nah. I mean, did he bottom, sure, to, um, all sorts of things. But we were like I said to you." He eyed Dominick. "*Versatile*. Didn't you see in the pictures in his room? But, see, he's talking *forever* in here, did you see that in his mail or anything? Forever is...forever!"

"You got others?" Dominick asked.

"Sure! I got the one that told me when they were getting here... I got this one that's kinda dirty...I got this one that says we could share his boy...I knew he said something about that...Look, here's one where he gets kinda...affectionate and all that." He handed the phone to Dominick who read the screen.

Rebecca asked, "You were saying that going to the gym had nothing to do with you being with him except he told you... what?"

"Oh. Well, you know, he was supposed to help me with the contest and all." He sighed. "And seriously, I just don't give a flying rat's ass right now about this whole thing, but the Newark Manacle—that's my bar, that sponsored me for the contest? They insisted I had to do it. They even got me a costume for my leather fantasy image thing since you got all my leather." He laughed. "Like I got any chance after last night, right? But whatever. Anyway, Mack was supposed to help me, but maybe he was gonna be disqualified as a judge 'cause of what he did at the bar that night. So, he says, this other judge—and I don't wanna name names—is kinda easy, why don't I go, like, *talk* to him. Know what I'm sayin' here? So, I was checking that out. I texted him and he answered he was down there, so I went. A little after one, maybe?"

Rebecca took a deep breath. "So that would be George Santos."

Giuliano looked impressed. "Wow, you guys really do your investigatin'! Yeah, him. So, I met him, we messed around a little. But that was it, I swear on all the saints, after that I was back in my room—by two!—and sleeping all night."

"I got one thing," Dominick said, handing the contestant's phone back to him. "Why would I know Mack was...like you say, versatile—by the pictures in his room? All the pictures we've seen were his manly-man calendar shots."

"No, the ones *I* brought him!" Giuliano laughed. "From back in the day! Like the one with the yellow panties?"

The detectives stared at him.

"Do you have copies?" Rebecca asked.

"Hell, yeah! I wasn't gonna give him all I had. I got 'em in my bag at the, waddayacallit, the concierge."

"We'd really like to see them," Dominick said.

"I'll get 'em back, though, right? Because...I ain't got nothing else from him now, you even got the panties." Suddenly, his posturing fell away, and he looked punched and deflated.

"Let's see them and then maybe you can keep most of them." The two of them walked with him, hearing sounds of hammering, thumping, spurts of music and static and shouting coming from the main ballroom and the steady buzz of the crowds waiting to get in.

Nancy Nichols sent her article on Dr. Abraham and the Zod books to one of the few genre literary magazine/websites that paid; she knew the *Record* wouldn't care. And what was worse was there was little else about this event the *Record* would care about. Vic had already suggested she take the rest of the day off and head out tomorrow to cover some sort of protest by the teachers' union or the city clerks union or some other union where she was guaranteed not to see any people dressed in leather versions of a Roman centurion's armor.

And more's the pity, she thought as she pondered her options. Woodrow was let go, it seemed he wasn't the killer. The detectives were still wandering around—she saw at least one of them in the lobby. But it was pretty clear this story was tapped out. She should do her targeted interviews and grab some Thai on the way home and put her feet up while she waited on responses from editors of various other places she'd contacted to place stories. It wasn't that she—or anyone in the real world—would care who won this crazy thing.

And yet...it was a free show. And who knows, there might be a stage collapse. Or, she thought with a giggle, a wardrobe malfunction. How they would be able to tell with what people wore in this scene, she couldn't imagine. And maybe the fantasies would be funny.

"Hi, Nancy!" shouted Phedre, waving excitedly from across the lobby. She threaded herself through the pockets and lines of people with a matador's skill, and this in four-inch platform heels. She'd gone for a '60s fusion look in a leather miniskirt and vest, both striped in candy colors, and ropes of Mardi Gras beads around her neck and wrists. Trailing after her with the video camera was a slender white-haired man in black trousers and a white shirt and leather jacket, looking somewhat like a steakhouse waiter. But instead of a bowtie, he had what looked like a pink dog collar around his neck.

"Isn't this the best contest, ever?" Phedre said breathlessly when she got to where Nancy had tucked herself. "I have never seen crowds like this for the contest! Ready, boy?"

"Yes, mistress," the older man said, raising the camera.

"I take it he's your boy," Nancy observed.

"You catch on fast! Hey, when are we gonna do that interview on polyamory? I want to make sure all my peeps will be there. Okay, boy, in three…two…Hi and welcome to the Mr. and Ms. Global Leather and Bootblack Contest here in New York, New York! It's Phedre Lysande, your in the scene reporter, on the scene, and it's a capacity crowd for the first time since this contest was for men only! Mr. Newark Leather is back in the running and there will be a special, final tribute to Mack Steel and we can count on a real nail biter as we get closer to finding out who will be this year's Global Leather Champions!"

Nancy leaned back and watched the taping and decided to stay. It wasn't like she was going to come back to see this next year.

And there was just this feeling she had that the story wasn't quite over yet.

CHAPTER 40

MACK STEEL—OR RATHER, ALBERT CLARENCE STAHL, HAD looked quite cute in drag. Without a mustache and with a dark curly wig cascading down over his shoulders, he looked like a rather strong-jawed Mediterranean beauty. In one photo along some shoreline spot in New Jersey that placed the Manhattan skyline behind him, he mimicked a classic calendar girl pose, with both hands on his bent knees, head leaning toward the camera, lips pursed. In another, he was on a hotel bed in an odd parallel to the crime scene photos taken at his murder, wearing nothing but those yellow panties and a smile. And in a third, he was bent over what looked like the edge of a desk, leaning on one elbow with his face coyly turned to the camera, his feet in enormous high-heeled mules, but otherwise completely nude.

"Those legs!" Rebecca couldn't help but saying, as she shuffled through the pictures. She remembered the man in his dead naked state as being muscular and handsome, but in his younger days he was lighter and more lithe than cut. His legs were gorgeous, long and curved in exactly the right places, the arch of his calf astonishingly erotic, considering her orientation and the context. It almost seemed unfair to women that they looked so damn good. In his billowing party dress and strappy heels, he could easily have adorned many a tool and die calendar.

Giuliano nodded with a slight smile. "Right? He was always proud of his legs. Man, he had a trick who'd pay him fifty bucks just to rub against his damn calves. Weirdo. But yeah, I'd always go for, you know, a longer line skirt. But he got legs, ya know? He used to dance to that song." He sighed. "And you didn't find these pictures in his room? I left him with five!"

"I'd like to make copies of these," Rebecca said. "If you don't mind. Do you have them scanned?"

He shook his head. "No, I had 'em in an envelope, I don't have a scanner. I just took them to this place and had copies made."

"So, you wouldn't have given these to anyone else?" Rebecca asked.

"No way! Who would I give them to?"

"We know Mack sent you pictures from time to time; did you ever share those with anyone else? Email them to anyone?"

He chuckled. "Aw, hell no. Why? They were for me. And since he was all sensitive about him being Global Leatherman, I figured he got enough guys who wanna do him 'cause he's famous. So, it wasn't like I was bragging or anything about hooking up with him. Can I keep 'em? You can make as many copies as you like. Shit, make a thousand copies to hand out here; let 'em all see what their Global Leatherman was really like."

"No, I don't think that's necessary," Dominick said. "I think this event had enough riots by now."

"You're tellin' me!" Ferri shook his head. "I really don't wanna stay. But if I can this, I'd have to like, move, 'cause all my bar friends are here. And I gotta sit through one more tribute to Mack and not say anything! I am gonna be so happy to go home tonight, I'll tell you that."

"I'm sorry it's been so hard for you," Rebecca said. "It might have been easier if you'd simply told us everything, earlier."

"Yeah, I know. But sorry, when you had the kinda history I had, you don't spill all your guts to the cops, even when you got nothing to hide." He half grinned.

"Well, you don't have to worry about having to sit through the memorial—Earl told us he canceled it," said Dominick.

"Yeah, but then Paul found out and came over all upset. And know what I think? I think he'll win. Because some parts of Mack musta rubbed off on him, he seems to get his way a lot. When can I get those pictures back?"

"I'll copy them now," said Rebecca. After she had her copies made and let Ferri return to the contest, she realized the key to the killer might finally, literally, be in her hands. All she had to do was figure out how to use it.

"I'm staying for the contest," she told Dominick. "I'm not completely convinced Ferri is in the clear, but I *am* convinced that for some reason or another, he and Steel did have a romantic connection. Although from all accounts, I can't imagine what he saw in the man."

"I hear that. But the world is full of people lovin' the wrong people, and it's still a damn good chance he's lying. Maybe Steel erased his ol' romantic emails and such because he decided he wasn't going to pursue anything, and once again we're back to Ferri. Funny how winning this thing was so important to him he'd go...*influencing* two judges, but now he's all sour on it."

"You just don't want to lose your bet. I'm sticking with Paul, though." She shook the envelope with the copies of the photos. "If Ferri did it, why would he tell us about pictures he removed himself?"

"That's assuming he removed them! Maybe he killed Steel, stomped off, Paul gets in, sees the scene, panics, and collects anything he thinks is detrimental to his...master's memory. I liked the idea of them doing it together, but so far there's no real suggestion of that. But they both could have been involved in setting it up or hiding the evidence, just at different junctures. Paul might have seen Mack dead with pictures of this cross-dressing scattered and just took off with them to destroy them."

"But he leaves the panties?"

They looked at each other, then thought in silence for a few moments. "And who sent that picture to Ravenfyre? We have Mack and Paul's computers, so where did it come from? And why send it to her?" Rebecca added. "Did that even have anything to do with the murder at all? The fact it didn't occur to her to make up a new email address for herself pretty much tells me there's no way she could have pulled off the actual murder and hid so much potential evidence. The email address used to send it to her is set up through KinkyNet; I'll put in a request to trace it first thing tomorrow. Who knows, maybe it'll be someone else's primary account."

Dominick shook his head. "It's amazing how much some of these people put out there in the world so's they can be found out as...different. They write about what sex they're havin' with who and doin' what and they take pictures all dressed up in their fetish outfits, and if you ask them one little thing, you wind up getting details you might never want to know!"

Rebecca smiled. "You mean how you and Ferri had a long conversation about how *versatile* he and Mack were 'back in the day'?"

Dominick nodded and made an invisible check mark in the air with his finger. "Exactly! Did I ask? No! But the man has to tell me that he and Mack used every condom they had they were so randy. Really? I did not need to know that. Although, I guess it'll make it easier to identify the samples you pulled from the trash."

"Ludivico is going to blow a gasket when he sees how many tests I want on all this crap," Rebecca said. "All the condoms, huh? Any idea how many constitutes 'all'?"

"Didn't ask. We still have time to grab him. He don't care about the contest anyway."

Rebecca checked her watch. "I'm thinking to let it go tonight. He's just across the river; we can grab him anytime. NJPD is very cooperative. And tomorrow we'll have phone and credit card records for Ferri and Paul, and we'll see if my request also gets access to their emails. But seeing as he will be going back all the way to California, I am thinking we might want to grab Mr. Helms and really work on that story of his. Do we do it now, or let him do his tribute? If you'd rather split, I'll stay and have a chat after his appearance."

"You *surely* did not think I was going to miss the contest after all this, did you? Let him have his last chance at being Mack's, uh, boyfriend. We can catch him later. And I bet you ten bucks the old guy wins."

"Fine. My money's on the pretty little guy. And for the girls?"

"Oh, the lady in the harem girl costume, definitely."

"I'll enjoy spending your money, Detective Dom. The one with the grey hair is going to run away with it."

He started to argue, and then saw something down a corridor that made him pause. "I do b'lieve," he said, looking down at his shoes, "I will get a shine. I'll see you at the contest."

Rebecca watched him head off to the bootblack stand and decided to go with the flow on this one. She showed her badge automatically as she passed the levels of security on the way to the ballroom and something he'd said just a little bit before that ticked her memory.

They used *all* the condoms?

She jogged up the stairs and then off to the side when she passed the front of the line of ticket holders waiting to be let in. And she made a couple of phone calls.

CHAPTER 41

"LADIES AND GENTLEMEN! DOMS, SWITCHES AND SUBS! BOYS and girls! Masters and Mistresses! Perverts one and all! Welcome to the Mr. and Ms. Global Leather...and Bootblack Contest!"

The cheers were so loud Earl Stemple thought for a moment that something had artificially raised the sound system volume. But it was remarkably static free and bounced off the walls with a resounding roar; he gripped the edge of the chair he was leaning against and felt the vibrations through it. The room was packed to the walls, with people actually standing—and not just people like nervous producers and stage crew with far too many chocolate-covered espresso beans coursing through their nervous systems. No, people were *standing* to watch his contest.

It started a mere fifteen minutes late, which for most leather community events was practically early. People were still coming in as the MC read the obligatory thanks to almost everyone Earl could think of; such lists had been scattered through the script. The volunteers, the underpaid temporary staff, the vendors, craftspeople, everyone who donated prizes, advertising, web page design, the sponsorship for a smaller contest or event that took place during the weekend...the list was several pages long, and some of the mentions had exact wording.

But the buzz of movement as the crowd navigated through the seats quieted down quite well by the time the two remaining winners from last year were re-introduced. House lights went down for their final appearance in their winner's sashes, and Ravenfyre was in the lead. Cheers were loud and sustained, but Earl could definitely hear some hissing in the background as well. Oh, dear. But there was nothing he could do about it now. It was already getting around that Ravenfyre's slave was moving on, telling stories of incompetence, neglect and impotence as well as being used as a ghost writer. This mixed with Mickey's outing had made Ravenfyre almost as unpopular as Mack. But she got to wear her sash one last time like any winner could, and it was hardly Earl's fault her slavegirl had a loud mouth and Dick had a limp...

Then, after the two of them took their bows, all the other former Global Leather titleholders in attendance were called up. It turned out that there were seven at the event, including Kelly Manning. They all got to stand behind Ravenfyre and Ferral as they waved for their farewell photos, and then both would be back later as the contest continued.

To his surprise and relief, things seemed to be going very smoothly! He could see elbows bumping against the scrims as the crew got the props ready for the first fantasy and the MC did the annual recap of the rules. Each Leather Fantasy Image could last for a maximum of thirty seconds, twenty-five of which could be narrated from a recording. There could be up to five people participating, including any required to manipulate the scenery or props. But the performers themselves, after assuming their poses, could not perform any dramatic movements. Technically, there shouldn't be any movement at all, but over the years they had discovered people had issues holding a pose for thirty seconds and that small movements sometimes created a heightened feeling of drama or eroticism to scenes. Whether movement was used at all and how was part of how the judges determined the score. People became creative with lighting, narration and other sound effects, which added complexity without too many potential accidents.

Lacking a true stage with a grand curtain and the mechanical means to raise and lower expensive material Earl couldn't afford anyway, his volunteer stage designer had come up with a two-layer scrim made of collapsible panels covered with a rough material that allowed for two special effects. If lit from the front, the scrim obscured everything behind it, making it perfect for hiding backstage goings-on. When lit from behind, it could allow a silhouetted version of the performers to be seen, perfect for more abstract Fantasy Images. And except for one year when a clumsy fantasy participant kicked them all over and then stepped through one trying to get up, the screens worked excellently. Using them in two layers allowed the contestants to set up hidden from the audience and then get revealed as the front screens were pulled aside.

"For our first Leather Fantasy Image, we present...Lennon Munro!"

Two black-clad crew members pulled the front panels away. Len was dressed in a black cambric shirt, open down his chest, with a black bandana knotted around his neck. Tight jeans were encircled around his hips by crossed black leather gunbelts showing the silvery glitter of plastic revolvers. He was wearing a black cowboy hat and under it, his eyes were shaded by a sculpted black mask. Under the heel of one raised western-style boot was a muscular man wearing nothing but a heavy leather body harness that held a horse's tail at his firm, rock-hard rump; and on his head was a leather fetish mask molded to look like a horse's head, with alert, perked ears. Behind Len was a smaller man in a predictable loincloth, buckskin boots and feather headdress costume; his was much less detailed than Len's. And although he strained for a noble, stoic demeanor, his pale skin and the tattoo of a dancing animal that could be a bear, a wombat or an overweight badger, slightly ruined his plausibility. That, plus the Donald Duck on his buttcheek.

The audience hardly needed the "William Tell Overture" to inform them of Len's identity as the Lone Ranger, so the voiceover of, "A fiery horse with the speed of light, a cloud of dust and a hearty Hi-Yo Silver...the Lone Ranger!" was a bit of overkill. But that was Len, thought Earl with satisfaction. It felt good to know that he could still rely on some things remaining the same after this crazy weekend. He felt, at last, that he could actually sit down for a while.

Rebecca edged her way into the packed ballroom, astonished at the crowd and the excitement level. Was it only a few days ago that she had no familiarity with this community whatsoever? Yet here was a decent theatre-sized crowd eagerly watching people pose like grade-school children in a pageant, earnestly and perhaps even passionately caring who won.

And to what purpose, she was still a little unsure. Even after these few days, it seemed that once people got these much-coveted titles, what they then did was—*this* for a whole year, traveling all over the country and getting dressed up for kinky fashion shows.

Maybe Trudy could explain it to her. Over coffee. After the case was closed. Maybe over a cocktail.

She's into this stuff, she reminded herself firmly. Do you really want to go there? She watched as the screens were returned to hide Len and his faithful companions and the room applauded with enthusiasm. No, it was silly to think about Trudy at all, when this was the world she chose to socialize in.

There was an open space to one side of the stage, and as she approached, she could see that it was taped off behind the tables where the judges sat, little lights clamped in front of them, illuminating just enough of the tabletop for them to write notes. Boi Jack then collected those notes. Ah, no doubt they were scores. Jack counted them and sealed them in an envelope—actually put a paper seal over the flap.

That was some security. Rebecca was about to turn back to find another spot to stand, but as Boi Jack came out of the judges' pen, she swept her arm to one side, inviting the detective in.

"Hey, wow, how nice of you to come," she said. "I guess you can sit back here, if you want. Did the other cop stay, too?"

"Yes, he's around here somewhere." He'd truly vanished after heading off for his shine, and that was almost an hour ago. Perhaps he had decided to grab Paul after all. Rebecca figured he'd call or text if he needed help or discovered anything new. Meanwhile, she tried to keep from checking her phone, waiting for a response to the favor she'd asked of one of the detectives back at the precinct.

"I'll radio security; if they see him, they'll tell him he can come up. Enjoy the show!" She slid past the tapes to deliver her envelope and Rebecca took an empty chair behind the judges. George Santos was almost directly in front of her; she wondered if any of the other contestants had known he was "easy." Seeing a box filled with an assortment of office supplies, she pulled out a legal pad, printed a question on it and folded the page. She tapped Santos on one shoulder and handed it to him; he looked at her and then at the paper in surprise. He unfolded it and even in the dim lighting of the room, she could see him go slightly pale.

Well, it looked like Giuliano Ferri had not been lying about influencing this particular judge. Rebecca raised an eyebrow, shook her head like a disappointed mom and took her seat again. George nodded to her with a guilty expression, folded the paper up even smaller and shoved it in his pocket. He leaned forward, pressing his fingertips to his forehead, and Rebecca wondered, for a split second, what he might do next. Then, her phone buzzed.

As the MC announced, "From the great nation of Canada, welcome Benjamin Sykes!" she read the text on her screen and nodded. Then, grabbing the envelope of photos, she left the judges' pen again, looking for some help.

There were extra patrols checking on the hotel, as she had requested after Woody's arrest. Rebecca made her way to the back of the ballroom, by the main doors, to run into Officer Wright again; he was cheerfully watching Mr. Alberta Leather frozen in what looked like the act of rubbing fire over the back of a beautiful dark-skinned man bound to a wooden frame in the middle of the stage. From such a great distance away, it was unclear what was making the red flickering effect in his hands, but the music was a sultry version of "Baby It's Cold Outside," complete with the snapping and crackling of a fireplace.

"Hey, Detective," Wright said, elbows bent casually as he rested his wrists alongside his firearm and nightstick. "How do you think they're doing that? Little LED lights or something?"

She shook her head. "Don't know. Are you stationed here?"

"No, I just dropped in to see what a kinky contest looks like."

"I need a favor." She explained, and he nodded. Beside them, an event security volunteer gave them a "*Shush*," but Wright looked at her with disdain and she backed off.

When he understood what needed to be done, he nodded again. "Yeah, I can figure out a way to do that…but how quick do you want it?"

"As soon as possible?" Rebecca shrugged and gave him her cell phone number. "It could really help."

He glanced toward the stage and sighed. "Okay, you got it. I'll let you know when I get back here." He left during the applause, and Rebecca headed back through the room to look for Earl.

CHAPTER 42

THE ANARCHY BACKSTAGE DID NOT CEASE BECAUSE THE FRONT of the house seemed orderly. Dominick had to keep moving to avoid the transfer of props and cast members, the nervously pacing contestants, the wildly gesturing stage manager and the various squads of not-quite-helpful backstage volunteers who didn't seem to know exactly what to do.

But not all the contestants were waiting for their turn to present an image. His meeting with the bootblack had been quite the learning experience. He eyed one shoe with admiration, turning the toe to allow the leather to catch light and gleam. His shoes had never looked so good, and his feet felt...amazing. Ferral's hands had been strong, fingers pressing points through the shoe leather that Dominick didn't even know could feel pleasure or relief. No, he'd never perched in a chair at an airport or bus station and gotten a damn foot massage as well as a shine. But the conversation had been even more enlightening.

"What's on your mind, sir?" Ferral had asked with a deceptively casual tone.

"You a dude or a lady?" Dominick asked directly.

Ferral had laughed, and the other bootblacks as well. Before the doors opened, they were all still working, although officially, their contest was done, with nothing left but the revelation of the winner. "No time off?" had been Dominick's first question, and they all gave him the same shrug.

"We all got plenty of breaks. But now, there's a thousand people coming in and some of 'em will want to touch up their gear. We can do that, remind them who we are and what we do."

"Believe me, no one makes us work," LeatherDreamz giggled. "We're just pigs for leather. Blame Ferral, though, for betting us we can work until the last minute before stage time. Because, wow, I am a sucker for a bet!"

"Well, then, I came for that shine you promised me."

As Ferral started, a woman took a seat in Eddie's chair and LeatherDreamz started meticulously packing her case of tools and polishes. Beside her, Timmy was rubbing his hands with moisturizer. And then Dominick asked his question.

"Oh, you can say I'm both or neither," Ferral said easily. "You want to see my ID, it'll say I'm a boy. Tomorrow maybe I'll be as girly as Dreamz."

"Yeah, right," she scoffed.

"This scene is a place where it feels like anything goes," Dominick continued. "You got people dressin' up all kinds of ways, you got slaves and masters and bondage and torture games, and fetishes and all that...but are you really all that open-minded? Is *anything* really okay with any of you?"

"Well, you know about safe, sane..." Ferral stopped as he saw Dominick nod, and then picked up a can and scooped light-colored goop onto his fingers. He began spreading it over the detective's shoes with quick, confident motions. "Well, there it is. If you don't have permission, if you're a flaming idiot, if you're bothering people...then you're not welcome here."

"And that's it? No other taboos?"

"Everyone has taboos, and everyone has tastes and limits. I don't like being pigeonholed as a boy or a girl, I like being just Ferral. Sometimes, that pisses people off—they see the world as up or down, black or white. But here at least, I can say, call me *this* not *that*—and they mostly respect it."

Dominick nodded and considered how to ask what he wanted to know. He held back a groan of pleasure as Ferral's fingers found a spot that apparently wanted rubbing very much. "Mostly?"

"Hey, I don't live in fantasy land. There are always people who don't get it and don't want to. Some people don't like looking at anything that threatens their own identity, right? So, if some woman looks at me and thinks I'm sexy, but she sees me as a boy and she's a dyke—she says, wow, am I straight?" Ferral gave an exasperated sigh. "And men are worse. Some men. But that's their karma, you know?"

"Well, I'm thinking it's gotta be a lot of people that way around here," Dominick argued, leaning forward. "Everything here is in pairs, one or the other."

"Top or bottom!" Eddie interjected. "Daddy or boy."

Dominick nodded. "Like that. So, if you're all into that big masculine trip— like, uh, the..."

"Zodians?" snickered LeatherDreamz. She closed her case and wiped down the outside with a damp paper towel.

"Sure, like that. There's no space there for someone in between."

"You'd be surprised! Remember, this is our get out and party weekend, this isn't how we live full time!"

"Speak for yourself, dude," LeatherDreamz said. "I'm totally lifestyle."

"Yeah, okay, so except for Dreamz. What I mean is...some guy is in there with a sword and axe and big boots, and his wife is dressed in slave silks and all that. They go home, and he lets the dog out and takes out the trash. She opens the mail and pops open a couple of beers, and they sit on the couch and watch something on the DVR. Tomorrow, they go to work, no helmets and horns, no collars and bells. Maybe he likes to garden; maybe she drives a monster truck. How would we know?" Ferral shrugged.

"But if it got back here that he was making flower arrangements while she was fixing carburetors, you think they'd be embarrassed?"

Eddie laughed. "Man, they'd be run outta their Zodian confederation club so fast!"

"So, it matters," Dominick said.

"To some people, but not to most, is what I'm saying," Ferral insisted. "There's always extremists. The people who don't want to see me as my own person, and insist I pick a gender. The people who think it's weak to bottom, or humiliating to serve or to..."

"Polish boots!" said the other three simultaneously.

"Right."

"Or for a guy to wear women's clothes?" suggested Dominick.

Ferral nodded. "Exactly. You're always gonna have those people, even in the scene. But they're the minority, I promise you." He leaned back and looked at his job with a critical eye. "There you go, what do you think?"

Dominick looked down and nodded. "Beautiful. Just beautiful."

They all smiled at him and then prepared to go into the contest.

CHAPTER 43

EARL LISTENED TO REBECCA AS SHE OUTLINED WHAT SHE wanted to do. He frowned and had her explain it again and nervously bit his lower lip. "What exactly do you think will happen?" he asked.

"I think Mack's killer will be outraged and show it," she said with complete honesty. "And then we will grab him."

"I don't know," he fretted. He looked around nervously; she had asked for some privacy, and a space away from the contest management areas, so they were on the now empty hallway leading to the other conference rooms on that floor. "It sounds dangerous. Why not just...arrest whoever you think it is? Quietly?"

"This is a risk," she admitted. "And what will *probably* happen is absolutely nothing. But I'll have someone posted right by the stage, and I'll be there with my part—with Detective DeCosta."

Earl sighed. "There's no way around this, is there? If I say no, I might be letting an opportunity to catch a murderer go. If I say yes, you might actually catch one right here on my stage! And that means—it's one of *us*!" He ran his hand through his hair and shook his head. "Oh, this is just awful."

"I know." Rebecca nodded sympathetically. "But I need to know, can we do this, or not?"

He swallowed and nodded. "All right. But you need to promise me that everyone will be safe!" He wondered what his insurance broker would say if he ever decided to produce this again. Surely there was an additional fee for potential crazed killers? His phone buzzed and he trudged back to the ballroom, thinking of a return to retail. How peaceful that sounded. How secure and safe and completely without these sorts of decisions.

The scrim parted to reveal Jazz Dean dressed as her drag alter ego, Andrew Gyne, dressed in a long-line black crepe suit, spit-shined wing-tips and a fluorescent orange tie. She had sideburns and a mustache and her hair slicked back, and she had swiveled her body into a microphone-caressing pose. Behind her, dressed identically in leather microskirts, high heels and torpedo push-up bras under skimpy sweaters, were three women posed as her backup singers. A crash of drums, guitar and saxophone came from the speakers along with a voiceover decrying the state of youth today and their wild music. The applause was steady, if not thunderous. When the stage lights dimmed again, the MC came out and was spotlit to make a few more thanks.

Rebecca ran into Dominick outside the main doors and drew him aside to describe what she planned. At first he was shocked; then, he laughed. And then he found another uniform and called in more bodies to station around the area—one by the stage, one by the doors leading down the hall. Rebecca sent a text to Officer Wright, letting him know where to find her and then she took Dominick to the area behind the judges.

After a few minutes of vamping, including a few regretful

puns, the MC said, "And next up, we have, for your pleasure, Maurice Berezovsky!"

Dominick put his fingers in his mouth and gave a whistle. A few of the judges turned in confusion and he grinned and waved at them.

The scrim panels parted to reveal Maurice dressed in rubber jodhpurs, tall boots and a long-tailed coat, almost like a hunting outfit. Behind him, hanging from the bondage frame, was another outfit, of soft, grey cotton trousers and a white shirt with a camel-colored cardigan sweater over it; they hung as a complete outfit, ready for him, obviously well worn. A pair of docksiders were on the stage under the trousers, and a cap hung from one corner of the frame, with a cane next to it—clothing and accessories for an old man, retired to Palm Springs.

The man in question, resplendent in his rubber, back straight and eyes fixed to the audience, held a large cup, from which poured a long line of colored squares of rubber, each one knotted to the next by a corner, so it looked like they were spilling from his hands out onto the floor and down the stage to where two young men were sitting, looking at each other. Each one of them held one of the trailing squares, the line taut between them, like they were collecting them, or catching them as they fell.

Maurice winked.

The narration was a sprightly piece of music made slightly melancholy with the sound of a clarinet. Rebecca immediately recognized it as Klezmer, a sort of Eastern European Jewish jazz. The narration was Maurice's own voice.

"What do I have for you? A little color, a little smoothness. Rubber gives a little, but it's strong. That's a metaphor, so pay attention! Time I don't have so much left, but I can give you a touch of something so hot you'll *schvitz* like a *mamzer*, so cool, you'll strut like a peacock. I'll tell you my stories, I'll give you a taste. But it's up to you to say if you want more. And even if you don't wear rubber like mine...be sure to wear the little rubber hat on your *schmeckle*. Because whatever you wear, you should wear it in good health!"

And then the lights dimmed.

This time, the applause and cheers were thunderous and sustained. Dominick whistled again and grinned at Rebecca. "I like him. What's a *mamzer*?"

"A...a bastard."

"And a *schmeckle*?"

Rebecca grinned. "A little penis."

Dominick laughed and clapped harder.

As the stage was reset, the MC struggled to keep the attention of the crowd. Scores were run back to the tally-masters. They had missed Angelina's Fantasy Image—apparently she had been some sort of magical instructor with a boy and girl posed for her to beat with a wand. The wand was suspended with invisible thread, which was a cute special effect.

Also, Kevin McDonald had appeared in some sort of Arabian Nights tableau, with his wife and two other slaves arrayed for his pleasure. Jason Asada had been the only one actually bound so far, for his Roman galley slave fantasy.

Blade Guthrie's fantasy was just being in her leathers, straddling an imaginary bike while a punk version of "Bad to the Bone" played. She grinned and waved from time to time, making revving sounds. Mistress Ravenfyre asked for one of the volunteers to bring her some Tylenol, please.

By the time Chevalier Franklin's fantasy of two men in motley bound and suspended from the frame was first set and then cleared, Rebecca had started to worry about her big plan. She had another inspiration and went to find whoever was in charge of music and sound.

Giuliano Ferri was next, and his scene was set up so quickly it caught the audience by surprise when the stage lights changed. The scrims shot back and one spot hit him standing in a motorcycle cop's uniform, holding a man bent over in front of him, nightstick poised for personal insult. For the music, Sammy Hagar complained about being unable to drive the speed limit. There was no voiceover.

"Boring," murmured Mickey Abraham.

Indeed, the audience seemed to think so as well. The music was cut off instead of trailing, and Ferri started to move before the spot turned off. It wasn't a disaster, but it was the worst staged fantasy of the night.

It was getting close to the end. The MC ran out of people to thank and instead started asking the audience if they were having a good time. After some more vamping, during which Rebecca just kept her phone in her hand, in case she didn't feel the vibrations of an incoming call while it was pocketed, she finally found the sound man. He had three laptops open on a table and a folded script on a stand; he spoke quietly into a headset microphone as Kelly Manning was announced.

Manning's fantasy involved him wearing a headdress of a somewhat ungainly set of stag's horns; his legs were in rough brown suede and his chest bare under a suede vest covered with layers of cut suede leaves in a variety of autumnal colors. He was standing with one leg on a stool wrapped in a sheet that mimicked tree bark; he had one hand holding a long staff with green leaves spurting from the top; the other hand was held open in welcome to a slender woman dressed in a very skimpy green frock, with vines and flowers wound through her hair. She was reaching up for him from a position leaning on one hip, a perfect picture of yearning. The soundman tapped and music came up, sounding like it was from the *Lord of the Rings* soundtrack. It included a voiceover intoning a short poem about the horned man and the coming of spring.

Rebecca decided her sneaky plan wasn't going to work and sighed. Should she ask about the music anyway? Why not? She tapped the man when the Fantasy ended and the MC came back, and when he tried to shoo her away, showed him her shield. Then, he was all cooperation, especially since she knew exactly what she wanted.

But as the MC was introducing "Slave phyl'ta!" the text from Officer Wright came through, and Rebecca sent a text to Dominick to let him know she was heading back to meet the patrolman. Dominick smiled grimly and studied how to move around the table; he spotted the uniform by the stage and went over to confer with her. But he did pause long enough to cheer for phyl'ta.

"It's not on foam or anything, Detective," Wright said, handing the package to her. They met by the main doors again, this time not bothered by any volunteers. "There wasn't anything open nearby that could do that. But I got some cardboard..."

She felt it and nodded. "This is perfect, Wright, thank you. Do you think you can stick around until the end? At least until I tell you we're done here? I'd like you to keep an eye on this side of the room." She pointed and then swept her arm, and gave him the layout of the floor. He was more than happy to move into the room and take up a position against the wall, closer to the stage and comfortably situated to watch the show.

"This is fun," he said, before moving into his spot. "It's crazy, right? But fun. I might bring my girlfriend to one of these things. Is this the only one?"

"No," Rebecca said, with a slight hesitation. "They have these...all over."

"Awesome."

The world was very strange, Rebecca thought, as she headed the long way around, to the other side of the ballroom, to where the props were being carried away from all the previous fantasies and the stage crew was preparing for the final one.

In no big surprise to anyone, phyl'ta's Fantasy Image was straight out of Zod. To the strains of Middle Eastern techno pop, the scrims revealed her bound to the frame, her layers of silk seemingly removed from her and draped over the uprights or tossed into silky puddles of bright, rainbow-colored sparkles. Her ample rear was mostly covered by one last layer of lavender silk, her large breasts barely contained in a jeweled bra. She was facing the audience at an angle, strings of beads and bells draped around her hips and wound around her surprisingly dainty ankles. Her head was thrown back with a look of orgasmic agony on her face.

Two Zodian men were in the scene with her, one brandishing the short truncheon described in the books as a slave goad, the other with a multitailed whip. Both men were additionally armed with their honor knives and fully helmed and adorned with the usual fur and leather armor. The applause for the scene nearly drowned out Mickey Abraham's giggles.

"Shh!" Zenu managed, before a little snort of his own.

"Is that a *dildo* he's holding?" asked Chava Negilla, leaning forward to look. "Oh, my God, it is!"

Mickey covered her own mouth and shook in laughter; Laertes glared at her and wrote down a perfect score.

The Boys Jack furiously texted each other at the same time.

"Is it over yet????"

Bitsy and Tom reached the elevator already tearing at each other's clothing. "I need you so much," he growled into her ear as he ran his hands down her hips. She turned to catch his kisses on her mouth, smearing her perfectly applied lipstick, and they almost fell out at his floor. "But shouldn't you...don't you have to..."

"It's all over but the fat lady singing," she said, licking his jaw.

"And I am hoping you'll be making *this* fat lady sing real loud in about twelve minutes."

"How about three," he gasped as they hurried down the hall to her room. "And then again in about ten more?"

She giggled as she thrust her keycard in the door. "Yes, master!"

"And, for the last time; let us remember our lost comrade, Mack Steel, Mr. Global Leather, with a re-staging of his winning Leather Image Fantasy."

The applause now was scattered as conversation continued, even though there were plenty of loud shushing sounds from all around the vast room. Chairs scraped as people adjusted their positions. The lights went dark and the scrims were pulled back in that darkness. A single spot illuminated a man dressed in a T-shirt and jeans with a baseball cap on his head, trying to look like a teenager. He looked half-scared and half-confused; perhaps the direction had been lacking, but it worked for the theme.

"Last year's youth was better," whispered George Santos. He got a few nods, but most of the judges were busy putting their final scores down for Boi Jack to collect.

A Janet Jackson song came up after a moment of silence, and the crowd seemed to relax. Over the sound of the song, a deep man's voice said, "A boy has hungers, desires and needs..."

Nancy Nichols stared at the stage and wished she'd gone home. Not only had the tableaus been astoundingly dull and pretentious, but the periodic delays as they changed the stage and thanked about a million people were interminable as well. How could they make kinky sex look so staid and dull? She checked her watch and pondered whether to wait to see who won. She could get Phedre to text her, surely? She got up and worked her way down the row to leave, ignoring the mutters of the people she temporarily blocked from seeing this overblown piece of...

A sudden rise in audience sound made her turn.

On the stage, as the narration droned on, the spot shifted to Paul, who was standing erect, his head tilted to one side, looking slightly up, in his shorts and boots and leather shirt. His leather collar was a slender dark slash across his taut throat and locked in the front and he was holding one hand over his heart in what might have been a posture of loss or grief...except it looked like he was about to recite the pledge of allegiance.

A few wags snickered here and there followed by waves of hissing commands to be quiet and whispered arguments.

Then, the sound cut out entirely and Paul turned his head in anger; there was silence for two, three seconds, and then ZZ Top blared out of the speakers, and the spot shifted to position three.

On a stylized podium borrowed from the hotel gift shop was a pair of black boots, bright under the white lights. On top of them was a leather cap—neither of these actually belonged to Mack, but no one could have known that.

Paul opened his mouth and shouted something, but the music covered whatever he said. And then the laughter and applause from the audience drowned out any possible chance he had of being heard, as they saw what was propped on top of the leather hat.

It was a poster of a young and very beautiful Mack Steel in a classic pinup pose. He was caught kneeling by an ottoman, his ass thrust out toward the viewer, his hands reaching for the other side. He was dressed in a short skirt hiked up his perfect, shapely legs, revealing stockings underneath, and a conical longline bra. The smile on his face was completely open and his eyes merry; the bland, cheap motel room background added to the naughty 1950s feel of the photo.

Several people rose and cheered lustily, soon followed by more. Row by row, people stood to clap and laugh and make wolf whistles. Some of the contestants, hearing this, crowded around the back door leading to the stage, but the crew pushed them back. The Zodians, who had not yet gathered up all their gear and left, blocked stage left as they tried to see what the audience was reacting to.

"No!" screamed Paul, staring at the poster. "No!"

But the room was stamping and drowning him out, with only the people closest to the stage clearly seeing the anger and shock on his face. The judges were almost all laughing; Ravenfyre was sitting with her mouth open in shock; Mickey spit her seltzer across the table and splattered a passing volunteer. Chava was on her feet cheering and waving her feather boa.

Rebecca and Dominick moved in closer from both sides of the stage as ZZ Top continued their tribute to legs.

"No!" Paul shrieked, finally topping the sound system. He grabbed the poster, tried to rip it, but when the cardboard backing Officer Wright had improvised refused to tear easily, he wrestled and folded the poster in half and threw it to the stage and stomped on it. "It's not true! It's impossible! You liars! You fakes and liars! He was never like that!"

The man next to him put a hand on Paul's shoulder and Paul punched him in the stomach, hard. That made the uniform by stage right step up; the stage crew were getting frantic instructions to back off and move out of the way, now! They scattered, one of them shoving into a confused Zodian, who stumbled out of the wings onto stage left.

Paul saw the cop coming and darted to one side, looking around in a panic. When he saw the reeling Zodian, he ran over, pushed him violently, and grabbed his honor blade out of the sheath. He brandished it at the patrol officer, who cocked her head to one side and held her hands up, trying to speak in a reassuring voice. The sound system cut off just in time for some people to hear her saying, loudly, "Now come on, you don't want to hurt anyone..."

"It's a lie! Tell them that's a lie! He was never a fairy! He was *real* leather! He was *old guard*! He was a *real master*!" He waved the knife from side to side, and the front rows of the audience started backing away from the stage. Rebecca came up stage left and put herself behind him; she could see the uniform still coming forward. With one hand, she slipped the handcuffs from the back of her belt.

"Sure he was," she said, startling Paul and making him spin around. He hit the rear scrim and it crashed down. "He was a master and he was a drag performer, and he was JB's lover and was going to be again!"

"No! Nooo!" His face was so red he looked about to burst; his eyes were wild as he swung back to the patrolwoman and stabbed at the air in front of him before whirling back toward Rebecca. "He would never...I was his only...I was his boy! He was mine! Mine!" Suddenly, he broke and ran toward the uniform, and she dodged out of the way of the knife but put up an arm to block him. It was well-executed and should have gotten him, but he kicked at the fallen scrim and leapt off the back of the stage, heading toward the rear doors.

"Shit," Rebecca cursed; no way was she drawing her firearm in a crowded room of people all dressed in black. She jumped off the back as well and turned sharply to the right, and saw Paul threatening one of the stage crew, who was diving to the floor. Smart man; she pushed herself into a run to catch the lithe, angry young killer. But the backstage area was crossed with cables and cluttered with the remnants of props, and she cursed as her heel caught on something; she reeled and stumbled and barely caught herself against the rear wall before she hit the floor with her face.

A strong arm helped her up and then let her go; Detective DeCosta was a blur as he leapt the tangle of props and the downed stage manager and hit Paul from behind with a tackle that would have made any Hall of Famer proud. The ring of contestants that had been blocking the door first gasped and then started to cheer; the audience on the other side of the stage was shouting and screaming questions, and there was a steady thunder of feet as people milled in different directions trying to figure out where it was safe.

Earl clutched his heart and sank down into an empty chair in the front row. Nancy Nichols was taking photos in all directions while running toward the stage, cursing that she'd been pointed the wrong way for this amazing chaos! "Press! Press!" she shouted, as she struggled against the waves of people.

Boi Jack found herself standing in front of the judges' table with her clipboard held in front of her like a shield. Had she actually thought she could defend them? She dropped it and thumbed her headset. "Jack! Is everyone all right? Jack?"

Two uniformed police officers came out on stage and started waving people down; they were cheered as loudly as any fantasy during the contest, and they grinned and continued to wave.

Back stage, Dominick held Paul firmly, while he cursed, spit, and frothed at the corners of his mouth. "He *deserved* it! He was abusing me! He *lied* to me!"

"Paul Helms, you are under arrest for murder," said Rebecca, finally fixing the cuffs on his wrists.

"It was his fault, all his fault!" he wailed.

Boy Jack, standing with his contestants crowded around him, thumbed the switch on his headset. "It was totally Paul," he said.

"Oh. Em. Gee," said Boi Jack.

"You know," said Mickey Abraham, appearing from under the table, "I think I should write some more Zod books. I *love* this community!"

CHAPTER 44

THIS TIME, REBECCA TOLD DOMINICK TO TAKE THEIR SUSPECT in. "You brought him down, you get the collar." They were waiting down in the lobby with a subdued Paul, who kept shaking his head and muttering, "It wasn't my fault." A patrol car was on the way to get them.

"Hey, you actually solved the mystery. Now, remind me again how you did that?"

"You told me Ferri said they used the last of the condoms when they had their little reunion. But when I first saw the room, there was a fresh box of condoms on the dresser, along with a ton of paper trash. It was all in the evidence box. Obviously someone went out to buy them. I had one of the guys back at the precinct go over to the locker and look through the receipts and find the sale. Almost one A.M., from a Duane Reade pharmacy down the block. Ferri was in the gym at 1:15 with two witnesses. And, the condoms were bought with Steel's credit card. We'll see about a security camera image tomorrow, but it's pretty clear Paul went back to the room and was sent out shopping."

"Damn, that's cold. You go away because your...partner...is getting it on and when you get back, you need to go buy more sex stuff?"

"I'm guessing Mack was his usual charming self, wasn't he, Paul?"

Paul shook his head. "I was his slave, I would do whatever he said, and I was his good boy. He loved me. Not anyone else. Ever!"

"Yeah, we know that's not true. He loved Julie. He loved the time they spent dressing up in girly clothing and being together..."

"No, no, no!" Paul shook his head, eyes tightly closed.

"You can destroy the pictures, but you can't destroy history, Paul. You could kill Mack, but not a man who loved him for years after he was gone. But why did you send his picture to Ravenfyre? It was easy enough for you to make a new mail account for yourself, and I'm betting that very picture is on your phone. But why send it to her?"

He opened his eyes and laughed suddenly. "That bitch! I saw her slinking around that night and thought she'd see the picture and come in screaming the next day how much she hated him!" He almost looked proud.

Rebecca nodded. "Well, that wasn't the smartest thing you did. Neither was continuing to use a similar password on your new KinkyNet account. ASSword2 popped it right open. I can't wait to cover all the ways you hid your bloody clothing—rinsing it in the shower at the gym, or dunking it into the Jacuzzi there... leaving your own leather in lockers or toybags until you had the time and privacy to clean it..."

"Cleaning up and makin' your boots smell like they was covered in turpentine, cause you had to scrub the blood off!" Dominick said with a nod.

"Wearing the chain collar instead of the thin leather one you have on tonight." She pointed at it. "You even found or maybe bought another leather collar—you were wearing it on Friday night—but you had to have the real one back tonight."

He dropped his head. "*My* collar. Mine. He shouldn't have said those things. He should have stayed with me." And then he pressed his lips together, and his shoulders shook as he started to quietly cry.

"You sure you're not coming down now to get this?" Dominick asked. "You're senior, you're the first on the scene."

"Yeah. But now *you* have to do the paperwork. I'll be in tomorrow, and we'll see what we can get out of him when I present the full timeline. Congratulations and thank you, Detective." She looked into his eyes and nodded. "I'd have you at my back any time." The lights from the top of a car flashed through the front doors, and she bid him goodnight.

He nodded serenely back and didn't grin until after he stowed Paul into the back of a squad car and climbed into the front. His first homicide collar as a full detective! *Sweet.*

Back in the ballroom, it took almost a half hour to get the audience and participants to settle back down. A few dozen people left, fleeing a feared arrival of mainstream press, but Phedre, Cary and Nancy were the only ones gathering this story, and the three of them had completely unique viewpoints.

"Well, after that excitement, we actually have some winners," the MC said, looking disheveled and sounding exhausted. But the crowd was cheering already, and one of the two cash bars was out of drinks.

"For the sister and brotherhood awards, voted upon by their fellow contestants, representing the contestants who showed the best spirit of friendship and support to their new brothers and sisters...Kelly Manning, the former, uh, Ms. Global Leather, and slave phyl'ta of the Nevada Zodian Confederation!"

Pity Dominick missed hearing that, Rebecca thought as she

re-entered the room. She looked around for Earl and spotted him up front, by the judges.

"And the new Global Leather Bootblack is….Timmy!"

Loud cheers rose as the man came out on stage, waving his muscular, bare arms. Kelly and phyl'ta both hugged and kissed him and the three of them moved to one side.

"The new Ms. Global Leather is…Angelina Swiderski!"

She looked genuinely shocked, almost as if she had to be pushed to come forward from the wings. But the crowd cheered her, and she accepted the plaque with a smile and a wide wave to her NuKnk posse.

"The youngest Ms. Global Leather, ever!" the MC exclaimed.

Rebecca stopped at the judges' table and heard Mickey Abraham say, "The revolution will be twittered; she's barely old enough to drink."

"And finally…the new Mr. Global Leather is… Maurice Berezovsky?"

Rebecca couldn't help it; she laughed and started to cheer. So did the judges, who seemed united in their support. The audience leapt up in an ovation and Maurice looked, if anything, twice as shocked as Angelina. He came out and stood next to her, looking old enough to be her great-grandfather. As he accepted another plaque, Rebecca could see his lips moving in a very familiar way. Although she couldn't hear it, she knew he had said, "*Gevalt.*"

"The oldest Mr. Global Leather and the youngest Ms.?" Rebecca asked Earl.

"It sure looks that way," he said weakly. "Is everyone all right?"

She nodded assuringly. "Everyone is fine, even Paul."

He shook his head sadly. "I didn't want it to be some weird sex thing with someone in our community. We're not like that, really."

"But it wasn't," Rebecca said. Nancy Nichols popped up beside the two of them looking positively energized.

"It wasn't? What are you talking about? 'Sex Slave Murders Master With Mistress's Knife!' There's even cross-dressing!"

Rebecca shook her head with a smile. "Sorry, but it really had nothing to do with kinky sex or the BDSM scene or masters and mistresses. More like 'jealous boyfriend finds out his lover was taking up with someone else.' Paul talked a lot about being a slave or a boy, or whatever. And maybe he was. But Mack loved someone else, who loved him back for so long that the *minute* they got back in contact, they were immediately planning to stay together forever. And even worse for Paul, it wasn't even a man who lived the same life Mack did—a leatherman, a celebrity titleholder, someone who was always masculine and sexy. Instead, the man was a newbie, someone who was doing it just for fun. Someone who shared a history of playing with drag and being, uh...more relaxed about roles. This was a threat to his place in Mack's life. The knife? They probably brought it to make fun of it in some way, taunt Ravenfyre with it. It was handy, and he used it."

Nancy deflated a little. "You are *kidding* me."

"Sorry! But it really didn't have anything to do with sex, or role-playing, or even cross-dressing. It was just plain...jealousy."

Earl brightened. "Oh! Well...it's still bad. But it's...ordinary."

"Damn," Nancy said, "Fine. I'll get one more story out of it. Two if you'll give me an interview, Mr. Stemple?"

He gave her an incredulous look and she shrugged. "Gotta ask. So, Detective, did my question help?"

"Yes, actually. I realized what Mack was going to do after his title year was...*anything he wanted to.* If he wanted a lover who wasn't a slave, he could have one. If he wanted to keep both, he believed he could. If he wanted to dress up like he used to when he was young, he could even do that!"

"But he could always have done that!" Earl said in exasperation. "I wouldn't have cared! No one would have!"

"Don't be silly," Mickey Abraham said, raising a lowball glass to them. "He couldn't do drag while he was Mr. Global Leather because there was a *Ms.* Global Leather. He wasn't going to risk anyone comparing him to Ravenfyre there! He hated women! While he was…symbolically tied to one, so to speak, there was *no way* he'd put on a dress, even if he enjoyed it. Although, judging by that picture, he really should have."

"You solved it, you solved it!" came an excited cry from behind Rebecca. Everyone turned as Trudy shot from the crowd and once again threw herself at Rebecca, who had a very brief thought that she'd have to tell her not to do that any more. And then she felt a thrill of pleasure at realizing, once more, how good Trudy felt in her arms.

Nancy Nichols considered a picture and then deliberately turned away. She would interview the detective tomorrow, and get the scoop on how it all went down, one more "exclusive to the *Record*" story. And she would bank this goodwill for future use.

Earl was grinning, and then his headset and phone started clicking and buzzing as the breakdown began and crowds of people headed down to the lobby bar or to the special afterparty at the Shaft. Also he had to meet with the winners and have them sign their contracts; the hotel wanted to know if he had a count on how many rooms he'd need tomorrow night, and the clean-up crew was waiting to get into the ballroom. He grabbed the phone and switched on the headset and went back to work.

Next year, for sure, he'd have a full-time, paid assistant. Where the hell was Bitsy?

"You really shouldn't be doing this when I'm on the job," Rebecca murmured.

"But you solved it! It's all over, right?" Tonight, Trudy was wearing black jeans and a soft black suede shirt that opened at the throat into a wave of ruffles.

"Yes, it looks like it's all done."

"Well...then..." Trudy looked around with wide, green-flecked eyes, framed by those cute-as-hell nerd-girl frames. She carefully determined no one was listening and leaned in close. "You didn't answer me when I asked before. Are you seeing someone?"

"I...no. Maybe we could have dinner..."

"Love to. I have a place on the Lower East Side. We can go for Chinese or Indian." She grinned and shrugged. "Or, we can go to my place and order pizza. Wanna come over for...herbal tea?"

The repeat of her invitation to their first date made Rebecca feel dizzier than when she almost hit the wall after stumbling. "Let's grab a cab," she said.

This is a bad idea, she thought as they left. So bad. Remember where you are.

She paid for the cab.

Bitsy and Tom wandered down to the lobby dressed to go out in search of ice cream or cupcakes. Both wore half-dazed masks of pleasure and adoration as they walked past excited knots of people loudly discussing the contest aftermath while they spread the news all over social media.

Just before they reached the front doors, though, Bitsy paused and looked around. Such an animated crowd! Earl must be happy, she decided, cuddling closer to Tom. Even after all these years, people got excited over who won! Not that she cared in the slightest right now. Tom checked his phone and said, "There's a place on Third Avenue open until two! Damn, and I have ten messages?" He laughed and pocketed the phone. "We can find out who won later."

"Whatever you say, *sir*."

He puffed up a little and held her tighter as they walked out into the night.

CHAPTER 45

"So you're not a strict vegetarian any more, either," Rebecca teased.

"I'm not a strict anything any more," Trudy giggled, tasting of pepperoni. Her lips were soft and warm and parted just slightly, teasing Rebecca to kiss her harder, run the tip of her tongue between them and pushing just hard enough to feel the ridges of her teeth.

"God, you are hotter than I even remembered," she said, running her hands along Rebecca's spine. "You're still doing karate, I bet."

"And when I saw you, I thought you were working out."

Trudy nodded and nuzzled Rebecca's throat. "I do, a little. When I remember. I have these friends I work out with, but we're all so busy...I need, um...someone to be more forceful with me, get me to go."

Rebecca pulled back. "I'm not into that..."

"I'm joking, I'm having fun," Trudy said, her eyes dancing. "Still so serious. How can you be single?"

Rebecca ran a finger down those soft lips and across Trudy's chin. "Busy. Picky. Not politically correct." Gun shy after you, she didn't say. "Why are you?"

Trudy shrugged and ran a hand down Rebecca's leg, smoothing the light fabric down. "Busy. Picky. Definitely not politically correct." She grinned, gave that lilting laugh. "I dated around last year, got myself into trouble a few times. No, not seriously! Just...went looking for the wrong kind of women. I kept looking for...I don't know. A woman who identified as a top, I guess. And too many of them wanted to push me in all these ways I didn't want to go."

Rebecca shook her head. "They didn't really know you."

"Not like you did."

They kissed some more.

"Are we really doing this?" Rebecca said with a slight gasp when they parted. She looked at her blazer by the door, shield and firearm wrapped inside the pocket, holster on top. "I'm the same woman I was. Still a cop..."

"You're the hottest cop on the planet." Trudy got up on her knees on the couch and then straddled Rebecca's lap. "I wanted you that first night I saw you. I've been thinking of you since then. Like...*really* thinking of you. Like every night when I went to sleep thinking of you. Are we doing this? If this means, will you come and make love with me, hell, yeah, I really want to do that."

And Rebecca gave up rational thought and started getting that soft suede shirt open. Luckily, it had snaps.

She couldn't call what they did wrestling for position, because as soon as she pushed or pulled, Trudy was happy to move, change her posture, shift over or under. Their shirts got left in the main room; they got to the bed with pants still on, but Trudy started kicking hers off fairly quickly.

It was almost completely dark, except the lights from various

401

businesses illuminated her bedroom in red and gold and green stripes. Rebecca rolled on top of her and heard the sighs and moans that had haunted her own evening thoughts many times, despite the pain of the breakup. Yes, she though, yes. We do feel so good together. No one ever fit me as well as you...

"Oh, God, Becca, I want...I want..."

"What, sweetheart?"

"I want you to say it."

"Say what?"

"You know...Oh, like that! Yes, like that!" Rebecca spread her body on top of Trudy's and let their skin touch, pressing down. Trudy nodded and threw her head back against her pillows. "God, I love that!"

Running her hand up Trudy's side, then across her shoulder and down the length of her arm, raising goose bumps on the way, Rebecca twined her fingers with Trudy's and pressed the back of her hand down against the bed.

"Yeah! Oh, Becca, yeah!" Trudy bucked up and Rebecca almost pulled away, but Trudy grabbed at her with her free hand. "No, just like that, please! And say it!"

Rebecca started to get a clue. "You mean..."

"Please! Now, please!"

She leaned in close, and whispered it into Trudy's ear. "You... have the right to remain silent..."

"Oh, God, oh, God, oh, God, Becca, yes, yes, yes!"

Maybe they could make this work after all, Rebecca thought, much later, as she began to fall asleep. After all, they're really not all *that* strange, those people. Just about as strange as...everyone else.

ABOUT THE AUTHOR

LAURA ANTONIOU IS THE AUTHOR OF THE WELL-KNOWN *Marketplace* series of erotic novels, in addition to dozens of short stories, essays and other works in various genres. Her work has been translated into Spanish, German, Japanese and Hebrew. Winner of the NLA Lifetime Achievement Award and the Pantheon of Leather Lifetime Achievement Award, she nevertheless intends to keep living for quite some time. A popular speaker on topics relating to alternative sexual practices—aka kinky sex—Laura has presented, taught and ranted at over 150 conferences and events since the 1980s, delivering enlightenment, entertainment and indictments. She has also appeared at colleges and universities, including Harvard, NYU, Rutgers, Columbia and the University of Washington.

In 2010, she hit the world of e-books as the *Marketplace* moved to a new publisher, and Laura came out as Christopher Morgan, bestselling writer of *Muscle-Bound* and other gay male erotica. Together with her wife, Karen Taylor, Laura has written a ritually correct leather Passover seder, titled *Avadim Chayanu*.

Laura is featured in the collections *Writing Below the Belt: Conversations with Erotic Authors*, by Michael Rowe, and *The Burning Pen: Sex Writers on Sex Writing*, by M. Christian. Her short story, *The Man with the Phoenix Tattoo*, won the John Preston Short Fiction Award. The story was originally published in *Take Me There*, Tristan Taormino's 2011 Lambda Literary Award-winning collection of transgender erotica. Laura was also a columnist for *Girlfriends* magazine and Alt.com, editor of *Badboy* and *Bi-Curious*, and a regular contributor to the *Sand-MUtopia Guardian* from 1993-2000.

Laura plans more novels in the Marketplace series as well as delving into other genres. All of her available works can be found at her website, lantoniou.com.

The Bestselling Novels of James Lear

The Mitch Mitchell Mystery Series

The Back Passage
By James Lear

"Lear's lusty homage to the classic whodunit format (sorry, Agatha) is wonderfully witty, mordantly mysterious, and enthusiastically, unabashedly erotic!" —Richard Labonté, Book Marks, Q Syndicate
ISBN 978-1-57344-423-5 $13.95

The Secret Tunnel
By James Lear

"Lear's prose is vibrant and colourful...This isn't porn accompanied by a wahwah guitar, this is porn to the strains of Beethoven's *Ode to Joy*, each vividly realised ejaculation accompanied by a fanfare and the crashing of cymbals."—*Time Out London*
ISBN 978-1-57344-329-6 $13.95

A Sticky End
A Mitch Mitchell Mystery
By James Lear

To absolve his best friend and sometime lover from murder charges, Mitch races around London finding clues while bedding the many men eager to lend a hand—or more.
ISBN 978-1-57344-395-1 $14.95

The Low Road
By James Lear

Author James Lear expertly interweaves spies and counterspies, scheming servants and sadistic captains, tavern trysts and prison orgies into this delightfully erotic work.
ISBN 978-1-57344-364-7 $14.95

Hot Valley
By James Lear

"Lear's depiction of sweaty orgies...trumps his Southern war plot, making the violent history a mere inconsequential backdrop to all of Jack and Aaron's sticky mischief. Nice job." —*Bay Area Reporter*
ISBN 978-1-57344-279-4 $14.95

Ordering is easy! Call us toll free or fax us to place your MC/VISA order.
You can also mail the order form below with payment to:
Cleis Press, 2246 Sixth St., Berkeley, CA 94710.

ORDER FORM

QTY	TITLE	PRICE
_____	_____	_____
_____	_____	_____
_____	_____	_____
_____	_____	_____
_____	_____	_____
_____	_____	_____
_____	_____	_____
_____	_____	_____

SUBTOTAL _____

SHIPPING _____

SALES TAX _____

TOTAL _____

Add $3.95 postage/handling for the first book ordered and $1.00 for each additional book. Outside North America, please contact us for shipping rates. California residents add 9% sales tax. Payment in U.S. dollars only.

* Free book of equal or lesser value. Shipping and applicable sales tax extra.

Cleis Press • Phone: (800) 780-2279 • Fax: (510) 845-8001
orders@cleispress.com • www.cleispress.com
You'll find more great books on our website

Follow us on Twitter @cleispress • Friend/fan us on Facebook